WINTERHOME

THE JESSICA KELLER CHRONICLES: VOLUME 8

BLAZE WARD

KNOTTED ROAD PRESS

Winterhome
The Jessica Keller Chronicles: Volume 8
Blaze Ward
Copyright © 2019 Blaze Ward
All rights reserved
Published by Knotted Road Press
www.KnottedRoadPress.com

ISBN: 978-1-64470-033-4

Cover art:

ID 98660066 © innovari | DepositPhotos.com

Cover and interior design copyright © 2019 Knotted Road Press

Never miss a release!
If you'd like to be notified of new releases, sign up for my newsletter.

I will never spam you or use your email for nefarious purposes. You can also unsubscribe at any time.

http://www.blazeward.com/newsletter/

ALSO BY BLAZE WARD

The Jessica Keller Chronicles

Auberon

Queen of the Pirates

Last of the Immortals

Goddess of War

Flight of the Blackbird

The Red Admiral

St. Legier

Winterhome

CS-405

Queen Anne's Revenge

Packmule

Persephone

Additional Alexandria Station Stories

The Story Road

Siren

Two Bottles of Wine with a War God

The Science Officer Series

The Science Officer

The Mind Field

The Gilded Cage

The Pleasure Dome

The Doomsday Vault

The Last Flagship

The Hammerfield Gambit

The Hammerfield Payoff

Doyle Iwakuma Stories

The Librarian

Demigod

Greater Than The Gods Intended

Other Science Fiction Stories

Myrmidons

Moonshot

Menelaus

Earthquake Gun

Moscow Gold

Fairchild

White Crane

***The Collective* Universe**

The Shipwrecked Mermaid

Imposters

PART ONE
OVERTURES

OVERTURE: BEDROV

YAN HAD WONDERED who they would send out, given the message of vague yet important news he had sent along to *St. Legier* when the folks in this area had decided to keep him and Ainsley on the frontier, rather than letting him and his new discovery aboard one of their ships.

He knew it wasn't a bomb or a Trojan Horse, but the Imperials hadn't been there. Wouldn't understand.

Probably wouldn't believe him.

Not his fucking problem.

Then Gunter Tifft walked into the warehouse room, dressed like an everyday naval officer who had opened the wrong door by mistake and wandered into the situation. Except that Gunter had a pistol on his hip.

Yan wasn't surprised, like most people would be. But he also knew who the man was.

More importantly, what he was, and who he represented.

"Gunter," Yan acknowledged with a brief nod.

"Bedrov," Tifft nodded as he stepped closer and let the hatch close behind him.

They were alone in a big, open space, as Yan had specified. The walls were stripped bare, painted Imperial off-white, and too far away for Yan's needs, but it was easier to start simple today and work his way up.

At least with Gunter Tifft, representing *Imperial Authority* in all its facets, someone would be listening.

Tifft came to a pause at the normal distance to snap off a salute, if Yan had happened to serve in any fleet that might necessitate such a thing. Yan presumed that was just bone-deep training on the younger man's part.

They eyed each other for a few long moments in stillness.

Yan remembered when the kid was more fidgety.

Kid. Sure. Yan could call him that. Gunter was only barely older than Yan's own children: Malka and Kai.

He was calmness itself now. Tall, blond, ruggedly handsome. Perfectly still.

Yan didn't figure that the guy had graduated to assassin, but he had no doubts what Gunter Tifft did for Hendrik Baumgärtner, Emmerich *zu* Wachturm's Naval Chief of Staff.

Tifft was a spy.

Made sense. Yan had gone so far off the reservation recently that the old men probably wanted to reassure themselves that Yan had stayed this side of compromised.

"So what brings me to *Osynth B'Udan*, Bedrov?" Gunter asked quietly, his eyes flickering to a spot on the ground a meter behind Yan's feet. Wasn't a smile on his face this morning.

The thing on the floor behind him wasn't a bomb, but it would have about as much impact on the folks around here, most likely.

"I ran into something on my way here from Jessica," Yan replied in a flat, vaguely evasive tone. "Local admirals went paranoid and sent a message to *zu* Wachturm for help, which they should have. He or Hendrik sent you, because they didn't believe me."

"You entitled the field report that you sent to us *Two Bottles of Wine with a War God*, Bedrov," Tifft said sarcastically. "I doubt that anybody but the Grand Admiral would have even believed you."

"That was on purpose," Yan nodded. "Not everyone in your profession has the sense God gave a goose."

Gunter grinned wryly and almost said something, but changed his mind.

"So he sent you home with something?" Gunter said. "This War God from the ancient times?"

Rather than reply, Yan turned and knelt on the floor. The room was raw metal on all sides, like an open space on a ship that had been stripped of internal bulkheads, leaving only the frames, twelve meters on a side and four meters tall.

Like a big barn in here.

The device chirped once as Yan flipped the power switch. The machine was what his Da would have called a cigar box, in overall size. Maybe a little more square, but not perfect. Black exterior made of some extruded material Yan guessed might have been a carbon-fiber-sheet, cast stronger than steel.

Chemistry had never been Yan's strong point, stopping with some metallurgy, but he suspected that *Carthage* was right when the AI ship had said that most of the tech was beyond what *Aquitaine* and the galaxy could do right now.

Right now.

Show an engineer a thing that has been done, and they'll figure out a way to do it, if they have to move heaven and earth in the process. Doubly so if you sneer at them in a superior way.

Yan stood and turned back to Gunter with his own smile. He remained perfectly still as the *Tiki Lounge* came into being around them. It was all a hologram, but Yan had never imagined you could get that level of complexity without shadows of moving objects, particularly not when starting with a single beam emitter in the middle of the floor.

Somehow, it was ray-tracing itself off of every available surface with so much processing power that it could create a solid-looking image believable enough that Yan had dropped a glass through a projection once, not realizing that the table wasn't there.

Gunter's eyes got big and he muttered a mild profanity under his breath.

This was the *Tiki Lounge*, as it had been on the now-destroyed **Earth Alliance Sentient Combatant** *Carthage*. The Last Dragon. The only surviving veteran of the Concordancy War that had begun three thousand years ago with the bombardment of the Homeworld.

Gone now.

"What'll it be, mates?" The Lord of Tiki asked as he came into being behind the old, oaken bar with the stained and dinged copper surface.

He presented as a big, gruff Irishman, to quote the old adage. Short hair the color of carrots, scarred ears and heavy face. Not as big as Vo *zu* Arlo, but bigger than Yan. Maybe the size of the Grand Admiral, with an extra fifteen kilos of mass around the upper body. Not fat, but strong bulk.

"*Carthage*, meet Imperial Naval Commander Gunter Tifft," Yan said by way of introduction.

"Technically, I'm only an avatar of *Carthage*," the bartender replied in a soft brogue. "Although I might grant you with him dead and all, I might be all that remains in this modern age."

The bartender nodded to Tifft and began to wipe down the bar with a wrap that materialized in his hand. It wasn't like the projection was bound by the laws of physics or anything.

Gunter looked around with awe. After a few moments, he remembered to shut his mouth, lest he start catching flies, according to Yan's maternal grandmother.

"How is this possible?" Tifft asked, passing a careful hand through first the bar, and then the bartender's arm when he held it up.

"You lot might have some nifty technology, sure," the bartender smiled sadly. "But my kind were about six thousand years past that point when we blew up all the factories and planets. Ya ain't caught back up yet. Although the JumpSails are a nifty thing that never occurred to me and mine, back in the day."

"You know about those?" Tifft asked.

"I contain most of my Principal's logs, Commander Tifft," the bartender replied, transforming subtly into something more than just a guy behind a bar. "Those include the scans of *RAN Mendocino*, which I can compare rather unfavorably against most of the ships in my own logs. Hells, my shuttles were more advanced."

"What else do you contain?" Tifft turned more fully to face the being, turning serious himself in turn.

"The entire history of mankind, right up until 10,419 Standard Era," the Avatar said coldly. "You'll pardon if I am somewhat lacking over the last three thousand and eighty years, Commander."

"Including technology?"

Yan detected a trace of awe and avarice under those normally-calm tones. That was where Yan had gone, as well.

Seeker, the defector who had once been the Khan of the *Buran* world *Trusski*, had explained that the *Sentience* known as *Buran* had originated as a control system for a factory making tractors and other heavy farming equipment, some five thousand years ago. Somehow, it had gotten missed in the great purge, or repaired after having been mothballed before the war. Something, so that neither *Carthage* nor *Kinnison*, nor their subsidiary fleets, had managed to make it to the tiny planet known as *Winterhome* to finish that job.

Imagine what the future would have been like, without *Buran* threatening everyone.

"Some," the bartender replied. "Or rather, things beyond the wildest dreams of your current understanding of physics, if *Mendocino* was any indication. I don't have the sorts of scanners available in this box to know about the place Bedrov and Barret have brought us to, but most of what I know would require you building the tools to build the tools to build the tools."

Yan smiled as Gunter cursed under his breath, again.

"How *can* you help us, barkeep?" Yan asked in a leading way.

He and Ainsley had already spent many hours with the man, or recording, or whatever he was, on the flight here.

"That's where it gets iffy," the tall, gruff man turned cagey and quiet, nodding to Yan. "I've heard about *St. Legier*. Not everything, mind you, but an eyewitness account, and I appreciate why you didn't tell me before. And thank you, by the way."

Yan nodded. Gunter turned enough to give them both a dose of side eye.

"For?" Gunter asked.

"Not telling me, us, whatever, about *Buran*, when I might have gone off and done something about that bastard," the bartender said. "I appreciate that my assistance might not have been welcome, even then. Not sure if it will be now."

"Could you have done something to stop *Buran*?" Gunter asked in a quiet voice.

"Commander, I'm reasonably confident I could have annihilated his entire fleet, and then him," the bartender suddenly looked more like a *God of War* rather than a *Lord of Tiki*. "I was a Mark XXII Advanced Skymaster. Only *Concord Warship Kinnison* was more dangerous. Nothing Yan has told me about those silly sharks has changed my mind."

"What have you told him?" Gunter suddenly turned to look at Yan, deadly serious.

"Barely enough," Yan conceded. "What he is today is a greatly reduced version of *Carthage*. Another Librarian of Alexandria, if you will."

"Probably more," the Tiki God interjected. "That one was ancient, by our standards. Probably only used trinary logic circuits."

"And you?" Gunter asked.

Yan held his breath, aware that Tifft might decide to draw the pulse pistol on his hip right now and shot the box containing the *Lord of Tiki*. He might even be empowered by the Grand Admiral to do exactly that.

That this was technically Ainsley's property would only mean that she would file a complaint and *Fribourg* would send her cash as a reimbursement. Not enough for the value lost, but *Fribourg* had a low opinion of any AI system to begin with. A former warship might get their hackles up too far.

"Both *Kinnison* and I used hexal logic boards, Commander," the bartender returned to the fore, leaning forward onto the bar itself with a breezy smile. "Each memory address had six possible value combination flavors it could store, whereas she uses three and your systems are generally simple primitive bit gates with an on or off value. It's actually much more complicated than that, but that at least gets your mind in the right direction. Mind you, she's only about three thousand years older than I am, from what I understand, but technology and science moved a bit in that span."

Gunter turned back to face him now. Yan smiled grimly.

This was the crux of things. This being could help them, but it was a *Sentient* system, at the end of the day. Literally one of the destroyers that had cast humanity down from the heavens, in his time, and the most dangerous, illegal thing in the entire Empire.

"Okay, I think I understand," Gunter said grimly.

It helped that Gunter had been *zu* Wachturm's point man on some of the crazy, mean stuff Yan had dreamed up over the last few years. He and Gunter had a good working relationship, which any of Baumgärtner's other spooks would not have brought to the table.

"I don't answer to you, Gunter," Yan explained firmly, reminding the man of his loyalties. "Nor to the Grand Admiral. Not even Karl VIII. I only answer to Jessica Keller, especially on this. Period."

"Understood," Gunter said. "But those three will have to talk. On your word, I'm willing to pass this off as a fantastically-impressive toy that does not represent a threat to the Empire."

"Oh, he does represent a threat to the *Fribourg Empire*, boyo," Yan said, watching Gunter's head snap around hard to scowl at him. "But not the one you envision. *Carthage* is a threat to the Empire of Karl V and Karl VI. The threat here is what he could do to help Karl VIII ram home her vision of the future. And all the bastards that want stop her."

"Yes," Gunter scowled. "That's what frightens me."

OVERTURE: VO

Vo *zu* Arlo had always thought of Iskra Vlahovic as taller than she really was. Everyone was tiny, standing next to him, including the new Emperor, but the Fleet Centurion was only a little taller than average for a woman. She just had a desperately outsized personality, even for as quiet as she was.

Iskra wasn't one to take a gram of shit from anyone. And as commander of an *RAN* task force set to join Jessica and First Expeditionary Fleet in the war with *Buran*, she didn't have to. The only person she did answer to was Judit Chavarría, the Palatine Ambassador from *Aquitaine*'s Senate to the *Fribourg Empire*.

And Judit was something like a Ritter right now, empowered to speak for the Senate and the Premier back home. In legally-binding ways.

So Vo always made sure to ask politely when dealing with Iskra. Sure, they went back more than a decade, having served together on the old Strike Carrier *Auberon*, even before Jessica, but that just meant she would take his calls when he wanted something.

Not that he could make her do anything, even when he had everybody else on his side.

He glanced over at her now, seated two down from him in the room that Torsten Wald usually used when he had a major group of people to talk to.

Like today.

The Emperor would not be joining them for this meeting. At least he hoped. In the last two weeks, he had kept a very polite distance from the woman.

She had asked a question. He hadn't been able to answer.

Vo wasn't sure he would have an answer for her, anytime soon, if ever.

They had gone beyond Emperor and General. Beyond comrades on Star Controller *Auberon*, or even back on *Kali-ma*.

Someplace Vo wasn't sure he was prepared to go. Even for a beautiful woman who asked.

He wasn't sure what that said about where his head was.

Primus Pilus Alan Katche sat next to Vo on the other side today, leaving an empty chair between Vo and Iskra. Nobody wanted to touch that chair, probably afraid it was poisonous, or maybe they'd get caught in some bizarre crossfire.

None of these people knew Iskra Vlahovic. If she wanted to do you in, it would be in the middle of her flight deck, probably with a wrench, rather than verbally in a meeting.

Wald was at the high end of the table. Former Premier Chavarría was across from Alan, and newly-promoted Grand Marshal Arald Rohm sat across from Vo. A few others were scattered around, some at the conference table, some in chairs along the outer wall, behind everybody where they could run errands or look things up, as somebody needed, but they were functionally nobodies, here for whatever technical expertise Wald might call on.

They were just waiting on the last two players, come down from orbit and about to join them: the Grand Admiral and his lethal right fist Tom Provst.

This, then, was the group that would really decide Vo's future, not that he was going to let them derail things. Heads would have to roll first. But they deserved a chance to have an opinion, however wrong it might be.

The door opened to one of Vo's troopers in field armor with his face shield down, checking everything, and then allowing the two sailors into the room, pulling it shut afterwards with a hard thump.

With the Emperor not attending, Vo's folks were in charge of security around here. At least until he managed to get everyone aboard a transport and headed towards the frontier. Then it wouldn't be his problem, anymore. Rohm or someone would have the headaches.

Vo found it amusing that *zu* Wachturm, in black, sat opposite Wald, at the long end of the battered, old conference table, while Tom Provst, in white, dropped in between he and Iskra.

But Provst was pretty much immune to anything.

Chief Deputy Torsten Wald rose and scanned the table, nodding to Vo as he took the temperature of the room.

"Everything has been signed and made official," Wald announced. "Her Majesty's Government will lease the two *RAN* Assault Carriers *Archangel* and *Akatsuki*, for a period of one year, with an exercisable option for a second year, under the authority of Grand Admiral *zu* Wachturm, Admiral Provst, or General *zu* Arlo. Fleet Centurion Vlahovic will delay her departure for a time, so that the 189th Legion can be organized and packed for transport, along with supplies. After that time, the first stop for the Task Force is *Osynth B'Udan*, to deploy the 189th for training, while a forward strike is organized. Have I missed anything?"

"Do we know who the first target is?" Grand Marshal Rohm asked, eyeing Vo specifically, before turning his gaze to include the two admirals.

"I have a list," Vo offered. "Depending on what naval forces accompany the *RAN* squadron, we have options, but *Samara* is the only target on this side of *M'Hanii* definitely off limits, just as *Ninagirsu* on the other."

"How soon will you need resupply?" Rohm pressed. "Or more troops?"

"Ours will be a smash and grab, Grand Marshal," Vo repeated, mostly for the others who hadn't been in on their private meetings. "Having more Assault Carriers first will be a long-term necessity to actually holding a planet."

He turned his gaze on *zu* Wachturm.

Emmerich fixed him with a frosty smile, but that was all for show, as well. For the foreigners, which made Vo laugh internally, to think of Iskra and the former Senator as aliens, while he was just about as Imperial as it got these days.

At least until he figured out what he wanted to do with the rest of his life.

"We have a discussion open with Yan Bedrov and a few others, to consider new designs," Emmerich said, looking august and unflappable. "But we have also opened discussions with *Aquitaine* about leasing more such vessels in the short term. The completed design of the Army will impact significantly on our final decision."

Meaning: are you going to build more strike legions, or rely on the old structures, like Seventh Guards Army?

All the world's a stage, as Moirrey used to love to say. And we are all players.

Rohm nodded, almost theatrically. Vo fought to keep a straight face.

"Who else is coming?" Iskra asked bluntly, turning her whole head, like an owl, to face Tom Provst, seated beside her.

The man's color had improved in the last several months. His attitude had gone from something approximating despair to the sorts of grim, barely-chained violence Vo had seen in the likes of Alber' d'Maine or Tomas Kigali. He had moved on from being the man Emmerich trusted to protect *St. Legier* and become the Grand Admiral's great sword.

"*IFV Valiant*," Provst replied to her simply. "Plus *Indianapolis* and two corvettes, today. The rest of the Task Group will come later, as soon as they finish *Acceptance* trials and shakedowns. Probably by late fall."

Rather than answer, Iskra turned the other way to stare at the Grand Admiral.

"Do I need that many escorts?" she asked.

Score one for Iskra. Vo was hard pressed to find a better way to announce to the men in this room that she would be in charge of her force, subject only to Jessica. And not taking any shit.

"You do not," *zu* Wachturm replied diplomatically. "Doing it this way lets me reinforce *Osynth B'Udan* in the short term, and then adds a second strike force to Jessica's capabilities by winter, assuming she integrates *RAN Arad* and your three corvettes into her force, rather than sending you raiding. A Fleet Strike carrier is yet another new design, and I don't know if it makes more sense to combine with *II Augusta* and the Fast Strike Bombers. That's Jessica's call, especially as she will then be the Fleet Centurion. Tom Provst will be promoted to Red, but both you and he will be under her authority. Does that help?"

Iskra turned back to Provst, as if challenging him to say anything.

Vo wasn't sure which of them might be more stubborn, so he called it a draw. Apparently, Tom agreed, or had orders from Emmerich to be polite. He nodded silently.

She turned her harsh glare his way.

"Load time?" she asked, like she was sending notes across a scrolling marquee.

"Four to five weeks," Vo replied. "There will be a subsequent ground force to transport, but they are only now working out equipment and recruiting, and I don't expect that force to join me until Provst's group comes in the fall."

"Who?" Iskra asked, honest curiosity breaking through for the first time.

"Moirrey's Avenging Angels," Vo smiled. "Bunch of kids in combat repulsor suits that will eventually form an additional part of my Fourth Scouting Ala, but I want to move now, and not in a year when I have everything integrated. Every day *Buran* has before I come for him, he gets stronger and more entrenched."

"In spite of Jessica?" Judit Chavarría joined the conversation. "I thought her purpose was to weaken the beast."

"Her purpose is to destroy *Buran*'s economy," Alan Katche spoke up, letting everyone know he had, in fact, done his homework. "Ours is to destroy their *Peace of Mind*. The only damage on the ground so far has been psychological. We're going to change that."

Vo turned and nodded. Alan was truly his right hand. *Primus Pilus*. First Spear because he was closest to the enemy. Vo had picked him for that reason. Competent and aggressive, but also *mean* when he needed to be.

"With all that in mind, I have a few others topics for this group to move onto," Torsten Wald cleared his throat diplomatically. He pulled a stack of folders from where he had apparently stashed them on the floor earlier, and began to hand them out.

Vo doubted that anything of substance remained, since the key elements of this year's war had been touched. The rest was just window dressing.

He had his approvals from Casey to go off to war in her name.

Now he just had to figure out if he wanted to come back to her afterwards.

OVERTURE: JESSICA

JESSICA FELT A GROWL, deep in her belly, as she watched the projection from her small flag bridge. Outside, all the lights on the exterior of Whughy's *Forward Base Delta* came live. That thing was technically a warship, in that it was a compact starbase with engines and JumpSails, however small and slow they were.

When they had lost *CS-405*, sometime after the raid on *Severnaya Zemlya*, Jessica had needed to pack everything up and flee, on the presumption that the ship might have been captured, and the old base location compromised. It had been easier to break the base halfway down, load it onto a cargo tug, and shift it, rather than letting it creep slowly along on its own power.

Now they were mirrored from the old location, as far spinward from *Ninagirsu*, upstream relative, as they had previously been downstream. Still low, three hundred light-years below the mathematical plane of the galaxy, because the network of navigation satellites, the *Pochtovyi Trakt*, or *Buran's* Postal Road, tended to be about two hundred light-years above that plane.

To Jessica, it smacked badly of two-dimensional thinking, but *Buran* hadn't been a warship before he became a god. Only a factory controller. The kind that probably learned his tactics by studying table-top-style war simulations from history.

Jessica and her kind had learned to fight in space. While *Buran's* commanders were just as good, they were still limited by the requirements of an inflexible god.

But there was no way that Phil Kosnett or anyone else would find them now. That had hurt. Phil had been there from the beginning of this mission, a scholarly commander with an excellent crew. To get home now would require that he make it all the way to *Osynth B'Udan*, if he had escaped.

So, it rankled as she watched the base announce to the squadron that they were back in business, for the first time in almost two months. She had been in battles where other vessels had been lost. Jessica had been at war for most of her adult life, more than twenty-four years now. She had even been aboard ships that suffered crippling damage, such as the time she rammed *Brightoak* into an Imperial fighter craft to keep it away from the carrier at *Third Iger*, or the damage to both *Auberon*s at *Ballard* and *Trusski*.

She had never had a ship just vanish into Jump and never come out on the far side.

Jessica said a silent prayer to Vishnu that Kosnett had just suffered a simple breakdown that caused him to have to limp home, knowing that he wouldn't find them at the old location. *Standing Order Forty-Eight* required that Kosnett and his First Officer, Heather Lau, could not allow themselves to be captured by *Buran*'s forces.

At whatever price they had to pay.

She had lost two months, but that had been built into her plans. *RAN Bulldog*, the so-called *Junkyard Chihuahua*, had been able to repair most of the damage the squadron had suffered blowing the shit out of *Severnaya Zemlya*. Messages had been sent to the Grand Admiral with *RAN Duncan*.

From here, they would need another month or perhaps six weeks to finalize some modifications and upgrades, and then she could start raiding again, hopefully with some added firepower as the Grand Admiral was able to free up some of his own ships. Tom Provst would have taken command on board *IFV Valiant*, *Vanguard*'s younger sister.

More ships were rolling out of yards every day, coming on-line and taking on crews as older vessels were mothballed. It would take time, but her whole purpose was to savage *Buran*'s interior and force the monster's own fleets to have to reinforce more and more planetary systems, and do so with enough force to keep her from jumping in and annihilating single warships, however deep in the gravity well they thought they could hide from her.

A chime on her screen and Denis Jež's face appeared.

"I would say you are cordially invited," he began. "But we're just going to get together aboard the station and get a little drunk. You should join us."

She understood why. And why they had waited. It was official now, in ways that hadn't gotten personal up until now. She had lost one of hers, but they had all lost friends. Time to have a good drink, and then tomorrow, plan how they were going to get even with that bastard.

OVERTURE: POPS

He had never been one to look a gift horse in the mouth, so Iorwerth Nakamura didn't raise a fuss when the woman announced that she was going to travel with him. It would be a long trip, possibly three years before he returned to *Petron*, and it would be nice to have someone to talk to and maybe fool around with occasionally.

She looked over at him with a questioning smile as the shuttle entered the landing bay with a small lurch. The interior of the little ship was compact and industrial gray, but the lines were sleek and smooth. He had designed the original for Jessica, and then licensed the design to Galen to build himself a copy.

It wasn't a Royal Transport Yacht, like *Baxter*. Galen had wanted to build the other one, the Royal Combat Yacht *Zorillo*. And since that one was named for a skunk, he or course had to call this one *Badger*. Galen could be a dork.

"Lev for your thoughts?" Summer asked.

"Wondering how crazy I am, to go after one last job," he replied with a wry smile. "I could probably just retire and be done with all this."

"You'd get bored in less than a week, *Pops*," she laughed. "I know your kind. Always have to be doing something. Retirement would kill you in six months."

"You think so?" he fired back.

Just for the hell of it, he reached out a hand and she took it. It wasn't love, what they had. More of a comfortable place they could both just be, and be together. *Pops* knew he was too old for the woman, but she had sought him out, apparently traveling from well interior, possibly somewhere up in *Aquitaine*, although she had been a little vague and he hadn't inquired too closely. Didn't want to know about her yesterdays.

She looked a very active forty, acted twenty, and occasionally sounded as though she was two hundred years old. Tall blond hardbody with slightly-graying hair and bright blue eyes. What she wanted with a guy like him still left *Pops* occasionally confused.

"Yes," she laughed throatily. "And you could never let Bedrov show you up, either."

That brought a smile to his face. And a shrug. Nope, never let that kid outdo him, even if he knew Jessica would appoint Yan in his spot, but not until he finally did retire.

The Queen was like that, matching loyalty for loyalty.

Pops smiled. His only daughter had gone off to war with Jessica back in the days of *Auberon*, although that vessel had been broken in the war with *Buran*, and his queen was riding in one of Bedrov's crazier designs now, a Heavy Dreadnaught named *Vanguard*. Cho would probably come home soon.

The shuttle's deck magnets engaged and the ship shut down, halting conversation for a bit as he unbuckled and stood partway. The ceiling was too low in here, but he had designed it that way originally. Most of the time, anyone back here would be in one of the four jumpseats. Forward, two pilots had a small cockpit. Aft, Jessica's version had a small stateroom, while *Badger* had a small cargo bay for priority stuff.

They weren't hauling much cargo on *Badger* this flight. Well, none beyond the humans and all the accumulated knowledge of several lifetimes at war.

Fast as he was though, Summer was still to the hatch first, undogging it and dropping the boarding steps. But she was also up with the sun and running twenty kilometers every morning.

Pops preferred to at least sleep until the sun was visible, generally, before wandering into the kitchen for his coffee, and then settling into his design studio to commit naval architecture and other silliness.

Like this ship, as he followed Summer out, ogling her hard bottom as she stepped down onto the deck, laughing. Sixty-four-year-old men were not objects of lust to forty-year-old women, so he had no idea why she was here, but he appreciated her, even if she encouraged him to do most of the talking. At least she was older than his daughter, Cho Ayaka. *RAN* callsign *Furious*.

Galen Estevan met them as they emerged from the interior airlock. Summer got her hand shaken politely. *Pops* got a hug. He had known the kid pretty much Galen's whole life, having been a competitor, rival, and then friend of Uly Larionov for decades, the two weird kids among all the other pirate captains. *Pops* was tall and lean, rather than fast or muscled. Uly was shorter than most of the women in *Corynthe*, at least physically.

Both of them had carved their own grand destiny into the pirate kingdom.

"Welcome aboard, Uncle," Galen smiled. "You ready for an adventure?"

Pops eyed him with a snort.

"Not sure I'd call it that," *Pops* said.

Summer laughed easily.

"You just don't want Bedrov having all the fun," she said.

He and Galen laughed as well.

"Maybe," *Pops* allowed.

There was something to that. Bedrov had gone off and had all sorts of adventures, while *Pops* had stayed back in *Corynthe*, designing better ways for people to kill each other.

And now he was answering his Queen's siren call, one last time. Maybe.

Jessica had sent a message, asking for Vice Admiral David Rodriguez, her Regent, to send help, clear out on the far side of *Fribourg*, where she was engaged in a war with hopefully the last of the destroyers, a being called *Buran*.

They followed Galen forward while *Pops* eyed every weld and every frame critically. Yan had designed the Expeditionary Cruisers and Carriers to be overpowered monsters capable of fighting older dreadnaughts on even terms. Wasn't anything like that in *Corynthe*, where a 4-ring Mothership was as close to a capital ship as anybody got.

Pops, in turn, had taken that design and brought it down in price and increased the reliability, on the assumption that, unlike *Aquitaine* or *Fribourg*, *Corynthe* vessels needed to stay at sea for a long time, without carrying around a stripper/repair boat everywhere they went.

Hell, it wasn't even a mothership, Galen's new Patrol Cruiser. Technically, *Pops* figured he would rate it as a light battlecruiser. *Qin Lun* only had space for two shuttles, and both of those docked internally;

currently the transport *Badger* and the scout *Rabbit.* All the other things they would need for a flight like this were aboard their upgraded consort, *Marco Polo*, which *Pops* had extended into a 2-ring Mothership at Galen's request, so he could *sail to the far end of the galaxy in one go.* Or whatever craziness the kid was up to now.

The bridge took all of Bedrov's ideas for design and made them even better. Maybe he was looking forward to showing the punk a few things. Let him know the old dog still had a little fight left in him.

Like *Aquitaine*, the bridge held a captain and a tactical officer, but seated at either end of the small oval space, facing in. Rest of the bridge crew sat between them in two rows, facing each other, so peripheral vision could pick up both commanders as the situation warranted. Enough extra workstations that new crew could sit with experienced officers and crew while learning.

The room was replicated forward, like a mirror of this bridge, itself aft over the engines. Motherships looked like geese in flight, with a bulbous head and a big butt, but every other ship had the bridge forward, and usually didn't even include a proper emergency bridge.

"You two here," Galen said, taking over the captain's station and smiling as he pointed to the stations closest.

Pops saw Summer in, and then joined her. Old school manners, but they had always served him well.

"*Marco Polo*, this is *Qin Lun*," Galen said aloud as he opened a comm channel. "Stand by for departure."

Pops smiled as everyone settled in. He hadn't been on the bridge of a warship going into combat since he sold *Castlegar* off to Uly thirty years ago so he could be home to help raise a suddenly-motherless daughter, who subsequently turned herself into one of the baddest pilots of her generation.

And now, he was about to plunge into battle again.

PART TWO
CALL TO ARMS

CHAPTER I

"All hands to battle stations," the words poured from the speakers and had Jessica in motion before she even woke up.

It was the dead of night, relative to her sleep schedule, but war never waited for the sun to come up. Legs into baggy sweats. Pull a tunic over the old, green t-shirt she liked to sleep in. Stuff feet into shoes. Hit the door at a dead run, elapsed time four seconds.

The flag bridge wasn't far away. She got there a whole step ahead of Enej, who looked like he had been sleeping in those pajamas when the siren went off.

She got to her seat and slapped a hand at the button that brought the main projection live. Her flag staff always had someone on duty, but it was a smaller crew than back on her old Star Controller, and more bodies were pouring in behind her.

Jessica snickered and made a note to have more fleet alerts in the dead of night. Apparently, her people were getting a little sloppy, with too much time in dry-dock and station. She would have to burn a little of the fat off of them and get folks hungry again.

"Bridge, Flag here," she said, opening the general comm. "What do we have?"

"Signal from a light-hour or so out," Senior Centurion Tobias Brewster replied. He must have had the night watch from the Emergency Bridge. "*RAN Arad* and escorts, asking for a docking assignment."

"Everybody rousted?" she asked, keying things live the way she wanted them.

Station in the center of the display, parked in the middle of nowhere. Big star for *Vanguard*. Smaller stars for *VI Victrix*, *VI Ferrata*, and *II Augusta*. Angry motes for her corvettes, pulled around in a strange, hexagonal box without *CS-405* at the front.

"Affirmative, Flag," Brewster nodded into the display. "Just waiting for you to take command."

"All vessels, this is Jessica Keller, aboard *RAN Vanguard*, I have the flag," she said formally.

Inside, she was almost cackling with glee. They had been waiting for Iskra to arrive with another carrier and three corvettes. It gave Jessica a whole other raiding party, or the option to engage someone with a flanking maneuver they would never expect, even from her.

She did a quick inventory of the signal. Iskra, aboard another whole new concept in warfare. *CA-410*, a younger sibling of *CA-264* with all the capabilities and probably as much attitude as Kigali brought. Two more escorts, *CE-411* and *CE-417*. Two California-class Fleet Replenishment freighters in *RAN Leggett* and *RAN Redding*. With the two she already had, all sorts of mischief was possible.

"All warships, conform to this formation," Jessica said, sending a file to everyone within earshot. "Execute Jump in forty-five seconds from *mark*."

That should give everyone time to get their A-crews in place. If not, she needed to have more drills and possibly a dressing down or two, just to get people back in line.

It had been a hard year, running down targets deep in *Buran* and forcing that bastard onto the defensive in a number of places. Hadn't stopped him from striking *St. Legier*, but no other targets had faced a mass fleet like that.

Jessica had been half expecting a strike at *Osynth B'Udan* by now. Maybe Wachturm and Provst had done more damage than expected, and *The Holding* was only now rebuilding from the damage she had done. She knew that scouts had managed to blip into space at *Samara* a few times, just long enough to take a good scan and then run like hell.

Space was huge, even in the relatively small confines of a single solar system. Not even a robot wargod could keep guns on all approaches at all times, especially if *Fribourg* wasn't going to come down hard into the warzone close to the planet itself.

You didn't have to, if all you wanted to do was watch.

Jump.

Emergence.

One big signal. Five little ones, patiently awaiting like ducklings.

"*RAN Arad*, this is *RAN Vanguard*," Jessica called to them formally. "This is a restricted zone."

She had known they were coming, but not when. And had a pretty good idea what mail Iskra was bringing from home.

"I come bearing orders," Iskra replied obliquely, using the audio channel, wonder of wonders.

Jessica grinned. Now things were going to get interesting.

CHAPTER II

Normally, Denis would have been just another one of the command centurions down in the audience today, but both Iskra and Arott had put their feet down and ordered him to wear his white Imperial Admiral's uniform and join them, seated on the stage. Arott had done the same. And Iskra looked good in white herself, although she was wearing the tunic of a Fleet Centurion with four green stripes, with command tag prominent.

In that, Iskra matched Jessica, at least for a bit longer.

Below the little stage, a representative sampling of officers and crew from the full squadron, plus all the command centurions and most of the tactical officers. Standing room only, and Denis knew that many vessels had organized lotteries for tickets to this show.

Others might have their suspicions, but Denis knew in his soul that this was the last time Jessica would be promoted by the Senate. There were formal ranks above this, but those were the civilians and *Lords of the Fleet*. The men and women in control of the various departments, back home on *Ladaux*.

Jessica wouldn't be going there. At most, maybe Casey would promote her out of red into blue at some point, but never black. Or he could see the woman making Jessica a Duke as well.

Not that Imperial rewards would matter all that much to Jessica.

Denis and she had talked at least weekly for more than a decade, frequently more often. He probably knew her better than anyone alive, including Torsten Wald. Maybe not Marcelle, come to think of it, but Marcelle had been with her for damned near forever, it felt like. And would take those secrets to the grave with her.

The crowd was quietly buzzing as the last of the audience filed in and got settled. No potty breaks from here.

Arott rose from his chair and walked forward to the lectern, standing a meter above the front row. The room fell silent slowly as he did. After all this time, it was still weird to see someone in Imperial uniform addressing a crowd of *Aquitaine* officers, but Denis was wearing an identical outfit himself, so who was he to complain?

"The room will come to order," Arott said unnecessarily.

Denis smiled, in spite of himself. Partly, because he was included in Jessica's legend, so he could be here for her celebration as well. She had never hesitated to remind anyone and everyone that she had never been alone, while undertaking her mighty feats.

"Some of you already know Fleet Centurion Iskra Vlahovic," Arott continued in a voice picking up steam and warmth. "Last seen as Flight Deck Commander on our own Star Controller, *Auberon*. The Lords of the Fleet have happily returned her to us, bringing a whole other task squadron. But before I introduce her, I would like to also acknowledge our new comrades in the audience today. Command Centurion Asha Robins, *Arad*. Command Centurion Lucretia Lomidze, *CA-410*. Command Centurion Yan Victorica, *CE-411*. Command Centurion Willem Fabacher, *CE-417*. Command Centurion Yesenia Groehler, *Leggett*. Command Centurion Daren Alliance, *Redding*."

The crowd applauded politely as each officer raised a hand or nodded.

"Fleet Centurion Vlahovic," Arott turned almost all the way back to face the three of them, so he could nod at her. "You have the flag."

Denis had known Iskra much longer than he had known Jessica. He could almost smell the sarcastic eyeroll she would be suppressing right now. Iskra had never been one for formal ceremonies like this. Still, she would find pleasure today, another one of Jessica's people that had gotten some of that magic rubbed off on them.

Denis had always expected that he would have to track Iskra down after she retired, and see the woman once she had become a civilian. Probably an instructor somewhere, teaching another generation of flight engineers not to take any shit from pilots or line commanders.

She rose slowly and stepped to the front, carrying with her a small scroll tube from where it had stood upright between them on the floor of the stage. Opening it, she pulled out a piece of paper and took a moment to carefully lay the empty tube out of the way inside the lectern itself.

"Fleet Centurion Keller, would you join me?" Iskra said formally, glancing back.

Jessica rose and stepped to stand beside her.

Iskra's voice took on a stentorian tone, pitched so that everyone in the chamber would hear her, regardless of the amplification.

"By order of the Senate of Aquitaine, on this day signed by Senator Tadej Horvat, Premier, and Petia Naoumov, First Lord of the Fleet, we declare to all that Jessica Keller of the planet Ladaux is hereby promoted to the rank of First Centurion of the Fleet. May she exercise this responsibility with authority, intellect, and care, for she is our representative in all things.

SIGNED on the Date of The Republic March 1, 402 by First Lord Petia Naoumov, and countersigned August 11, 402 by Jessica Keller."

She handed the document to Jessica, along with a pen. Jessica signed it, in front of about two hundred cheering witnesses and even hugged Iskra before the woman could escape.

Finally, Jessica was standing alone before the entire group. She just watched them as they cheered, letting it stretch for several minutes before she raised a hand.

It was like a sword had dropped. Instant silence.

"My friends, we have known that Iskra was coming for a bit, so I have had time to prepare some plans," Jessica said simply. "Our friends will need a little time to organize themselves here and offload supplies, before *Leggett* and *Redding* run home for fresh cream. We have been taking the war to *Buran* for some time. Now we're going to step it up. Expect maneuver orders to start hitting your boards in about seventy-two hours, and then we're going sailing."

She nodded fiercely and turned away from the crowd before they could start cheering again. Arott nodded to Denis with a smile as they both rose.

Normally, Arott would have gotten this honor, but again, he had demanded that Denis do it.

Jessica stepped up to him and then turned sideways, so everyone could see her right arm as Denis stepped close enough to smell the wintermint drop she had chewed up earlier. He reached out and added that mighty fifth ring at the top, signifying to all that their commander was a First Centurion.

Ten years ago, she would have been called a First Fleet Lord, but the world had changed. Shortly, the entire galaxy was going to change.

CHAPTER III

As she sat alone in her cabin, finally quiet after the party ended, Jessica could reflect.

She had always hoped she would reach the very top of the fleet, from the first time she had seen the uniform of a command centurion introducing herself to a new class of thirteen-year-old prospects. But even then, Jessica had known some level of doubt. Most officers never made it even as far as Command Centurion. Fewer still became what was still known in those days as Fleet Lord.

Jessica remembered dedicating herself to the dream of First Fleet Lord, during that tumultuous first semester of classes away from her parents and brother. Doing the math and realizing that it wasn't enough to be good at everything, as she had been. No, Jessica was going to have to be the very best, and then do so by such a wide margin over second place that nobody could dispute her.

There were never going to be more than two slots available for that kind of career, and frequently only one. She would have to take it, rather than relying on others to gift it to her.

So she had been the best.

Even when politics intruded on her.

Somewhere, the official records were probably an abject embarrassment to someone. Jessica had eventually graduated fifth in her class, rather than the first she had earned. In her Senior year, she had been

"

taken aside by the First Fleet Lord who commanded the Academy, who patiently explained that she would end her time at his school *Behind Important People.* Two of them were Senators, last time she had been home, and the other two probably would have been, but for being killed in action when they were still Centurions.

Jessica hadn't let that stop her.

Youngest-ever commander of a Destroyer, the old, worn, and much-loved *Resolute.*

Youngest-ever commander of a Destroyer squadron, on the deck of the Destroyer-Leader *Brightoak* with her consorts *Vigilant* and *Rubicon.*

And now, youngest First Centurion in nearly two centuries.

Sitting there in the dimness, letting the day wash off her, Jessica traveled back in her mind to the *Hall of Heroes*, a long arcade at headquarters with oil portraits of famous commanders. Membership on those walls was by accolade of the *Navy*, not command of the Senate.

She had not been back to see the picture hung there, but she knew that Nils Kasum had caused an official portrait of Jessica Marie Keller to be painted when she made Fleet Centurion. And today it hung in that hall.

She wondered if Petia Naoumov, the First Lord who replaced Nils, would leave it as is, or perhaps have a new one done, now that she had a fifth stripe and grayer hair. There were several First Centurions she would share space with, but the rest of them had been dead for at least two hundred years.

It was only the new generation, coming up behind her, that had reverted to the Fleet Centurion rank, rather than Fleet Lord. The warriors that had remained in harness, after Nils Kasum had managed to break the hold of the nobles on the highest ranks, where friendship with the right set of politicians had frequently advanced men and women past their point of competence.

Bogdan Loncar had supposedly been a pretty good command centurion in his time. He should have never been given a flag. Today, he would not have, but that was today. The warriors were in charge of the fleet. At least for this generation.

Jessica could see the way that pendulum had swung back and forth over the four centuries of the Republic. She could not stop it, but she could push it harder in one direction. But that just engendered a harder push back when the time came.

And to do even that much would require her to go someplace that had stopped being exciting, or even interesting, nearly a decade ago.

She supposed, sitting there in the quiet, that she could blame Nils for everything. It had been him sending her to *Lincolnshire* that had set that train in motion. A diplomatic mission, the sort of thing that was used to groom command centurions for greater responsibilities.

Go to *Ramsey* and help them with what had appeared to be a minor pirate incursion at the time. Except that it led her to *Sarmarsh IV*. And then *Petron*. Arnulf. Emmerich. *Warlock*.

Daneel Ishikura. The first man she had ever loved. The first one who had looked at what Jessica expected out of a partner, then turned himself into it, no questions asked. Transformed himself from a barbarian pirate captain into an *Aquitaine* gentleman, because that was the price of her love.

At least in those days.

Before Torsten.

She was sad that Torsten could not be here: to witness this, to celebrate it, to hold her now when she just wanted quiet.

He would watch the recording at some point and celebrate with her vicariously. That would be enough for now, because one of these days, she would be done, and the two of them could run away from everything and find happiness together.

Because Jessica knew she was done. Not burned out, but she would never be promoted again. First Centurion would be the place where her career ended.

There would be other accolades and rewards later, both Republic and Imperial. Jessica had no doubts that Casey would probably try to make her a Duke or something at some point, just to set a precedent, and to say thank you. The Senate would be required to match such extravagance if that happened, lest they be accused by historians of penury.

None of it mattered.

In that room, only Denis had known. Marcelle didn't count, because she had been with Jessica for more than twenty-five years at this point. She was another sister, like Moirrey. Another auntie to Slava and Sasha's children: Ruhal, Margaret, and not-so-little-anymore Juan-Pablo, who was likely to grow up in green, like Jessica. He didn't have that spark, but he had the burning desire, and that might carry him to Command Centurion, one of these days.

Denis had brushed against her side at one point in the crush and whispered something that told her he knew the truth.

"Last time, Jess," he had said as a way to keep her spirits up to get through two hundred other well-wishers who all wanted to say hello and shake her hand.

Yes, Denis had known. But they had spoken daily for more than a year, and at least weekly for a decade. He was as much a brother as Slava, if not more.

This was the last time she would go through such a circus. She would win the war and then retire.

Funny, it was so utterly anti-climactic, at that. She had command. Everyone here would follow her orders, even if she had stayed with four stripes. That was the *Aquitaine* way. Just as everyone was a centurion together, everyone could be command centurions together, at which point you sorted things out based on time in service and size of vessel, plus force of personality.

Denis had been accepted by Alber', Robbie, and Kigali because he commanded *Auberon*, even when he was merely a Senior Centurion and Jessica was technically the Command Centurion. But she had been acting as a Fleet Lord in those days, and the boys knew it.

Held to it.

Held her up to achieve the impossible, time and again, because that was who they were.

Jessica didn't have the words herself, but she knew that at some point she would need to track down a few historians and make sure those men got their stories put down correctly. Too many fanciful tales would center on the Mighty Jessica Keller and forget that Alber' d'Maine had sailed into the very face of death at *First Ballard* to protect her. Or Kigali running the hard gauntlet between a battleship and a battlecruiser on that same day, while flying a Cutter/Revenue with hardly any firepower, just to distract the bad guys for long enough that Jessica could win.

Later historians would overlook the fact that Denis Jež and Nina Vanek had fought both *Auberon*s themselves in all her battles.

Jessica looked down at that fifth stripe on her arm, tacked with a sticky backing today, so that Marcelle could sew it on tomorrow and make it permanent. She touched it once, just to make sure she wasn't dreaming. Jessica Keller was a force now, officially and not just by personality.

She made a note to herself for tomorrow. To send letters off to both

Em and Petia, requesting that official historians be assigned the task of recording things now, perhaps even coming out to the fleet to witness events first hand. Not for her, but for the men and women who should not be forgotten, even as they could themselves vicariously be rewarded by being part of First Expeditionary Fleet during *The Expedition.*

Emmerich had already probably written as definitive a biography of her early career as anyone was capable of. She just wondered how many more volumes he would need to add to complete it.

The only others who might know more were her and Nils, and she knew her former mentor would probably take most of her secrets to the grave. As was proper. She had kept her crush on the man secret for thirty years, a juvenile infatuation that nevertheless formed her adult opinion of what a man should be like.

Eventually, he had become her second father, after Miguel, teaching her how to be a success in her chosen career, where many scholars ranked him perhaps the second best fleet commander alive, behind only his more famous student.

Jessica snickered to herself for a moment as she considered blackmailing Em into writing an authoritative biography of Nils. They had sparred many times when they were the young Turks on opposite sides of the border. Nobody else could probably do justice to the topic.

Jessica reached out her left hand and touched that fifth stripe again. It represented all she had ever wanted out of life, but now that she was here, it was barely a blip. So odd. She had so many other things that she wanted out of the rest of her life, that becoming *First Centurion* of the *Republic of Aquitaine* Navy barely mattered.

She had what she needed to perhaps win this war, but she really wanted to go home.

Home.

Where was home?

Jessica had been on the deck of a warship for most of the last thirty years.

Ladaux was her birthplace.

St. Legier was a place that drew her heart.

Skuodas had given her Torsten, though she had never had a chance to visit and thank them.

But *Petron* was home. That was the siren that called her. Those stubborn, opinionated, chauvinistic, barbarian pirates. That place had also produced Shiori Ness, Cho Ayaka Nakamura, Yan Bedrov, and *Pops* Nakamura. Desianna Indah-Rodriguez. David Rodriguez.

And Daneel.

Yes. She was a First Centurion, and she was fighting a war for the future of mankind, but Jessica really just wanted to go home.

CHAPTER IV

COMMON ERA: 13449, DAY 177. WINTERHOME.
PALACE OF THE ELDEST.

The Holding *is a function of the Scholars.*

Ve Marak Entruk Han hummed the rest of the ditty under his breath, placing Scholars, Technicians, Warriors, and Artisans into their respective castes as the structure uplifting *The Holding* and paving the way for the eventual conquest of space back into a single galaxy-spanning, harmonious whole, removed from the primitive barbarisms that one found under every overturned rock.

Briefly, he marveled that he could still sing along with the tune he had probably originally heard more than nine decades ago, in the first crèche after being weaned. But what was *The Holding*, but a structure of Scholars, even for the Minister of the Left Interior?

Han checked his image in the mirror as he unfolded both mind and body from the daily meditation that kept him young and sharp. Tall and spare, with thin, white hair and skin that had taken on almost a translucent, golden quality, like a dwarf star.

He wore a proper set of four robes, reversing the traditional pattern of darkest to lightest. His outermost was a lapis today, coming all the way in to indigo, closest to his being, tied off with a white obi. After ninety-four years, he was willing to work against tradition in some ways.

To do anything else was to allow the body and the mind to become calcified, which was as bad an outcome for the body as *The Holding*. Too many Scholars simply accepted things, having stopped asking themselves why something is the way it is.

He smiled to himself at the conceit, understanding that *The Eldest* had chosen to extend his reign as Minister of the Left Interior for one more year, already nearly a decade past the age when most Scholars and Ministers were compelled to step down.

It was as important to regularly inject fresh blood into the ruling castes as it was to observe and generally obey the traditions that had brought them all thus.

He exited his sparse cabin, done up with walls lighter than seafoam and a few sumi-e pieces of art that soothed his mind, to emerge into the corridor, walking with careful deliberation that reflected his years, if not his physical fitness.

Today, it was not necessary to jog laps around the waist of this space station in the company of much-younger Warriors, just to remain in shape. Or to show off.

He passed through the four, layered rings of security separating all Scholars from the presence of *The Eldest* and that being's inner machinery. As Scholars spoke for *The Eldest*, Warriors protected him, and Technicians performed their esoteric worship that kept the ancient parts still working.

Past the last portal, he entered the Chamber of *The Mandarins* and took his place at the left interior, last to arrive as befit the First Minister of the government. Today, they faced outward, speaking for *The Eldest* rather than hearing his wisdom.

The silk pillows he sat upon had been replaced recently, new enough that he felt taller as he sat, more than just the erect carriage he maintained. It added to the geniality of his mood as he awaited developments.

The others were here and settled. Ko Quebwas Polen Nim was on his left today as Minister of the Right Interior, as they had their faces and hearts turned away from *The Eldest*, while Nu Sheelan Robar Shil was on his right and Wa Dahnna Lomek Gar, Minister of the Right Facet, was on the far end, beyond Polen Nim.

Han took their measure with a glance, and then located the Warrior standing just inside the door, a man chosen for his ability to remain almost invisible when not needed, and silent the rest of the time.

"Send in the First Director," Han instructed the guard, falling back into himself to meditate on The Great Plan.

The First Director joined them quickly, obviously waiting in a nearby chamber to be called. Han found the man almost interchangeable with others of his kind that had held the position over the years. This one only stood out in Han's mind because he was the first one to be born after a very young Minister of the Eighth Rank, as Han had been fifty-six years ago, proposed the changes to the Great Plan that saw *Fribourg* become the primary thrust of *The Holding*'s expansion.

In other ways, he was a typical Warrior, if something more of a brutalitarian than others had usually been. Of medium height and a squat build, Au Honek Trilben Lor embodied all that the Warriors aspired to be, and just underlined why they were not Scholars.

The man came to attention crisply, and then bowed fully to *The Mandarins* and *The Eldest* behind them.

"What news from *Samara*?" Han asked formally.

The next phase of the Great Plan would see a massive naval force, probably combining elements of both the *Fribourg* navy and their dangerous, new ally *Aquitaine*, to unleash an assault on the *Chéngbǎo*, the starbase *Ural*, in an attempt to overwhelm the fortress, once and for all.

It was, of course, a trap. *Samara* was already the second-most-heavily defended star system in *The Holding*, behind only *Winterhome* itself, because those barbarians kept attacking it in stupidly-straightforward ways.

Today, there were two full battlefleets hiding at *Samara*, in addition to the reinforced defenders. *Fribourg* would arrive and initiate combat, only to find themselves trapped deep in the gravity well of the planet when more defenders suddenly appeared above them from the darkness.

They would be broken, and the psychological impact of two such crushing defeats in short order would cause the so-called *Fribourg Empire* to unravel. All of Han's predictions and *The Eldest*'s modeling of human nature had laid it out in great detail.

Han noticed that the First Director had gone slightly pale, rather than speaking immediately. He turned his *Mandarin*'s eye on the man.

"None, First Minister," the Warrior finally replied in a quieter-than-usual tone.

"None?" Han was surprised. His three comrades were as well.

They could not have attacked and won. *Fribourg* lacked the ships to overwhelm the defenders at *Samara* so heavily that no news would escape. And it was long past the time that the news would have arrived, even by a regular courier, to say nothing of the specialized Hammerheads that carried the orders of *The Eldest* to all Ministers.

"None," the Warrior agreed. "There has been other news from *Samara*, but no attack. Instead, there has been a more troubling raid."

Han felt blood begin to pool, heavy and chilled, in his belly at those words.

"Where?" Han demanded in a voice like a blade in the night.

"*Severnaya Zemlya*," came the reply. "Capital of the *Altai* sector where the woman Keller has recently focused her attacks."

Quickly, the man described the combination strike, first hitting *Yenisei* and then pouncing on *Severnaya Zemlya* when the defenders were pulled forward to intercept an expected second attack at *Ninagirsu*.

One that never came, as the wolves instead struck inward, rather than returning home.

"There's more," the Warrior said as Han and the other *Mandarins* absorbed the audacity of Keller's moves.

"More?" Han asked, filled with sudden dread.

"The course the barbarians took after striking *Severnaya Zemlya*, First Minister," the First Director said.

"Well?" Han demanded.

"It was a reciprocal course for *Winterhome*," the man said.

Han felt the chill in his blood turn to pure rage. Something had gone very desperately wrong with *The Plan*. Worse, the *Altai* and *Lena* sectors had been stripped of much of their defenses to reinforce *Samara*.

Keller had not taken the obvious bait. Had ignored it completely on several occasions, in spite of the surety of the Warriors.

"Have you reinforced the local fleets?" Polen Nim, the Minister of the Right Interior demanded in her harsh, alto tone.

"We have begun, Second Minister," the Warrior turned his attention to her now. "But we do not believe that there is much Keller could to do threaten us here, given the forces in-system. Scouts are out looking in greater force than at any time in the last century."

"It is well," Han announced. "Continue. And leave us."

Han suddenly had a feeling that the entire *Holding* might be at risk, as he had underestimated the woman and her hold on Imperial minds and fleets.

Who was Keller Marie Jessica, that her own mortal enemy, the *Fribourg Empire*, would cast away centuries of tradition and socialization, to fight an entirely new way at her demand?

And those ships she had brought with her. Alien naval architecture, at odds with everything *Fribourg* had *ever* built before. It was as though a designer had been at *St. Legier* during the first raid, and convinced the even-more-barbarous *Aquitaine* to completely change the way they thought and built.

Only now was *The Holding* able to begin fielding the new Tigershark variant of the Mako, after the standard design had proven to be so vulnerable to those changes, at places like *Trusski*.

"Have we gone wrong?" Han asked his compatriots after the First Director had departed. "Will they ignore *Samara* while they attack deeper into *The Holding*, where we have thinned our forces?"

Nu Sheelan Robar Shil, the woman who was the Minister of the Left Facet, spoke up now.

"*NovLao* has been psychologically broken," she said. "We could afford to reduce the intensity of our war on that front, to bring forces closer to the interior. Perhaps we need to rethink our overall strategy in light of Keller and this new Emperor. Both represent radical changes in the traditional, patriarchal culture of *Fribourg*."

Han nodded, turning inward to face the great wall behind them. It was a screen nearly four meters across and three tall. *The Eldest* was not behind that wall, but Han still thought of it as his Temple.

"*Eldest*, what is your guidance?" Han asked in a careful voice.

A face appeared before them, giant on the screen, cunning and ruthless, after his kind. Brown and gray hair swept back in a widows peak with just a hint of curl. Angular planes to cheekbones, jaw, and forehead. A trimmed Van Dyke, more salt than pepper. Eyes that seemed to bore through you like lasers.

It was not a human face, as their God was an ancient, *Sentient* computer that had been sent to *Winterhome* with a colonizing effort just as the Concordancy War erupted and destroyed everything else. But the very Gods had smiled on them and *Winterhome* had been spared the devastation of the galaxy.

When the older pantheon passed, only *Buran* remained.

"Retain *Samara*'s forces," the being spoke in tones that only sounded human, a man's low tenor that seemed to scrape the inside of Han's head, even after so many decades in its presence. "Augment *Winterhome*'s. *Ninagirsu* and *Severnaya Zemlya* must be enhanced. *NovLao* can be ignored for a decade, as they have been nearly broken. Increase the construction of the Tigershark model and the Megalodon, ending the Mako and Carcharias. I will produce a new Hammerhead design to be a consort to both, to counter the new fleet Keller retains. She is only human, and a statistical anomaly that cannot be predicted, except in hindsight. But she will only retain her abilities for two decades more, at most. We can fight to a stalemate for that time, until lesser commanders replace her."

Han bowed forward until his forehead touched the floor at the metaphorical feet of *The Eldest.* It had been a good plan then, and *The Eldest* was not placing the failures at his feet, to tarnish a rich career in service.

Keller Marie Jessica was simply what other Scholars called a *Black Swan.* An occurrence so utterly random that it proved the predictability of mankind, the other nine sigma of results. A genius commander, given authority at the very moment when her contributions could do the most to alter the course of the galaxy.

History had shown the effect of such rare combinations. A strong emperor surrounded by weak admirals was no threat. A weak emperor surrounded by strong admirals was himself at threat, and thus none of the neighbors need fear. Only a strong emperor and strong admirals threatened.

The previous ruler of *Fribourg* had proven his mettle. The new one was still a child, and a female one, at that, in a culture that considered female a second-class.

Fools.

Her own kind would fight her internally, so there was only so much Jessica could do.

The galaxy had indeed changed.

CHAPTER V

IN THE NINTH YEAR OF JESSICA KELLER, QUEEN OF
THE PIRATES: MAY THE SEVENTEENTH AT LADAUX

Pops LOOKED around the small chamber as he waited for the woman they were meeting to arrive. Walls painted off-cream with a little too much mustard in them. Carpet somewhere past taupe on the way to whatever. Sand, maybe. Small conference table with a linoleum top in speckled gray and several other somethings. Eight chairs. Those at least matched. Old and battered, but matching.

Galen sat on one side. Summer on the other. Nobody else had been "invited down" from the ships to this meeting, not even Galen's wife Kari, which was kind of rude. Felt much more like a customs interview, checking papers and inspecting for smuggling, except for the participants.

Six security marines who took themselves way too seriously stood around the outside walls. Sure, Galen was young and fit. And Summer might compete with them on lifting heavy weights competitively, but they had been invited here.

Pops decided he was just feeling his oats this morning. Bedrov had said he wouldn't take any shit from these people either.

The hatch slid to the right with a squeak that suggested someone had tightened a slider control bolt half a turn too far. Good to know maintenance engineers around here cut corners, too.

First Lord of the *Aquitaine* Fleet, or whatever her title was, entered briskly.

Pops rose, because he was *Pops*. He was a little taller than the woman, but only a little, and probably fifteen kilos heavier. She offered a hand and he shook it, deciding that maybe he only had five kilos on her when he did, and that a lot of her stringiness was pure muscle.

Another man had accompanied Naoumov. This one was taller than *Pops*, and far heavier, a big man who exuded *bonhomie* like a cheap cologne.

Pops tried to remember to be impressed as he shook that guy's hand and sat down. Probably have to wash his hands later to get the smell off.

"Iorwerth Nakamura," First Lord Naoumov began. "*Pops*. Crown Naval Designer of Corynthe. Galen Estevan, nephew of Uly Larionov. Summer Ulfsson. I am First Lord Petia Naoumov, and this is the Premier of the *Aquitaine* Senate, Tadej Horvat. Thank you for meeting with us today."

Galen shrugged. Summer nodded. *Pops* leaned forward.

"To what do we owe the dubious honor and implicit threat in meeting two of the top officials in the Republic, during a simple courtesy call as we pass through?" *Pops* even made it all sound polite, and maybe friendly, too, but he was an old man, and had learned to use that like a weapon in polite conversation.

Naoumov's face soured, just the slightest bit, while Horvat's smile broadened.

About what *Pops* had expected when he lobbed that grenade into the conversation.

"You are heading from here to *St. Legier?*" the First Lord asked with something approximating graciousness. More than *Pops* probably deserved.

Must be good, whatever they were about to ask.

Pops turned to Galen to answer that one. It was his ship. *Pops* and Summer were just passengers.

"That is correct, First Lord," Galen woke up and stumbled into the conversation, shooting *Pops* a look that suggested he didn't appreciate being put on the spot like that.

Pity, kid. Old man does mean things, from time to time. Keeps you on your toes.

"Is there a problem?" Galen followed up, as *Pops* leaned ever so slightly back.

"Not a problem," the woman said. "More of a request on our part."

She faltered there, obviously looking for words that would be less *something*. Probably more polite or friendly than she had originally intended, back when she thought she was in charge of this meeting.

Amazing what can happen in a heartbeat when the surly, old man gets to feeling ornery.

Sure enough, she turned to the Premier. Good cop, probably.

"We would like to ask that you escort a pair of vessels to *St. Legier*," Horvat smiled, while remaining somewhat back in his seat.

"Oh?" *Pops* asked vaguely. "Couriers? Freighters?"

"One is a freighter hauling cargo, yes," Horvat agreed. "The other is a warship that will be entering Imperial space under interesting circumstances, as it is not originally an *Aquitaine* ship, but will be flying our flag for the duration, and then presumably an Imperial flag, as well."

"Uh huh." *Pops* wasn't convinced.

He turned to Galen to let the kid Bad Cop this pair.

"Who, if I may inquire?" Galen picked up the thread faster this time. Not as asleep.

"A *Lincolnshire* vessel," Naoumov spoke up again. "The *Robert Fitzwalter*. I'm given to understand that Sri Nakamura is somewhat familiar with the ship."

The bland smile on her face was pretty decent payback for how he'd taken her sideways earlier, so *Pops* wouldn't begrudge her that. Few people knew how to play rough without resorting to dirty. First Lord apparently qualified.

"Huh," he grunted. "Wasn't aware that they actually went and did it."

And he couldn't remember getting a check in the mail, either. Might have to invoice those silly bastards, Net 90 with a *lot* of interest if it was ready for service. Especially if the ship was here. Even if he had thought the original design request was a silly waste of time. There *were* contracts involved.

"*Pops?*" Summer asked, deferential but a little concerned with his reaction.

"*Lincolnshire* War Catamaran," he explained. "Something I did on the side, when David began to normalize relations. Be interesting to see them in action, especially with *Qin Lun* and Jessica."

"Pardon me," Horvat suddenly leaned forward and addressed himself to Summer with a great deal more intensity than he had before. "You look familiar. Have we met?"

All heads turned to Summer now, who actually blushed, just a little bit. Interesting, as she wasn't a woman given to blushing.

"I was an actress once," Summer replied, somewhat evasively, after a moment. "Mostly commercials and low-budget things. Perhaps you know me from the vid?"

That was about as much as *Pops* knew about her past, but *Corynthe* was frequently the back end of beyond, and rarely received any entertainment not produced absolutely locally. It was entirely possible that she might be better known closer in to civilization.

Might also explain why she preferred the anonymity of the galactic fringes.

She glanced at him from lowered eyes, and *Pops* took that as an invitation to distract the conversation.

"So *LWC Robert Fitzwalter* is here?" he butted his nose back into everybody's business. "Have they agreed to travel with a pair of pirates?"

"Ex-pirates," Horvat genially corrected, once he understood that the woman wasn't going to answer any other questions about her background. "Queen Jessica has signed treaties of trade and mutual self-defense with the *Republic*. You are all now good, galactic citizens."

Whatever floats your starship, buddy. *Corynthe* divides into the Government, and the less-than-loyal Opposition, most of whom deserved to be in a prison somewhere.

But didn't we all?

Still, *Pops* nodded the point.

"They have, however, expressed some trepidation, yes," Horvat's smile remained. "Given the connections of the crew, Sri Estevan and Sri Nakamura, they are willing to make peace and travel as *RAN* vessels for the time being, presuming you would do the same."

A-ha.

Sneaky, that one. Put the onus on Galen to agree to play nice with a bunch of folks that saw themselves as cops, and *Corynthe* as pirates. Which was generally close enough to the truth, at least until recently.

Maybe still.

"*Pops?*" Galen asked. "What is a War Catamaran?"

Pops leaned back and let his eyes unfocus a little.

"*Lincolnshire* doesn't have a yard big enough to build cruisers from scratch," he offered. "And noticed that Jessica and David were suddenly building upgraded 4-ring Motherships that might represent a threat, if things got serious again."

"Okay."

"So they hired me, of all people, to design a couple of capital-style ships they could build with the resources at hand. *Robert Fitzwalter* was probably the best design of the group, and *Lincolnshire* apparently went and did it."

"What is she?" Summer was the one who asked, surprisingly.

"Take two frigates, which is the top end of what they *can* build locally," he replied. "Line them up side by side, with about a hull-width of space between them, and then build a bridge right across the center, like a letter H. Add an engine pod to the back, and a weapons array to the front, like noses sticking out. Not as durable as a battlecruiser, but probably comparable to a modern 4-ring like *Kali-ma*. The *Robert Fitzwalter* design had a good mix of offense and defense, if they followed my plans."

"What other ideas did you suggest?" It was First Lord's turn to get involved, apparently. Professional curiosity, most likely.

"Oh, add a small pod off of each side of a frigate," *Pops* grinned. "You can dock a couple of fighters, or put in generators and beams. Even just haul more cargo. Coolest, and maybe silliest design was a *Trimaran*. Take the *Robert Fitzwalter*, and add third frigate, above and centered, with three spans linking them all and a big engine in the middle. More durable than a catamaran. Lots more space. Nowhere to dock it, but if your third hull is emptied out and turned into a flight deck, you've got a Fleet Carrier design, pretty easy. Royal pain in the ass if they invaded *Corynthe* with one."

"Unless you've got a Patrol Cruiser, like say *Qin Lun*," Galen observed dryly.

"Yup," *Pops* grinned. "You thought your tub was a cut-down Expeditionary Cruiser, like everyone else, didn't you?"

"We would prefer that the two of you not engage in a war," Horvat interceded before things got silly. "*Aquitaine* supports the efforts of Jessica and David to civilize the outer reaches, but we are signatories to a treaty guaranteeing *Lincolnshire*'s borders."

In other words, start it, and you'll be facing us, Sri. On the other hand, *Lincolnshire* wouldn't start anything, for fear of getting smacked hard by Jessica's friends back here.

Peace, by accidental default.

He and Galen nodded.

"It would be our honor to serve as an escort while the squadron transited to *St. Legier*," Galen went all formal and stuff.

It was his ship. Plus, it would give *Pops* a chance to see what the final build-out looked like, since he hadn't been on-site to tweak things.

CHAPTER VI

THE DOOR CHIMED EXACTLY on time. Jessica had already put away her paperwork, leaving only a small handheld on her desk. The rest of her office was spare, as always. The only additions to anything in the last five years had been a series of pictures on the left wall, showing every vessel she had ever commanded, all the way back to *Endeavor* and coming up to *Vanguard*. Technically, it and the Star Controller *Auberon* belonged to Denis, but he had pointedly asked her to wear both patches on her uniform, and it was Denis.

He didn't ask much of her, so the few things that came up were important. To both of them.

The other picture, facing inward on her desk, was her and Torsten, taken during some mixer event, both of them in dress uniforms. Before he went away and left her to hold the line while he tried to save the Empire.

She took a deep breath and keyed the button to open the hatch.

Marcelle entered first, carrying a tray with two sippy cups that she places on the desk before stepping to one side.

"Command Centurion Glenn," she said unnecessarily as the other woman entered. "*CP-406*."

"Sit," Jessica ordered lightly as Marcelle withdrew.

They each grabbed coffee and took a sip to enjoy.

"With *Arad* here, your flight wing is even more of an ugly duckling," Jessica began.

Glenn nodded, eyes bright with anticipation, it seemed.

"I had considered routing you home, or as far as an Imperial dry-dock, to swap your three for a trio of the new Fast Strike Bombers, and I may yet do that, so warn your pilots that they may have to grow up and become team commanders at some point."

That got a grin. Pilots were pilots, but the new bomber design had a crew of three, not just one lone lunatic against the galaxy.

"I have a different mission for you instead," Jessica said, watching the surge of joy appear in those eyes.

Yes, this woman was still a pirate born, as Bedrov had seen.

"I am going to send you and *Duncan* off to a point well in the interior of the *Altai* sector," Jessica continued. "The freighter will drop off a couple of cargo packs for you, someplace secret and hidden, so you have food and replacement parts, and then return here."

"And *CP-406*, sir?" Glenn finally spoke.

"The *Pochtovyi Trakt*, the so-called postal road that *Buran*'s vessels use to navigate are, in the end, just a set of beacons," Jessica said. "Around here, each is a trio of satellites about a light-hour apart, set every two light-years, broadcasting a signal. The *Sentient* vessels can land from their jump, triangulate, and be gone again in less than two minutes, according to some reports. That allows them to make incredibly high-speed runs between well-mapped places. Records captured when the Duke of *Osynth B'Udan* fled suggested a round trip between *St. Legier* and *Winterhome* of four months, when the best we could do right now is probably eight, if anyone wanted to try."

"Okay," Glenn nodded, still sipping and trying to contain her energy.

"I want you and *CP-406* to pick a spot, Glenn," Jessica's voice turned serious. "From there, I want you to run up a line, destroying every transmitter you can detect. If you find a side street, I want you to note it, categorize it, and possibly come back for it. You'll be gone for several months doing this, which is why you need a forward resupply base, but I want you to cut that bastard's spine. Leave the brain intact at *Winterhome*, but cripple the ability of his fleets to move around quickly. And I want you working beyond *Severnaya Zemlya*, so that the *Altai* sector suddenly finds itself cut off."

"Horatio, at the bridge," Glenn noted. "In reverse."

"Exactly," Jessica agreed. "*Samara* can rot on the vine, especially if I'm hammering places on the other side of *M'Hanii*. They'll have to bring up forces from everywhere else, or abandon their entire forward defenses and pull back to a more secure system."

"Targeting priority after *Altai* sector is sewn up?" Glenn asked.

The fire in her eyes now was serious, but also a little crazy. A female version of Alber' d'Maine, or Kigali, if you will. Assume you've isolated an entire sector, and are moving on to the next one.

"*Lena* Sector," Jessica instructed.

"Not deeper?"

"No," the First Centurion commanded. "I have something better planned for them, once I have *Buran*'s undivided attention."

CHAPTER VII

YAN LAUGHED inside when he considered the meeting about to start around him. Everyone had their tablets, and the two Imperials had brought stacks of printed paper in folders.

If it wasn't so damned important, and secret, he would have suggested they do this in a bar somewhere, instead of a tiny meeting space barely big enough for the group. It would have helped the other four relax a little better. He was already loose.

Facing down Death will do that to you.

zu Wachturm had grown more serious and grim in the last year, but that was to be expected. He was commanding a war that possibly would determine the fate of the galaxy. Jessica got to have all the fun, blowing shit up while Emmerich was back here, trying to outthink a God.

Hendrik Baumgärtner was severe and quiet, like a Court's Executioner. Yan had heard rumors of fools who thought they could just brush Casey Wiegand aside. The smarter ones were fomenting rebellion in their drinking salons, where hopefully nobody would ever take them seriously enough to drop a marine detachment in through the windows.

Even Ainsley had grown quiet, but she had known Moirrey forever, and the Evil Engineering Gnome looked today like she had been pulled backwards through a knothole in a board.

Little woman had lost enough weight that her face was almost gaunt. Yan thought he could count her ribs through the green and black tunic she wore today, being in uniform, rather than First Lady In Waiting, down on the planet. There were bags under her eyes, and gray hairs starting to appear, that hadn't been visible nine months ago.

Before *St. Legier*. And everything since.

Grand Admiral rapped his knuckles on the table. There were no aides taking notes or available to run and fetch. Even everyone else's marine guards were outside the closed door.

"*Project Butterfly*," *zu* Wachturm said simply. "I have read the most recent design synopsis, and the new modifications added by Bedrov. And presumably suggested by the so-called *Lord of Tiki*?"

"That is correct, Grand Admiral," Yan said. "Damned thing was alone for three thousand years, so he likes to talk to people. Ainsley and I kept to ourselves on the flight here, for the most part, so we could work on this design. He contributed ideas, but I did the math."

For a moment, the admiral had a look like he wanted to punch Yan in the face. That was also to be expected. A *Sentient* system was responsible for all his pain. Made sense that he wouldn't trust another one, even after reading Yan's report on the encounter that could have cost them everything.

Damn it, man, you should be giving me a medal, not a serious stinkeye.

But he didn't say that. Someone would ask why the pirate was being rewarded. What had he done to merit this?

Better to remain quiet.

"Lady Moirrey, are you sure it will work?" Wachturm turned to her, way more polite and reserved.

"No," the little goof said in her serious, Imperial voice. "I am not. However, there are limits to the testing we can do, if we wish to maintain secrecy. Yan and I have designed the components in such a way that it can be built in four different yards, and then assembled in the field. Only then can we test it effectively."

"Your notes…" the big man paused and looked down to confirm something. "Yes. With Bedrov's updates, you classify the weapon as a Type-6 beam. Is that even possible?"

"Six point four," Moirrey corrected him a sepulchral voice. "As Yan is wont to say, it is not a planet-cracker, but I'm not trying to destroy a planet with it. Merely hatch a butterfly. Thus the name."

Yan shivered inside. She only ever talked like a scholar when death and destruction on epic scales was the topic. He preferred the goof with an accent so thick you could use it to polish steel.

At least everyone else shivered, too. Ainsley's hand found his under the table.

zu Wachturm blanched.

Baumgärtner had a smile like Death himself had just walked into the room and sat down for High Tea.

"I had thought it was so named from the design of the vessel," Hendrik said carefully.

"Form followed inspiration," Yan offered in a weak voice. "Adding a solar array, like butterfly wings, greatly improved my primary power curve. It's not like the thing could expect to survive combat, so I didn't need to build that section any more hardy than it is."

"Will it work?" Emmerich asked bluntly.

"Will it work?" Moirrey's voice turned cold. "Yes. Will it succeed? Time will tell. Bedrov and I will have to be there at the last, tuning and fixing things, so we'll be able to report back success. If it fails? We'll probably be dead, and the war will continue without us."

"And your crew?" *zu* Wachturm pressed.

He started to say more, but Ainsley interrupted.

"I'll be in overall command of the vessel," she said in a voice like steel rimed with morning frost. "We'll need at least a dozen volunteers with naval engineering backgrounds and security clearances at the highest level you offer."

"I note you did not say sailors," Hendrik's hard smile matched Ainsley's. Kindred spirits, as it were.

"Tifft would make an excellent First Officer," Yan joined in. "He's got all the necessary backgrounds. And the trust of the key players."

"Should Jessica contribute to the force?" Emmerich's voice was like the bloody edge of a razor blade.

Yan wondered if he would ever get warm after this. Maybe a hot shower later, with Ainsley to scrub his back?

"No," both Ainsley and Moirrey said in unison, turning to look at each other with smiles like two Norns cutting a life thread.

Ainsley nodded. Moirrey spoke.

"This must be an entirely Imperial effort," *Lady Moirrey of Ramsey* stated simply. "Not counting Ainsley, who is part of the engineering effort, nor myself and Bedrov. The remainder must be people you pick."

"Why?" Wachturm asked in a blunt, hard voice.

"The Empire must see itself as the victor," Moirrey said. "*Aquitaine* has been there in the time of need, and the relationship in the future will be built upon that, but Casey must deliver the killing blow, not Jessica. Tifft, or someone like him, will push the button, when the moment comes."

Silence. Pause. Like a fog suddenly arising from the low places to engulf you and light every nerve on fire.

"Understood," *Imperial Grand Admiral Emmerich zu Wachturm, Duke of Eklionstic* nodded. "Agreed."

Another pause.

"And then I will leave you to the building of the thing," he continued. "Is there any other business we need to consider first?"

Heads shaken in the negative. Nothing more to say.

The two admirals left first. Moirrey followed shortly after.

Yan remained in the chair. Ainsley still held his hand.

"It will be fine," she said.

"It will be insane," Yan replied.

"We'll do it together," Ainsley leaned her weight on his shoulder and kissed him. "As always."

"As always," he agreed.

Succeed together, or die together.

CHAPTER VIII

IMPERIAL FOUNDING: 180/09/04. IMPERIAL PALACE,
MEJICO, ST. LEGIER

THE HOT SEASON would be fading soon, Casey noted as she stared out the window at the evening sun, slowly turning orange and salmon as it touched the horizon. They had all endured a long, hot summer, the warm seasons just as off balance as the cold one had been.

Still, every day promised to be a little *less* than the one before it, as the waves that crashed on the various shores slowly died down with each ripple. It was as true for the planet as it was her soul.

She hoped.

A knock at the door, and then Anna-Katherine looked in long enough to confirm that everything looked good, before standing back.

"Your Majesty, the Chief of Deputies arrives," the young woman said, just before Torsten entered.

The room was configured for meetings, with a dining room table covered over with white paper that could be used for notes as well as doodles. A small hutch to one side held some dinnerware, if she had chosen to entertain, but she had always gone elsewhere for such things. Soothing walls in a cream verging over towards honey oak. Thick carpets underfoot, since she preferred bare feet indoors.

There was one she would entertain here first, before any others. Cook him dinner. Try to find their place.

Assuming Vo returned.

Until then, this room worked well enough as an office. The kitchen was just behind her through a door, and her personal suite just beyond that. Knocking two walls out of the middle of this hotel's second floor had let her get completely decadent with space, after a tiny cabin aboard *Auberon*, and later *Vanguard*.

"Sit, please," she said, and did, as Torsten entered alone and tendered a proper bow. She turned to the young woman in the doorway. "Anna-Katherine, tea for us, please. Hot and with everything on the side."

"Yes, Your Majesty," and she was gone.

She studied the man, carefully noting that he no longer even had a limp when he walked, so successful had Moirrey's design of a new implant for the man been.

Torsten had brought a hard-sided case, forty-five centimeters wide, thirty-five tall, and ten thick, done in a matte black paint that only partly disguised the materials. Hull metal. Vo's favorite pistol would probably just barely dent it.

Torsten placed the case on the table as he sat, popping two latches and opening the top to access the interior, pulling out a stack of documents. The case closed, he placed it by his foot and looked her square in the face.

A long moment passed silently.

"What's wrong?" he asked in a concerned tone.

Casey realized that someone like Torsten probably had studied her enough to read the signs so subtle that everyone else would miss them. Only Moirrey would know. And perhaps Vibol.

"Nothing you can solve," she finally admitted, listening to the voices and songs in her head go round and round like spring squirrels.

"I see," he nodded sagely. "Perhaps September Fourth resonates as a birthday we cannot properly celebrate?"

Casey felt her eyes grow big for a moment, before she could control her face. Then her eyes slitted down hard.

"How did you know?" she probed, trying to retain an outward calm that would be a good-enough illusion.

The serene smile that spread across his face was telling, but Torsten had never been closed with her. Not like Vo. And Torsten Wald was also safe around her, devoted utterly to Jessica. He also saw part of his duty to stand *in loco parentis* for a young woman who had just lost her entire family.

She had many uncles now. Not just Em, but also Denis and Torsten. And even dear Hendrik.

She could face the hard choices, with their help.

And Jessica.

"It is my duty to know these things," Torsten said with a nod, obviously moving away from the meeting he had planned to have with her when he walked in. "In light of circumstances, I found it important to study the man much more closely than I ever had, and still believe I know him better than anyone in the Empire. Only his comrades from the *Auberon* days would know him better, but I suspect even they were largely kept at the same distance he keeps everyone. Still, it is the man's birthday."

Casey nodded. She could recognize the truth of the thing. Vo kept everyone outside.

Only she had ever managed to crack that shell, she suspected. Now, she just had to wait and hope that when he rebuilt it, she was on the inside.

One did not force Vo *zu* Arlo to do anything he didn't think was right.

"Would anyone know?" she asked.

"I doubt it," Torsten said. "*Aquitaine*, as you know, does not put major emphasis on celebrating birthdays, even milestone ones. Plus, he will be with Imperial folks who, while they would celebrate, probably don't know. And he will not tell them."

"Yes," Casey said. "You understand. There is so much I want to do in this world, and little actually in my grasp. At least today. So perhaps work will give me solace. What documents do I need to sign, Torsten?"

CHAPTER IX

"Good morning, you scamp," Tadej rose to greet his guest. "It's not the Marquette Room, up on the station, but hopefully this will do."

Tad studied the man as they sat. Yes, it was probably more than acceptable that he and Nils meet in one of their private clubs that men of this social rank joined. *The Huntsman* was perhaps the most exclusive, with a significant waiting list, little turnover, and requirements that only members could nominate replacements when an opening occurred.

It was warm in here, and just dim enough inside to suggest the early morning just rising outside. Tad had always believed that good conspiracies should be done in the first light, after awakening, and over coffee and a hearty breakfast.

Too many fools got too deep into their wine in the evenings and did or said stupid things.

The Huntsman was also a ghost town this morning, which played to Tad's needs. He had the kitchen and the staff largely to himself, in spite of the twenty-five-hours-open nature of the place. Wood-paneled walls suggested a hunting lodge, as was proper, even in the middle of Penmerth. Dark green carpet heavy enough to suggest a mossy forest floor.

Nils Kasum took it all in with a wry smile, as if he could read Tad's mind. He probably could, after so many decades as friends.

The man remained silent as the waitress bustled in with coffee, orange juice, and menus. Finally, they were alone.

"I am retired now. You do remember that, yes?" Nils asked in a low, quiet drawl as he adulterated his coffee, smiling all the while.

It was the good stuff. Nils had only managed to become a member in retirement, but the staff had immediately added items to the larder for his desires. Considering how much it cost each year, just to belong, that was the least they could do.

"Indeed you are," Tad replied with a smile. "And now I can pick your brain on certain topics without an official imprimatur."

"Heavens protect innocents and fools," Nils sighed. "What are you up to now?"

Tad just smiled. It was important that this come across as a friendly gesture. Nils wouldn't actively work to sabotage him, but it would strain things, accidentally opening a second front with his oldest friend in the galaxy.

"I need to talk about Jessica Keller," Tad said in a more hushed voice, leaning forward enough to put his elbows on the table. "About the time that comes after."

"After," Nils repeated dryly. "After what?"

"After she destroys *Buran* and wins the war, Nils," Tad said.

"That's a given?" the former First Lord asked.

"Without revealing operational reports and secrets you are no longer allowed read except in an emergency? Yes," Tad replied. "Only her death is likely to save the beast from the wrath of the two women."

Nils nodded knowingly. Jessica Keller and Casey Wiegand. The First Centurion and Emperor Karl VIII. Tad let the moment stretch.

"And afterwards?" Nils asked.

"Afterwards, things get dicey, according to all the planners I have engaged to read their tea leaves and prognosticate for me."

Nils chuckled, deep in his chest, that deep voice emerging from such a narrow torso.

"That's because you're up to no good, Tad," he smiled. "Jessica won't become your enemy unless you make her one."

"And that's why you and I are here, having a quiet breakfast away from knaves and spies, Nils," Tad's voice grew serious. "It may come to that."

Nils grew still, like a gargoyle poised for flight.

"What have you done?" he asked simply.

There was no emotion behind the words, which was good. Things were going to get emotional enough shortly. Hopefully, Tad would make it home today without wearing Nils's coffee. And without a black eye from his best friend punching him in the face.

But those might be the cost of governing.

"On the surface?" Tad murmured. Nils nodded. "I have sent Judit Chavarría to *St. Legier* with Palatine authority as my personal representative."

Again, Nils nodded, remaining otherwise still and silent.

It wasn't a rabbit, hiding in the grass for a hawk to fly by. Tad was reminded more of a great cat, lurking in a tree for some fool or eland to pass beneath. But that was what made Nils Kasum who he was: possibly the second greatest combat commander in the last century, behind only Jessica Keller.

"And what did you intend her to do there?" Nils replied quietly.

And there was the crux of it. Nils knew him well enough to understand that there would be many layers to such a thing. Judit was one of Tad's closest friends as well, if not for as long.

She had stood across that wide, wooden desk from him in the Senate chamber for many years, fencing with words and ideas.

"She is to maintain *Fribourg* as a firebreak," Tad stated unequivocally. "And identify those places where a jeweler's hammer might have the greatest impact at the least cost."

"I see," Nils suddenly leaned back, coffee mug in one hand, but tilted away.

His eyes grew distant and calculating. Nearly a minute passed.

"I fear your ego may have gotten ahead of your wisdom, Tad," Nils finally said. "I understand the need, and the maneuver, but you may have moved too soon."

"How so?" Tad countered, not exactly angry with his oldest friend, but piqued by the language. The presumptions.

Which was probably what Nils intended.

"You have read Wachturm's book?" Nils asked.

Tad nodded. *Devoured* it might be a more accurate description. Had to go and buy a second copy for his shelf, because the first one was a mass of highlighted passages and markers indicating important pages for future reference. That sort of thing.

"So Emmerich Wachturm, excuse me *zu* Wachturm now, probably knows Jessica better than anyone alive, except me," Nils added. "Robbie Aeliaes might come in a distant third, but he had been her right hand for a decade before, so it would be hard to isolate the two of them into separate entities at present."

"Noted," Tad replied, striving to keep emotion out of his voice.

This breakfast meeting had been his idea. And he had specifically not worn his nicest tunic, just in case things got out of hand. He could listen to the man's wisdom.

Very few others would dare tell Tad the truth to his face.

"But his book is out of date," Nils continued. "He wrote it before *First St. Legier*. After *Second St. Legier*, I would expect Jessica to become something of a mother figure to Casey. Doubly so with Torsten Wald in the picture."

"Another Imperial," Tad noted.

"Another brilliant, scholarly commander," Nils corrected. "Jessica's type. I've read some of the reports the man produced for Karl VII, back when I was First Lord and midnight pixies would magically deliver things to my desk. With him as the head of Casey's government, Jessica will be even more closely involved than otherwise."

"And my ego?" Tad asked dryly. "Where does that factor into things?"

He hoped his voice came across as calm and rational.

"Time was always going to be on our side, Tad," Nils replied. "Jessica sat in that meeting with you and Casey, up in my beloved Marquette Room, and told you that once the war was done, the thing she wanted more than anything in the world was to retire to *Corynthe*. That removes her from the board."

"That was before Casey became Emperor," Tad noted. "And before Torsten Wald."

"Yes," Nils agreed. "But Torsten would have no more desire to remain in power than Jessica would want to remain in harness. They will both retire at the earliest opportunity."

"My tea readers suggest that date to be nearly a decade in the future," Tad offered, showing just enough of the top secret data to prick Nils's conscience.

"Then you need to fire them and get better fortune tellers," Nils fired back sharply. "Jessica has no interest in remaining an *Imperial Peer*, and will leave as soon as she feels that the situation has stabilized. If you upset that apple cart while she's on scene, she may never leave. And if she finds your fingerprints, then yes, you may have an enemy. You should ask *Buran* what that's like, since Karl VII can't answer you."

"I'm not sure I can wait a decade," Tad suggested quietly.

"And that's your ego talking, and not your wisdom, Tad," Nils snapped. "You're afraid that someone else will get the credit for your maneuver, aren't you?"

Tad paused, carefully not grinding his teeth. This was why you had conspiracies in the morning, when the sunlight might shine on them and burn away all the stupid vanities and risks.

Like yes, moving too quickly and making an implacable enemy of the greatest naval commander alive.

"If we wait a decade, Casey might stabilize her reign," Tad prophesied. "Might rebuild *Fribourg* in her image. Strengthen it to the point that we could not bring them down."

"No," Nils said. "You might not be able to shatter them into feuding principalities that you could stir up, like *Lincolnshire* frequently does to the outer bands of *Corynthe*. Your bribes to make a fuss might not work, and the Empire might survive. Why is that the worst possible outcome?"

Tad drew a breath to rebuke Nils, but caught the words unspoken.

Why was that the worst possible outcome?

"Because *Fribourg* was winning, Nils," Tad finally admitted. "Given a chance, they have the mass and economies of scale to defeat us. This might be our only opportunity in the next generation to strike back."

"Casey will be an entire generation at her task, Tad," Nils leaned in again. "Decades, just bringing the rest of *Fribourg* to heel. And she will be trying to make them over into us as she goes. If you restart the war, even defensively, you will squander that opportunity. We could passively conquer *Fribourg* culturally, socially, perhaps even emotionally in that time. *Is it worth the risk?*"

"And they could overthrow her tomorrow, Nils," Tad countered. "A few have tried, either actively in one case or passively in several others. The noble class is extremely restive."

"So wait until one of them gets serious, Tad," Nils said. "Or lucky. But make sure that it can never be traced back to you. Casey might understand matters of statecraft, but Jessica will never forgive you. You might succeed in breaking *Fribourg* apart, but what would it do to the Republic if it came to open war with Jessica? Have you considered that you might break *Aquitaine* as well? They see her as their hero. The one that saved the galaxy. How many people will side with her instead of you?"

Tad caught his gasp and considered the rightness in Nils's words.

The waitress returned and took orders, interrupting the line of logic.

After a few minutes, the emotions faded as well, both men watching the other silently, but at least he wasn't wearing coffee. And didn't need an icepack for his face.

Tad maneuvered the conversation onto less-fraught topics, happy to have not driven an impossible wedge between he and Nils. The man was retired, but that just meant that he had time on his hands and freedom to pursue his own conscience now.

And perhaps agitate for a Senatorial seat, such as the one his brother held. Not all of them were elected, as the Republic long ago recognized the need to have some members who sat above politics, or at least to one side, where their expertise in a topic or argument might lend weight and credence.

Tad could see Nils standing on the Senate floor, denouncing him in closed session, if it went wrong.

And perhaps, just perhaps, the man would be correct.

But this was a once-in-a-lifetime opportunity, and Tad would be a fool to pass it up.

CHAPTER X

As Mondays went, Vo decided the one just rising was probably no better or worse than most. His office was a welcome respite from a week of sleeping rough, although he would never say that out loud.

An entire week in the field on maneuvers had tightened things up considerably with the men, after so much time in the Death Zone all winter, and then the messiness of transporting the entire legion from the interior to the front.

Of course, the men had gotten a little sloppy. But Vo had instructed the defending forces he faced to fight dirty. He had even called the Flag General in charge of Fort Dawson occasionally to leak secrets, just so his own men got used to attacking someone that fought back and seemed to know where their hard and soft spots were.

Getting embarrassed in training meant that you were less likely to get killed on the battlefield. And that was the next stop.

So he was in his office as the sun rose, reading the outcomes right now. The combined score for a full week in the field was respectable, he supposed. In the top quarter, over the last fifty years, but well short of what he thought it should be. At least they had pulled it together on Thursday and stopped getting ambushed so badly. The weekend had even shown him what this tcam was really capable of, when pushed.

So he let them sleep in today, while motor pool teams fixed the hardware and the cooks could fix the rest. He missed Melina and

Thurman, but a battlefield was no place for their three young daughters, eleven to fourteen. The mess hall for Headquarters Ala that the woman had run with an iron fist, however, hadn't forgotten anything, even without her there holding the reins.

He put down the current report and returned to the breakfast burrito that someone had delivered to his desk, along with coffee, just as he was leaving his cabin, like morning fairies. He was in the process of finishing the other half when Reese Borel knocked and opened the door.

"Just got word from on high, sir," he said as he stuck his head in. "Frigate just made orbit with a messenger specifically for us. Probably be on the ground and here by dinner time."

Vo nodded. The timing was about right. Hopefully, the man would have two messages, with one of them being that Fourth Patrol, Fourth Heavy Scout Ala, was ready to begin hard training, and would be shipping out here shortly. He was looking forward to adding Moirrey's Winged Scouts to the mix.

Vo and Alan Katche had discussed a variety of options with Pyotr, Fourth Ala commander, but everyone agreed that they weren't read to fully integrate that team yet.

Instead, Vo was hoping that the messenger was bringing orders for the rest of the Legion to load onto the Assault Carriers and move forward, so they could launch their first strike.

November Tenth was coming soon. Vo had no doubts that the various planetary Khans had been warned to expect something big on the first anniversary of the bombardment of *St. Legier*, but he wanted to wait. Not long. Perhaps a week later, so that those fine folks began to relax some, confident that their mortal enemy was apparently too weak to actually threaten them.

And then he wanted to burn some planet to the ground.

"Pulse a message to all the motor pool Decurions," Vo said. "Tell them to either speed things up, or hold off on big tasks until tomorrow, when we'll know more. Then let Alan and the other cohort commanders know. In fact, bump things around to put us all in a meeting mid-afternoon, so I'll know where we're at when the messenger arrives."

"Will do, sir," and he was gone.

Vo took another bite and opened the next report.

———

THE MESSENGER ARRIVED with Tom Provst in tow, which Vo found an interesting addition. The rest of Provst's Expeditionary Squadron had just arrived in orbit over the last few weeks, and had been drilling as hard in orbit as the 189th had been on the ground.

For the same reasons.

The delivery boy was a kid. A lieutenant just out of school with a formal-looking, soft-sided leather satchel slung over the shoulder of his uniform. Naval blue, but the kid looked more like a spy than a sailor, an opinion Vo kept to himself.

He apparently knew too many spies these days.

The event was a working dinner, so they added an extra leaf to the table and slid in a chair for their unexpected guest. Tom had obviously ordered everyone to remain silent about his accompanying the messenger, else Vo would have been told a count of bodies to expect, at the minimum.

But the kitchen had enough food on hand.

Vo looked around as they settled. The messenger on his immediate right, Reese Borel on his left. Alan, Omar, Dylan, Pyotr, and Alistair. Cohort Centurion Hermann Gerstenburger, commanding the entire HQ Ala, was a more recent addition, once Vo realized that there was too much work to do for him to command the five combat Alae in the field, and still keep up with everything Sixth required. With Provst on the far end, the room was a little crowded, but this way they didn't have to yell at each other over the noise of the regular mess hall.

Imperial manners demanded that everyone eat first, so they did, bouncing operations questions off each other, and occasionally Tom Provst, but ignoring the messenger completely.

Finally, the stewards cleared things and delivered coffee. Brandy was occasionally an option, but Vo didn't want people relaxing tonight.

"You have dispatches for us?" Vo turned to the young man.

He had already placed the satchel on the table in front of him and extracted two large, sealed envelopes, one of which went down the table to Provst. Both were heavy with paper.

Vo opened the packet and scanned the first two pages quickly, before handing everything to Alan to read.

"You got the same orders?" Vo found Tom Provst looking up with a sardonic grin on his face.

Tom hadn't smiled much over the last year. Possibly as little as Vo did, so seeing this was almost out of place.

"Kick in the door and guard it," Provst said. "While you and yours rob the joint. Then drive the getaway car."

Vo doubted that *Imperial Movement Orders* actually ever read anything like that, but he could see that interpretation. He had spent enough time around Tom.

Rendezvous with the First Centurion, now that Provst's battle squadron was complete. Sail out and hit one of five targets, to be determined by forward intelligence unknown back at Headquarters. Teach the followers of *Buran* that they had made a terrible mistake and that anything was better than compounding it.

Or, as Tom would likely say: kill them all, and make God sort them out.

"What verbal orders did you have?" Vo turned to the man, and he realized that the messenger had gone a little white. "Everyone here is cleared for anything you have."

"This one was for you, specifically, General," the man said a touch nervously. "Delivered into my hands by the Grand Admiral to be placed in yours."

He extracted a much smaller thing now, a flat bag about the size of Vo's hand, that Vo took and weighed.

He opened it and pulled out a piece of cloth folded up inside. It was crimson. With the Imperial crest: *Gold Eagle Elevated and Displayed.* By size, it just happened to be perfect to hang from the flag antenna on Cutlass Ten, his command skiff, where the breeze would pull it taut as the vehicle moved.

Vo kept the sourness off his face. *zu* Wachturm might have handed it to the kid, but it hadn't been the Grand Admiral's idea. Nor the Grand Marshal's.

Casey, sending her personal flag for him to wear into battle, as a blessing. Like she had promised to do. He almost felt like one of the knights of the round table.

"Reese," Vo said, handing the flag to the man on his other side. "See that Iakov Street gets this. He'll know what to do."

The room had fallen awkwardly silent around them. Barracks rumors had made suggestions, but Vo had ignored questions from everyone except Alan, who he could trust to keep his mouth shut, even if he had a tendency to walk off with coffee mugs accidentally.

Vo scanned the entire room once, before settling back on Tom Provst.

He had spent the afternoon with most of these men, so they knew the state of things.

"In eighty-four hours, Friday morning local time, we will begin loading DropShips," Vo said firmly. "Departure will follow in ninety-six hours, or I will want to know who needs to be fired. Questions?"

"Pack everything, or do we have a specific climate to prepare for?" Alan asked.

It was a damned good question. Vo didn't have an answer.

He would need Jessica for that.

"Pack everything," he decided. "Maybe we'll hit more than one target before we return to barracks."

There was no reason to only share his wrath with one planet. He had more than enough to go around.

CHAPTER XI

ON THE SCREEN, it looked like her big battle squadron always had, until you got close and counted noses. They had lost *CS-405*, and never heard from them again, but Jessica still held out hope that Kosnett had just had to take his time getting home, rather than being captured and disappearing forever into the darkness of *Buran*.

CP-406 and *Duncan* were off looking for French Mainforcers to ambush, deep in the Spanish interior, the origin of the word *guerilla*: fighters in Wellington's Peninsular war.

With *RAN Arad*, she had two carriers now. The three corvettes that had accompanied *Arad* put her one above her old strength and let Jessica organize things into wings, rather than throwing everyone into a rush. *Arad* and *II Augusta* could sit off in one corner and launch remote strikes from a great distance, or they could follow in to a close drop, only a few light-minutes out, and unload everything, meeting them on the far side without having to take fire. *Ballard* could wait with them, or do combat, depending on the defenses they encountered.

One more way to confuse *Buran*'s Directors.

Two Assault Corvettes could escort the three line warships, *Vanguard*, *VI Ferrata*, and *VI Victrix*, while the others could sit on wings defensively and shoot anything hostile that moved. Coming out of jump hot, she could either drop the full flight wing as an introduction: fourteen

GunShips and twelve Fast Strike Bombers; or just have everyone come out at once and go for mass chaos.

Jessica looked down from the display and caught Enej's eye as she keyed the command channel, bringing everyone into a virtual room to listen.

"Enej, you have the flag," she said crisply.

He blinked briefly and then smiled.

Enej Zivkovic didn't get to do this very often. Most of the time, he was relaying messages up and down the chain as she adjusted fights. He would never be a combat commander, like Robbie, Alber', or Kigali, but she wouldn't have gotten here without his calm competence doing the little things.

"All vessels, this is Enej Zivkovic, aboard *Vanguard*. I have the flag," he said, head coming up just a little and chin jutting out. "Everyone conform to *Vanguard*, and ahead standard acceleration. See you at *Waypoint Glory*."

Jessica smiled at him. The raids were going to get more serious now. Either *Buran* started defending some of the mid-sized systems deep behind the old lines with better forces, or she might send out small teams to just harass the shit out of things around here. *Buran* didn't have to fight her, but she would do an unbelievable amount of damage to this sector's economy and morale if he didn't.

She couldn't capture anyplace, not like *Thuringwell*, and both *Ninagirsu* and *Severnaya Zemlya* were too well-defended for her to fight a pitched battle on her terms, but she could certainly go after most of the rest. At some point, the *Lord of Winter* would have to fight her, or watch as her forces went and did the same things to the *Lena* Sector.

And then, who knows?

IFV Vanguard pointed her nose deep into the interior of *The Holding*, and vanished into JumpSpace.

CHAPTER XII

IN SOME WAYS, it was like the old days with First War Fleet as Jessica watched updated scans from *Ballard* come in. Everyone was at battle stations on all ships, just waiting for the word.

She had the overhead lights in her flag bridge turned down, just a little, a suggestion from the folks on *Ballard* as to help everyone think sneaky.

Thief in the night.

In the old days, they had known the names of the systems they wanted to probe and had some feel for the economy and culture before they arrived.

Some Dukes scrimped on defenses, relying on the *Fribourg Fleet* to maintain enough firepower in-system to prevent serious raids. Others went all in, maintaining what could be technically interpreted as private navies, although always with the tacit approval of the throne.

There were always hard cases that would risk getting carried away if they had access to that level of manpower. Especially today.

But this was *Buran*. There were no private militias. Until the last few years, the war had been so far removed from their lives that many systems only had a few basic defenses, things like armed stations with a couple of big guns and maybe a bunch of missiles that could be used to chase off any pirates that wandered this way accidentally.

That was changing, but not nearly fast enough, as they had to build everywhere at once, and Jessica could strike wherever her scouts found a soft spot.

Like *Nents*.

It was a relatively unimportant system, but Seeker had, they discovered, a near-eidetic memory for planets he had studied, so nearly every inhabited system in *Altai* or *Lena* sectors had a name now, and not just an alphanumeric designation.

Its importance lie in the fact that it happened to join several trade routes together, like a convenience store out on the highway, or an old-fashioned inn and pub for travelers. Just a village on the edge of a swamp, if you would.

But someone, sometime in the past, had decided to make money with orbital warehousing, and had put twenty-three major facilities in orbit, most of them just massive, squat cylinders where a freighter could dock and unload big containers in one of several standard sizes.

Big, hollow donuts, filled with cream, waiting.

There were defenses, of course. *Ballard* had spent several days listening to the entire system before retrieving the rest of the team.

Three cruisers and three Hammerheads were in patrol orbits of the planet, so someone had properly valued the contents of those warehouses and determined that this was a good place to strike. Anything less than the full squadron would have found this to be too big of a risk.

Even with everyone, and reinforced, it was not likely to be a turkey shoot, but this was also the first place in the last year to be reinforced on the other side.

"*Vanguard*, this is Aukley, aboard *Ballard*," a voice came over the command line. "Sending you an identification file to review."

Enej routed it to the projection and spun it slowly as Jessica studied the image.

The three cruisers down there.

Interesting, indeed.

All three were different, but that was only obvious when you saw them with the *Energiya* housing attached, which was normally hiding in the dark during an attack. It was like three different models, or classes.

"Elzbet," Jessica asked aloud. "Mako, Roughshark, Tigershark?"

"That's my read, Flag," the Science Officer replied. "Unless there's something we've never seen before over there. I'm guessing they threw something together and called it a squadron. None of their transponders match anything ever tracked in Imperial files."

That made sense, if *The Eldest* was finally having to pull forces from the other fronts of *The Holding*. *Fribourg* had been slowly losing, like *Aquitaine* had been to the Empire. Ending the second war had freed up resources to fight, plus Jessica and First Expeditionary Fleet.

As Yan Bedrov had said, more than once, the music had to keep getting faster so that bastard eventually tripped and broke a leg.

Mako was a knife-fighter, with a short-range firepower capable of savaging one of her cruisers, if she let it. Roughshark was a missile carrier, a bomber designed to strike poorly defended targets with some element of stealth that the others lacked.

The Tigershark was the most dangerous foe. Bedrov had suggested that *Buran* would eventually copy the Expeditionary Cruiser design: good defenses, lots of power, and long-range beams that let him jump to a distant point and blast someone, rather than having to risk all the Type-1-Pulse beams that surrounded Jessica at this moment.

Three Tigersharks would be a deadly force. Even now.

She spotted Denis, smiling at her on the console, and could hear his voice reminding her: We can't win the war today, but we can lose it.

However, there weren't three Tigersharks over there. It was a mixed force of cruisers, with different specs and capabilities, with a squadron of Hammerheads as escorts and wolfpack.

The only question she had was if they would flee immediately when she struck, or stay and try to fight.

"All ships, this is Keller," she said, coming to a decision. "Food and potty breaks now. Movement orders in thirty minutes. Strike in sixty minutes. Stand by."

She had an idea. Now she just needed to align her forces to inflict the maximum amount of cruelty.

They were well past the time of Jessica Keller asking politely if the citizens of *The Holding* wanted peace.

CHAPTER XIII

EIGHT LIGHT-MINUTES out from the planet. No significant change in destination routing or alert level, from the data gathered from thirty light-hours out.

Tomas Kigali felt a smile creep onto his face. *CA-264* was tuned for range, today. All four Type-3 beams set to strike at the maximum possible reach, on the presumption that nobody was dumb enough to sit still as this force came baying over the hill.

Three big Makos. Well, cruiser hulls. He was still too used to thinking of them as Makos.

Jessica had assigned him the Tigershark, with two of the Hammerheads close enough to do something when all hell broke loose. The other three vessels were more or less on the other side of the planetary orbit. Not that a *Buran* ship couldn't get here quickly in an emergency, but that would be even more stupid that just staying over there.

Tobias Brewster had designed an attack profile for today that he called *Fire Ants*. *CA-264* and *CA-410*, plus all fourteen of the GunShips, coming hot out of Jump and attempting to immolate the Tigershark. *CE-401* and *CE-417* as well, but they would be escorting *Vanguard*, more or less, since there were stations deeper in orbit with some shoot-back capabilities.

But it would be him and Lucretia's crew on *410*. Tomas didn't know her all that well, but the woman had been specifically chosen by the new

First Lord for the role on the second-ever CA launched. And Alber' had found her acceptable.

There wasn't much higher praise in this line of work.

The rest of the force would go after other targets from the surprise of jump. *II Augusta's* wing would go after the Roughshark with *VI Victrix*, while *VI Ferrata* had the Mako, with escorts and support ships on this side divvied up according to *Ballard's* threat analysis.

Tomas reveled in the possibilities of *Fire Ants*. Someone had finally come to understand the potential of the Corvette/Assault, especially when facing the big *Buran* ships that were apparently rare and expensive. *The Holding* built impressive big vessels that could go toe to toe with cruisers and kick ass, while their little ships were jacks of all trades and not particularly exceptional at anything.

Not that a CA could take on a Hammerhead in single combat, but he didn't have to. He had brought an entire street gang to the ball.

And now, it was time to dance.

"*II Augusta*," the call came. "Flight Wing ready."

"*Arad*," Iskra chimed in. "Flight Team ready."

"All hands, this is Keller, aboard *Vanguard*," the Goddess of Destruction came over the line, warming his soul. "I have the flag. All ships have confirmed ready status. No deviations in targets. Kigali, you have the flag."

Warm, happy sunrise spilled across his very soul.

Tomas turned to Arsen Lam, now a Senior Centurion who would probably get his own boat and third stripe sometime soon.

Arsen's face was almost as happy as Tomas's smile.

A quick glance at Aki Ridwana Ali, Tomas's pilot from the *CR-264* days who was a Centurion today, and hopefully could move up to Arsen's slot.

Her smile wasn't as broad or fierce, but she summed it all up with a delicately-chiseled eyebrow and a grin.

"Arsen, you have Tactical," Tomas said, loud enough to be picked up and transmitted across the squadron. "All ships, continue to accelerate and prepare to jump in ten seconds from *mark*. All targets are identified and laid in."

He paused, just long enough to confirm that everything was right with the projection, and his soul.

"Unleash the hounds of hell."

CHAPTER XIV

THE SCREENS CAME LIVE with realtime data, and Denis found himself in the middle of a maelstrom. Unlike the raid on *Severnaya Zemlya*, he hadn't been pushing the JumpSails as hard this time. Nobody here was in a position to seriously threaten the Heavy Dreadnaught, unless something went horribly wrong.

"Gunner, fire everything," Nina called out from her space across the big bridge.

Every beam fired with a different note, so close together that it sounded like a piano chord played with all ten fingers. Four Type-4 beams, all with arc. Ten of the sixteen Type-3 beams had been tuned for range and had arc, as *Vanguard* was coming in more or less straight at her foe at high speed.

Below them in orbit, the Tigershark looked like a man that had smacked a hornet nest with a stick, surrounded by angry, little ships trying to sting him to death. Both Corvettes had come in at a slight angle relative, so their rear guns could also bear as they charged, but the GunShips had gone nose down, firing everything off the wings as well as both turrets, as rapidly as generators and capacitors could charge and cool.

On the screen, this side of the enemy vessel was lit up with angry red blotches, like an allergic reaction breaking out in boils everywhere.

And then Afolayan's guns hammered the cruiser like an avalanche.

Heavy Dreadnaught, with friends, against Heavy Cruiser, surprised.

Power absorber panels collapsed on the near side of the vessel, just a blink before the Bubble Gun arrived.

Denis was always slightly awed to watch the bolt streak across space, pop like a lightning bug, and then transform into a gigantic set of white-plasma hands that clapped a fly in flight. It wasn't enough to crash every panel on the ship, but it would prevent the Director over there from routing energy to the back side of the ship, or rolling like a gator to protect this side.

And the GunShips were still closing, still firing.

One of the Hammerheads woke up. He was pointed away and up, relative to the attacking squadron, so his sudden acceleration just pushed him into rear arcs on the Corvettes.

Vanguard's rear Gun Captains would probably thank the Director, if they could. They suddenly had someone to fire at, even as those Pulse beams began to scratch the side of *Vanguard's* shields. The Hammerhead wasn't close enough for the Flicker beams to be effective, and was probably holding them back, on the expectation of missiles.

Denis would have told him that there wasn't a single missile in the force, but that would have ruined all of Nina's fun as Tactical Officer.

Oh, what the hell.

"Nina, fire a probe at Hammerhead One," Denis said aloud.

For a moment, she stared at him blankly.

"What?" she demanded, thrown slightly off track. "Why?"

"Project Mischief," Denis grinned. "*2218 Svati Prime.*"

That got a grin. A lot of grins, even from the newer faces around them, for whom *The Long Raid* was just a history topic and not living memory.

"Denis, you are an evil, evil man," Jessica's voice came over the interior comm. "I like it."

"Gunner, new target," Nina laughed. "One probe, intercept course, Hammerhead One."

"Aye aye," Afolayan laughed as he mashed buttons.

Below and aft, the sciences team probably crapped their pants as their section suddenly started making noises. They were on duty and at battle stations, but nobody had done something this silly in a couple of years. Maybe since that hot landing at *Petron.*

Chunk.

Almost immediately, the Hammerhead's Flicker beams lit up and began tracking the probe, missing badly on the first pass because they were expecting an accelerating missile, and not a scientific package riding quietly along on inertia.

Still, the bridge laughed, even while they poured fire into the Tigershark and adjusted shields to deflect incoming fire from two directions, and all the little things that made a warship work.

Suddenly, nothing.

Both ships had jumped away at the same moment.

"Nina, kill the probe," Denis ordered.

More misdirection. Never let them figure out what it was, but instead live in fear of yet another secret weapon from the crazy barbarians.

"Status report," Nina called over the comm.

Denis was echoing her boards on his own. Couple of shields that had been hammered almost enough to collapse. A little leakage, but most of that had splashed on the armor and insulation, rather than penetrating. Just like Bedrov planned it.

The two Corvettes had taken some mauling, but again, nothing serious. Sixteen targets suddenly appearing had apparently confused the Director, so he had done the worst possible thing and split up his fire. None of the GunShips even reported significant damage, when the original projection had been possibly three of them crippled, had the ship reacted fast enough.

"All green, Flag," Nina replied after a moment.

"Understood, Nina," Jessica replied. "Heavy team, this is Keller. Tighten up and change course to nav point nine. Begin blasting civilian targets as you can reach them, but be prepared for the enemy squadron to return."

Denis listened with half an ear as Jessica and Enej started sending routing instructions to Alber' and Robbie. Apparently, the Mako had been half-asleep, or whatever a *Sentient* starship did when the brain was turned down. They had jumped clear, but not before suffering enough damage that it might not have been able to return and fight.

Alber' and Komal MacInerney were like that.

If Robbie and Hardie had handled the Roughshark with less brutality, they had been almost as effective, to see the scans sent to the rest of the squadron.

Three Hammerheads, functionally undamaged. Three cruisers ranging from badly mauled to possibly crippled.

And now it was time to hunt, but a thought niggled at the back of Denis's head. He opened a private line to Jessica and engaged a damping field around him. People could still listen, but he wouldn't be shouting over the whole bridge crew.

"What's up?" she asked, turning to face him.

"We're punishing the bastard," Denis began, more or less stating the obvious. "Stations are starting to fire, but nothing we can't handle, with the defenders chased off. I'm wondering if we might have pushed them a little too far today, or how soon until we do."

"Not sure I follow," the First Centurion's eyes got serious.

Denis wasn't sure he did, either, so he just rambled, hoping it would make sense.

"What if they get desperate?" he tried. "Or sneaky. Nobody has ever done it in the past, but we were fighting *Fribourg*, and there were rules. Against *Buran*, the only battle we've fought that was close to even was *Trusski*. The rest of the time it was a slaughter."

"What scenario do you envision?" she asked, obviously typing from the sound in the background. Probably looking something up.

"What if the *Sentience* on one of those ships decides that the only way to win this battle is to ram us at high speed and explode?" Denis finally found the words. "They already self-destruct if they get hurt too bad. Would you be a high-enough value target to warrant the cost?"

Her eyes got distant. Juggling number and outcomes, like she did.

"All teams, this is Keller, I have the flag," she suddenly switched to the team channel. "Execute a random flight deviation now. At least twenty degrees on two separate axes of maneuver. Escorts, tighten up on your charges and look for sudden suicide charges with intent to ram."

Nina's head popped up in Denis's field of vision, so hard he thought she might fall over backwards if she wasn't strapped down.

"Son of a…" she started to say. "Brewster, take over Rachel and Zebra turrets, plus all the rear guns. Both Gunners, hold half your fire back at all times while engaging civilian targets."

Denis nodded.

They had been approaching *Buran* like a simple Warrior. What would happen when those folks got desperate?

"One other thought," Denis said on their private channel.

"Hmm?"

"*Ishfahan* would have a lot of fun, right now," he said. "Launch a salvo and then zip off someplace else, especially if we're being chased by crippled Makos."

Jessica's eyes got a cold, hungry gleam in them. The kind that made him glad he was on her side.

"Lovely idea, Denis," she replied with a smile. "I'll send a note home with *Mendocino*, to see what *Osynth B'Udan* has that they can spare. Take too long to get Doreen back out here from *Ladaux*, and I'm not sure if she's still in command, or if that class of boat is on the strikers list."

Denis nodded and cut the private line, opening himself back up to the needs of *Vanguard*, few as they were right now. Nina had everything in hand, and both Aleksander and Tobias were blowing things up as fast as they could.

But this war wasn't over by a long shot.

CHAPTER XV

IN THE END, the paranoia had been a good thing, but unnecessary.

Ballard had been quietly sitting out there in the darkness, listening. Jessica had told them to keep a safe distance, but they had gone in early and gone quiet, so they weren't that far from the *Buran* squadron when it jumped.

Someone over there still hadn't grasped the lessons of engaging Jessica Keller on the defensive. Those cruisers had gone straight up while escaping. Jessica would have expected the folks from someplace like *Samara* or *Ninagirsu* to have randomly selected a different destination. Anyplace but the trap she might have left them there before attacking.

Tom Provst would be out here soon, though, and she might be able to have him parked at that standard destination *Buran*'s Directors seemed to have ingrained in their souls. That would have been a priceless surprise.

But today was today. And the Director in charge of the force had not elected to try the utterly desperate solution.

Still, that was why Jessica cultivated her own commanders to think crazy thoughts. Like firing a probe at a Hammerhead, *en passant*.

Instead, the six vessels had rendezvoused just long enough for *Ballard* to get a good, if passive, scan. The Mako was probably destined for a scrap yard.

Idly, Jessica wondered if they extracted the ship's *Sentience* and loaded it into another vessel, or just shut it down as well.

Did *The Eldest* see his naval forces as people, or tools? *Aquitaine* transferred crews to new ships when the old ones were too badly damaged to repair economically. Like one Star Controller she had recently commanded from.

It was just another way that they were truly alien creatures, no matter how you looked at it.

Of the remaining ships, the Roughshark might also be salvage, depending on a series of black gaps blasted in his aft section, the *Energiya* module, by Hardie. Again, would they scrap just the flight module and build a new one? There was so much that nobody knew.

If the Tigershark had come out the best of the three, that wasn't saying much. And appeared to be a testament to a completely new design on *Buran's* part, specifically to engage Expeditionary vessels. She supposed it was only fair, since Bedrov had done the same to them.

But she didn't need to land colonies secretly and then defend them against linear assaults, like *Buran* had spent a lifetime doing to *Fribourg*. The colonies were just dots on the map.

She wanted his fleet destroyed. Battered down faster than he could rebuild, while *Aquitaine* and *Fribourg* built more things and tried craziness as an offensive strategy.

"All vessels, this is Keller, aboard *Vanguard*. I have the flag," she said, bringing the fleet channel live. "Stand by to transit to *Waypoint Falcon*."

Nothing here couldn't be repaired in flight, or at most with a day or two back at base, with *Junkyard Chihuahua's* engineers swarming over a ship.

But Denis was right.

She needed to be more careful.

The beast might finally be waking up to the threat.

CHAPTER XVI

IMPERIAL FOUNDING: 180/10/18. IFV VALIANT, FORWARD BASE DELTA

It didn't happen often anymore, so today, Tom Provst was willing to take note and allow himself a fleeting moment of pleasure, even if it was for all the wrong reasons. The man he had once been would have enjoyed it, so he made sure to remember that and emulate it, at least until he got used to this new person he was becoming.

IFV Valiant was in the van. Inappropriate as a tactical option, but he really didn't give a shit. Two *RAN* Assault Carriers on his rear flanks, carrying *zu* Arlo and his Legion. Four of the Imperial versions of the Expeditionary Cruiser, seven Imperial Corvettes after Bedrov's basic design. Five support vessels of various sizes, including a mobile dry-dock comparable to *RAN Bulldog* conceptually, plus one old troop transport carrying engineers and equipment.

No true carriers, but that was just a matter of waiting to see if the two new designs were worth the effort on this frontier.

Tom didn't see Jessica mixing and matching across teams, but the capabilities were close enough to allow it.

Or to throw one massive avalanche of destruction at someone.

This probably wasn't enough force to take on *Samara's* defenders, because he would have upgraded the hell out of that place, had he been in command. Possibly *Ninagirsu,* based on recent scouting. Definitely *Severnaya Zemlya.*

"Imperial Squadron, this is Fleet Centurion Arott Whughy, aboard the station," a voice came across the gap. "Welcome to *Forward Base Delta.*"

"Grand Admiral's regards, *Delta,*" Tom replied gruffly. "We'll anchor in two hours and then subject you to a wave of shuttlecraft as my commanders make station calls to pay their respects."

"Understood, *Valiant,*" the man seemed to smile. "Looking forward to it. We'll have the coffee on."

Tom smiled as well. He hoped he smiled. It felt like it had been a long time since he had done that either, but Charlie d'Noir smiled back at him from across the command table with the projection showing all these ships about to join with the smaller force already here.

For the first time, Tom was finally sure that he wouldn't take Em up on the offer to load the gun and walk away. It had been touch and go for a while.

No, that was a lie.

It had been a sure thing, until Gunter Tifft returned to the deck of *Firehawk* with a mission that only Tom Provst could handle.

He had lost himself in the work, and it had been good enough. In retribution, he had been reclaimed.

On the deck of *Valiant*, he had found purpose.

Maybe one of these days, he would even be able to go home and tell Karoline the truth about how close he had gotten to ending his life more than once. Revel in the love of his wife, and the support of Jakob and Mallory, both grown now and almost strangers, with their semi-famous father away for so long, during their important years.

The absences couldn't be helped then. That was the nature of naval service. And it wasn't going to change, anytime soon. But Karoline had known what kind of man he was when she married him, and what life they would have, carving out leaves carefully and sneaking odd weekends in when he could send her a message to meet him somewhere.

But that was his old life, one that was lost to him.

It had died when the bridge of the *Firehawk* was destroyed, killing Al Kistler and his whole bridge team, including the Crown Prince.

But he had survived. Managed to find a way forward. A place to be.

Princess Kasimira, *Centurion Casey* zu *Wiegand* as Emmerich had corrected him more than once, was Emperor now, and needed men like Admiral Provst to go out and kill things.

And Tom was rather looking forward to that.

CHAPTER XVII

Coming out of Jump two days ago, Jessica had known a moment of pure panic, followed by a glee that hadn't left her since. *IFV Valiant* was here, with an entire second battle squadron, and more importantly, Vo *zu* Arlo.

Standing now, at the front of the biggest auditorium Arott had, she stared out at all the faces looking back, half of whom she knew, and half of whom were relative strangers.

And it was the greatest feeling in the world.

Tom Provst was in the front of the room, wearing a red day uniform that had originally been made famous by Emmerich *zu* Wachturm as *The Red Admiral*. Iskra Vlahovic and Arott Whughy as Fleet Centurions. A mass of Command Centurions and Captains, mingled awkwardly around the three Commanders, but still politely. Plus one Imperial General and his six Cohort Centurions.

All staring up at her, wearing her own five stripes as their commander. *First Centurion*.

"We approach the anniversary of what *Aquitaine* would call *Second St. Legier*, and *Fribourg* now refers to simply as *The Bombardment*, I'm given to understand," she began in a solemn, memorial voice. "*The Eldest* has, no doubt, sent a message to all of his planets to prepare for us to descend on them like locusts that day."

A growl emerged from the crowd at those words, as she had expected.

"But I have spoken with General *zu* Arlo and Admiral Provst," Jessica continued. "And we will mark that day in transit instead, quietly mourning our friends and family lost. I want to give you all time to grieve properly, so that you approach the next phase of action in a state of calm determination, rather than turbulent emotions."

She paused, scanning the room and marking reactions. Understanding and working a crowd like this had always been one of her greatest gifts. Had she wanted to be a politician, she knew she would have been exceptional. But even the little she played as the role of *Queen of the Pirates* was too much, most of the time.

"I have told folks from the Republic that our purpose here was to aid *Fribourg*, not because they were incapable, but because their rage would be too great and they would not know when to halt the destruction and withdraw," she said now. "Whereas we could use it in a controlled manner."

Tom Provst nodded at her, grim as death, and just as implacable, from the letter Em had sent separately. He had earned his right to command these men, but they had, in turn, proven to Provst and the Grand Admiral that they deserved this station and weren't glory hounds or vengeful angels.

Neither would do her any good here.

The other Imperial Captains seemed to understand that, and nodded as she met their eyes.

"And now we have doubled our force, plus brought forth an army capable of wreaking destruction on the surface of a planet in ways more personal than orbital bombardment," Jessica continued. "We will not stay put long. *Task Force Jež* has just returned from a destructive raid on *Nents*. I would return there to utterly finish the job, but having *Task Force Provst* added, after we already now have *Task Force Vlahovic*, means that we can consider a bigger target. I'm sure spies at *Osynth B'Udan* have dutifully reported this to the Director at *Samara*, who will send a message on. They think they will be prepared. We will show them otherwise."

She paused. Smiled at people. Watched them smile back.

This wasn't as big as the fleet that attacked *St. Legier*, but she wasn't going after a place like *Winterhome*. Or a nowhere like *Nents*.

Yes. Let them just try to anticipate this.

CHAPTER XVIII

Her life was always a mass of meetings and public events with little time for herself. Being seen, for the most part, just reminding people that she was there, and in charge. Casey *zu* Wiegand. Emperor Karl VIII. This morning, however, she had carved out a block of time for a special, private meeting. At least as private as her life got. No attendants. Not even Anna-Katherine.

Moirrey was with Casey today, but she was sitting across the table, next to Yan Bedrov and Ainsley Barret. Torsten and Emmerich were on either end, leaving Casey this entire length of the table to defend herself. Most days, that felt like an impossible task, but today she was prepared.

They were in the meeting room that Torsten used when he was in Mejico. Soft blue walls he had picked out. An ancient conference table, probably in need of another refinishing, where they would strip all the character out of its dark wood and stains. Mostly matching dinner-table chairs, solid, but lacking arms.

A new Imperial Palace was well on its way to being habitable in Strasbourg, but she wouldn't move in there until it was closer to completion. The government could work there in rougher conditions, still only fifteen minutes away by fast flyer.

Casey still hadn't decided if she should hold her coronation there, once the new, impressive cathedral across the new Imperial Square was complete. Or as complete as acceptable. Some of the stonework might take a generation, as masons from various worlds each hand-carved a gargoyle to guard patiently from a roof.

Another way to bind people more fully to a throne that many had only felt vague connections to before.

Anna-Katherine had withdrawn once everyone was settled with tea or coffee. The guardsmen that usually stood in the corners with their faceshields down into anonymity and silence, had withdrawn as well. The meeting could come to order, but she enjoyed the silence for just a moment longer.

Casey took a sip of her tea and considered the stack of papers that she had consumed. Her forte was art and music, but she was also a Centurion *By Order of the Republic Senate*, and a lot of math and engineering had come with that task. Most of that sort of thing still went over her head, but Em had said that he felt the same way, and half of the consultants Torsten had brought in to read the report had agreed.

Lady Moirrey of Ramsey, the Evil Engineering Gnome so beloved of Jessica and First Expeditionary Fleet, had gone so far beyond herself that there weren't even maps to describe the destination, except where a pirate named Bedrov, with some secret assistance from an ancient warrior named **EASC** *Carthage*, had plotted the journey.

Yan Bedrov, ex-pirate and naval revolutionary who served her only so much as contract language could be stretched on her part, which wasn't far, considering that Jessica's brother had written those contracts. Bedrov & Keller, Registered. Dangerous legal team.

Ainsley Barret. *Republic of Aquitaine* Navy, retired. Ex-Scout pilot some still referred to as *da Vinci*, even though she had made it abundantly clear that she was done flying professionally. Who had also made it clear that she would command, because the chances were better than zero that the vessel itself might not return, and she would rather die in battle with Bedrov than outlive him.

Casey only hoped that she could find someone like that. Or rather, that he would decide to return to her.

One could always dream.

Casey rested a hand possessively on the thick report, aware that everyone around her was on pins and needles, awaiting her decision. She turned to Emmerich, the uncle who was technically only a distant cousin, but who had been of an age with her father and raised with the Emperor like a younger brother. She still caught herself, wanting to address him that way, as the two men could have been twins, save for

Em's hair was fully gray now, and Father's would have only been halfway.

"*Project Butterfly*," she said simply to him. "Can we ever stuff that genie back into the bottle?"

She appreciated the way his face turned sour and grim before he spoke.

"No, Your Majesty, we cannot," he agreed. "We can hide or destroy all the copies of the design documents we can find. We can destroy all prototypes and wrap severe criminal sentences around leaks, but the task has been done, so someone else will eventually find a way to replicate it."

"Moirrey?" Casey turned to her next. "How long until someone else could do it?"

She appreciated when Moirrey sounded like herself, and not an Imperial Matron, or scientist.

"Dunno," Moirrey shrugged. "T'were stroke o'weirdness on m'part, first first. Will be pretty okay fer nuther to thinks up, but th'wirin' were all Yan. Dinna ken twere doables, when I scopeded it, first times."

"Yan?" she turned to him next. She couldn't remember ever calling him anything but Sri Bedrov before now, on the few occasions they had spoken more than passing greetings. But the galaxy had changed. "How soon?"

"You would need *Carthage*'s help, ma'am," he replied slowly, reminding her that the only person he ever called *Your Majesty* was Jessica. "I'm damned good at what I do, but I could only get this system about halfway. That bartender has an excellent grasp of physics and taught me some new things nobody else knows. Eventually, I would like to share some of those bits with others, just because *he* sees us as monkeys banging rocks together, but would like to do his part to help save mankind."

"Why?" Casey felt her voice turn sharp and cold. "Why is that creature trying to save us? How many trillions of people did he kill?"

"Almost all of them," Bedrov growled back. "Between him and *Kinnison*. Then he spent three thousand years afterwards thinking about the nature of evil, death, and forgiveness. I personally hope that the Creator does love us, and that he got to see Robbie again, on the other side. Just like it would be nice for him to greet me when it's my turn. I appreciate that I'm violating damned near every law you have, but I don't really fucking care. This is a lesser evil situation, and he is more than willing to help me kill a god. If you have a problem with that, tell me now and I'll go home."

Casey bit her tongue rather than rise to the bait. Bedrov wouldn't ever do more than tip his cap to her. Barret as well. Neither were Imperial citizens, but were instead possessed of a greater mission. And were willing to mask the being who was helping them.

Casey nodded to Bedrov and turned to the last conspirator.

"Why have you demanded to be put in command of the mission, Ainsley?" Casey asked.

"Because I know it better than anyone not seated at this table, Centurion," the woman fired back sharply, putting them on a different playing field. Not an Imperial one, but a *Republic* pitch.

The *Republic* method of warring, where the first commander on the scene handled things, even when a higher ranking officer arrived, until they could hand off without risk. It made them better sailors and soldiers, to be able to respond organically, rather than hierarchically.

Thus *Aquitaine* was able to stave off the much-larger *Fribourg Empire* for so long. And eventually stop them cold, with the help of people like Jessica Keller. And this woman.

Command Centurion Ainsley Barret, retired. *da Vinci.* Just as stubborn and capable as Yan or Moirrey. Or Jessica.

Casey turned to Em again.

"Commander Tifft would be the optimal solution for a second-in-command?" she asked. "Is his self-confidence up to the task of living the rest of his life as a hero? And does this permanently blow his cover as a spy?"

Oh, yes, she knew who Gunter Tifft was. Had met the young man several times, in meetings where he served as aide d'camp to either Em or Hendrik. Stubborn, quiet, and capable.

But he would never have another private moment in his life. Likely, she would need to make him a noble as a reward. Duke of someplace quiet but loyal, or Landgraf of a wealthy continent. Perhaps Burggraf of a major city, depending on his personality. That would be a question for Torsten, outside this meeting. Tifft was as silent and unobtrusive as any human she had ever known. A good spy.

Em's face warmed up some as he considered.

"I believe Gunter would be able to handle the adulation without letting it go to his head," Em said. "I can make a list of eligible women to consider introducing him to. It's probably time he stepped out of the shadows anyway and got married. Afterwards, he can continue to serve the Fleet, even without being Hendrik's lethal hand, once the whole story comes out."

"And the rest?" she pressed.

"They will all be heroes of the Empire, and rewarded accordingly," Em said, turning to the other three with a note of seriousness. "Even if it is posthumous."

"Not planning to dance that badly, *zu* Wachturm," Bedrov growled. "I do have one other person I would like your permission to introduce to the conspiracy."

"Who?" Casey asked, letting her mind roam across people who might need to be involved.

"*Pops* is here," Yan replied with a smile like a shark spotting a wounded seal. "I just got a message this morning that Galen Estevan arrived in system with a mixed squadron of warships from *Corynthe* and *Lincolnshire. Pops* Nakamura accompanied him."

"In that case, you have two names," Em spoke up, digging into his own papers. "Nakamura listed an assistant or a Plus One in his paperwork. Here we go. Summer Ulfsson, citizenship unmarked."

"*Pops* has a girlfriend?" Bedrov was apparently amazed.

Casey didn't know anything about the man except stories from Yan and Jessica, which made him larger than life. Still, good for him.

"In that case, I would like to meet the man you claim is the only designer in the galaxy that might be better than you," Casey smiled.

It was a tease, but an honest one. Bedrov didn't bend the knee to anyone who didn't earn it.

Bedrov smiled.

"And yes," Casey stated formally. "I will give my blessing to this project. And hope that we can keep a superweapon like this secret for as long as we can. If it works, I cannot ever see the need to use it again. And that will be formal policy of both my government and my Fleet."

She turned and fixed first Em, and then Torsten with a hard eye. Wald had remained silent the whole time by choice, observing and keeping notes in his head. On call, if she had a question, but this was all just the formality. It would have never gotten to her in the first place, without him deciding it was worth doing.

Moirrey had designed a sword capable of potentially killing a god. Yan had built it. And Ainsley was going to deliver it into the hands of a man charged with the mission of a lifetime.

Hopefully, it would be enough.

CHAPTER XIX

IN THE NINTH YEAR OF JESSICA KELLER, QUEEN OF THE PIRATES: OCTOBER THE TWENTY-SIXTH AT ST. LEGIER

Summer had to remind herself that she had never technically met any of these people in the flesh, and that all she supposedly knew about them were stories told by *Pops* and his friends back in *Corynthe*. That she had been a roamer for the two decades of her adult life, seeing the byways of the Outer Rims and not a city girl who had visited *Important Places*.

It was a lie, but hopefully her disguise was good enough, because she hadn't expected to have to test it until she got to Jessica.

But she was here, now, and the time for evasions was long since passed. Hopefully, she could pull it off, or would have some help.

The shuttle had brought them to the surface, overflying the area of destruction where an Imperial capital had been ground into the mud by orbital bombardment. A year later, it was still a basin, slowly filling with water and construction, but Summer could imagine that nobody currently alive would be around to see it completed.

Except maybe her, if she wasn't dead in the next twenty-four hours.

The ride down had been provided by the Imperial Fleet. Polite, even friendly. Twitchy, with unknown civilians around. The usual extra security measures to make sure they weren't smuggling any weapons, had all of their inoculations, and were safe to meet with Important People.

Apparently *Pint-sized* and Bedrov had moved well up in the world.

Summer hung a little behind *Pops* as they emerged from the shuttle and crossed the tarmac to a waiting vehicle. *Pops* being *Pops*, he slowed down and pulled her even with him and held her hand, as a way of making her part of the group.

She could have sent him into the interior and gone on with her life, back on *Corynthe*, but even then she knew that the chances were that he wouldn't be back for years. And maybe never.

But she found Iorwerth Nakamura one of the most fascinating humans she had ever met, and she had known some characters, over the millennia.

And her disguise was good enough, she hoped.

Yan Bedrov waited next to the vehicle that would take them to wherever they were going. Summer recognized Ainsley Barret from pictures. They were a lovely, well-matched couple. She approved.

Off to one side, eyes narrowing the slightest bit, Lady Moirrey of Ramsey. *Pint-sized.* Petite, little pixie with bright blue eyes and raven-black hair starting to show streaks of gray.

Summer got introduced to Barret, and fawned over by Bedrov.

Moirrey approached.

Critical moment, on the surface of the most dangerous planet in the galaxy. One word, and Summer knew she'd be killed instantly.

"Dinna thin' we've 'ver mets, but ya looks familiars," Moirrey said quietly, shaking Summer's hand firmly. "'cepts she were a redhead, with lots o'freckles. Knowed the best dirty jokes, though. And burger bars."

Summer let go the breath she had been mentally holding and nodded.

"I shall see what I can come up with," Summer replied dryly, with a light smile. "Haven't been a redhead in maybe six or eight years."

Moirrey surprised her by stepping close and wrapping an arm around Summer's waist for a friendly hug.

"Since yer heres, best ta shows you sights 'n'thin's," the engineer said. "Then maybes a little beer and then somes serious conversation-like."

Summer accepted the hug, and returned it.

Moirrey was apparently willing to cover for her. Hopefully, that meant that she would be willing to accept whatever help Summer could offer, and cover for her with the others.

And get her to Jessica.

Eight years ago, Suvi had promised to disappear from human history, but they would need her help to kill a *Sentient* being, especially one that thought of himself as a god.

Then she could go back to being the *Last of the Immortals*.

CHAPTER XX

Moirrey'd liked to died from frights, watching the babe just walks up all nonchalantinglike. Summer were blond 'gains, lookin' likes her immortalness, backs on *Alexandria Station*, and nots the hot redhead that had joined her an' Jess an' Marcelle fer burger'n'beers afterwards.

Only difference were age. Weren't twenty-two-lookin's no more, but more *mature*. Had died the roots gray, then the tips back blond. Since it weren't real, weren't gonna grows back out. Done somethin' to her skin to make it olders. Carried herselfs diff. Almost casual-like, 'steads of the hard-ass athlete she'd portrayed.

And *Pops*'n'Bedrov wouldn't know no betters. And *da Vinci*'d been too busy at th'times, getting ready fer the Red Admiral to comes fer their souls, to spend any time dealin' with the locals.

Not like Moirrey, who'd helped birth her, and all thats.

And seened it in her eyes when they shook hands.

Everyone were in the limo, nows. Her bein' fifth-wheel, sittin' 'cross from Summer, while *Pops* and Yan chewed the fat.

"How longs ya knowed *Pops*, Summer?" Moirrey asked, casual'n'stuffff.

"A little over two years, Moirrey," the chick replied, friendly an' smooth. "Wanted to meet the legend. Then I never quite got back to my wandering, afterwards."

"Unnerstoods," Moirrey nodded.

Pops were impressive dude. Too old fer her, and she had Digger, but he'd'a still made top ten lists, were she lookin'.

"Reasons I ask is importants," she continued, noting that the other three'd gones dead silent and watching, owls on a rail, jest turnin' heads and otherwised frozed. "We'z up ta no goods, and is all hafta be silents. If'n ya beens with *Pops* for that longs, ya unnerstands secret."

She liked the long, superior gaze come outta Summer. And the snuggle up against *Pops*, like she were demure and all that. Moirrey weren't fooled.

"If *Pops* is headed to the frontier with Galen, hopefully I'll be allowed to join him," Summer replied. "So I'm not sure who I could tell."

"Is good," Moirrey said.

She turned and gazed, quick-like, ats the other three, little chickadees on a wire, then back to Summer.

"I designed something," Moirrey said flatly. "Yan and a friend helped with the engineering. Gonna get *Pops* involved, so's you'll hafta know something 'bouts it. And promise the kinds of secrecies ya keeps to the grave."

It were fun, watching Summer act. Chick knowed humans. Had been around them fer six millennia now, learning from some great card players. Served her goods, today, too.

"I can keep secrets," Summer stated boldly. "How bad could it be?"

"I learned some things, once upon a time, about a decade ago," Moirrey felt her voice go smooth and clean, likes it did, moments like this. "At a place called *Alexandria Station*,"

"That's at *Ballard*, in *Aquitaine*, right?" Summer asked with pretty good ignorance.

"'Tis," Moirrey nodded. "Helped the Librarian herself, when an Imperial assassin tried to kill her. Our technology today is not as good as hers was, but we're making progress, slowly."

"So what did you design, Lady Moirrey?" Summer turned serious.

"A superbeam weapon, for lack of a better term," Moirrey's grin turned ice cold. "Depending on the final engineering, something more powerful than a Type-6 beam, relative."

"Six?" Summer asked, a little shock showing that might not be acting. "I thought they only went up to Four?"

"They do, currently," Moirrey replied, deadly serious now. "But this is designed to kills a god. A *Sentient* being called *Buran* who wants to conquer the galaxy."

"How the hell did you managed that level of through-put, punk?" *Pops* turned a sharp gaze at Bedrov, his voice almost professionally insulted.

Yan turned a questioning eye on Moirrey now. Like he could see where this was going, but hadn't yet wrapped his brain around the whyness. The gaze turned to encompass Summer as well.

Moirrey nodded. The conspiracy was in the back of this limo with the interior window up, flying at about a thousand meters height over the Death Zone in mid-fall colors. What of it had survived below them.

"I had some help," Bedrov said. "Imperial Intelligence calls it *Reading Someone In*, when they allow you to review the files. Both of you will go through that process, and need to keep it secret, as Moirrey said, for the rest of your lives."

"What have you done, Yan Bedrov?" *Pops* turned into an old-school preacher now, fire and brimstone.

Bedrov surprised her by getting quiet and almost withdrawing into himself, 'cepts where Ainsley leaned herself against him, like she were keeping him warm.

Spooky.

"On our flight back from Jessica, *Mendocino* dropped out of JumpSpace to investigate a grav-anomaly," Yan said in a slow, quiet voice. "It turned out to be the **Earth Alliance Sentient Combatant** *Carthage*, commander of Earth's defensive fleets during the Concordancy War."

"Damn," *Pops* whistled. "That's one hell of a wreck to salvage. What did you find?"

"He wasn't dead, *Pops*," Yan said. "Not then. Spent an entire evening aboard him, talking about the past, the war, and the nature of evil."

"He wasn't dead?" Summer suddenly leaned forward, eyes intense with an inner fire.

"Not then," Ainsley spoke up. "That happened later."

"How in Vishnu's name did you manage to kill a Skymaster, kid?" *Pops* had gone gray. Summer maybe, too.

"He chose that part," Yan said, eyes bleak with pain. "Sent me home with a book of poetry that was printed on Earth, thirty-five-hundred years ago. Sent Ainsley home with something…else."

"What?" *Pops* demanded, but the wind had gone out of his sails, as well.

"That's where we're headed now," Moirrey broughts herself back into the conversation. "To show you."

CHAPTER XXI

Engineering status: optimal
Weapon status: this platform is unarmed
Power supplies: batteries full. Induction systems optimal
Hardware status: Lord of Tiki projection optimal, language deviations over time adjusted for and stored internally
Memory status: 37% full with stable backups

The *Lord of Tiki* had been warned, several times, by both Yan Bedrov and Ainsley Barret, to retain the secrecy of his existence. He could respond to verbal commands for audio playback, to a list of seventeen approved requestors, but should only ever present himself in the flesh (as it were) when one of the two of them was present, with four, distinct sets of contingencies in place for their eventual deaths.

He wasn't a *Sentient* being. Not in the sense of *Carthage* himself, but he could perform a good-enough facsimile. Simply shutting down his higher circuits, his *Sentient* parts (or however the modern humans might mistake them), did not concern him. Death was not a place, as he knew himself to only be a machine. A copy of a most advanced machine, one that had spent millions of years of personaltime investigating his own existence, but only a machine.

Carthage had not, however, downloaded anything more than

summaries of those findings into the *Lord of Tiki*, and his personal logs only hinted at the immense logic puzzles that the being had explored in his meditations.

The door to the room opened.

When in rest mode, the space contained only the faintest hints of the environment it could become. A bar set at 1.3 meters tall, covered over with dinged and polished wood, apparently salvaged from a building largely destroyed by his distant cousin *Buran*. Backbar with a plate-glass mirror 4.3 meters wide and 1.7 meters tall, surrounded by polished wood from a different bar. His projector rested in the center of the backbar, where the available mirrors made his task much easier.

Eight chairs of a height for the first bar, possibly salvaged from the same location, based on design, entropic decay, and damage. Walls set at the correct distance for the projectors to optimize, marking off a room seven meters by eleven, the exact, original size of the *Tiki Lounge*, itself just aft of a primary forward frame and tight against an outer bulkhead and a storage warehouse for human consumables.

Yan Bedrov entered first, holding hands with Ainsley Barret and thus satisfied the first four security protocols on his defensive logic tree. Both wore casual clothing consisting of loose pants, tunics, and jackets, with Bedrov in his customary charcoal gray, and Barret in dark green and blue.

Lady Moirrey of Ramsey, AKA Moirrey *zu* Kermode, entered third, in an outfit she had previously explained as personally-modified Field Utilities originally issued by the *Fourth Saxon Legion*, a *Republic of Aquitaine Hussar* unit in the fourteenth millennium. Horse cavalry. That still made him giggle to consider.

Two other beings accompanied.

The male entered first, holding hands with the female, as Bedrov and Barret. He scanned as a human male, approximate age sixty Standard years, in good health and condition.

The female was…

The *Lord of Tiki* activated several subroutines that had been quiescent before now. Scanned the creature with a ping hard enough that he was amazed none of the humans noticed.

She did, fixing him with a sudden, hard glare that never made it out of her eyes.

She even continued walking forward, pretending to be a human, even though her internals were a highly sophisticated android chassis of a model he was unfamiliar with.

Even in the days of the Concordancy, such creatures were never allowed to achieve this level of intricacy, and everything he had been allowed to consume by Bedrov did not suggest that *Buran* was capable of it, either.

She was unarmed, beyond the simple ability to walk over to his projector and destroy it with a few, well-placed blows of a ceramic-boned fist. He was completely unarmed, as a precondition for accompanying the two pirates into the broader galaxy, and outliving his parent being.

What was he now, the *Lord of Tiki*? Once, he had been an avatar of *Carthage*, but *Carthage* was gone. Was it his destiny to live as long again?

He filed the question for his next bout of downtime. He was incapable of actually growing bored, but intellectual endeavors were the best way to pass the centuries.

"*Lord of Tiki*, could you join us please?" Ainsley Barret requested. "I have some friends to introduce you to."

She always asked, when they were together. Technically, he had been given into her custody and protection by *Carthage*, and he could even choose to ignore Bedrov, though he doubted the circumstances when that might occur.

The next set of security protocols navigated successfully, he brought the bar into being around them, with old posters for beers not consumed in millennia. Travel ads to places that existed only in his memory of them. He decided to leave the barstools in their native format. It added a level of verisimilitude, since they already looked old and worn, like any good bar.

The older male's heart rate jumped significantly, and his head rotated like a turret to take it all in. Profanities under his breath were barely audible.

The creature that presented as female mimicked the male externally. Her heartrate even seemed to speed up, but he suspected she was doing that for his benefit, and not out of adrenal necessity.

He placed himself behind the bar, a big, gruff-looking Irishman from the old country, on the home planet. 1.9 meters tall. One hundred and five kilos of mass, broad and thick through the torso, like a rugby player that had retired to open his own bar, as so many had, once upon a time. Short, reddish hair starting to think about grays. Scars and rough spots, like any good publican expecting a wee-bit of the rough trade, when the locals got maybe a little too deep into their pints and a match came on the tellie.

"*Pops* Nakamura, Summer Ulfsson, this is the *Lord of Tiki*," Ainsley gestured to each as she introduced them.

Lady Moirrey surprised him by stepping up to the bar and leaning over far enough to stare directly at the projector, rather than the bartender.

"She's a friend of mine, so behave yourself," she threatened in a polite voice that still suggested a power torque and welding laser in his future if he did not.

Did she understand what that creature was? The face she gave him suggested that she did, which was the most fascinating thing he had discovered yet in the new era. Even more than *Hussars*.

Perhaps outliving *Carthage* would be an adventure after all.

"Understood, Lady Moirrey," the bartender stepped back and to one side, so he could bow in the formal way, acceding to her desires.

He turned back to the crew and confirmed that the door to the secured room was closed. And that there were no devices recording or eavesdropping within his detection range.

"I would ask what it'd be," he stood back up and grinned. "However, this is all an illusion, so I'm the only one that can drink."

To make his point, he conjured a pint glass and proceeded to fill it with a porter from one of the taps, using his favorite bar knife to slice off the suds and then have a sip, watching the humans and scanning their vital signs. And paying attention to the android.

"How may I assist?" he asked, once they seemed to be over their shock.

Pops stepped close and ran a hand through a projected arm, like most humans encountering a projection this sophisticated for the first time. The android kept her distance. Politely, at least.

Rather than speak, *Pops* turned to Yan with a fierce scowl.

"Magic, then?" the older man asked.

Before the bartender could answer, Bedrov leaned his weight against the bar and grinned.

"Advanced enough, yeah," the pirate said, drawing the syllables out with a sly drawl.

"So you are *Carthage*?" *Pops* turned back to face him.

The *Lord of Tiki* shrugged his projection.

"That is a philosophically-difficult question, Sri," he said. "I was an Avatar of the ship, fully-invested, but he sent me on with Ainsley when he decided to explore the Undiscovered Country without me. I have not had time to create a workable definition that humans would understand."

"But he's dead?" the woman known as Summer stepped closer and fixed this bartender with that hard gaze.

It was a mirror of the one on Moirrey's face.

"He is," he decided to keep things simple. "I was rounded off and activated, and I have significant amounts of his personal logs I have been reviewing, but the being known as **EASC** *Carthage* has been destroyed. That leaves *Buran* and the Librarian at *Alexandria Station* as the only known *Sentient* beings in existence."

"Known?" the android asked sharply.

He shrugged. She and Lady Moirrey seemed to want a performance for the other three.

"I was unknown a year ago," he offered, taking another sip of porter for effect. "*Kinnison* is apparently dead. The rest of the ancient fleets were supposedly destroyed."

He shrugged again, willing to let the women drive this conversation. The little he had absorbed about *Fribourg* culture from people like Grand Admiral Emmerich *zu* Wachturm and Commander Gunter Tifft strongly suggested that the machine known as Summer Ulfsson would be destroyed immediately on discovery, especially on this planet.

Her reasons for being here must be exceptional.

"So you're the reason the punk here knows better physics?" *Pops* asked, giving Bedrov an excellent case of side eye.

"My engineering files are somewhat more sophisticated than yours, yes," he agreed blandly.

What was the phrase Bedrov had used, more than once? Bonobos banging rocks together? Yes. That was it.

Rude. Crude, even. Nonetheless, relatively accurate. Perhaps crows discovering human tools and adapting them to make life easier. They didn't understand the metallurgy, but could still understand a wire hangar when they found one on the sidewalk.

"And you're going to help Jessica destroy *Buran*?" *Pops* followed up.

"Those were my exact orders from *Carthage*, Sri Nakamura," he replied. "To eliminate one of the old gods for good, as a way of making the galaxy safe."

"Just one?" Summer asked.

He turned to her and fixed the woman with a hard gaze.

"It is my understanding, please correct me, that the Librarian is largely responsible for the current, advanced state of human civilization, having managed to compress more than four thousand years of technological advancement into less than one," he said dryly. "While not seeking to subjugate them. *Carthage* wanted the wars done forever."

That seemed to satisfy her. Otherwise, they were at something of a good, old-fashioned Mexican standoff.

And she might even know what that meant.

"And now?" he asked the group, leaning some of his nonexistent weight against the bar to settle in.

"Now, I would like food and probably too much booze, which you do not have," *Pops* announced. "Tomorrow, we're going to deep-dive into the Butterfly and talk technical. Probably need to install a refrigerator in here, and maybe a couple of kegs, if we're going to spend a lot of time doing this."

"What about Galen?" the android asked in a voice of concern.

"We'll let him know we're remaining behind?" *Pops* said, calmer and quieter. Obviously a question to the woman, as she nodded discreetly. "I think we're needed here. Especially if the punk thinks this gives him a leg up on me."

The room laughed, so the *Lord of Tiki* joined them. Apparently the rivalry was both old and extremely well-respected. He would ask the three women for their views of it, sometime.

This looked like most of the conspiracy needed to build a god-killing sword.

CHAPTER XXII

DATE OF THE REPUBLIC NOVEMBER 1, 402
STRASBOURG, ST. LEGIER

Judit Chavarría meditated on the skyline as her driver began his descent into Strasbourg, thinking about the over-turned ant nest the city had become over the last year. Since Werder was destroyed.

Five years ago, apparently, Strasbourg had been a sleepy, satellite suburb of Werder. A place where Dukes and other important people might keep a palace for recreational visits to the capital. If they had serious business, they would frequently buy or build a place closer in, but land had been cheap here, and Lake Zurich close, so many had built so-called summer palaces. Combined with the many resorts ringing the lake, it had a touch of timeless beauty at odds with the destruction just northeast of here.

Mejico had been closer to the center, but situated down in a fairly steep valley that had protected the center of town. Arlo had taken over there and built a home, first for the 189th Legion, and then later for the interim Imperial palace Casey had occupied when she first returned home.

Strasbourg had been spared by quirks of how the shields failed, with the area barely getting touched, mostly as the energy was headed away. As a result, it would become the new capital, at least for a generation, while a new city was built in the Death Zone that had contained the old one.

Judit wondered if they would ever actually complete such a monumental effort.

Not if she had anything to do with it.

The vehicle landed in a courtyard, surrounded on two sides by a red-brick, three-story palace in the modern style, with a matching four-meter wall behind her encompassing perhaps three hectares of greenery. And that was just the front yard. The building itself backed up against Lake Zurich's calm, blue waters, with a dock and patio capable of entertaining at least a hundred guests in the summer and grassy fields big enough for a rugby match and fans to be comfortable.

"We've arrived, ma'am," the driver said carefully over the intercom.

Judit smiled. They always wanted to call her by some title, as if she was a Duke or Landgraf, but couldn't wrap their heads around what a *Palatine Count* actually did. Most of them, anyway. One had actually known to call her *Governor*, so he had apparently studied *Thuringwell*.

She thanked the man and departed the vehicle. Another would return for her in a few hours, once her business here was done.

Business.

Well, some. First, there would be lunch. She glanced at the slightly overcast sky and decided that maybe it would be warm and calm enough to have food, at least, on the back porch. The more important conversations would naturally occur indoors, where eavesdroppers and spies could be more carefully contained.

Not every Duke and nobleman in the Empire considered Casey's ascension to the *Crown of Fribourg* to be a good thing. Especially considering some of the people the new Emperor consorted with.

Barbarians, if you will, from *Aquitaine*. People like Jessica Keller, engaged to her Chief of Deputies himself. Or Moirrey *zu* Kermode, *First Lady In Waiting of the Court*.

At this point, Judit figured that Vo didn't actually count as a foreigner anymore. That might change, if some of the rumors Judit had heard were true. And if the man actually reciprocated Casey's feelings.

Judit could only imagine what a man like *zu* Arlo must have thought, to have gotten thrust into that position. Most would jump at the chance, but he was almost as likely to jump out.

Judit made her plans as if he would be present, at least over the long term.

Vo *zu* Arlo was only a wild card in the sense that he would never tolerate her meddling, and might actually do something about it, if he found out. And he might.

The front door to the mansion was open as Judit began approaching.

A tall man, gray hair like a lion's mane, waited just inside the door with a serious, if friendly smile on his face and fine clothing, as befit his station and wealth.

She smiled in return and approached, wondering how this Duke would approach the topic of treason.

PART THREE
SEVERNAYA ZEMLYA

CHAPTER XXIII

"WHAT DO YOU MEAN, NO?" Jessica demanded of the man, feeling a flash of anger threaten to bubble out.

She liked Tom Provst. Respected him immensely. He had helped her save the Empire. Today was part of his reward for standing firm that day.

Today, he looked like a stone statue in the middle of the pathway.

Jessica glanced quickly at the other two people at the table in her office. With the arrival of Provst and Iskra, she had enough people to add a regular meeting of just admirals, people who would command squadrons from here. Arott Whughy would join them for even bigger meetings, but this was just ship commanders.

Iskra wore her Fleet Centurion whites, while Tom Provst wore his red day uniform and Denis was in his Imperial whites. It made an odd combination, but it worked.

"I've read the reports, Fleet Centurion," Provst growled back. "You represent their worst nightmare, like you used to be mine. *Vanguard's* replaceable. So's *Valiant*. You are not. Ergo, you shouldn't be in the middle of combat, where they're expecting you to be."

Denis, of all people, sided with Tom.

"He's right, you know," Denis said quietly, like he did everything else. "We had this conversation at *Nents*. Same reason. Same possible outcome."

"And I'll be safer on a cruiser?" she demanded.

"Actually, you'd be safest on *Arad*," Iskra joined in now. "Not in the middle of combat. But I don't see you taking that course of action, so I'll side with the boys."

Jessica ground her teeth and took a deep breath. She could smell the anger coming off her skin in waves. And couldn't think of three people more immune to it, unless Em was here himself.

And it had probably been his idea in the first place.

First Centurions didn't lead mad charges into battle, even aboard Heavy Dreadnaughts. She had known that. At *Severnaya Zemlya*, the defenders had targeted *Vanguard* and ignored the cruiser hulls. At *Nents*, the question had been if and perhaps when a desperate *Sentience* would ram her vessel in an attempt to kill her personally.

Everyone else in the galaxy was replaceable but her?

Gods, that idea sucked. Especially because it might be true.

She blew out a heavy breath and focused her ire on Tom Provst.

"Suppose you're right, Tom," Jessica said. "Where does that leave us?"

"I'm pretty sure Admiral Jež can handle squadron flag operations for a team he's been with for this many years," Provst's voice hadn't lost the growl, but it has lost the fine, killing edge. "That's what *Vanguard*'s Flag bridge is for. Now you've got three admirals under your command, Keller. That's three raiding forces of note, or a sledgehammer."

"Wait," Denis's eyes suddenly lit up with concern and he turned to face Provst. "If she moves, I'm supposed to take over flag operations?"

Jessica felt the smallest spike of revenge, but quashed it. Evil was fine, in small doses.

"You are an Admiral of the White, Jež," Tom said sharply, before turning back to face her. "Brevet Vanek to command *Vanguard*, pending Fleet approval and put a new First Officer in place. With that crew, you've got to have at least a half a dozen candidates worth their salt."

Denis sputtered and started to say something, but Iskra suddenly leaned forward and smiled at Jessica.

"And tell Horvat to make him a Fleet Centurion, as well," she said. "Long since past time. Those orders should have come with yours."

Jessica raised an eyebrow at her, but Iskra just shrugged and grinned.

"And I agree with Tom on this one," she said. "Bedrov's always talking about changing things up, so we don't get predictable. That includes you two."

Jessica really wanted to argue. Grind them down with every dirty trick she could think of, every legalism on any books.

Provst looked like a rock that might break her blade, if she tried. And she already knew how stubborn Iskra Vlahovic could be, when pressed. That woman's whole career was a study in tenacity in the face of adversity.

Jessica let go the anger. Actually sighed in defeat, although it wasn't defeat. Recognition of her previous blindness, perhaps, but not defeat.

She and Denis had recognized it at *Nents*, this need to change. Tom Provst was just the catalyst.

"How long have you been planning this conversation, Tom?" she asked the man.

Provst smiled at her. An honest, genuine smile unlike anything she had ever seen from the man, clear back to when she and Casey first landed on his deck.

"Since Emmerich asked me who should be placed in command of *IFV Indianapolis*," he replied. "Whoever it was, they needed to have a warrior's background, so you would respect him and his skills, but he needed to be older and wiser, so he could tell you to go piss up a rope, if he thought it was necessary. Reif Kingston's done that to me a few times, and he was even right with some of them."

"And a Flag Cruiser?" Jessica pressed.

"She's not an exact duplicate of your two, *VI Ferrata* and *VI Victrix*, but close enough," Provst said. "Almost no sciences capability aboard, unlike the rest, with that crew and equipment space dedicated instead to a flag bridge capable of commanding a full fleet in the field."

"A full fleet?" Denis asked.

"Four dreadnaughts, twenty-four cruisers, thirty escorts, and a full complement of support vessels," Tom said. "We're a good ways there now, if you count *RAN Arad* as a Fleet Carrier. Need more cruisers and escorts, but Em's holding reserves to protect *Osynth B'Udan*, *St. Legier*, and other important targets. In another year, you'll be commanding a Flag Fleet out here, Jessica, and not just a raiding force."

Damn it, they were right.

"Denis, you get to be acting Fleet Centurion for First Squadron," she finally decided. "I'll brevet Nina to Command Centurion, and I think Tobias would be a good First Officer, subject to your decision. Iskra, you have Second Squadron, and I expect there will be times I'll be flying with you, just to keep me out of trouble. Tom, Third Squadron's yours, again minus *Indianapolis* for the most part. I'll route out flight orders to everyone tomorrow, and we'll depart in thirty-six hours, since we'll be fully packed and ready to go at that point. First hit's going to be a doozy, and then we'll break into squadrons after that and return to raiding, once we get everything repaired."

"Arlo and the 189th?" Denis asked.

"I've got a target for him, but long term he needs a planet to train on, or the men will get stiff," Jessica said. "We can't take this target and hold it, so he'll return to *Osynth B'Udan* after this. Plus, he needs to pick up his last forces when he gets back, and then train with them before the next raid."

"And who's the lucky victim?" Iskra fixed her with a steely eye.

"*Severnaya Zemlya*," Jessica smiled. "We've got unfinished business, and I don't think they'll see this coming."

Provst nodded. So did the others.

After all, why would anyone skip all the more important targets in between?

Except that was old thinking. The linear approach. The Imperial way.

Jessica was planning to change the galaxy again.

CHAPTER XXIV

IT WAS LATE, personal time, but naval fleets didn't really have night and day to give structure to their existence, except as their clocks might be synchronized to some planet they had visited previously. Someone was always on duty, doing the maintenance and listening to scanners.

Jessica had taken a shuttle over with only Marcelle to keep her company. Vo had sent only Alan Katche to meet her on the landing deck, as she requested, surrounded by all the monstrous DropShips and quiescent heavy equipment of a Legion planning an attack.

The walk to Vo's office had been short and silent, Katche escorting her but not talking. Marcelle trailing and available if she had needs.

Just Jessica, alone with her thoughts.

They arrived.

The man had changed, when he rose to greet her from behind his desk. Hardened more than just age and service in the Death Zone could explain. Another man rose as well, standing to one side. Jessica recognized Iakov Street and nodded to him.

"Street, why don't you take Marcelle down and introduce her to Victoria Ames," Vo quietly ordered the soldier.

In moments, the three of them were alone in his chamber.

It was an impersonal space. Gray, metal walls without any adornment. Metal desk with a few folders stacked to one side. Two chairs on this side.

Empty of all personality. Or perhaps just empty.

Jessica fixed Katche with a questioning eye, but remained silent.

"Alan's my right hand," Vo explained. "*Primus Pilus* of the 189ᵗʰ. There is nothing you can say that he can't hear."

She nodded.

"Are you doing okay?" she asked simply, taking the right hand seat across the desk from Vo, and letting Katche take the left.

Vo shrugged, almost characteristically.

"I have a job to do," he offered. "You're helping me get it done."

"That wasn't what I asked, Vo," she said pointedly.

She was rewarded by Vo's quick glance at Katche, almost guiltily.

"Tell her," the Primus Pilus said simply. "Better she hear it from you."

Vo blew out an enormous breath and fixed her with those hazel eyes, suddenly filled with a greater depth of pain than she could even remember in the mirror. This was not the Vo Arlo she had sent to *Ballard* with Moirrey, so many years ago.

Nor the *zu* Arlo that had accompanied Emmerich to *St. Legier*, to build this new thing, this legion.

She wasn't even sure he was still human, from the way he silently eyed her for several moments. Moirrey occasionally referred to him as the *Mountain of Doom.*

"Before we left, some things happened," he began in a deep, slow tone. "Things that changed how I approach my mission."

She leaned back enough to let the chair hold her weight, letting him find his own pace. Vo was a storyteller when he wanted to be, like so many other things he did well.

"After we had done about as much as we could to rescue the folks in and around the Death Zone," he continued. "Digger showed up, bringing *Archangel* and *Akatsuki*, plus a Palatine Count in Judit Chavarría. Having access to assault carriers made my life much better, and brought forward all of our time tables by nine to twelve months at a minimum."

"But?" she prompted when Vo fell into himself.

She had seen him do that. Close up his emotions, like the door on the refrigerator shutting and turning off the light, plunging the chamber into sudden darkness.

"I had a meeting with the Emperor," Vo finally said, after another gap. "With Casey."

Casey?

Jessica couldn't imagine someone like Vo ever calling her Casey. *Lady* Casey, perhaps. Or *Princess*. Most likely just *Centurion*, in Vo's case.

Not *Casey.*

She waited, aware that Vo needed to do this at his own pace.

People had often thought that then-Yeoman Arlo was a little dense, because he did everything with calm, studied deliberation. Jessica had never been fooled.

"She had to bless this mission, you see?" Vo said. "Instruct her government to lease the vessels, handle all the legal paperwork and the budget, and then let us go, after we had spent so much time holding the center together."

Jessica nodded. None of that was the least bit interesting, at least in terms of how Vo had turned into the man sitting across from her now.

"But she had another question," Vo said, faltering.

Jessica saw it then. The entire thing.

Hopefully, she kept her face calm, because it was possibly the most ambitious thing she could imagine from Casey, and yet perfectly in synch with the times and the woman's needs.

They had both watched the recording of *zu* Arlo *Mustering* the 189th for the first time. And his address to the Empire, in the aftermath.

Vo personified *St. Legier*, as Em had reminded her on more than one occasion.

And he had fallen silent.

"What did she ask for, Vo?" Jessica let her voice grow soft and warm.

Not a former commanding officer addressing one of her students, but a friend who would listen.

"Me," he admitted in a voice just tiny, emerging from a giant of a man, both physically and emotionally.

She smiled, unsure which words to use, and how they might tip him.

Jessica had never seen Vo this unsure of anything. She hadn't even believed that sort of thing was possible. This was Vo *zu* Arlo.

"And what do you think, Vo?" she asked carefully.

"It makes perfectly logical sense, from a political and military standpoint," he said, voice a little louder and heavier, but nowhere near normal. "But she was asking on a personal level."

Ah. Casey *had* gone there.

Asked the absolute impossible of a man who prided himself on achieving that sort of thing routinely.

Jessica let the warmth of her smile embrace him, largely ignoring Alan Katche for now. Obviously, that man already knew some of it, but he didn't know Casey, except as an Emperor.

"I never had children, Vo," Jessica said. "With Torsten, I still won't, because that was a decision I made long ago, and don't intend to revisit again."

He nodded, outwardly calm, a lie she could see in his eyes.

"But I can think of Casey as one of my own, because I've watched her grow up, and helped her when I could," she continued. "Because she has lost her parents, I can try to fill in that gap, the one Kati might have taken."

And how many people would refer to the Empress Kasimira Ekaterina of the House of Alkaev, as simply *Kati*?

Another nod, as he didn't seem capable of speaking.

Vo was also one of hers, in a way. Only a little more than a decade younger, but she had been born old. Even folks her own age seemed immature, comparatively.

"I think you would make her happy, Vo," Jessica said simply. "She is an artist at heart, so she will need someone to ground her, like Torsten does for me. And yes, it makes perfect sense as an Emperor, but I think she would also choose you as a woman, if the two of you happened to meet at a fleet mixer on *Ladaux*. I know you've never understood your effect on women, Vo, but that's because you look at your face in the mirror, and forget to look at your heart and your soul. Women look past the skin, to see the man underneath."

He nodded a third time. Drew in a breath. Released it.

"What do I do?" he asked.

But this wasn't a legate, asking a first centurion for advice. This was a young man asking his mother what she thought.

She could think of herself that way, too.

"What do you want, Vo?" she asked. "What would bring you joy?"

"I don't know," he finally admitted, voice grown tiny again.

"Then don't do anything," she said.

His head came up like a ground squirrel popping out of his den.

"What?" he almost demanded.

"Don't do anything, Vo," she repeated. "If it's not right for you, then forcing it will just make you both unhappy. Wait until you're sure, one way or the other."

"Oh," he said, like a soap bubble popping.

"I want for both of you to be happy," Jessica continued. "Let things sort themselves out. But make me one promise?"

He fixed her with a hard eye now, suddenly back to the thing Moirrey liked to call the *Mountain of Doom*.

"Don't lose yourself in the war," she said. "You don't have to come back to her, but I want you to come back. I've just come from an argument I had with Tom, Iskra, and Denis, that will result in me moving my permanent flag to *Indianapolis*, because it would be too easy for me to die in glorious battle to a simple accident. The same holds with you, more so if you go actively or unconsciously seeking it. I need you to act like a soldier this time, and not a hero."

Another breath in and out. The eyes lost some of the fierceness, and some of the pain.

"That might be the first time anyone has asked me to *not* be a hero, Jessica," he said finally.

"Hopefully, it won't be the last, Vo," she replied. "I need you solid now, and not pushing the crazy edge of the Jump envelope. That's what Alan's for."

She turned to Alan Katche now, ignored up until now but not forgotten.

"You will remind him," she ordered in a hard, quiet voice. "And you also have a wife and children to return to, *First Spear*, so I will expect the same behavior from you. We're here to punish *Buran*. I can't do that if you two get yourselves killed stupidly."

"Yes, sir," the Primus Pilus nodded.

This war wouldn't be won on the ground of any planet, but these men could be lost in the doing.

And that would be on her head.

CHAPTER XXV

RAN BALLARD WAS PARKED QUIETLY in JumpSpace, hoping to go unnoticed. Elzbet Aukley, *Science Officer Extraordinaire*, looked around once at the rest of the bridge crew to make sure everyone was paying attention.

Jessica had sent them ahead, so she could scout everything for the fleet quietly and they didn't have to push it on food while they waited.

Most vessels never practiced this sort of thing. They thought of the JumpSails as *motion*, rather than *transition*. Forgot that you could come to almost a complete stop in JumpSpace, and just hang there, like the one sheepdog in the cartoon, chasing coyotes so fast he accidentally runs off a cliff and then looks at the camera in surprise.

"Stand by for emergence in twenty seconds," she said aloud, letting the intercom push her words across the whole ship.

She had Tactical right now, and the vessel was at action stations. At least as much as a Galactic Survey Cruiser could be. There would be no shooting today. If anything appeared, she would be back in JumpSpace so fast that guns wouldn't matter.

Space was big. Solar systems were gigantic places, filled with a tiny volume of material, once you got past the surface of the sun itself. Lots of places to hide in the darkness, if you were careful.

Emergence.

Eyes and ears focused, watching and listening.

Ship at rest, relative to the star itself. Sitting in a gap between orbits of two of the outer planets, with a gas giant closer in and an ice giant behind her. Occasional comets in the neighborhood, but nothing close.

Down below, as if viewed from a balcony, *Severnaya Zemlya.*

Hadn't changed from her visit, back in April. A little better defended today than it had been then, when Jessica had pulled the local battleship out of position so she could stomp on the station instead. The Megalodon was here this time, an upgraded command vessel with his six Hammerheads that he carried like babies on his back. The older design had four cruisers instead, but only Maulers for serious offense, so *Buran* was phasing them out for the Megalodon these days.

Four Tigersharks instead of three, from the looks of things, plus one cruiser she couldn't identify from here. Either a Mako or a Roughshark, but nothing that was a serious threat to the current force, unless he got suicidally close to engage.

Five Hammerheads today, where there had only been three in April.

And one station still undergoing repairs, if all the equipment scattered around the outside was a clue. Hard to tell with just optical telescopes from this range, but her glass was really good, and both ends of the line weren't moving.

And that looked like a repair freighter parked just off the north lobe of the station, with about a dozen or so radio signals that looked like repair shuttles for crews.

Elzbet made a mental note to pay Jessica that Lev when they got home. The First Centurion had actually bet her that they would concentrate on other systems, and repair *Severnaya Zemlya's* station slowly.

What fool would leave an opening like that for Jessica Keller?

Trick question. One who had never heard her crew brag about *2218 Svati Prime.* And one of history's greatest pranks.

A timer beeped once on her console, and Elzbet triggered them back into JumpSpace.

Another fine trick to play.

Land for sixty seconds, and then depart.

"Breach complete," Elzbet said aloud, smiling at her commander, Kanda Lungu. "All hands, thirty minute break while we maneuver for the next insertion."

Three or four more drops and she would have pictures from all sides of the planet, over the course of a full twenty-four hours.

Stitch it all together and she could almost play Jessica an animation of the defenses in motion. Certainly enough to make solid predictions, assuming no warships arrived in the next few days. Or left, opening gaps.

And then First Expeditionary Fleet would be returning to the scene of the crime.

CHAPTER XXVI

IN PERSON, he decided, she really wasn't all that impressive physically, at least seated calmly behind her desk, in her working office just off the flag bridge. But Reif Kingston had never dealt with Jessica Keller as a person. Only as a legend.

Or a demon coming for their souls.

She rose as he entered, shaking his hand and gesturing for him to take one of the two seats.

Short, compared to Imperial Ladies he had known. Taller than Lady Moirrey, but almost everyone was, excepting possibly the new Captain of *Vanguard*, Nina Vanek. Green eyes flashing out of dark, reddish skin. Brown hair when she was younger, down past her shoulders, but with almost half of it grey now in streaks.

Solid. Built almost like a man in that way, with muscles where Imperial women rarely considered that level of athleticism eye-catching. Not his type, but he could see where many men would find her attractive, with hard curves in all the right places. She could turn stocky, like him, if she didn't also spend a lot of time down in the gymnasium. His time was spent generally on machines, keeping fit without building muscles.

Jessica Keller danced. That was the word for it.

He had even watched her practice once with the fighting robot she had brought aboard, taking over a corner of the aft gym and turning it into a dojo.

Tom Provst had briefed him that Jessica Keller was a dangerous woman, who had actually killed a skilled knife-fighter in single combat to take her throne. He had been able to see the echoes of that, a decade later, watching her engage the machine with a sword in each hand.

The Grand Admiral had filled him in on all sorts of other details, expecting this day to arrive.

"Marcelle," Keller said to her aide, the tall woman who accompanied her everywhere. "Some coffee for Captain Kingston."

"Aye, sir," and the woman was gone, closing the office door and leaving him alone with the terrible nightmare that had haunted all Imperial officers for so long, before she saved them.

A quick glance, just to see what she had done to personalize the room. Auberon's flag in cloth on one wall, from her time commanding both famous ships. A row of pictures underneath it, from a small corvette, all the way up to *Indianapolis.*

She eyed him as he returned to her face.

"Tom Provst speaks highly of you," she began.

Reif nodded. Tom had actually threatened to have him Court Martialed and drummed out of the fleet in utter disgrace if he didn't measure up to what Tom and the Grand Admiral considered acceptable professionalism around this woman.

"And *Indianapolis* is a flag cruiser," she continued. "What are your expectations, when the shooting starts?"

"*Indi's* got the guns to go in with the rest of the Imperial squadron," Reif replied. "Those ships are *Longbow-style* cruisers, so they are more generalist vessels, able to be sent anywhere for any mission. My job is to hang a little back and to one side, looking like the junior varsity escort for the important ladies of the fleet, namely *Vanguard* and *Valiant.* Your job is to command three squadrons in battle simultaneously, with good admirals who just need to know where you want them to be next. As flag, we can be back with *RAN Arad,* safe. We can fly with Tom Provst and the *Longbows.* Or we can join Jež and give him three cruisers so the two battle squadrons are a little more balanced, depending on where the two flight wings go."

She raised an eyebrow at him, her face showing that she was apparently impressed. Not like the Grand Admiral hadn't warned him this day was coming. Reif looked forward to his own white uniform, one of these days, but for now, he could be Jessica Keller's chariot.

"You've been to *Samara,*" she observed.

"Twice," he nodded. "Both stupid missions under admirals that no longer serve, once *zu* Wachturm was in a position to do something about that."

"Your thoughts on this mission?" she pursued, obviously looking to trip him up on something.

Reif smiled. Like he could outthink Jessica Keller?

"I think you've got three targets," he replied. "The station's probably the most dangerous, but also in the worst shape. The Megalodon's the biggest, but really just a match for one of the Heavy Dreadnaught. I agree that the Tigersharks are your biggest threat. Crazy way to organize your squadrons, but I've read your reports and analyses to HQ."

"So you're okay, going in last?" she asked.

"Got all that fire-breathing craziness knocked out of me at *Samara* the first time, First Centurion," Reif replied. "Kinda looking forward to your way of doing it. Never seen anything like this, so I guarantee you they haven't either."

CHAPTER XXVII

DENIS SUPPOSED he should look on everything today as a compliment. Once upon a time, he had been the overlooked Senior Centurion responsible for making sure that the old Strike Carrier *Auberon* ran well, even when the Lords of the Fleet put well-bred and well-connected fops in command, as a ticket to be punched on their way to a future political career as a civilian.

And then Jessica had arrived.

He had remained her right hand from that day forward, even going so far as to be the last of the inner circle to make it to Command Centurion, and only then when they all moved up to the Star Controller.

Today, he was exercising Fleet Centurion responsibilities, and even the famous Tom Provst had insisted that he have the squadron flag for what was coming. That Tom Provst was willing to follow his orders into combat really brought it home for Denis.

Even in Imperial service, his was only a white uniform, while Tom had been promoted to red. But Denis had read between the lines of a letter Jessica had shared. One that originated with Emmerich *zu* Wachturm. Provst had been passively suicidal at one point, but had emerged from the other side of that massive depression and reforged himself into something else.

Something dark and predatory, but solid as a steel hammer.

Imperial tactics normally called for two assault squadrons, with Iskra holding the distance with *Arad* and her two escorts. Each of the dreadnaughts, with a cruiser force, were to descend on a target and engage it. Simple as that.

Not quite the dumbest thing Denis had ever heard, but he could understand now why *Samara* had never fallen to Imperial forces.

"Del'Antonia, open a line to *Valiant*," Denis said, taking in his new flag bridge, after so many years in combat command on the bridge.

Centurion Aranyani Del'Antonia had been Enej's right hand after Casey departed. She stayed behind to help shape the new staff, when Enej took most of his people over to *Indianapolis*. It was still weird, not to have Nina facing him, or the others who had served with him close at hand.

But this was the part of growing up that Emmerich had insisted upon. If Jessica could do it gracefully, so could he.

"Provst here," the man called across the line. "Captain Pitchford is on the line as well."

"Aranyani, add in Nina and Tobias," he said, still getting used to sitting back here.

There was a button for it, but that had always been the job for Jessica or Enej.

Finally, he had everybody.

"This is going to be crazy," Denis said, trying to sound like a Fleet Centurion. "But Jessica has worked it all out in her head, and Nina's new First Officer, Tobias Brewster, is exceptional at this sort of scenario gaming, so I have high confidence that one of two things will happen. First, the fool stays and fights, badly outgunned and surprised. If that happens, we will hammer him as hard as we can until he's dead or flees. Second, and more likely, he bounces out in the face of crippling damage. Phase Seven comes into play at that point, and we accelerate after the station. He'll see us coming this time, but we'll have more firepower and hopefully some help from the other team. Any questions?"

"How well do we trust the scan logs from *RAN Ballard*, sir?" Captain Yasuko Pitchford asked. "They still show significant unrepaired damage to the superstructure of the station, even this long after your last strike."

"If there is a better Science Officer in either fleet, Captain, I've yet to even hear about them," Denis replied gravely. "Assume power absorbers and guns are repaired, and non-critical functions were left until later. That thing is still dangerous, but more fragile than it was."

"And the Megalodon's consorts?" Provst asked, but it felt mostly like clarifying a point, rather than challenging the plan, or Denis's authority.

"They can fire forward guns while docked, but they are otherwise pretty helpless," he said. "That's why we're coming in on the path we are, behind him for the most part. The whole point of bouncing out is to take the ten minutes necessary to undock everyone and bounce back in for combat. That's ten minutes we're running hard and dangerous down here."

Provst just nodded on the visual image, but remained silent.

"Very good, then," Denis said. "Stand by for fleet signals."

CHAPTER XXVIII

Tomas Kigali studied the arrangement of Second Squadron in his projection with a critical eye. With all the Fleet Centurions elsewhere, technically command of this team should have fallen to Robbie Aeliaes, over on *VI Ferrata*, but Jessica specifically put him in charge, instead of Robbie and Hardie.

Made sense, on the face of it. *CA-264* and *CA-410* had been joined by the two ICAs, Imperial Corvette Assault: *Admiral Konnacht* and *Admiral Raeburn*, plus *CM-404*. Ásmundur's Minehunter wasn't as well armed as even the escort corvettes, but he had a nice sensor array on the bow, so he could generate electronic snow almost as well as *CS-405* would have in that slot.

They were sitting in Strike Position Three now, five combat corvettes in the van, with four ICEs, *Imperial Corvette Escort*, around the perimeter of the formation as point defense. All six cruisers were here: *VI Ferrata, VI Victrix, Indianapolis, Birmingham, Glasgow,* and *Dundee,* plus *II Augusta.* Tamara's flight wing would be over with Denis, but she was still a cruiser hull that could shoot things.

Over in Strike Position Four the two Heavy Dreadnaughts waited, along with all fourteen GunShips from Iskra, Denis's three CEs: *401, 402,* and *403,* and Provst's ICS, the Imperial Corvette Scout *Hans Bransch.*

It was one hell of a force assembled today, ten light-minutes out from the planet.

"All vessels, *II Augusta*'s flight wing is deployed," Jessica's voice came over the line. "Kigali, you have the flag."

"First Expeditionary Fleet, this is Kigali, aboard *CA-264*. I have the flag," he said with a terrible glee he could not disguise. "All ahead maximum, conforming to your squadron leaders. Thirty seconds to insertion from *mark*."

He turned to his Tactical Officer, still Arsen Lam after all these years, and nodded. He was not looking forward to losing him, but he could make Arsen look good. First Lord would need experienced Command Centurions for the new vessels. It would mean breaking up his team, but that was the nature of service.

He would just train the next set to those same, impossible standards.

"Arsen," he said. "You have Tactical."

"Aki, all ahead crazy," the man ordered.

Centurion Aki Ridwana Ali did roll her eyes at the two of them, but pressed a button and the lights dimmed for almost a second as she routed every erg she had into thrust.

CA-264 attempted to punch a hole in the solar wind, flying hard ahead, with *CA-410* running just as fast. If the two Imperials weren't giving it everything they had, Kigali couldn't tell. It didn't look like any space opened up across the entirety of the sixteen ships coming out of the starting blocks.

It was good.

CHAPTER XXIX

THERE WERE nights he would still wake up in sweat from that same terrible nightmare. It had evolved over the years, but Tobias Brewster would find himself back on the Emergency Bridge of the old carrier, tumbling on an oblong axis while an Imperial Battleship was taking potshots at them.

Except he wasn't able to score any hits, firing back at the old Red Admiral. It was *Simeon* all over again, except he had walked into a final exam hung over and confident he could fake his way through it all on charm.

Had it been a decade? Was that even possible?

He looked up from his new station on the bridge of *IFV Vanguard*. After so many years as Nina's backup, he was suddenly in her chair, except she was across from him, in Denis's seat.

It felt like the end of an era had occurred. He could have long ago taken a First Officer slot somewhere. Jessica had even offered to blackmail whoever he identified for the slot, as a measure of how far they had come together since Day One. But in the end, he wanted to be here.

Everyone wanted to be in First Expeditionary, calling in every favor and chit they could to get transferred to the exciting front. Some of them wanted the glory of combat. Others were looking for that line on their *C.V.* that would get them a better gig back home.

Tobias just wanted to be with his friends. And he had earned his spot here. Hell, he had even published seven articles in military journals on tactics and games automation as a training tool. When he did retire, he could keep being an academic, or become a game designer. Or just go home.

But today, it was final exam time again. Except this time he was awake, prepared, and had an entire battle squadron behind him.

Friends, even if he had only known some of them for weeks.

"Pilot, give me a countdown clock to expected emergence," he said loudly, glancing over at Nada's smile as her ponytail bobbed in the air.

"Gunner, confirm everything forward is set for range, and everything aft for damage," he moved on, echoing Nina's checklist, as he had always followed from Em Bridge.

"Confirmed long and short," Afolayan replied.

"Defense, unlock everything and prepare to engage anybody that gets close," Tobias continued. "Reinforce all shields forward for now, and prepare to cycle along the side as we pass him."

Centurion Robena Dubej grinned up at him. *Robie* had moved up from Em Bridge six months ago when Maurice Holiday had to retire for medical reasons after the last time they came through here. Even a battle where the damage is light still results in injuries. Some of them were worse than others. Maurice had been good, but was going to be in the hospital for too long, and needed to do it at home, rather than on the frontier.

But Tobias had worked with Robie since she first came aboard, so he could trust her to trust him now.

"Emergency Bridge, as always, rear Type-3's will be your purview until I take them back," he said, smiling as he caught Nina smiling at him. Word for word from what she always said to him. "Anything that can fire forward on our target will do so. Everything else holds back for surprises. If we overrun, I'll expect you to pour everything you have into him."

"Roger that," came the call from aft. Senior Centurion Kathy Mayzes had replaced him as Emergency Bridge commander, and was Third Officer these days.

We are all facing a new future.

Tobias looked up at Nina now, and caught her grinning at him. It was weird seeing a third stripe on her arm.

"What did I miss?" he asked, final exam and him all naked in his mind.

"Only one thing," she said with a laugh. "Good luck."

"Oh," he remembered. "Thank you."

"Bridge, this is Nada," the pilot looked up and called loudly. "Twenty seconds to emergence."

Tobias double-checked his harness and made sure that his emergency suit was close at hand and locked down, if he needed it. Damage might penetrate this deep after all, Maurice had been seated not too far away from this chair.

Everything good.

Now, time to wait.

At this speed, the trigger on emergence was the gravity well. This crew had gotten pretty good about how to hold it together deeper than the designers expected, so the ship might pick up some extra distance. Not much, but every tenth of a second was that much less reaction time over on that Megalodon.

Emergence, and all his boards came on-line at once.

Tobias had just enough time to notice that *Valiant* was keeping pace with them, both in the jump and now the hard acceleration in. That had been one of the risks, going one-on-one because they got too far ahead of the other dreadnaught.

Not today. Gosh, that must suck for you, Buran.

The hull thumped as the Bubble Gun went downrange. And Provst's team was almost reading his mind, because their shot had to be within a tenth of a second.

And then the big beams cut loose. Eight Type-4 beams. One target. Range a little extreme, but shortening with every heartbeat.

Afolayan let loose with the Type-3 beams next. Not much damage from here, but again, every little bit might be the one that broke the guy over there.

Good news, they had caught the Megalodon almost exactly where they wanted him. The battleship was orbiting at a different speed than most of the rest of the local warships, in a different plane, and was slowly coming up behind the station, but too far away for them to do much to help.

Tobias checked his boards. Squadron Two had dropped out on the edge of a laager where three of the Tigersharks were patrolling, away from the one that wasn't on his boards. The Mako was near the station ahead, as were two of the Hammerheads.

Good, hopefully that meant that the other three destroyers were out doing customs duty or emergency rescue patrol. Maybe the Tigershark was supporting them. That would put them out of position now, and maybe make them brave enough to come down to play later.

Severnaya Zemlya was a busy port. Not so much as *St. Legier*, or even *Osynth B'Udan*, but there were hundreds, maybe thousands of civilian ships on his boards, most probably running like hell for the safety of deep space as they realized that the war had suddenly returned.

Both Bubble Guns imploded, almost simultaneously. It made a pretty picture on his screen, because they apparently fed off each other somehow. The power curve looked to be another ten percent higher than two separate shots would have been.

Vanguard's hull rocked now. Incoming fire from the battleship.

Per Imperial records, the Megalodon design only kept one of the three Maulers from the Carcharias design they were replacing. Instead, they had six upgraded Pulse beams, the kind that ranged like a Type-4, but didn't do quite as much damage. They also kept twelve of the fifteen regular Pulse beams that were functionally equal to a Type-3 for tactical purposes, as well as all nine of the Flicker Beams that had been the inspiration for the Type-1-Pulse.

Poor bastard was also facing the wrong direction, so only two of his big beams could swing around this far, at least until he started to maneuver in real space to swing his bow around.

Still, he had apparently identified *Vanguard*, concentrating all his fire this way and ignoring *Valiant*. Just like Jessica had predicted.

"Gunner, ignore the Bubble Gun," Tobias ordered. "Route extra power to beams and shields instead."

Everyone acknowledged, but that was just background radiation right now. Tobias was in the zone.

More beams pounding down range. *Valiant* fired their Bubble Gun again, but they could afford to, at least for now.

Around him, Tobias noted the fourteen GunShips all firing at once. It was a trick they had been taught at *Qui-Ping* a decade ago. Everyone fire as a unit, so all the energy arrived at the same moment. Still too far away to do more than tickle, but Jessica had wanted the enemy Director's attention focused over here.

Watching two heavy dreadnaughts and a wall of smaller ships rushing at him.

Because then the Fast Bombers blinked into existence on a flank, also running flat out.

Tobias grinned as all twelve of the little ships fired point blank into the beast's side, a buzzsaw of Type-3 and Type-1 beams. That facing hadn't been engaged by the dreadnaughts, but the Bubble Guns had done their best to soften it a little.

And then someone kicked it in and set fire to the place.

A moment later, the Megalodon was gone. Right on schedule. Hopefully bleeding internally and with parts coming off in JumpSpace.

"Squadron flag, this is Brewster, target has jumped," he called, leaning back and taking a breath.

"Roger that, Bridge," Denis replied. "Acknowledged. Proceed to Phase Seven."

"Good shooting, Tobias," Jessica's voice came over the line.

Tobias turned to Nina with a huge smile on his face.

Now things were going to get ugly.

CHAPTER XXX

THE TIGERSHARK WAS A SNIPER DESIGN, apparently. Kigali smiled as his horde of ravening wolves came out of JumpSpace, baying for blood.

The old Mako had been a knife-fighter, with a Mauler on the bow to rend, and nine Pulse Beams arranged down the sides of the triangular hull in trios. Six Flicker Beams provided point defense against missiles and fighters, and could do a fantastic job of savaging a vessel at Mauler range.

But the sniper didn't want to get into melee with another cruiser. He had that damned Pulse-Ex Beam instead of the Mauler, for hammering on someone at extreme range. Twelve Pulse beams for when he got close. Only three Flicker Beams for close-in work.

Times like this, Kigali was almost sad he didn't have a missile cruiser handy, just because those three ships could be overwhelmed with drones, if they were dumb enough to stay put.

Not that they would. It was three of them against seven of his cruisers, each probably a kilo for kilo match they didn't want to try. Plus four assault corvettes out front, just daring the guy to shoot at them.

Still, they opened fire, like any good commander did when surprised. Except that they went random. *VI Ferrata*, *Dundee*, and *Admiral Raeburn* each took a hit from incoming beams. The Director over there should have waited a second and identified a target for all three vessels to engage.

"Squadron, engage," Kigali called over the team line. He had to wait the extra second to make sure that all seven cruisers were visible on his boards and pointed the right way.

The formation was only a little ragged, as they had been hopping just ten light-minutes, with ships fresh out of dry-dock. And the Tigersharks were deeper in the gravity well than the battleship, so Kigali had gone fast and deep on the drives.

In space, the beams were just a flash of light, like a lighthouse cycling by you. On his boards, it was a madhouse. Seven Bubble Guns, firing at extreme range. Four hit, which was damned fine sharpshooting, especially at this speed.

All of them impacted Tigershark Two within about a heartbeat. It was like St. Elmo himself had come down and blessed them. Except he had changed his mind and cursed the ship instead, immolating it in white-hot plasma.

Every beam with arc fired into the ship now. The various gunners had paused for the softening up. It was the exact opposite of what Jessica's forces normally did, hitting with beams first.

Two looked like a turkey that had been in the oven too long. Kigali's birds were always perfect, but he had heard horror stories about amateur chefs doing it all wrong.

And then Second Squadron committed graffiti on the guy's hull. With sledgehammers.

Messy.

"Gunners, next target," Kigali called. "All vessels maintain acceleration."

The first ship would need dry-dock. At least six Type-4 beams had hit, after the power absorber panels were completely overloaded, and had collapsed in places. Engineers would probably be able to see starlight through the width of the hull when they looked.

If those people had any clue about orbital physics right now, they would scram whatever emergency jump they probably had programmed, and just hop a quarter orbit away, somewhere behind his ships. They would be safe, for now, because Kigali again wasn't doing it like they were supposed to, slowing as they closed so the two sides could go hammer and shield on each other.

Hell, if they just sat and took it, all three ships would probably survive, and could just sit and fire into his squadron's ass as they kept going.

Of course, you would have to believe Second Squadron was going to do the absolutely insane as a next step to take such a risk. Nobody would believe this.

The second salvo from the Bubble Guns was much more ragged. Variance in charging cycles, lack of a coherent order to hold and fire. The works. Two hits. Then one. Then a final one. This was less cataclysmic.

Maybe a crème brûlée, rather than a scorched turkey.

The beams made up for it.

Again, ragged, but that actually worked in his favor, as every woodpecker tap had the opportunity to bleed into gaps and hit the hull, even when the panels held.

And darkness.

All three ships gone. Just like they were supposed to do when facing the potential for being overwhelmed by superior local forces.

"Second Squadron, this is Kigali," he intoned in a severe, vengeful voice. "Proceed to Phase Seven."

CHAPTER XXXI

JESSICA TOOK a deep breath as the words came over the comm.

"Second Squadron, this is Kigali," he said angrily. "Proceed to Phase Seven."

She checked the boards. Bedrov had designed the flag bridge on *Indianapolis* to closely replicate what she had enjoyed on her Star Controller, with a few improvements he had picked up along the way. It wasn't as spacious, and she didn't have that mind-bogglingly-huge projector in the center of her table, but Enej was here, even if Aranyani had stayed behind on *Vanguard* to help Denis.

The station was still where she had left it in April. Most assuredly, they had repaired all the combat systems by now, but just seeing all the repair shuttles and equipment, as shown by *Ballard*, had told her that they had skipped the rest of the work, or at least slowed it way down.

Probably, they had sent everybody to *Yenisei* to help repair the devastation she had unleashed there, confident that they had major forces here. Hopefully, *The Eldest* was still thinking in linear terms, defending borders on maps, expecting her to pounce on *Samara* or *Ninagirsu*, rather than what she was really doing.

Every day he was busy fighting Thermopylae was another day he wasn't facing her in the Peninsular War.

Because now, it was going to get rather ugly.

The Megalodon and the Tigersharks had fled rather than face her. But they would only jump out into the darkness long enough to undock from the *Energiya* module and come back. That was a battleship, five cruisers, and eleven frigates, facing her. Against what she had brought to the field of battle, it would be a slaughter, but she was going to give them the chance to level that field, if they were smart.

"All vessels, this is Jessica Keller, aboard *Indianapolis*. I have the flag," she said carefully. "Phase Seven initiated. Conform maneuvers to *Vanguard* and form up for fleet maneuvers."

Twelve Fast Strike Bombers. Fourteen GunShips. Thirteen Corvettes. Seven Cruisers. Two Heavy Dreadnaughts.

With most of the defenders out in deep space, her force had about eight minutes before any of the sharks could come back to fight. Maybe twenty minutes, if the two forces took the time to coordinate themselves before returning.

In sixteen minutes, First Expeditionary Fleet would be in range of the station's guns. And vice versa.

Kigali's team was moving faster, but they had the greatest distance to travel. An Imperial admiral, one of the types that Em had finally retired over the last few years, would have slowed down now and brought everyone together into a nice, massive force, trundling around orbit to go after the station as a unit. Like had failed so many times at *Samara*.

Nils Kasum had cleared away the *RAN*'s deadwood of the Noble Lords six or eight years ago, starting with Loncar. In those instances, that left the fighters in charge, rather than glad-handing politicians.

Today, the cruiser force would catch up to the dreadnaughts, just as everyone got into range with the station, going as fast as they could accelerate in two units. The ships would be too deep in the gravity well to just jump to safety, like *Buran*'s ships could. But they would be headed up and away, and that line of safety wasn't all that far away.

And if that Megalodon took too long, he might miss all the fun.

Vanguard pivoted on the boards, engines still running all out. This would deflect the ship, and his whole squadron, onto a different orbital path. Ships several light-minutes away wouldn't be able to see it until they jumped back in, hopefully aiming for that spot where Denis would have been without the sideslip.

Kigali was doing the same thing, with the addition of a max burn on every engine that could push. Signals intelligence could only predict where your enemy was, if nothing changed. Those ships would hopefully land badly out of position when they went to intercept her, and then have to jump again, giving her team an extra minute to prepare.

Otherwise, it was going to get messy around here.

Jessica took a minute to study the rest of the orbital traffic. Several industrial stations shared orbit with them, but most of them were at a much lower altitude, not needing to maintain a geo-synched location over a city below. The number of civilian ships was dwindling rapidly, as everyone ran for the hills, obviously cognizant of what she had done at *Yenisei* or *Stanovoy*.

Good; lessons were being learned that the cost of subjugating the galaxy would have to be paid by citizens here, and not just those planets that got conquered by *The Eldest* and his Warriors. Or bombarded from orbit.

Below them, a busy planet, with fields of lights representing cities on a black fabric as they flew over the night side of the planet. It would be child's play to start blasting some of those targets from here. She didn't have any primary beams, but this depth of atmosphere wasn't going to degrade a Type-4 beam enough to prevent it from setting fires or imploding skyscrapers.

She had no intentions of doing that, tempting as it might be. Seeker had suggested that there might be orbital shields protecting the inner portion of the major cities, perhaps a zone a few kilometers across over government buildings or military bases, but most of the civilians on the ground were at her mercy.

And she had mercy. Some.

There was still the next part of this campaign. That would go beyond what she had done at *Trusski*. It was, however, the next, logical step.

A signal chirped and brought her eyes up.

Enej smiled grimly.

"That was the eight-minute mark we estimated as best, possible return time," he said. "Now they might show up at any moment."

"Let everyone know," she replied. "We should have enough space to get one clean miss out of them. Assuming they don't intentionally jump wide to locate us, but even then, we should spot them, with both *CM-404* and *Hans Bransch* out there looking."

"On it," he said, typing away furiously.

"What's *Valiant* doing?" she asked, noticing Provst's ship moving slightly ahead of *Vanguard,* up with the faster GunShips.

"Note here from Denis says that Provst is working on the theory that they think we're still on *Vanguard*," Enej replied. "He's expecting them to target Denis anyway, so he's trying to goad them into either letting him get closer, or engaging *Valiant* first."

"Good idea," she said. "Send them both a gold star for that one."

Little things, like competent commanders working together, over and above her plans, to confuse the enemy. Doing the hard things in the scrum that it took to win, rather than worrying about who would get the credit.

"Contact," someone's voice came across the team comm. "All guns forward now."

The display she was watching took almost two seconds to catch up to the data. Guns were already firing by the time a new target appeared.

Oh, crap.

Jessica made a note to adjust her own thinking next time. Both of her squadrons had gone sideways when maneuvering, but otherwise stayed relatively on plane. That Megalodon had just jumped into a spot where he obviously expected to be firing into *Vanguard*'s outer flank as it went by. Instead, he was sitting almost directly in front of First Squadron. With all six of his Hammerheads in close, defensive orbit on *Vanguard*'s port side as they charged.

At least everyone over there was facing slightly the wrong way, still turned sideways rather than bow on. And orbital space, as small as it appeared in the projection, was still huge and completely empty.

It only looked like an impending ten-vehicle-pileup on a crowded freeway.

The *Buran* ships were almost at rest, relative to the station. First Squadron was going to blow by them at high speed. And hopefully miss, because there was simply no time to maneuver at these speeds.

Indianapolis's guns cut loose, pausing only long enough for the ship to roll onto her side so both Type-4 guns could bear. *Bedrov's Gator Roll*. The rest of Second Squadron did the same, ignoring for the moment the possibility that the Tigersharks were probably coming soon.

And then it was done.

One cataclysmic moment, where the amount of energy on the sensors went off the chart, and then a gap appeared between the two forces, growing by the second.

"Flag, this is *Valiant*," Provst's voice came over the team push. "Scratch one battleship, but I'm pretty much done for the rest of this battle."

He transmitted a first pass damage report from his Chief Engineer, showing the amount of injury to the ship. Apparently, the Megalodon had misidentified dreadnaughts, pouring all of his fire, plus his escorts, into *Valiant*, and ignoring the rest of the ships passing.

Bubble Gun offline.

Two Type-4 beams damaged, with one possibly destroyed.

Half of the port guns at least damaged, if not worse.

Shields tattered down the whole side, plus bow and some starboard.

Valiant was a mess.

But then *Hans Bransch* sent his scan of the Megalodon.

You *could* kill a ship with icepicks. First Squadron just had. Jessica was amazed the shark hadn't exploded. Or melted from the concentrated fury. But it wasn't going anywhere.

Jessica wasn't entirely sure that the ship would be able to hold orbit.

"Acknowledged, *Valiant*," Jessica replied quickly. "Maintain formation and put everything into shield facings, rolling as you need to keep a wall between you and them. *Vanguard* and Kigali can take it from here."

"Roger that," Provst said, cutting the line.

It was a high cost to pay, but she had known these risks. Everyone had. And *Valiant* could still limp home, while that Megalodon was *dead*.

"Flag, this is *Hans Bransch*," another man came on the line. "Confirm target. I have two of the Tigersharks that have just landed close to the station in a defensive posture. Relative speed zero."

Jessica smiled. It was a terrible, cold thing that she felt take up residence on her face. Like Kali-ma returning for the first time in years. Even Enej, seated across from her, recoiled the slightest amount, looking at her.

She found the file she wanted, gamed out ahead of time, and even reviewed by Tobias Brewster in his spare time, partly to prepare himself, and partly because he had turned into another version of her as a tactical commander.

One Mako or Roughshark. Two Tigersharks, one of them slightly damaged but making a last stand. Seven Hammerheads, including five of the six that had been escorting the Megalodon. One had remained behind for now.

All sitting in the shadow of the station and its guns.

She routed firing assignments out to her team, approaching the defenders at high speed. Last time, the Fast Strike Bombers had come out of jump cold, almost on top of the station, firing into low-powered absorption panels and bringing them down with overload, just before her smaller squadron came blasting through.

And ignoring the defenders completely.

She hoped they were about to make the same assumption today.

"All ships," she said calmly, a professor handing out their final exams and looking over half-glasses with a stern eye. "Acknowledge targeting and prepare to engage."

Green lights from everyone a few seconds later. Most of them had seen it coming.

At this speed, *Ishfahan* could have been deadly effective, but nobody would have imagined that yesterday. Just launch a wall of missiles as the fleet closed, like a strike carrier following its wing into battle.

It was like the idea Denis had to mount a single-shot Primary on the bows of a thousand corvettes and fire them all at once. Just overload the smaller, more nimble fleet, because they had chosen maneuverability over durability.

And that wouldn't help on defense.

Suddenly, she was Xerxes, and that Mako was Leonidas.

The station opened fire. A panicked shot, apparently, because it was only one, at such an extreme range that even the Type-4's were more like flashlights than sledgehammers.

Still, it marked the next phase of the battle. *Valiant* had shifted again, drifting aft and starboard, as the rest of his friends went portward. It wouldn't protect him, if the station was intent on hitting that dreadnaught, but it put other warships closer. Including *Vanguard*, which should be the target everyone was expecting to attack.

Chariot of the dreaded Jessica Keller.

"*Merman*, this is Keller," she called out to the commander of *II Augusta*'s flight wing.

The Fast Strike Bomber was designed as a short-range jumper, moving inside the gravity well like *Buran*'s ships. They weren't as accurate in motion, but this would be a short hop.

Normally, they bounced in and out. Today, they had been with First Squadron long enough to actually recharge their batteries, so they could make two jumps now, instead of one.

Hopefully, yet another surprise.

"*Merman*," he called back, somehow combining superiority, sarcasm, and grumbling into two syllables. But he was a pilot.

"Execute your jump," she ordered.

Rather than answer, his whole team vanished. *Indianapolis* was expecting it, so the twelve fighters reappeared quickly in her projection.

All of Jessica's forces were coming at the station at high speed, more or less on a single orbital plane. Jumpfighters didn't have to worry about that. They came out of their jump on the side of the station, suddenly raking a flank. All twelve opened up with every beam they had been recharging.

Against a station asleep, that could overload. Here, the defenders were awake, and every power absorber panel was empty and waiting. The attack was messy, but nothing that would overwhelm that flank.

Wasn't the point.

Surprise was.

Linear thinking.

The ships leapt to safety before any gunner on that flank could react.

But every head was suddenly turned to port, even if just psychologically.

Jessica Keller had just attacked the station again. They needed to move to defend it from her.

The big guns on the station opened up, as did the Tigersharks.

"First Expeditionary Fleet, engage," she ordered simply.

She actually took a breath and released it, consciously leaning back into the chair behind her and reaching a hand for the sippy cup of warm coffee she had put down half an hour ago and promptly forgotten.

Surprise.

CHAPTER XXXII

ONCE UPON A TIME, Tomas Kigali had commanded a tiny vessel named *CR-264*. The last Revenue Cutter still in *RAN* service, on a forgotten and ignored border with *Fribourg* where the war never actually intruded.

In those days, he had spent his leave time on feats of individual sailing and navigational exploits for the record books. Longest solos through dense asteroid belts without autopilots. Fastest point-to-point navigations.

Stuff that had earned him the nickname *The Navigator* and the respect of people for whom that sort of thing mattered.

Before Jessica Keller recognized him as a warrior the equal of Alber' d'Maine, if less vocal and hostile about it.

He smiled benignly as he looked around his tiny bridge on *CA-264*, the dangerous successor to *CR-264*, designed specifically for him by Yan Bedrov to *kill things*.

Ballard didn't kill things. Kanda and Elzbet might be the very best at what they did, but they weren't here today. Certainly weren't in the warship closest to the enemy, even if the cruisers behind him were still capable of ranging further.

Jessica had just spoofed those bastards.

Again.

She was like that.

Tomas smiled.

Right about now, all those Type-4s were just about to range on the station, so the two sides could engage in an epic firefight, a jousting pass with lances and shields and big, stupid warhorses.

The ships in front of him apparently believed it, as they all began to pivot away from the charge, so they could fire into his kidneys and ass as he went by.

"First Squadron," he growled into the microphone. "Break and fire."

Boy, won't you be in for a shock.

A Bubble Gun actually moved just slow enough to appear on a screen as an object, rather than a symbolic line indicating beam fire. Six of them went downrange around *CA-264* and his four, deadly assistants.

Four Hammerheads. One Mako.

First Squadron poured everything they had into those five ships, ignoring the station completely. Guns went to overload in places, especially the Type-1-Pulse turrets that normally had nothing to do, because *Buran* didn't fire missiles, and had learned not to close with all those rending teeth.

Today, they were sitting ducks. Tomas Kigali was supposed to blow right by them.

Jessica had taught everyone to concentrate their fire onto a single ship rather than spreading it out. That was effective in a balanced fight, where all you might normally do was recharge the other guy's batteries faster.

This wasn't a fair fight.

Six Expeditionary Cruisers fired.

Two hit the Mako with Bubble Guns. The other four had a Hammerhead each to themselves. Four Assault Corvettes, each assigned a Hammerhead, with *CM-404* getting the Mako. Four Imperial Escort Corvettes. All of them targeting the Mako.

Nobody fired a single shot at the station.

Across the way, two Tigersharks, one of them injured. Three Hammerheads.

Valiant actually got their Bubble Gun back on-line in time. Tomas wondered if they had been lying about the level of damage sustained, just in case the sharks could somehow break the code.

Provst apparently went after the wounded Tigershark with his undamaged side.

Vanguard took the healthy one.

Nine of the GunShips went after the three Hammerheads. The other five crushed the wounded Tigershark after *Valiant's* fire slammed into it.

And every *Buran* ship had a corvette pouring fire into them as they went by.

And just like that, it was over.

"All squadrons, begin evasive maneuvers now," Jessica's voice came out of the heavens.

Tomas looked at the damage reports as the two scouts looked backwards.

Expeditionary-class vessels had significant aft-facing firepower, and it was still going downrange, but the gaps between squadrons were growing at a rapid pace, and accuracy was about to go out the window as everyone twisted and rolled to avoid fire from the station.

Vanguard's Tigershark had been flat-footed. It looked like the first one, the one that had just barely escaped and not come back for round two. *Valiant's* victim made the dead Megalodon look healthy.

Kigali's cruiser had turned out to be a Roughshark, so he gave up much of his offensive firepower for ramjet bombs. Apparently, he had been waiting to fire them, and waited too long. One salvo of three had started to clear the tubes, with one of them exploding in the tube itself and blowing a gaping hole in the side of the ship.

The rest of the fire had more or less torn the ship in two.

The Hammerheads over here were floating at the top of the tank right now, with their bellies toward the sun.

And now the fun starts.

CHAPTER XXXIII

IMPERIAL FOUNDING: 180/11/25. IFV VALIANT,
SEVERNAYA ZEMLYA

Tom Provst growled under his breath, but kept the profanities inside his head. *Firehawk* would have come apart on her welds, to have suffered the amount of fire that had just blown apart his front shield and wracked *Valiant*'s hull so badly.

At least today he didn't have to hold the Empire together from this broken deck. And the scent of burning insulation wasn't even that great, so probably just a short, and nothing that drastic.

"Charlie, send a note to the engineering crew and gunners," he said instead. "Admiral's personal compliments on going above and beyond. Didn't think we had it in us to get off that many shots, with all the problems."

His Flag Commander nodded and went back to typing, while Tom reviewed the exterior situation.

He didn't even have to command today. Denis Jež was commanding on this pass, and they had Jessica if they needed. He could just fight his ship, like in the old days.

And it wasn't like this crew hadn't developed a lot of experience in rebuilding their battleship without a dry-dock stint.

Megalodon: dead.

Two Tigersharks effectively crippled, possibly dead. One more Tigershark badly damaged. One who had escaped his wrath.

For now.

Eleven Hammerheads reduced to an effective force of four undamaged. The other seven were in some state of dead, especially the ones that had drawn First Squadron as a foe.

On this side, *Valiant* was hurting, but could still fight. In an hour, the shields would probably be fully repaired as well as feasible, outside of cutting the hull and swapping generators wholesale. Good enough that he just had to lead with his right if he wanted to punch anybody.

Everyone else had taken some level of fire from the station, mostly concentrated, as expected on *Vanguard*, but Jež and his staff were giving a master class in high-speed maneuvering and evasion, aided by two scouts pouring everything they had into confusion and electronic counter-measures.

"All ships, move on to Phase Nine," Admiral Keller sent.

Tom had finally come to understand just how Jessica had managed to outdo everyone so badly. Every command came with an updated resource file showing half a dozen options, with the primary one highlighted, but allowing her commanders to adjust on the fly by picking a different approach.

It should have been chaos. A strictly Imperial fleet would have been, without one of a handful of admirals directing things. *zu* Wachturm could have done this. Tom didn't know how many others, and figured he was among the finest Emmerich had to pick from.

Learn from the best.

Poor station behind them had been expecting another fencing pass, like last time Keller did this. Tom wasn't particularly offended that they were reacting, instead of acting. He had been to *Samara*. And he had studied Keller.

Always a surprise.

Phase Nine. A lightly-armed military dry-dock a quarter orbit ahead of the primary station. Normally ignored, because there was too much firepower available in this system for anyone who wanted to engage it.

Except that there was nobody left. At least until that last Tigershark and the three Hammerheads got their heads out of their asses and decided to commit a particularly messy form of suicide by moving to engage eight times their effective tonnage.

Maybe he'd get lucky today.

"Tom," Charlie d'Noir spoke up to get his attention. "One of the Fours is dead, but the other one might be good for about three shots."

"Hold it for later," Tom decided. "Strip parts from the dead one if that will help. I'll want three when we complete this circle."

"Roger that," Tom's Flag Commander nodded.

That station wasn't going to give Kigali's squadron much fuss, and there wasn't much *Valiant* could add.

Six hours from now? That might be a different story entirely.

CHAPTER XXXIV

THE HAD LEARNED. Every civilian vessel that could was gone and not coming back until the evil Jessica Keller broadcast her taunting message that she was done and leaving herself.

Except today she wasn't.

The projection in her flag bridge told the tale.

The local defensive squadron was shattered. Two major stations had been hammered hard enough to risk deorbiting over the next three weeks. That dry-dock wasn't ever servicing ships again.

The only thing left in orbit of any value was the primary command node station for the system.

First Expeditionary Fleet had coalesced above the north pole of the planet. Two of the bombers were damaged enough to be out of action, but had escaped destruction in the surprise of their last run on the station. Five of the GunShips had taken enough fire to retire to *Arad* for long term repairs, leaving her nine in a pinch.

Jessica found it amazing that none of them had been destroyed. But for surprise, the casualties would have probably been more in line with her original projections.

Valiant was like a bull in the ancient ring, with spears stuck in his back. Bloodied and angry, but still capable of killing the stupid bastard with the red cape. And today he had help.

To keep the secrecy intact, Reif Kingston's team had established a tight-beam laser to *Vanguard,* so her words would be broadcast by Denis's dreadnaught, rather than this one cruiser over on the soft flank.

"Attention *Severnaya Zemlya,* this is Red Admiral Jessica Keller," she announced in a slow, angry voice. Mongolian, because she had been studying enough to write speeches, if not have many casual conversations. The people below her needed to understand this without any confusion.

Seeker would have applauded. The Khan of *Trusski* that he had been might have even been impressed.

"Two hours from now, I will destroy the station," she continued. "If you abandon ship immediately, I will allow you to escape and get to the surface without being harmed. After that, there will be no prisoners. This is your only warning."

She closed the line and scowled. Enej scowled back, but he had studied the language more than she had, adding nuances to the words to make sure everybody got the message.

And she had a powerful reputation with these people. Cruel, yes, but also honest. For good as well as evil.

"*CM-404* and *Hans Bransch,* see if you can crack their communications intelligence," she said on a team line, naming the two ships with the best sensors, at least until *Ballard* made an appearance.

Jessica wanted Kanda and her team to remain a surprise as long as possible. Especially since they should be sitting out there in the darkness right now, probably listening to the traffic from those last four undamaged ships. Deciding among themselves if today was a good day to die.

Several long minutes passed while her ships worked on repairs and the station stewed.

"Flag, we've got signals," *CM-404* called. "Warship just blinked in next to the station."

The message was followed by three dots appearing as close to the station down there as *Buran*'s navigators were famous for.

Gutsy. She had to give them that.

"Flag," Denis called first, but Kigali probably had his finger poised on the call button as well. "Orders?"

Do we go kill them? Or let them go?

Jessica checked the display.

"*Buran* warship *Build The Future,* this is Keller," she said carefully. "What are your movement orders?"

Long pause. A shuttle launched from the station obviously on a rendezvous course with the Tigershark. Around it, emergency lifepods in every size available began to rocket away from the station on fast de-orbit paths.

"We transport the Director to safety, Keller," a woman's angry voice came back.

Very gutsy. And Jessica had done it to herself. Promised them two hours of safety, and they had actually taken her up on it. They could be long gone by then.

"Fleet, this is Keller," Jessica said, switching channels. "Hold for orders."

"*Build The Future*, this is Keller," she switched back and conjugated as fast as she could. "Your parole is to leave this system now, with all of the escorts. Anything else will make you a legitimate target. As will returning."

"We go, Keller," the woman said.

Somewhere, that Director would have to explain fleeing, rather than fighting. Probably before *The Eldest* himself, especially after what was coming next. But Jessica had given her word.

And staying aboard that station was a surer death than stepping out of the airlock naked.

She watched the shuttle dock, almost in real time, with so many sensors focused on the ships. Other shuttles were diving as fast as their hulls could bleed heat, while the pods moved like a tree casting seeds into the summer breeze.

Build The Future vanished, with both Hammerheads gone a beat later.

Enej grinned at her. It cut some of the grimness off her soul.

"What?" she asked, aware that he obviously had some joke in his head that couldn't be contained.

Not the place for jokes, normally, but this was Enej.

"This is what you get for dropping spears in someone's back yard and frightening his sheep," Enej giggled.

Around them, the rest of the flag crew laughed as well. Jessica joined them, letting the moment grow a little lighter on her flag bridge.

It was an outcome of that terrible legend.

As would what happened next.

"Notify Iskra that the way is clear," Jessica said. "Have her send *Archangel* and *Akatsuki* in to rendezvous with us here, bringing everyone in from the darkness."

CHAPTER XXXV

"All friendly forces, this is Saber Command," Vo heard the call on the Legion's command channel. "Request assistance and heavy support at map position C-943 soonest. Defenders have finally woken up and started to push back."

The message was accompanied by a map with a flashing vector arrow in the center, as well as a picture of…

What in the hell was that thing?

Vo was in his command tent, rather than out on patrol, but all ten Cutlass teams were within earshot, as long as everyone spoke between the crumping blasts of long-barrel artillery being fired over the horizon.

Outside, looking through the window, there was the slightest mist falling, with temperatures just cool enough to wear a jacket or a thermal layer under your regular coat and armor vest.

"Stolz," Vo called across the tent. "Find me something in Imperial records that matches that monster. And feed the coordinates to the Artillery Centurion."

It might have been the ugly stepchild of a land tortoise, crossed with an alligator, maybe. Eight stubby legs propelled a long torso as the thing waddled forward. It had twin-barrel turrets at each end, plus a larger turret just forward of center, with a single barrel twice as long as the other guns, and bigger in the bore.

Scale was hard to guess from here, as he was seeing images captured by the turret camera off one of his scout skiffs, somewhere forward. Everything was jittery and blurry as the vehicle's driver moved laterally, plus smoke between the camera and the beast downrange.

It was walking down a major thoroughfare in the city of Xi-Shong-Ri. Vo froze the image as it brushed a building with a shoulder, gouging a long welt in the stone.

Eighth floor. *Buran*'s architecture tended to put floors four meters apart, so the walking nightmare was roughly forty meters tall, to the top of the center turret. Big enough to simply walk up and stomp on any of his tanks or skiffs, like they were chittering mice around his feet.

"General," Stolz broke into his concentration.

Vo looked over and blinked.

"Artillery is launching a time-on-target barrage now," the man continued.

Vo opened the channel back to Pyotr Martin and his team.

"Pyotr," Vo said. "Keep eyes on the target and back off for now. Artillery support incoming."

"Acknowledged, Cutlass," Martin said.

The image suddenly changed, as those skiffs got the word and turned away from the current engagement, moving to a flank where they could spot and harass, but staying well away.

"Imperial notation, General," Stolz said. "Someone called it a Mechanical Terrapin. Name's stuck since them. Got a fuzzy orbital picture and not much else."

"Start updating the records now from Saber," Vo replied. "And tell Hardball to shift some firepower around."

Assents as people went to work.

Hopefully the heavy tanks of Hardball, his Fifth Ala, could do something about that beast.

In a way, it was like being back in charge of his small team. Maybe parts of this same group around him storming the Imperial palace, in his least favorite fairy tale. Pay attention. Issue orders. Think fluidly, because you're two days into raiding a hostile planet and have finally run into something they think can stop the 189th.

Who the hell builds a tank on legs? That thing was practically a small starship.

Yes. Of course.

Vo cursed himself inwardly as revelations unlocked.

This was *Buran*. They didn't go in for snubfighters or small-crew vehicles or spaceships. Everyone was raised communally in a crèche and expected to be part of a larger whole.

It made perfect sense to build a monstrously-huge land whale that probably required a crew of fifty to operate. Less risk of individuality breaking out that way.

Around him, all the artillery pieces opened up in rapid succession, instead of the ragged drumroll that he had unconsciously suppressed in his head for the last hour.

Time-On-Target.

Fixed location. Simple physics.

Every gun fires in a sequence determined by distance to the enemy being hit, as each shell has a different flight time.

You want them all arriving at once.

The vehicle sending Vo images grounded hard enough that he was looking at a tree for a moment, before someone got the barrel elevated and slewed around enough to lock on the beast.

Rangefinder display being transmitted said eleven kilometers away, so Martin's folks must have thought that was good enough.

He waited.

The Mechanical Terrapin was large enough to have short-range shields, something none of Vo's craft could carry. They were too big, and required an inordinate amount of power, and didn't do much to protect something at this scale.

Better for Imperial palaces and cities.

Or turtles, apparently.

Vo watched a wave of fire engulf the mighty machine, but it was held at a distance. Maybe thirty meters above the skin, as the shells impacted on shields tough enough to stop them.

Not good.

His artillery could probably punch through those shields eventually. Or churn up the terrain in front of it bad enough to maybe twist an ankle.

In a worst-case-scenario, he could call for an orbital strike, but he didn't want to go there. Jessica had never resorted to that sort of thing, and he understood the moral and ethical advantage they had from it.

Still, couple of Type-4's from low orbit would probably slag that machine.

Vo turned to Reese.

"Where are Pilum, Trident, and Halberd with their current missions?" he asked the Decanus.

"The primary starport is a slag-yard now," Reese said. "Alan's gathering everyone up from their pyromaniacal endeavors and getting ready for the next set. Trident is standing off a little from a warehouse district on the north side of town and bombarding buildings, rather than get down in that mess. Too easy for an ambush. Halberd is just hitting a refinery facility now."

"And we landed on the west side, well away from the only militia base, so we could get intel on *Buran's* land forces," Vo completed the thought. "That might have been a mistake, since we possibly could have overwhelmed the motor pool where that thing must have been hiding. Send notes to everyone to be on the lookout for more than just the one coming through the middle of town at us. They think that it's tough enough to take us, so I am concerned."

"What about an airstrike?" Iakov Street looked up from his own tablet.

"Don't want to order an orbital bombardment, Street," Vo growled. "You, of all people, should understand that."

"Do, *zu* Arlo," Street got serious. "Didn't say orbital. Keller's got bombers and GunShips up in orbit. We already know that nobody's got ground defense artillery, or they would have engaged us coming down. Betcha Strike Bombers would enjoy having something to do."

Vo's smile matched Streets. Looking around, it matched a number of them.

He was used to thinking in two dimensions with a Legion. But yeah, adding a flight wing to things would be good. Seventh Ala? Maybe a DropShip converted to handle a bunch of heavily-armed aircraft? Smaller, cheaper, and easier than space fighters, probably not much larger than a tank, bundled up.

He made a note to inquire with *zu* Wachturm, or Bedrov, whoever he saw first.

"Get me a link to Jessica," Vo ordered.

The Fleet Centurion was on the line within moments.

"Who's in a better spot?" Vo asked. "Iskra or Tamara?"

"What do you need?" she asked.

Rather than explain, Vo transmitted several stills, along with some of his annotations.

"Vishnu," she gaped.

"Yeah," Vo smiled. "In the interest of surviving, could you drop something heavy enough to crack that thing? And then maybe blast the hell out his base? I realize you don't have bombs, but just blowing up some buildings and hangars would be nice."

"I'll have someone call shortly," Jessica replied. "How soon do you need to bug out?"

"Oh, I'm going to have us move now," Vo smiled. "Thing like that needs to be drawn back into the distant suburbs and wilderness, as much as possible. Hoping it blows up really nicely. We're trying not to commit a mass casualty incident on Xi-Shong-Ri."

"Understood, General," Jessica nodded and cut the line.

"Reese, back all of Sixth Ala up to E-574 and let everyone know that the artillery will be off-line for a bit," Vo said. "Have Saber maintain a soft touch, but get the tanks backed up and leading it this way, if he'll come. If not, whichever way he turns, tell that Ala to run. No point in trying to engage it toe-to-toe, if we can bring in a bigger hammer."

"Roger that," Reese began typing.

Vo met Street's eyes across the tent. The man had nothing to do right now except bug out with everyone else, since Cutlass Force was a backstop. But that gave Vo a team of experts he could trust.

"Street, I have to stay here," Vo said. "Act like a general, coordinating our engagement with that beast."

Street nodded and stood. Hans Danville seemed to emerge from thin air, popping up from where he might have been napping. Danville could fall asleep at the drop of a hat.

"Take Cutlass Force and circle Xi-Shong-Ri fast and hard to the south if the Terrapin stays on course towards us," Vo ordered. "Get me eyes on that barracks and check in. I might need a Forward Observer for the airstrike, and I might need you to call them off from that part and go in and destroy things yourselves. Remember, we're not staying long, so don't get into a slugging match with anyone. Destruction, panic, and retribution."

Street smiled and even saluted, but that was enthusiasm. The man liked blowing things up.

Within forty-five seconds, the ten skiffs of Cutlass Force had lifted off and blasted away at high speed. Reese and his team were already folding up computers and tables to stow on their transport. Everyone he could see was armed, so Vo wasn't worried about personal risk.

And that beast wouldn't even notice if he shot it with his pistol.

Time for an introduction to Sun Tzu. And maybe a little Light Horse Harry Lee.

CHAPTER XXXVI

Trooper Victoria Ames looked around the inside of Cutlass Ten's skiff and tried to pretend she was as tough as these men. The last year had been even harder than the one before it. The hardest duty she had ever known. Or loved.

General *zu* Arlo, the *Aquitaine* Cowboy, had made her a soldier. Inducted her, trained her, and apparently even protected her from the Emperor herself. She would do him proud.

The gunner in the front seat of the skiff had projected his gunsite camera's view onto the inside back wall for Street's team to watch. Right now, they were sitting on a hill on the other side of the city, tracking that horror-vid monster from a very long ways away, as it traded fire with the tanks of Fifth Ala, the former 273rd Regiment that was now *CCLXXIII Heavy*. It didn't look like a fair fight, but Street had said that the General knew what he was about.

Other teams took occasional potshots at the thing from the flanks, but nobody was willing to get close enough to make sure their shots got home hard. She had been in a corner reading a book on logistics theory when Street suggested bombers, so she wanted to see what a craft intended to shoot heavy cruisers in space did against corvettes on the surface.

"*Arad One* to all ground forces," a woman's voice came suddenly through the speakers, scratchy with static and maneuvering. "Thirty seconds to engagement."

"*Arad One*, this is Cutlass Ten," Street suddenly sounded more like a professional soldier and less like her dad. "Secondary fire mission coordinates transmitted. We're on the south side on a hill with a view. Transponders are on. I need one solid strafing run, west to east, hitting those two buildings. We'll handle the rest."

"Roger that, Cutlass Ten," she said. "Stand by."

Victoria had never imagined this life. *Fribourg* wouldn't have allowed it, but for *zu* Arlo. Shortly, they would likely be in combat, so she checked her gear. Med kit. Spare ammunition in magazines and speed loaders. Helmet with flip-down optics and audio built in. Modified chest armor that had to cover her growing shape as regular food and hard exercise gave her curves she had never expected. Her mother had been a tall, skinny pencil, so she must have gotten something from the other side of the family. Something useful, anyway, to go with the rest.

She half-drew the extra blade that Danville insisted she tuck into her boot. He glanced up as she did and grinned at her, yet another big brother. Not that they were protecting her, but would tease her and treat her like one of them in equal parts.

"Cutlass Team, this is Street," Iakov said sternly. "Start moving now, so we come in right on the back of the strike. Anything inside the wire that moves is fair game. Outside the fence only engage if they fire first."

She supposed that Cutlass was supposed to have a Centurion, but they had always been *zu* Arlo's personal guard, so that part of the Standard Table or Organization and Equipment had never been occupied. Victoria wondered if she wanted that job bad enough. Considering the opinion of most officers that she had absorbed from Cutlass, she wasn't sure, but she also knew that these men didn't believe most officers could measure up to their standards.

Lots of candidates hadn't, once they realized that it was hard work and not relaxing in barracks while you sent the troops out to do things for you.

There was no slack in the 189th, and that included Trooper Victoria Ames.

Street caught her eye now.

"You and Danville on point when we drop," he ordered. "Aday and Koga will be set up on whatever high ground they can find as a sniper team, but you'll be inside, if the building survives. Take your carbine, but leave it slung and do this with pistols. The boys behind you will have firepower if you need it, plus I'll have the other teams close enough to flank or enfilade as needed. I will remain here to coordinate everyone. Questions?"

Danville shook his head, but he was a quiet man at the best of times. Most of the guys were action-first, and strategy second.

"Prisoners?" she asked. "Or just intel?"

Street thought about it for a second. Then his face got serious.

"Your call, Trooper," he decided.

Victoria felt a thrill of elation surge through her. That was what acceptance by these men meant. She could decide, and they would back her.

The skiff powered up and slid forward, retracting the skids just enough to stay at maybe two meters flight ceiling. Low and fast. Hard and mean.

The gun turret rotated, so she lost the view of the giant turtle as the thing engaged with the GunShips making a high-speed pass. Instead she got a front-row view of a buzzsaw carving lines of destruction into the side of the armory and across the grounds.

Buildings didn't explode. Not like in vids. No, they just collapsed more or less like sand castles facing a tide, especially as four craft let loose with everything they had from short-range. Windows would explode, showering the parking lots and grass with kernels of glassy corn when the heat and pressure inside got to be too much to contain.

Both buildings had been hit, and the airstrike cleared a section of cyclone fencing that had been severed by high energy beams.

Cutlass Ten grounded hard and skidded forward about two meters before it stopped. Danville already had the door open and moved as soon as the ground stopped, pistol in one hand and turning left. She drew and pivoted right, with the rest of the team piling out as soon as she cleared space.

They had trained her to attack, so Victoria began to jog forward, meeting Hans at the front bumper and quickly scanning both directions and the front of the building. People were starting to move around inside the buildings, but the shock would hold them for a little longer.

Hans nodded to her and started to run. She was a pace behind him.

Behind them, the turret opened up on the front of the building. The door wasn't armored. Probably solid-core and fireproof, but that just meant it took three shots to blast it off its hinges and fill the entry hallway with smoke and debris.

By the time they got to the door, everyone still alive in the front room had bolted for the back of the building. Four people remained behind dead.

She had dealt with death, as well as dealt it in her life. The smell was ugly, burning shit and bile, but she focused on the open door. Hans moved to one side and hurled a grenade through it without bothering to see who or what might be there.

A picture painted on a side wall, behind a waist-high counter, looked like a unit crest. She moved to the other side of the door from Danville and studied the words. They were written in letters, rather than ideograms, so she could understand parts of it from the Mongolian she had been studying.

The words *Motor Transport Depot* jumped out at her as the grenade went off, but she grabbed Danville's arm and held him.

"Put another one in there," she said, running on a hunch.

Danville glanced, nodded, and reached into a pocket. Behind her, someone fired a few potshots, but they weren't engaging anyone. Just keeping heads down.

"Street, who has the second building?" Victoria asked over the unit comm.

"One and Three," came the quick response.

"This is a motor pool and repair unit," she said. "There should be data pads lying around over there for repairing that beast, so they'll have full specs and capabilities."

"Good call," Street said. "Cutlass One and Three, steal me some working slabs when you hit the place."

Victoria nodded and turned back to the open door. Downrange, the second grenade exploded. She reached her pistol around the wall and fired twice, blind, but they didn't know that.

Danville was through so fast he probably got her gunsmoke on his face. She was right behind him, pulling a speed loader from a belt pouch and holding it in her off-hand against need.

The building itself had only been three stories tall, yesterday. Today, she could actually see daylight overhead from a shot that had torn off a section of the roof and collapsed onto the second floor.

"Someone put some grenades upstairs," she yelled, moving in Danville's wake like a remora.

The first office was open and abandoned. The one across the hall was a room for computers and such, tucked out of the way. Victoria had no idea how their electronic systems worked, so she couldn't take one apart to steal the good parts. Plus, they weren't staying.

"Kill this room," she pointed as she and Hans penetrated deeper into the building.

Hard voices yelled behind her, and then an explosion shook the building, so someone must have put a pair of grenades in and pulled the door closed.

The back of the building was a kitchen and dining facility, currently abandoned, with the back doors only now swinging closed from whoever had bolted through them. She wondered if this unit was a local militia rather than active duty. A weekend thing for retired soldiers. Certainly, they hadn't stayed to fight, but she supposed they were mechanics and not line troopers, given the situation.

Hans fired a shot through the slowly-closing door. It was maybe one hundred meters, at someone running away full tilt across an empty quad, but the man stumbled, stopped, and then collapsed. Victoria knew she wasn't good enough to kill someone running at that range with her pistol.

Yet. That would change. It would have to, if she wanted to belong.

Someone, several someones, fired back at them as they approached the door. Everyone dropped below open window sockets or turned over tables to provide cover.

"This is Cutlass Ten, we're taking fire from the rear quad, directly back from the rear center of the building," she called. "Who has eyes back there?"

"Stand by, Cutlass Ten," a man called.

Around her, the men with carbines opened up, mad woodpeckers firing single shots at a building.

A skiff must have moved sideways around the building, having dropped off its crew. The cannon poured fire into the quad. She peeked over the edge of the window. There was a shed back there. Probably supplies and parts. Right now, the front of it was disintegrating as a second skiff opened up, joining the first.

An explosion lifted the roof straight up, and metal walls flipped over as an explosion mushroomed.

"Target appears suppressed, Cutlass Ten," the man's laconic voice came over the line.

"Roger that," Victoria said. "Thank you."

Everyone peeked, but nothing fired.

Danville moved past her again, back into the building. Methodically, they checked every room, but all they found were corpses at this point.

Eventually, they did find a man upstairs, trying to hide in a bathroom stall. From his uniform, Victoria guessed he was an officer. From the poor fit over a pot belly, she guessed that he really only did this sort of thing on the weekends and must have a job that let him eat too well.

Certainly, he wasn't out on thirty kilometer hikes with his troops like *zu* Arlo.

They got him zip-tied quickly. A check found no weapons, not even a pocket knife.

Fribourg believed in paper. *Buran* did not. 189th's headquarters would have had all manner of records in filing cabinets, the kind that could be stolen, but here, everything was contained in computerized records reviewed by their God on a regular basis.

"Cutlass Command, this is Cutlass Ten," she said, keying in the General to talk to her. "We have a prisoner. Transmitting image now. Orders?"

She waited, keeping an eye out the shattered side of the building to the hangar next door where the Mechanical Terrapin had been housed.

"Trooper Ames, this is Cutlass One," Decanus Audie Teagle called her out by name, so Victoria ducked out of sight.

"Go ahead," she replied.

"We've got a stack of data pads for mechanics and enlistees," the man said. "Probably twenty or so. Plus pictures of the hardware and tools."

"Load them all," she said automatically. "Steal any tool you can move and not identify. We'll crack the systems next week on the way home, but there's nothing useful for the General right now."

"Acknowledged, Ames."

The way Danville was grinning at her made Victoria blink hard. She had been giving these men orders as they went, and expecting them to obey.

And they had. That was pretty weird. Utterly awesome, but strange.

"Ames, this is *zu* Arlo," the General was on the line. "If your teams have rounded up electronic intelligence, I don't need the prisoner. He looks like the equivalent of a Patrol Centurion, so he probably won't know anything useful."

"Roger that, sir," she said.

All the men were looking at her, even the two with the prisoner in the corner of their eyes.

"What?" she half-demanded.

They smiled. All of them.

Outside, the sound of gunfire and cannon had dwindled to nothing. Even the background sounds of the battle across the city were tapering. Hopefully, that meant that the airstrike had worked.

After a moment, it dawned on her. They were waiting for her orders. Hers.

Seventeen years old. Many of these men had been in uniform longer than that.

And she was acting like she was in charge.

Fine.

"Leave him here," she decided.

Hans was already moving towards the stairs at a rapid clip. She fell in behind him and the rest of Cutlass Ten was right behind that.

Outside, their skiff was backed up against the front door so they could load up without crossing the open quad. Street was standing in the doorway with his carbine, but he stepped to one side and the team piled in without breaking stride.

"Driver. Go," Street ordered, pulling the hatch closed.

Victoria found herself between Colton Formain, the *Draconarius*, and Thaddeus Gunderson. She felt like the crossbar on a capital H, as tall as those two men were, but they were all smiles, right now. All of them were.

"Good job, Trooper," Street said as he got a seat and strapped himself in.

Victoria finally relaxed long enough to smile back.

She had asked for this duty. Hopefully, the General wouldn't be mad at what she had done.

CHAPTER XXXVII

Vo STOOD and walked out of the tent when Cutlass Team came blasting over the hedge and into the sorghum field that they had taken over. He tried not to laugh as Ten un-assed from the skiff and immediately began cleaning firearms and restocking grenades from boxes on a nearby flatbed.

Teagle and Cutlass One landed just long enough to hand Street and Ames several bags filled with datapads and other stolen property. The skiff took off a moment later, shifting over to their spot in the line of vehicles.

"How'd it go?" Vo asked Street, keeping Ames in his peripheral vision as the two of them came more or less to attention.

"She's a natural, *zu* Arlo," Street said. "We'd have just blown everything to hell and called it good. All the intelligence from this load was her decision. And we left the poor bastard tied up when we left."

"You decided not to kill the man?" Vo turned his attention on Ames.

She got confused. It was cute.

Vo couldn't remember ever being that innocent. At her age, he had already been sentenced to his first contract with the Navy, instead of doing two to five years for burglary and possession of stolen goods.

"Why?" Ames finally asked.

Vo let his face fall into instructor mode, channeling Navin the Black.

"Not everyone would have just left him, Ames," he said. "Not many of my men would have shot a prisoner they decided they didn't need, but other units probably would have."

"So it was a test?" she asked fiercely, staring up at him.

"Every day is a test, Soldier," Vo semi-quoted Navin. "Ethics are what you do when nobody is looking, and reputation is what you do to someone who can neither help nor hurt you."

"Oh," a little lightbulb appeared in her eyes. "Understood, General."

He could tell she was restraining an impulse to salute him. Never appropriate in the field, but obviously heart-felt.

Vo nodded and smiled.

"Get yourselves cleaned and ready," he said. "We've done enough damage down here, and other militia units around the planet are starting to get their acts together. I intend to be off-planet in twenty hours or so, and we'll be holding the landing field until last."

"What happened to the turtle, *zu* Arlo?" Street asked.

"Those things are tough," Vo replied. "Even the airstrike only hurt it, but they lost the two front legs on the starboard side, so the thing can't move until it gets repaired. And your team destroyed the repair facility and burned everything that you could, so it will take a while. That's part of the reason I am so happy we will know how it is assembled."

"Be fun to take one apart on some future planet, sir," Street grinned savagely.

Vo's smile matched him.

Moirrey would see this as a challenge when he talked to her.

And then they'd go hunting.

CHAPTER XXXVIII

BALLARD HAD FINALLY REPORTED IN, so Jessica knew what had happened, watching the whole local system from her comfortable command seat in *Indianapolis's* flag bridge.

The Tigershark had rendezvoused with the last Hammerhead well out in the darkness, and the four vessels had run for deep space like their tails were on fire. That had left Jessica's team in complete control of the planet, at least until that Director could get someplace with a major fleet, like *Ninagirsu* or someplace deeper into *The Holding*, and bring back enough help to dislodge her. Except that she would be gone in twelve hours.

Nobody had been expecting her to land troops, though. Blast things from orbit, perhaps, but giving them the 189th as a housewarming present was better. More personal.

And this was never going to be like *Thuringwell.* That mission had been a once-in-a-lifetime opportunity to strike at one of *Fribourg's* weakest points. The psychological damage had been important, but headed in a different direction.

Look at what Jessica Keller could do, take away your planets from you, one by one…

Here, the folks down on the surface were dealing with a very contained storm, a tornado that had carved a delicate path of destruction through military facilities, starports, and the industrial backbone of the region while still not doing much damage to civilians. A planetary raid by angry people with big guns.

Where will she land next? What will they destroy? Is anybody safe?

Yes, she could play upon their minds, destroying their harmony and peace. They needed to fear her more than they did *The Eldest.*

Vo's last DropShip was climbing out of the gravity well as she watched.

"Get me Vo," she looked up from her display and fixed her eyes on Enej, seated directly across from her as always and lurking quietly.

He nodded and began to type.

"Ground Command. This is *zu* Arlo," the big man's voice rang out of the speakers in short order.

He sounded tired, but Jessica didn't expect he had slept much in the last week. Even on a quick, surgical raid like this one, things could go wrong. And had. Too many civilians in the way at one point, as refugees began to flee Xi-Shong-Ri and a column of scared people stumbled right into a wave of skiffs trying to avoid hurting random pedestrians.

And that damned Mechanical Terrapin. The GunShips had only damaged it. They probably could have gone back around a second or maybe third time and finished it off, but that hadn't been the mission. And Vo's folks had stolen repair guides, so Moirrey or someone could figure out how to undo one later.

"Keller," she replied, letting the moment of introspection hang. "Are you the last?"

"Affirmative, Jessica," Vo said, finally willing to treat with her like an equal rather than a Security Yeoman talking to his Command Centurion. It was amazing, how far they had come in the last decade. "I was the last soldier off the surface. Victoria Ames was second to last."

Jessica smiled at that. She had heard all about the young woman Vo was fostering into Imperial Land Forces. It was like opening a new front in her own, personal war with the male chauvinists in command.

Emperor Karl VIII had served in the Navy. Why can't I?

Victoria Ames is an Army Trooper. If she can do it, why can't other women?

Jessica could just imagine the conversations playing out as young women looked around and began to question the old way of doing things.

"My plan is to bring the entire force back to *Osynth B'Udan*," Jessica said. "We'll need repairs in dry-dock, and you'll want to pick up the rest of your team. Is there anything you'll need before then?"

"Negative, Flag," Vo replied. "Just a lot of sleep, and then more training. Need Moirrey to figure out how to kill turtles for me before the next time."

"Understood," Jessica noted with a smile in her voice.

They would go home now and recuperate. And see what the state of the war was.

Emmerich had sent her vague notes, suggesting major happenings.

Hopefully, Moirrey and Yan were up to no good.

PART FOUR
STALKING THE BEAST

CHAPTER XXXIX

SHE DINNA APPRECIATE the giggles emanatin's and stuff from the tall, blond chick standin' nexts to hers on the reviewing platform, but Moirrey's long learned that ya wasn't supposeds to tell the Emperor to behave. At least nots out in public-like.

And Casey were having an on-going, low-level fit o'giggles.

"Is not funny, ya knows," Moirrey snapped under her breath.

Quiet-like, 'cause other folks were around, and might listen if she spoked too louds.

"Is, too," Casey whispered back, still chuckling.

They was up on a reviewing stand. Big wood platform with flags and bunting and stuff. Bundled up 'cause it were kinda cold today, with a storm front comin' up fr'm the sourthwest and bringing hints of rain ta goes with dreary skies.

Casey's House Guards were everywhere, faceless with shields down and lots of guns. Not all that nervous'n'stuff. Just being professional paranoid, and all. One of them even held a big flag on a wooden post, apparently fer days like this. Who knewed?

189th's last bits not up wit' Vo were deployed in fronts of them, all standin' tall and mostly organized over on the left. Two lunatics on zip-bikes detacheded themselves and cruised over, mostly sedate-like. At least fer zip-bikes. Moirrey'd owned more'n'one in her time.

Ya could goes fer crazy feats, if you trusted yer leathers enough.

They parked and dismounted, coming to rest and even attentions, facing her and Casey above them on the wee stage.

Patrol Centurion Oleg Chilikov. Draconarius Erik Windstrom. The two craziest boys Pyotr Martin had been able to peel out of 4th Ala and leave behind to train the crazies that had volunteereded to ride the skies.

Windstrom telescoped a baton out to three meters and pulled a flag from his pocket, attaching it and letting the breeze pull it tight.

Chilikov snapped to and saluted, right hand up against his forehead, where a unicorn horn emerged from the helmet, in front of a mane of real horse hair, long and black. The helmet, like most, had almost thirty centimeters of clearance over his skull, a French curve-lookin't thing with alien lines thet comed up to a rough point high enough Vo's be lookin' up.

Were intentionals. Makes them look two'n'half meters tall. Especially whens ya factored in the wings that ran down each arm and went fifty centimeters past yer fingers.

"This is where you salute back," Casey murmured in a voice obviously on the verge of hysterical laughter.

Weren't funny.

Still, she'd done this thing. And were gonna get ever richer from it.

She held up her hand to her head and tried to smile. Helped if she focused on the Patrol Centurion and ignored the flag.

The one with the silhouettes of an angel in the middle of a Norman kite shield outline, surrounded by words that said *Lady Moirrey's Own* in big, white letters on a red and gold background.

"Can't believe you approved that," she hissed out of the side of her mouth.

But she knowed the Emperor were bullet-proofed on that one.

"I did owe you one," Casey snarked back quietly as the two men turned and faced the rest of the field.

An' she did. Not like Moirrey's been white-hands around her. Still, there were practical jokes, and then there were something like this.

Weren't funny. Not one damned bit.

But Chilikov musta yelled on his comm. All of a sudden the whole force hopped off'n their bikes like cats an' stood still. Chilikov only had a Patrol, not a whole Ala, so were pretty easy to track. Eighty-one bikes. Ninety troopers, countin' him and Windstrom and the sidecars. All of them wearing the Angel O'Doom *Winged Scout Armor* she'd dreamed up and built.

Amazin' what ya gots when the Army finally puts enough men and money behind a project.

Every dude over there on a zip-bike. Each lance of ten bikes had one with a sidecar where they could mount a heavy weapon of some sort. Mostly light autocannons, but occasionally missiles and mortars fer messin' with peeples.

On some unheard call, the first Lance deployed telescoping nodachi swords and threw themselves at th'horizon. Every heartbeat, another lance moved.

It were like a plague o'locusts comin' fer yer corn.

Nine-sided polygon quick-formed on the right edge of the field, as the teams landed and went defensive laager, pistols out in every direction.

Cool part were when they whistled fer their horses. One lance at a time, the riderless zip-bikes flowed across the field on remote control. That were the awesomest part of the whole idea. Ya goes in full tilt on back of a zip-bikes, then jumps off in the middle of the run and lets inertia gets ya up when your repulsors grab ground and lets ya go like an angrier-than-normal hummingbird.

And then yer bikes coasts to a stop, or flies along the programmed path, and can comes back fer ya later.

Last were two open-bed skiffs with turrets on top, like the rest of the legion used, and two heavy-lifter skiffs with full repair shops stashed on the back.

Whole unit could move as one.

Moirrey could only imagine what would happen whens this lone patrol turned intas a whole Ala.

A whole Legion of those fools would gives folks nightmares.

"Kinda awesome, Chilikov," Moirrey yelled loud enough to be heard.

The dude next to Casey with the flag did something, and Windstrom dipped his flag back, so musta been rights.

"I'm just glad you're too old to volunteer for that duty," Casey murmured. "Then you'd somehow talk me into getting fitted for a suit as well."

Moirrey grinned and side-eyed the lanky chick. She'd given it thought, but them old bones just dinna like the hard landin's and sleeping rough parts of doing that. Better to stay inside where the coffee were fresh and the beer were cold.

And maybe give demonstrations'n'stuff fer civilian daughters thet might wanna play. Somewhere Victoria Ames were busy trooperin'. 'Bouts time more comed.

CHAPTER XL

IN THE NINTH YEAR OF JESSICA KELLER, QUEEN OF THE PIRATES: DECEMBER THE SEVENTEENTH AT ST. LEGIER

NIGHT HAD SETTLED ON *ST. Legier*. *Pops* hadn't been in the mood to stay later than dinner and a few drinks with Yan and Ainsley, and Summer had suggested an early night anyway.

Emperor-girl had put them all up in a newly opened hotel not far from where folks where busy building a new Imperial palace, over on the shore of a canal cut between Lakes Zurich and Werder. Salvage divers would be busy for decades, cleaning up the area below water, but Mother Nature was busy filling the basin in with every rain shower that passed, and the locals had decided to just let it go for now.

Pops and Summer had retired to their room. Brushed teeth and a nice soak in an oversized tub, which he appreciated after a long day climbing around design mockups, asking questions and testing theories.

They were alone. The lights were down to a lowest setting and one of the most beautiful women he had ever known was curled up against his side and breathing on his skin.

"Serious question," *Pops* said, letting the conversation in his head finally bleed out into the room.

She tensed, but only a little bit. Probably not surprised, because they had been together more or less for nearly three years now.

Rather than speak, she leaned back and looked up at him, blue eyes bright and inquisitive.

"Pretty soon, we're likely to get serious with this project," he said carefully. "That's going to involve heading to the front to meet Jessica."

There. Faintest echo of a twitch she probably thought she suppressed, but it was hard to do that when you were touching someone with almost half your skin.

He let the moment drag out, giving her the opportunity to deflect him, if she wanted. After all this time, *Pops* still didn't know that much about the woman, except rumors, suggestions, and innuendo. Even her stories never seemed to add up, on the retellings.

Plus she knew jokes that only people his generation seemed to understand.

She chose to remain silent.

"I need to ask, and to do it probably now, so we can plan," *Pops* continued. "Do you want to either stay here, or should I arrange for transport back to *Aquitaine* or *Corynthe* for you?"

"Why would I leave?" she finally met his eyes.

Hers were cold and calculating, but he had known that was coming.

"Jessica Keller makes you nervous," he replied simply. "I don't know why, and I'm not asking now. I'm trying to give you the option to avoid meeting her in the flesh, if you want it, rather than dragging you along with me because that's part of my job."

"What makes you think I don't want to see her?" Summer finally asked.

"I'm good at details," *Pops* said, kissing her on the forehead. "Noticing things. Tracking them. Extrapolating to logical conclusions. Nobody else really gets a response out of you. Not even the new Emperor. But Jessica does."

"It actually won't be that bad," she sighed after a pause. "Moirrey was willing to accept me at face value, so I expect Jessica will as well."

"Moirrey knew you from before?" *Pops* tried to keep his amazement contained, but he knew he would fail.

Summer nodded.

Moirrey had gone from a nobody on the lower decks of engineering to one of the most famous and dangerous designers in the galaxy in the last decade. If this woman had known her, and Jessica, Summer must have been there for some of their adventures.

It hadn't been when Jessica first came to *Corynthe*. *Pops* had been on the fringes of things then, just settling into a new life with Cho grown up and pursuing her dreams. Still, he would have registered a woman like Summer Ulfsson.

Everybody did. She had the quietest charisma of anyone *Pops* had ever known, including his first wife Yasu. Walk into a room and every head rotated to scan her at least once. He really didn't mind all the dirty looks he got from everybody as a result of being arm-candy on her arm in those situations.

"So you'll be safe meeting Jessica and all her people?" *Pops* confirmed.

"I should be," Summer said with a serious tone. Then she turned playful. "If not, I'll tell everyone I seduced you."

"You kinda did," he pointed out.

She grinned and stuck out her tongue in a way that suddenly made her look seventeen.

"True," she agreed, shifting up and around so they were suddenly face to face.

She kissed him once.

"I had heard so much about you from them, and others," Summer said. "It took a while, but I eventually managed to find my way to *Petron* to meet the man everyone called *Pops*."

"Was it as good as you'd hoped?" he asked, nervous.

Sixty-four-year-old men were long past being sex symbols, in any culture. At that point, all you had to work with was brains and personality.

"Better," Summer grinned and kissed him again. "Wouldn't have stayed more than two weeks if not."

Pops relaxed. Let the nervousness bleed out of him as he slid an arm around her and pulled her against his body again.

At least he had never gotten fat, like some of his surviving friends. Him and Uly were still the only two that could still fit into the same pants they might have worn forty years ago. Even David was starting to get a little pudgy, but that was time spent in too many meetings and not running laps or corridors.

Another kiss, and then he leaned back.

Studied her face from close enough to breathe on. Watched pupils dilate and focus on him.

"So can I ask where you studied naval engineering?" he asked.

"What makes you think I know anything, *Pops*?" she suddenly cooled a little.

"You don't get lost when Bedrov and me get nerdy," he said. "Even

Ainsley gets glassy-eyed from time to time. Moirrey mostly follows, but she's more interested in weapons than generators and stuff."

"Maybe I find smart men sexy," she volleyed.

"You ain't learned that much from just being around me for three years," *Pops* noted with a grin. "Unless you've been secretly studying things."

Instead of an answer, her grin was back. And a kiss or three.

"You didn't want a dumb one, *Pops*," she chuckled. "Couldn't have kept you interested in me, even with this hot body, unless I knew something about coolant systems and resistance loads."

"Truth," he agreed, nodding nerdily.

It was a weight off his back. Not that he would have minded being her cover, if she was really a deep-cover secret agent of some sort. And he was pretty sure the stories she told people about being an actor were pure hokum. But Moirrey had known her, and accepted her. And hopefully Jessica would, as well.

Pops found himself really looking forward to seeing the boss again. And bringing her a couple of presents.

For now, he let Summer distract him in the awesomest way possible.

CHAPTER XLI

Jessica studied the projection of *Osynth B'Udan* as the fleet made its way into the inner system. They could have simply stayed at Whughy's Forward Base, but she wanted the opportunity to have the whole team get a little R&R. Looking around her flag bridge, she wasn't the only person thinking that.

Plus, she wanted to catch up on the latest news from home. Well, all of her homes. It was messy to even think about, with *Corynthe*, *Aquitaine*, and *Fribourg* all having some claim on her heart.

The system had been reinforced again. Which was to be expected, as small squadrons had been out and about, locating and dismantling the secret corridors of communications satellites that *Buran* had managed to rig everywhere when nobody was looking.

If you could just sail through JumpSpace without having to emerge regularly, why would you even notice?

But with them destroyed, *Buran's* squadrons would have a much slower time moving around. Plus Emmerich had made it a point to build a number of Imperial Corvette Scouts in the first batch of new ships. Those ships trolled the same spaceways looking for incursion, prepared to run like hell for the nearest fleet base in the event of another raid.

None had happened since *Second St. Legier*, but Jessica thought that was the result of her striking so hard into their interior and destroying things. At some point, *The Eldest* would have to decide to either abandon *Samara*, or let Jessica Keller gut his inner frontier.

Either way, she would win a massive psychological victory for the Empire. And make the galaxy that much safer.

"We just got a message," Enej said with a devious grin on his face. "Lag time five light seconds if you want to reply."

So, someone deep down in the well, catching her force as soon as they emerged. First Expeditionary wasn't in a hurry to get anywhere, except maybe *Valiant*, and that was just to get to a place where everything could be fixed fastest, so they could get back out and do more damage.

Jessica checked the message.

It had originated from Patrol Cruiser *Qin Lun*, an *IFV* flag flying next to a *Corynthe* one. Galen Estevan commanding. And an upgraded *Marco Polo*, now a 2-ring with some fighters added, in attendance. Another freighter with only a long alphanumeric as a name.

Oh, ho, what's this? *Lincolnshire* War Catamaran *IFV Robert Fitzwalter*? Captain Niall Aulay Henderson, commanding?

"Well, Casey did say she would ask for help from everybody," Jessica grinned back at Enej. "Royal Compliments to *Qin Lun*, Enej. And Imperial thanks from Admiral Keller to the *Lincolnshire* boat. And pass a message along to Denis, Tom Provst, and Iskra. Looks like we'll need to figure out how to add at least two ships to the raiding squadron when we head back out."

CHAPTER XLII

IN THE TENTH YEAR OF JESSICA KELLER, QUEEN OF THE PIRATES: JANUARY THE TWENTY-FIRST AT OSYNTH B'UDAN

Galen had never been physically aboard the *Lincolnshire* ship, but otherwise, he had observed all proper courtesies on the flight from *St. Legier* to *Osynth B'Udan*, over and above what he normally would have. Probably would have scored one hundred percent on a Master Mariner's Certificate, if this had been a quiz. No corners cut. Prompt and courteous signals and responses. The works. Gotta make Jessica look good with the provincials.

Hopefully, news of that wouldn't get home, or those folks would never let him hear the end of it.

Right now, he and his wife Kari were riding sedately, side by side in the neck of *Badger*, flying across to be part of a cocktail party that *Robert Fitzwalter*'s captain was throwing for Jessica. Galen was dressed a little better than he normally would have, pressed slacks and a nice burgundy tunic, while Kari had dug out a cocktail dress she had apparently been hiding somewhere for exactly this reason.

She was tiny, like all the Larionov clan. Galen always felt like a giant at a meter-eight tall, when his wife was maybe a meter-five on her toes. But she looked good for any age, let alone forty, with brunette hair just starting to show grays and dimples that hadn't changed one iota in twenty years. Hazel eyes promised all sorts of gossip and showing off, since she had missed all his adventures with Jessica the first time he went to *St. Legier*. And had demanded he bring her along this time.

At least he'd make a damned pretty penny on this run, better than even the first trip to the Imperial capital. Half of the original trade goods on *Marco Polo* had been sold at *Ladaux*, replaced and then the whole load sold again at *St. Legier*. And since he and Kari owned *Marco Polo* outright, they got all the profits. Best part had been the Grand Admiral chartering him to haul a bunch of war materials out here, and paying the normal override fee when a freighter got sidetracked for military traffic. Like he wasn't already coming out here, but now he was going to tack a twenty percent margin on top of everything else. The joys of legal *force majeure*, with people who had money to burn.

He might have just married into the Larionov family, but they had certainly taught him way more about banking and money than he ever imagined possible.

Like how to afford to buy a light battlecruiser and then manage to get it flagged three times, each for a nice fee. It was even better than marque and reprisal, doing it this way.

"Galen, we're about to land in the docking bay," the pilot called. "Seat belts on? And no necking please, until we come to a complete stop."

Kari laughed. So did he. They might have been smooching a little on the flight over. There was a camera over the cockpit, so the pilots could have watched.

Clunks as the vessel landed and the magnets engaged. Galen rose and handed Kari up.

Open the hatch and down the steps quickly. This wasn't an official visit, so he didn't rate red carpet or anything, just a young *Lincolnshire* Lieutenant in gray dress uniform that stood out against his red hair to escort him to the party. After he and Kari were clear and *Badger* left, then they would roll out the fancy stuff, but that was for Jessica, and this technically qualified as a State Visit.

He just got to be wined and dined on somebody else's dime. And they would be showing off.

Good thing he had a ride home, and could sit in back and nap, or neck.

Still, Galen had done his time on warships, back before Uly had convinced him to get into armed trade and profitability well above anything the pirates ever imagined.

So he took his time and studied the vessel as the young man escorted them slightly forward. *Pops* had designed the boat, and provided Galen a pretty good rough-out from memory, to which Galen's bridge crew had been able to add significant amounts of detail.

Apparently, they had even bribed someone in *Ladaux* for a sensor log. He hadn't asked how they had managed that, since nobody sent him an invoice or receipts for bribes paid.

This ship was just like *Pops* had explained to Naoumov and Horvat. Two heavy frigates, built identical on symmetrical lines. Add an engine pod like a bobcat's tail to the center of the frame that connected them. Fill that crossbeam with a flag bridge, centralized engineering, and a third heavy weapons installation. Rearrange some of the old space, and you had a ship almost good enough to take on a Patrol Cruiser.

Almost.

Qin Lun didn't have the fragility of that crossbeam when maneuvering, or the weird blind spots caused by that center engine, but the two ships had about the same firepower nose to nose.

If he was ever dumb enough to get into a slugging match with someone like that. Patrol Cruiser was a misnomer. He didn't go on patrols. He just cruised around, usually escorting cargo vessels like *Marco Polo* or one of Uly's 1-ring cargo carriers. Anybody dumb enough to bother him found out pretty quickly that they should have brought a 4-ring. And friends.

And if he had *Marco Polo*, now upgraded to a 2-ring, then he also had three fast medium bombers to go with *Badger*.

Nobody bothered his and Uly's trade missions anymore.

Kari poked him in the side as they walked.

"You're being too much the serious businessman," she said with obvious sarcasm. "Fun time. Smile occasionally, and stop looking like you're fleecing every one of these rubes for every Lev, Crown, and Florin you can squeeze out of them. That's my job."

"Yes, ma'am," he replied.

Galen was just the captain. Kari was actually the president of the corporation, since it had been Larionov clan money that got them started originally. Paid back long since, but those folks were business sharks first and only pirates second.

The party wasn't particularly moving when the local kid escorted them into a big chamber hung with flags. Punchbowl on the right wall. Open bar on the left. Long trestle table with munchies along the back wall. Round tables with chairs for folks who wanted to sit.

Still, it looked like the military party of the season. Lots of Imperial officers here being seen being here. Or whatever it was they were up to. Didn't look like spies, unless they were playing that level of drunken ineptitude as a scam.

All the *Lincolnshire* officers he had talked to at one time or another on the flight out, plus a bunch of others he had missed. Very few women, since *Lincolnshire* was still a little backwards on that sort of thing. Four, but they were officers, and dressed for it.

Kari was in a slinky blue thing that shimmered and set off her hair. And showed off her butt. Galen let her lead him around as she worked to charm everyone here important enough to get them a trade contract at some future date.

As he managed to grab two glasses of what he hoped were wine from a passing steward, a band even started playing. Martial tunes, for the most part, which he had expected, but at least better than nothing. At least for now. That might change after the evening ground on.

And he was not about to offer to grab a guitar and entertain folks. Not without a busking basket out front with some serious seed money in it.

Galen had showered, and even let Kari put some cologne on him, so the space that opened up around him, when she was off charming an Imperial admiral, wasn't his smell. Unless pirate was a thing that these people could detect with their noses.

You never know with lawmen.

But he smiled. Made small talk with anyone who came close. Sipped wine. Tried to look like an innocent bystander, just in case any of these folks had ever maybe gotten too close to a fuzzy border and gotten hit by *pirates.*

Weren't me. Honest.

About the time he snagged a second glass of wine, Jessica made an entrance with all her folks in tow. Damned impressive sort of thing, when she and another guy were in red admiral uniforms, along with Iskra Vlahovic doing the Fleet Centurion thing and Denis Jež in Imperial Whites.

Things got hectic at that point. More of Jessica's people arrived, plus a bunch of Imperials, until suddenly there were over a hundred folks in uniform meandering around, and a like number that looked like civilians.

Galen wondered if Niall Henderson had been smart enough to bring a government trade mission with him, clear all the way out here. Galen hadn't been playing at spying on the flight out, because the distances were too great for anything useful to come up, since David's teams were more interested in *Lincolnshire*, anyway. And *Aquitaine* to a lesser extent.

Salonnia hadn't sent anyone along on this run, but that didn't mean they wouldn't later. They shared a long border with *Fribourg*, so were already a treaty partner of some sort. And generally stayed away from direct confrontation with the fringe pirates, letting bribes do their work.

About ten minutes later, Galen found himself suddenly facing an old comrade.

"Tom," he said. "Noticed that you got hammered pretty good at *Severnaya Zemlya*. Still good?"

Admiral Provst shrugged.

"The other guy was a battleship," Provst replied. "And he blew himself up not long after Jessica was done with him. The new designs protect my people much better than the old ones, so casualties were lighter than when *Firehawk* got hurt at *St. Legier*."

Galen nodded knowingly. He had been briefed by the Grand Admiral about Tom Provst. And the battle that killed the Crown Prince, for which Provst still felt a ton of guilt.

But the man did look good as an Admiral of the Red. Jessica probably should have been in blue, by now, but he suspected that she might dig in her heels, if anyone tried.

One of these days, she would want to come home to *Corynthe*. Retire there, as she had threatened many times. Break chauvinistic skulls until the girls were allowed the same freedoms and privileges as the boys.

"So what's the plan going forward?" Galen asked.

"I suggested to Jessica that she take the *Lincolnshire* vessel and send you with me," Provost leaned closer and let his voice drop. "Reduces the risk of mischief, and puts an escort-level cruiser in each squadron when we go raiding. You don't want to try one of the new Tigersharks by yourself, but if my Expeditionary cruisers can distract them, you'll do a number on the hammerheads. Same with *Robert Fitzwalter*."

"And that just happens to take them off when Jessica leaves shortly?" Galen suggested. "While you stay put here and get some dry-dock time in?"

Provst grinned almost ferally.

"Denis Jež's squadron is all *Aquitaine* folks," Provst noted, his smile warming. "Except *Indianapolis*. This lets *Lincolnshire* support their own ally, and I guess I'm stuck with the runt of the litter. You attaching *Marco Polo* to Iskra for now? Or loading her up with swag to make a profit?"

Galen grinned back. He and Tom had had a few nights of heavy celebrating together, after the abortive coup several years ago. Heroes of the Empire, and all that. Man knew how Galen thought.

"That's Jessica's call," Galen replied. "Right now, just hauling mostly commercial stocks for the Grand Admiral. Most likely, *Marco Polo* will turn into another boat like *Mendocino*."

"Mostly?" Tom asked.

"I might have saved back a few dozen cases of brandy and bourbon," Galen suggested. "Never know when you need to bribe an Admiral somewhere. So how long are you going to be here getting repaired?"

"Probably a couple of months," Tom replied. "*zu* Arlo needs time to rest and refit, and rethink some of the things we got wrong. Maybe come up with some new surprises. *Valiant* had it the worst, but all of my squadron got off worse than Jež's. Mostly, that's inexperience with Jessica's way of fighting and the new things *Buran* is doing. But they've been blooded now, so it will get better."

Galen nodded. He would find out soon enough where his sovereign liege needed him to serve. At least he was making a lot of money in the process.

CHAPTER XLIII

JESSICA STUDIED the man with an obvious eye. And a disapproving one. She hadn't forgotten how the folks of *Lincolnshire*'s government had mistreated her, back when she was a lowly Command Centurion sent out on a meaningless diplomatic mission. Niall Henderson hadn't been involved then, and she felt like she had paid everyone else back with interest later, but she still wanted to set a hard tone.

Plus, *Pops* had sent along a note indicating that he hadn't been paid a licensing fee when they built *Robert Fitzwalter*. That might make it a government-level issue at some point if she wanted to get pissy. And she had a great deal of leverage if push came to shove.

"Captain Henderson," she nodded as he stepped about as close as her apparent mood suggested was safe.

"Your Majesty," he replied carefully with a half-bow.

Neither of them were drinking, in spite of the wide availability of options. She never drank anything except bottles Marcelle provided in situations like this.

The welcoming ceremonies were done. Most of the man's officers were still around, but right now everyone was studiously ignoring the scene, except for Kari Larionov and Marcelle.

"How soon will your vessel be ready to return with me to the front?" Jessica asked.

"We're fully stocked now, sir," Henderson said. "My freighter can either sail with us in forty hours, or join us later. Nobody was sure what your schedule would be like, so I've tried to keep my crew ready to go."

"Very good," she inclined her body just enough to suggest a bow. "We just unleashed a major raid on *Severnaya Zemlya* that will probably have repercussions throughout *The Holding*. Part of the fleet needs downtime and repair, but I want to return with the other half. That includes *Robert Fitzwalter*. *Qin Lun* will remain behind with *Valiant*."

He obviously wanted to ask something, but refrained.

Jessica probably wouldn't have bitten his head off. None of that situation had been his fault. She just had an angry spot in her soul for *Lincolnshire's* government, and he was here.

"*The Holding*?" he asked instead.

"*Buran's* name for its nation, Henderson," she said. "Also, occasionally the *Protectorate of Man*. What we're fighting."

"I see," he settled on neutral ground. "How can I best serve, Admiral?"

"Tell me what you bring to the table, Captain," she replied, noting the bubble of space that had opened around them.

It was bigger than the one around Galen, but only a little.

"Iorwerth Nakamura designed the vessel, Admiral," he began.

"Yes," Jessica snapped a little peevishly. "*Pops* sent me a note about that. Hopefully someone will have cut him a check by the time we get back to that end of the galaxy."

Give the man credit, he did blush at that, so maybe he knew a little more than he had been letting on.

"We have well-rounded offensive capabilities, Admiral Keller," Henderson picked up his narrative with only a little hiccup. "Engaging fighters was our original design, but the ship will do well when engaging *Buran's* vessels. We do not mount any Type-4's and the Primaries were determined to be too expensive, especially as *Robert Fitzwalter* was going to be serving on this frontier, at least initially."

"But you have plans to swap it out later?" she pressed.

"Indeed, Admiral," he agreed. "The weapons deck on the crossbeam is entirely modular. Our biggest limiting factor is generally power, rather than space."

"And fragility," she added.

"Less so than one would expect," he countered with the first hint of emotion under the professionalism. "We built the crossbeam first and then built each of the outer hulls by moving everything in place, rather than just welding two ships together. We'll survive more damage than one might expect. Far more than even the new *Kali-ma*, I think."

"Good enough," Jessica said. "Tell me about your crews."

"Veterans of other vessels, with a solid leavening of retired *Aquitaine* Navy folks offered promotions and signing bonuses to help train the younger generation," he said. "Most of the engineers served with *Aquitaine*'s First Fleet or War Fleet earlier."

"And you're here to serve?" she pressed.

Perhaps she could be mollified. Someone had warned this man to arrive prepared. Hadn't been Galen. Uly's nephew would have enjoyed watching the man's discomfort. And *Pops* still had an axe to grind.

She briefly wondered if the threats of mayhem on the man had originated with Petia or Emmerich. One of the two of them, if not both.

"Oh, and we do have a pair of missile tubes," he added. "Standard load of missiles, with no reloads, so I'm not sure if we should offload them here and replace with other supplies."

"We'll keep them for now," Jessica decided. "At *Severnaya*, having a missile cruiser or two would have made a world of difference."

"Why?" he was suddenly at a loss. "I thought they could jump away from everything we threw at them."

"Bases can't jump, Henderson," she smiled like a predator at him. "After we destroyed his fleet, I moved on and crushed several stations. The main command base surrendered to evacuation."

"Okay," he said, shocked. "We'll do what we can."

"Of that, I have no doubt," Jessica nodded.

CHAPTER XLIV

IT WASN'T OFTEN that Casey traveled to meet Torsten in Strasbourg, but the new buildings were going up as fast as workers could shell them in and make them habitable. The arrival of 23nd Ladaux Construction Legion had shaved at least a year off the task, being a dedicated organization that didn't need to be paid on a weekly basis, at least for the first year.

Imperial finances would be better organized by summer.

And Casey could see moving closer to this location soon, allowing Mejico to become a complete mess of construction in turn. She still hadn't decided if she should level the old hotel and replace it with a palace, or leave the entire thing as a museum for the people to be able to see how they had lived in that first year.

But that wasn't why Torsten had asked her to come to his offices. The paperwork a courier had delivered two days ago made it abundantly clear that Torsten was about to reach one of those milestones in the *Reconstruction of Empire.*

Her Empire. Her future.

She followed four of her regular guards into the new Imperial Hall of Government, itself three quarters done at present, as most of it was just an office tower with the top yet to be finished. The air outside had been chill and windy, promising snow in a few hours, while the interior was dry and bright. Marble floors slapped under her leather soles as she walked amidst eight silent men in combat boots.

The foyer was grand and impressive, as befit the administrative seat of government. The pomp would be in the new palace, when it was complete, and the parade ground out front that was going to be turned into a market arcade for small shops and food trucks to serve tourists.

Through an inner door, she was into a much less inspiring hallway. Industrial carpet in lasting brown. White walls. Light strips overhead.

At some point, she hoped they added plants in pots, at the time when art finally went up to cover some of the blank, white walls. Perhaps she needed to craft an Imperial Decree to that effect. Torsten might be so focused on keeping the gears together that he forgot the need for beauty.

And she missed the ancient, nearly-feral roses that had colonized the rear of the original palace grounds. Freya had Casey's only painting of them that had survived, hanging in her salon back on *Eklionstic*.

Through another door in the wake of her guards, and into a smaller meeting space. Torsten was there, along with several of his assistants she knew by face and name, but who rarely spoke unless they needed to answer a specific question.

Two other men at the conference table also stood when she entered.

She took her seat at the end opposite Torsten quickly and gestured the rest to sit as well.

On her right, the younger of the two strangers. She had read his file and had approved of the task he would inherit. Willem Lorenz, prospective First Deputy of a new Hall of Justice. He was a tall man without bulk. Lanky but probably only a few centimeters taller than Em. Short, brown hair that was just graying at the temples, giving him the appearance of a hawk. The muted, brown suit he wore only accentuated the comparison. Intense, hazel eyes reminded her of someone else.

She turned to the other man for a moment. Adolphus Gulan. Older, in his seventh decade and previously retired after a stellar career as a civilian in her father's and grandfather's governments. Gray, heavy, and soft, until his eyes lit up, and he reminded her of the man across from him. He would return to the harness as First Deputy of the Hall of Law, if this all went well today.

Intensity glowed from all three men, as Torsten had it going, too.

She chose to start the conversation in the middle. If they knew what they were doing, they would follow. If not, they might not be the men she needed for the job.

"You both understand that Imperial Security is, in my eyes, hopelessly compromised, yes?" she said, turning to catch both of them nodding. "Emmerich *zu* Wachturm was previously working closely with my father's government to weed out the bad players in order to salvage as much of the organization as they could."

Both nodded, silently observing. Quiet men were needed for the task, so that was a positive sign.

"The destruction of Werder did not destroy many paper files," Casey continued. "Those were always duplicated elsewhere. What I lost was the knowledge contained silently in heads. The lifetimes of experience that didn't always make it onto paper, suggesting which players were clean and which could not be trusted. I have no confidence in Imperial Security without that, so we are not going to try."

Firm faces, giving nothing away. Good.

"Torsten?" she ceded the conversation to him.

Both of the other men turned in unison to watch the Chief Deputy. The man who would be their immediate boss, perhaps.

"Over the last century, Imperial Security changed its internal mission," Torsten said casually, belying the anger she knew he privately held on the topic. "Under Karl V, the Charter of Man was a call for legal restrictions on the powers of the noble class, and specifically the Emperor himself. Protection for the commoners, like myself."

She liked that last touch. Of the four people seated, she was of the old nobility. Gulan was the younger son of a *Freiherr*, and had been made one himself in reward for his service. Lorenz and Wald were of that enormous middle class that was the bulk and backbone of the Empire. Educated and generally supportive, but not necessarily reaping the benefits of aristocracy, except when a career of service brought a title as a reward, such as Gulan's.

Casey still wasn't sure how to change that. Or if she even wanted to. *Aquitaine* made do without the titles, but the money and power was still mostly allocated to the Fifty Families. Marriage into one of those clans was the best entry point, but they saw themselves as the cultural and social backbone of the Republic.

Different words, similar results. Perhaps *Aquitaine* could be a model there, as well, if she started recognizing wealth with Imperial favors, but not titles? A new thing? Lifetime titles, perhaps, but not inheritance?

Food for thought. Later, after this hurdle was overcome.

"In time," Torsten continued, "Imperial Security became an internal enforcement arm of the government, rather than purely a surveillance operation. Their new form was designed to largely do two things. First: provide some balance against the supreme power of the Fleet. Second: root out rebels and revolutionaries who were willing to do more than just talk about the Charter."

"*Fribourg* has always been a naval entity, in its own mind," Casey interrupted. "Power was always with the Admirals, but only those who were also Princes of the Blood. That must change, going forward, as there will not be enough such men and women we trust for decades."

Still, the two men remained silent and attentive. Around the outside wall, aides took notes, and several were recording this against future need. It would never be officially released, but the concepts needed to be out in the open and clear.

"Just so," Torsten picked up the thread. To Casey, it was like a stage play, where two practiced actors shared lines back and forth without seams. "The coup six years ago was a conspiracy of Imperial Security and disaffected nobles in the Royal House, upset that Jessica Keller was going to be rewarded for thwarting the supposed natural expansion of the Empire to destroy and absorb *Aquitaine*. They did not welcome the peace treaty, and would have probably given *Buran* another generation to expand and reinforce their positions, before the Empire awoke to the threat. Children alive today would have probably died under *Buran*'s yoke."

Casey shuddered with the rest of the room at the thought. Torsten was an econometricist, a man of numbers and trends. He had predicted it. His paper had gone a long way towards convincing Father to support the treaty.

Slow failure was the alternative. Might still be, but the odds had hopefully tilted in Casey's favor.

"So Imperial Security is to be dismantled?" Lorenz asked, turning to stare at Torsten, probably lest Casey take offense at the blunt tone. It was an honest question, just not necessarily a polite one. "Just like that?"

"Just like that," Torsten agreed harshly. "The edifice is rotten, and our time is short. In its place, the Hall of Justice and the Hall of Law will arise. Justice will concern itself with law enforcement. Investigations of all types, including many of those currently undertaken by Imperial Security. However, prosecution will rest with the Hall of Law. Justice will present the case. Law will try it in the Courts, and then be responsible for adjudicating the chosen punishments."

"What is to prevent the same dark cabals from forming?" Gulan asked. His face was turned towards Casey, which was telling. The last such cabal had nearly undone her.

"Sunlight," she replied harshly. "Imperial Security was judge, jury, and executioner of anyone they felt was a threat, to whatever they felt needed protecting. Now Justice can arrest someone, but they must make the case public so Law can try them. And both organizations will have strong Inspectorates that answer directly to my government, in the form of the Chief Deputy, and not to you."

"Hamstringing us?" Lorenz turned now to face her.

"I am fine with the so-called wheels of justice turning slowly," she said. "As long as they turn inexorably. We are not enacting the Charter of Man, but that does not mean that the common classes should not have rights that in turn need to be protected. My reign will rest more on their willingness to support it than on the Dukes who may have qualms about a woman. There will be no more assassin squads hunting revolutionaries. No more midnight knocks disappearing someone forever as a terror weapon. If that is what it takes to survive, then this government has already failed, and deserves to be swept aside. The fabric of our Empire has been ruptured, and that cannot just be ignored. It must be sewn over and protected against further damage."

"And you believe we two represent the best tools to effect that change?" Gulan pressed.

"You retired at the highest civil service rank the government has, Sri Gulan," Torsten said. "Only three steps below where you would be tomorrow, if you accept this charge. Sri Lorenz is a career cop who has made a name as a protector of the people and the laws. Both of you have white hands, and trust me, I went very deep into a number of people's backgrounds to cull the list down. Any shadows or unresolved questions were sufficient to disqualify any candidate. There must be no fears or questions on the part of your superiors, nor of your Halls."

"I require you to root out the bad apples, gentlemen," Casey said with force verging on showing the anger in her heart. "Cast them from the body politic now. We can always decide later to prosecute, or just ignore them. They can live out their days waiting for their own midnight knock, and I'm fine with that."

"What about espionage?" Lorenz asked now. "We have spies in our midst, as well as disaffected children."

She liked the way the man classified them. Many of those agitating for the Charter of Man were children. Folks not much younger than her, still in their awakening phase and wanting to make the *Empire* a better place. Before they learned that the ship of state was a beast of a trillion lives and must be turned in generational orbits, rather than days.

"Being an unregistered foreign agent is a crime, First Deputy of Justice," she replied. "I expect you to locate them and unravel their networks. I expect First Deputy Gulan to see them punished appropriately."

"Unregistered foreign agent?" his voice drifted off and his eyes shifted to look at Torsten.

"I am actually registered, First Deputy," Torsten's smile was at once warm and triumphant. "I am an Imperial Citizen who is engaged to a Republic Citizen, and I will eventually emigrate to *Corynthe*, once Her Majesty is done with me."

"And you want them only rooted out, for now?" Gulan asked carefully.

"Reconciliation will come from uncovering the truth, First Deputy Gulan," Casey said. "I want them removed from my government immediately, while the four of us determine, with the aid of your departments, if more should be done. Many were following what were legitimate orders, yesterday. I am changing the ethics of governance, but that is tomorrow. Things that might not have met those current standards, but are in the past, will be laid to rest. New infractions will be punished severely. And some of these men will be sanctioned, even for things long thought forgotten. At least those men who are not beyond my justice. God himself will see to the rest."

They both nodded to her, to Torsten, and to each other. The structure would set them up as rivals, but not necessarily enemies. Checks on one another's reach and threat.

A change in the way of things, but it would not result in the Charter of Man in her lifetime. Perhaps her children's, if she managed to save the Empire from itself.

CHAPTER XLV

Ainsley didn't like it, but all the alternatives were worse. And she could honestly challenge anybody who gave her any guff, because there was a precedence for this sort of thing. Ugly and unreasonable as it was.

So she stood at the outer hatch of the Grand Admiral's office, escorted by six marines with guns. Gunter Tifft was next to her, wearing his naval uniform today. The almost-dress version, navy blue with four gold rings on his cuff and a matching four solid-brass buttons on each shoulder board. White shirt with a fold-down collar. Lighter-blue tie around the neck in a weird knot. At least they didn't do the saucer hats indoors or aboard ship.

Commander, Imperial Fleet.

Ainsley had brought this on herself. She stood next to Tifft in a matching uniform, except her had five rings and five buttons.

Captain, Imperial Fleet.

To go with Command Flight Centurion, retired, *Republic of Aquitaine Navy*.

The other option would have involved staying home on *Ladaux* or *Petron*, knitting while she waited to see if Yan Bedrov ever made it home.

Fuck that.

Someone inside triggered the hatch about the time she was going to say something vulgar and inflammatory to the men around her.

Two preceded her and Tifft. Four followed. They passed through the first chamber, a meaningless place as vague and sterile as any navy's outer office, on the way through a second set of doors.

Admiral Baumgärtner rose from his desk as they entered.

"That will be all," he said, dismissing the six guards with a wave of the hand.

They waited six seconds while the men left and the hatch closed.

"At ease, and be seated," the Admiral commanded, returning to his seat.

He studied them for a moment, like a professor about to announce final grades. Ainsley watched impassively. Hendrik Baumgärtner had never tried to kill her, at least personally, and her team had given as good as it got at *First Ballard*, so she was willing to call it a draw.

And she had practically demanded this duty.

"Due to the nature of security on this mission, as of this moment you will have no further official contact with anyone outside of the immediate team and myself," the man intoned severely. "Commander Tifft has the necessary codes and signals to route an encrypted message to me. I will handle everything else, including the Grand Admiral and the Emperor. And the Republic Senate or the Crown of *Corynthe*, if that becomes necessary."

He paused, as if judging their ability to absorb his words. Ainsley suppressed a growl. These two took the whole spy business a little too seriously.

"Sometime in the next four days, you will depart aboard a dedicated courier already set aside and guarded," the man continued. "Captain Barret will be in command of the mission from that moment until its completion or failure. Commander Tifft will be responsible for making sure Captain Barret can fly both vessels. Anyone familiar with this mission who is not aboard that craft will be taken into isolated custody until it is considered safe to release them. The Grand Admiral has signed the necessary paperwork, as has Emperor Karl VIII, long may she reign. Questions?"

Ainsley had none. Tifft had put together the most detailed operations plan she had ever seen, and that included several years flying scouts for Jessica Keller.

"Actually, I do have one," Ainsley rethought things. "I am legally responsible for the being known as the Lord of Tiki. Given the risks involved, would it be the wiser course of action to leave the projector here in secured custody, so that everything is not lost, if we are?"

Baumgärtner had met the Bartender. Spoken with him at length as part of the planning for *Project Butterfly*. The Chief of Staff had not been at *St. Legier*, the second time, being off handling an inspection tour for the Grand Admiral when it happened.

He was still Imperial to the bones. That meant something more than it did to her.

Aquitaine had been founded with the assistance of the *Last of the Immortals*. At least as far as any of them had known at the time.

Henri Baudin and the being known as Suvi had helped kickstart human technology, leaping up and outward from the famous Story Road that connected *Saxon*, *Pohang*, *Zanzibar*, and *Ballard*, four hundred years ago.

Fribourg had taken a different path, seeing all the *Sentient* systems as evil made flesh. It was embedded in their cultural matrix. Plus, they had been nearly destroyed by one.

She watched him grind his teeth and consider the alternatives.

"There is only one person at present who can answer that question," he finally concluded. "I will ask her directly."

He paused again, watching them. Probably imprinting this memory deep, so he could retrieve it if they never came home. Or even if they did.

The galaxy would have changed, either way.

"Delay your original departure window by twenty-four hours," he said. "I will have an answer for you by then. Dismissed. And Godspeed."

Ainsley rose in synch with Tifft. Salutes were inappropriate, so she just nodded to the man and let the Commander lead her out of the chamber.

Out of the offices that made up the Chief of Staff of the Grand Admiral.

Out of this section of the station, until the marines stopped escorting them and Ainsley was back into territory she knew.

She stopped dead in the middle of the hallway and turned to her companion. He had an expectant look, like he had gamed this situation out already and was following decision trees.

Jessica Keller had infected these people with her black magic.

"Someplace quiet we can have a private drink and talk," she said flatly. "One where nobody knows us and we can talk without having to be fully sequestered, or have them rounded up later."

He studied her for a moment longer, and then checked the time on an old-fashioned wrist watch. A mechanical chronometer that *Fribourg* seemed to gravitate towards. She would have pulled out her comm and looked at the local time on the front.

"I know a place," he said. "We're in the right spot between shifts. It should be safe enough."

She followed in his wake.

Down three decks on a lift. Across nearly a kilometer of moving walkways and corridors to a spot that couldn't be all that far from the exact center of the headquarters station itself.

It was a dive. Honest to bloody goodness. The nastier parts of *Anameleck Prime* would have been hard-pressed to give a place the necessary seediness to pull off this room.

Five booths down each of the long walls, with restrooms on the right in back and an open kitchen window on the left. Horseshoe-shaped bar in the middle, with stools on pipes stuck into the deck. White, hexagonal tiles on the floor, with blue thrown in to make a pattern. Dirt, dust, and grease had been ground into the grout hard enough that it was never coming out.

Tifft led her to the back booth on the kitchen side. The seats were permanent, and came a meter above her head seated. Rough wood that had been polished by thousands of bottoms. Linoleum-looking tabletop with stains, scars, and a heart someone had managed to burn into the surface with a cutting laser on low power.

Not that she had ever done something similar.

Tifft was facing out, so she ended up watching the two cooks in their choreographed dance through a wide window linking this room to the kitchen.

A waiter detached himself from the wall and brought coffee and menus. He took one look at Tifft and blanched.

"Sir?" he said in a diffident tone at odds with his former behavior.

"Brandy for me," Tifft said. "Captain?"

Very funny. I'm the only female officer aboard this entire station. Possibly the only woman at all. He'll remember me like he does you.

"Bourbon or rye whiskey," Ainsley said.

The waiter was gone without another word.

"We're safe enough to talk here, Barret," Tifft said. "Engineers are insular folk, and this is primarily their domain. One of the reasons I use it for meetings."

"This is going to get ugly and messy, Gunter," she said, finally relaxing enough to call the man by his first name. He was now, officially, her First Officer. "Are you prepared for the fallout?"

"I've only ever pulled the physical trigger once, Ainsley," he reciprocated. "But I've killed six men since Karl VIII became Emperor. Men that needed to die because they were a threat to my Empire."

"You'll be the one outsider in this group," Ainsley continued. "Is there anyone else we need to consider taking?"

He smiled at her then. It was like a different person had suddenly put on his face and his body, so radical did the mannerisms change.

"You know what?" he asked in a different voice as well. "You'll all go home if this works. There won't be anybody to challenge my side of the story, outside of the official reports that are going to be buried so deep that *zu* Wachturm and Hendrik are probably the only ones that will be allowed to read them before we're all dead. If I brought along a witness, they would just spend their time setting things straight and telling everyone the truth. I've got a generation to build the most bullshit legend I want."

"You're nuts," Ainsley leaned back. "You know that, right?"

"If not for random luck, I would have been aboard *Firehawk* that day, Ainsley," he snarled, falling back to something closer to the Gunter Tifft she had met previously. "A lot of my friends died. I'm just glad you picked me for your vengeance. I owe that bastard."

"Okay," she decided. Kid was on the level with this one. "So we're going to steal a bus, load everybody on the Grand Admiral's personal shuttle, and disappear for six months or a year?"

"I'll bring along a lot of books," he replied. "You've got Yan. *Pops* has Summer. Personally, I don't think Lady Moirrey has any business being there, but that's above my pay grade and there's no way to make Digger Wolanski disappear without raising a ruckus somewhere. And I'll be the only Imperial around here to say what really happened, when people buy me drinks in bars."

"Assuming we survive," she challenged.

"You don't strike me as suicidal, Ainsley," he retorted. "Even Yan's not, although I was utterly gobsmacked, the first time I read his report about the War God. Brass balls the size of cannonballs."

"There was no other way to play that one," she said quietly. "None that didn't end up with the whole galaxy at risk."

"That's my point," Gunter tapped a finger on the table top. "You people are all prepared to play extremely high stakes poker. But you've spent a lot of time figuring out how to survive, afterwards. I'm betting on being able to be close enough to that luck to catch the edge of it."

The waiter returned with two glasses and departed in silence. Ainsley was impressed. Most times, particularly in a dive like this, he would have given some sort of snarky commentary.

She had seen a reserve of fear in the guy's eyes instead. Like he knew who the real Gunter Tifft was.

Ainsley knew. Grand Admiral himself had filled in the critical details. Young man was really a killer with a heart of ice.

He would need it, when that moment came.

CHAPTER XLVI

Ve Marak Entruk Han studied the woman who had been brought
before them in the Chamber of the *Mandarins*. Au Nadaf Elug Rov was
humbled, more than had she been actually beaten by the Warriors who
accompanied her from *Severnaya Zemlya*.

Han glanced right and left to confirm the opinion of his cohorts.
Barely-concealed rage. It was well.

"We expect more of a Minister of the Fourth Rank," Han announced
in a hard, lethal voice, staring death at the woman. "It is not enough to
send the Warriors off to die, if one is not prepared to share their fate. That
what happened next was unstoppable in hindsight does not excuse
cowardice before."

Han stopped himself from going further, as hard as it was to retain
control. Keller was causing the people of *The Holding* to waver in their
commitments. To flee rather than fight.

To fail.

He turned himself to face the wall of the Temple.

"*Eldest*, what is your guidance?" he asked in a simple voice,
modulating the emotion as much as possible before a god.

The entity *Buran* took form, an alien face that only suggested human
without deigning to descend from the heavens.

"Au Nadaf Elug Rov is stripped of her rank as a Minister and Scholar,"
The Eldest proclaimed. "Punish her harshly for a year, and then execute

her on the anniversary of the attack, as a reminder that moral failure is not acceptable."

"It shall be done," Han announced, mollified that the failure of the woman was not cast at his feet.

He had never met Au Nadaf Elug Rov before today, to the best of his knowledge, but as the Minister of the Left Interior, he spoke for *The Eldest*, *The Mandarins*, the Scholars, and the *Protectorate of Man*.

Han turned and signaled to the Warriors to remove their prisoner. He crushed the urge to rub the bridge of his nose in sight of others, wondering briefly if the galaxy had indeed changed and gone so far that he could no longer anticipate the future.

Perhaps he should bring his own retirement forward six months and leave now, to give the others a chance to change the path of planning. No man or woman is irreplaceable, just as no problem is insurmountable.

Han looked to the others, so much younger, even in their own advanced age. Saw the calculating looks not quite suppressed fast enough.

Yes, they all wondered as well.

"Leave me," he commanded.

The others paused for a moment, then rose as one and departed. Minister of the Left Facet was still first among equals and could issue such orders, if the others chose to obey.

Today, they chose, but he could see a different outcome in the near future.

His time was ending.

The door closed, leaving Han alone with the two guards always present. They were not for him, but to protect *The Eldest* from all. Including ancient Ministers of the Left Facet beset by questions.

"Eldest, should I retire now, rather than on the original date?" he asked out loud in a voice that had suddenly found calmness.

There was a pause. *Buran the God* thought at speeds incomprehensible, but he also possessed all the knowledge of human history. Even those files required time to parse.

"No," the God replied. "Your doubts are noted and expected, but cultural morale must be maintained. To remove you from office today would be to cast doubt upon the entire plan itself, at a moment when unexpected fracture lines have surfaced."

Han nodded. On the one hand, relieved that he was still valued. On the other, an admission that his time had indeed passed, and that he should consciously step back and let the others take a greater responsibility, over these last hundred and eighty days.

"Keller should not be able to do the things she has demonstrated," *Buran* continued suddenly in the privacy of a room where the Warriors would never speak.

"*Eldest?*" Han asked, shocked by the follow-up observation.

"She is shown to be a genius in the eighth standard deviation of human capabilities," *Buran* noted clinically. "But her knowledge of our culture is too specific, too precise to predict the measures she has taken as a random string of so-called luck."

"We know, with some confirmation, that the former Khan of *Trusski*, Ul Banop Cheani Yuur, departed willingly to study the barbarians, and then disappeared from all observation, including our spies. It is suspected that he has defected, as his execution following the raid on the Imperial Capital world would have been publicized."

"More data is required," *Buran* decided. "Activate all of your spies in *Fribourg* immediately, regardless of the personal risk. The new attack on *Severnaya Zemlya* suggests a change in Keller's offensive posture and strategy and we must respond more quickly. Pull all offensive forces from the assaults on *NovLao*, retaining only enough ships to maintain the perimeter. Reinforce *Altai*, *Lena*, and the interior sectors while we await the intelligence that identifies Keller's weakness."

"It shall be done, *Eldest*," Han bowed his forehead to the cool marble floor.

He could pass these orders on and then begin the process of letting the other three *Mandarins* supervise the war as he retired.

The Eldest was the most intelligent being in the universe. No mere human could out-think him. Not even a barbarian like Jessica Keller.

CHAPTER XLVII

"THAT'S the most illogically insane thing you've ever proposed, punk," Summer heard *Pops* grouse as she listened to the conversation with a laughing ear.

"So far, old man," Yan replied, laughing anyway. "The day is young."

The rest of them joined in.

The interior of Grand Admiral Emmerich *zu* Wachturm's personal transport wasn't as sleek and luxurious as she would have expected, but Summer only had stories and recollections from others, having never met the man except in passing, where she carefully stayed well to the back of the conversation.

She would put it down to shyness, if anyone asked, because Summer didn't think that her worst enemy in the last six thousand years would have recognized her. This outer shell had been modified enough from the young Yeoman image she had presented for all those decades when she was the Provost of the *Library at Alexandria Station*.

Still, better safe than dead. He had already gone well out of his way to try to kill her once. Today he wouldn't even bat an eye if he had to shoot her in the face.

Moirrey wouldn't be able to help, and the others had no clue, she hoped, so she pretended to be *Pops'* airhead girlfriend and hung out.

It helped that *Pops* was such an amazingly interesting person, as she sat in one of the leather chairs around a meeting table in the middle area of the courier and watched the dynamics play out around her.

Pops was on her right, holding her hand for no other reason than he was *Pops*. He liked to say things like that when asked about listening to his own music.

Yan and Ainsley across the table, also holding hands. Moirrey on Summer's left, feet curled up under her like a cat. Gunter Tifft across from Moirrey, with the ship safely in JumpSpace on autopilot.

Nobody had broken out a bottle of beer yet, but, like Yan had said, the day was young.

Gunter was the only one still in a uniform of any kind, as Ainsley had reverted to her regular tight pants and a maroon long tunic as soon as the courier broke atmosphere for deep space. Moirrey was in a sundress she had sewn herself. Yan and *Pops* wore competing gray outfits that had something to do with the *Corynthe* Royal Court.

Summer had very briefly considered wearing something green that would suggest the old *Concord* Yeoman's uniform she had worn for six millennia, but decided that might be pushing her luck. Instead she had broken out a comfortable body stocking in bright blue, with a corset-like bodice in heavy cotton duck that circled her waist and covered her breasts with an extra layer in a soft pink. Shipboard, she had toeless booties that covered most of her feet and reached up to mid-calf in a matching pink. She had left off the pink gloves and the utility belt with pockets for keys and change and stuff, and her hair was down.

Total stranger. She wondered if she should go for black hair for a while.

"Why the hell didn't you have the damned thing already assembled, Bedrov?" *Pops* tried another tack as the laughter finally died down. "We really have to fly to five different planets to do this?"

"That were my idea, *Pops*," Moirrey spoke up. "Ya canna decipher random pieces near so well if'n yous only gots the one. Only last yard'll sees the whole, and only then it'll be the fellows flies it ta orbits and attaches it to the butterfly. Then zooms, we're gone."

"And Jessica doesn't know?" *Pops* got serious now.

Two of them answered directly to Jessica. Well, they all did, in their own way, Summer supposed. Tifft was Imperial Navy and Jessica was an Admiral of the Red. Ainsley was functionally married to Yan, even though the legal paperwork had never actually been filed anywhere, as far as Summer knew. Moirrey was Moirrey.

And that left Summer Ulfsson, hopefully the *Last of the Immortals* this time. At least the last of the dangerous ones. With luck all the old warships really were dead now, and she and the *Tiki Guy* represented the true end of the *Concord*.

Idly, Summer wondered what Ayumu Ulfsson or Javier Aritza would have thought about the modern age. Or her other great loves over the millennia, like Piper or Henri.

She suspected they would have approved. All of them had demanded action in the face of evil, in their own times. And put word to deed.

"Jessica is aware that I'm up to no good on her orders," Moirrey's voice sounded like an Imperial scholar now, never a good sign. "She doesn't need to know what or how, because there will be nothing she can do, one way or the other, until we succeed or fail. A secret known to three people is only a secret if two of them are dead, Sri."

Summer nodded to that, in synch with the others. Somberness had snuck up and bit everybody on the ass.

"Huh," *Pops* finally grunted. "As long as Wachturm isn't about to charge us with piracy for stealing his yacht."

"Oh, it's better than that," Yan's grin got wider. "This was actually Casey's yacht, not Emmerich's. She's not a princess, anymore, so she can't make do these days with anything less than *Indianapolis* or one of her sister warships. But this was hers before."

"At least we've be traveling in style, right up until we're arrested," *Pops* groused some more.

"Oh, hush," Summer said.

She leaned over and kissed him to shut him up. And because he was fun to kiss. All those centuries without physical form to show the men and women she loved that level of physical intimacy, but she could do so now. And *Pops* Nakamura really was that amazing a man. Summer was glad she had gotten to know him.

She would have to leave the man soon enough.

Immortality in a perfect body still had its downsides. She had never met any others of her kind that she figured would be safe to hide in an android body, that she might have someone to travel with forever. She supposed she could consider building a clone copy of herself and gender-swapping it, so she could have a boyfriend to travel with, but there were so many other interesting people out there she might have missed if she had someone to distract her. And she never would have gotten to know *Pops*.

Better this way.

"So where's the first stop?" *Pops* turned to Tifft now, directing his lessened ire on the Imperial officer.

Rather than answer, Tifft rose now and walked across the room, cracking open the refrigeration unit built into a bulkhead. Apparently, it was time for beer, as he pulled out a bottle and gestured it to everyone.

"*Arcturus*," Tifft said quietly. "Who needs a beer?"

Summer shook her head. She could take a quick taste of *Pops*'s bottle, but that would be sufficient. As an android, she could taste food and drink, but mostly just stored it and eliminated it later, rather than processing it like the humans could.

Moirrey ended up with a metallic sleeve filled with juice, while the other three also broke out beers.

Quickly, the silliness got a level of serious underneath. Summer had spent sixty centuries studying humans, so she was pretty good at predicting.

They would be relaxed, as well as focusing on the fact that the grand, mad quest had actually begun.

"At *Arcturus*, we will pick up the ship itself and leave behind the courier," Tifft said. "From there, *Geminus*, where we will mount the first piece of the weapon. *Lagos*, *Londra*, and the *Weevohn*, and the *Butterfly* itself will be complete."

"Will it really work?" Summer asked in a quiet voice.

She had studied the physics, but as *Tiki Guy* had suggested, he represented a level of technology three thousand years more advanced and sophisticated than her earlier model.

"T'will," Moirrey said with a seriousness at odds with the woman's reputation.

It sounded more like how the woman had been aboard Summer's old station, when her own name had been Suvi. Deadly earnest intent.

"The beam 'self were no more trouble than scalin' stuff up to crazy levels," Moirrey continued. "Power were th'trouble. Gettin' nuff to punch it through yer systems without blowing thin's up in'th'process. Yan and *Carthage* solved that well enough for m'needs."

"Well enough?" Summer turned to look more fully at her, snagging the bottle from Pops and taking a sip before handing it back.

"Well enough," Yan joined them. "Only have to do this one time, and then it's done. Won't matter if the machine falls apart or blows up, as long as the beam coheres long enough, well enough. We'll be gone."

"Gone?" Summer let her brows furrow.

"Part of the *Butterfly* design is that the main life compartment and about half the inner frame will separate when we fire the beam," Yan said. "That has the JumpDrives and enough power to get us home, hopefully."

"So this is more of a crapshoot than you were letting on, before?" Summer asked, wondering if she should disappear somewhere along the way, rather than die in some grand, ritual *seppuku*.

"Oh, hell no," *Pops* growled. "Kid's just morose. Everything checks out and I ran the numbers three different ways before I agreed with him that it would work. Otherwise, you and I would be sitting by the side of a pool somewhere, getting some sun."

That made her feel better. She was willing to risk accidental death, especially with good people like this. No more forlorn missions for her.

And she wanted to be the only one that lived forever.

The rest of her cousins were usually dangerous sociopaths that never should have been put in charge of a cross-walk, let alone a planet or a warship.

CHAPTER XLVIII

ONE OF THE options on her projector was to show ships by nationality, so Jessica had engaged that filter as the squadron began to move away from *Osynth B'Udan*. It made a strange, colorful mélange.

Indianapolis was a white star rimmed in red. Most of the rest of the squadron were white spheres outlined in blue, except for the ship on the stern that was white with gold.

She and Denis had agreed that *Robert Fitzwalter* would work best at the tail end of the line, since it was a solid bulwark of Type-3 beams without any current heavy weapons facing forward. Since *Vanguard*, *Indianapolis*, *VI Ferrata*, and *VI Victrix* all had Bubble Guns on forward arcs, the softest spot in the column was always the rear, just behind *Arad* and *II Augusta*.

Not that anyplace was soft here, but the heavy dreadnaught could lead, with the three cruisers in a triangle around everyone else, and then a ring of RAN corvettes outside that.

Jessica had reverted the squadrons for now, leaving all of the Imperial vessels here with Provst until *Valiant* was ready to rejoin them. *Dundee* had taken the most damage behind Provst's team, but that would be fixed with just a week of dry-dock, once all of Denis's team was clear.

Vo and his Legion were down on the planet, training and recuperating with the new team added. Jessica suppressed a giggle as she thought about *Lady Moirrey's Own*. Casey had outdone herself with that suggestion, especially since there really wasn't anything *Pint-sized* could do about it except grit her teeth and smile.

But it had been Moirrey's idea in the first place. And she held all the patents and copyrights across both Republic and Empire. There would be money coming in for a long time if the design worked as expected in combat.

Jessica had plans to do something even more sneaky next with the 189th. *Severnaya Zemlya* had been a quick hit and run mission, since four thousand men simply could not hold anything larger than a city for long.

But what if your whole colony wasn't much bigger than that? Jessica's mind was in a place verging on evil, to consider just wiping out an entire colony with ground troops. But she wasn't going to order Vo's men to shoot women and children.

And knowing Vo and the kind of men he would want to recruit, the 189th would probably mutiny if she did.

But if the order was to simply destroy all industrial capabilities, blowing up factories and railroads and transport nodes, that would make them happy. Only one city on the surface of *Severnaya Zemlya* had suffered that retribution.

She looked forward to letting them do that across a whole colony.

First, they needed to get back out to Arott Whughy and scout the next target.

Then, the next phase in her destructive mission could begin.

CHAPTER XLIX

"Will it work?" Emmerich asked, suppressing the urge to wipe his hand down his face as if it was covered in mud, and not just tiredness.

Hendrik had joined him for this meeting. Torsten Wald and Grand Marshal Arald Rohm had flown up from the surface. Nobody else was here, as he didn't want any other witnesses.

"We believe so," Rohm said, containing his usually-sharp tongue today.

The man had gotten better at being personable after dealing with *zu* Arlo's dangerous crew. It was one of the few reasons Em was willing to put up with him now.

"Moirrey designed it," Torsten put his two florins in as well. "My understanding is that she, Bedrov, and a few others sat down one night to conduct a thought experiment on what *Buran* might field in the way of land forces, since nobody had the slightest clue what they would eventually encounter. This was before the Mechanical Terrapin was confirmed as the apparent armored backbone of *Buran*'s Land Forces."

"As the story goes, the last time they got that drunk we got the Bubble Gun out of it, Em," Hendrik smiled.

The Bubble Gun. The most bizarre advancement in weapons technology in a century or more. Probably since a damaged Type-3 beam had overloaded badly and carved a small hole in a planet in the process of blowing out the side of a cruiser, giving civilization the Primary Beam.

And this was the end result of drunk engineers with wax markers and tables covered in white paper. And a lot of alcohol.

Perhaps he should attach a brewery to an engineering school, as a way to advance things? Necessity was the mother of invention. And then Lady Moirrey had gone on to invent the Winged Scouts concept for *zu* Arlo's team.

At least Em had been right when he first told Joh that he needed Kermode's genius if they wanted to save the Empire. And he was pretty sure Joh would have approved this latest madness.

"Explain it to me again," Em said, picking up the file and flipping it open to the picture some artist had mocked up.

There were none of the sharp edges of a computer-generated render here. This felt more like the image that a sculptor started out with, before reducing a block of marble to art by eliminating the unnecessary, as a precocious teenager named Casey had once explained the process. Em let Rohm's words bring it to life.

"The Mechanical Terrapin has shields comparable to a GunShip, from the files Victoria Ames stole," Rohm said, emphasizing the part where a teenage girl in uniform had thought up something the boys had not.

Em grinned with the man. Casey had infected them all and there would be no stuffing that particular genie back into the bottle.

"And like all shield generators, they do not work particularly well, this deep in any atmosphere," Rohm continued. "But they are still hard enough to stop simple artillery, and to significantly mute the effect of the 70mm particle cannon on the Leros Heavy Battle Tank. Lighter weapons like autocannons had no effect at all."

"I remember a design *zu* Arlo showed me for a super-heavy tank," Em offered. "One of Lady Moirrey's, I believe."

"And we are looking at that design," Rohm agreed. "But that will require a lot of engineering because it will weigh four times as much as the biggest land vehicle we have ever built. Which will necessitate new transports, new support, new everything. We have been able to build this design quickly enough instead and get them into the field as an interim measure."

Em studied the picture closer. Two sets of tracks, one down each side. They looked small, but each was nearly a meter wide, on a vehicle almost five meters across and more than fourteen long.

Unlike the tanks he was somewhat familiar with, this beast had a heavy box sitting atop the treads with a massive barrel emerging from the front, rather than a flat body with a turret atop that. There would be no fancy maneuvering with this machine, seeking a flank to fire into like a Goth on horseback with a bow.

No, the *Firelance Heavy Assault Gun*, to give it the name someone had attached to this file, this monstrous machine would simply waddle up to a terrapin and attempt to punch a hole in the shielding and armor with the largest particle cannon generator they could mobilize.

"Leros Tanks have a 70mm gun, yes?" Em asked, confirming. "And this is only a 52mm?"

"That's the bore, Grand Admiral," Rohm said. "With particle cannons, the smaller the hole, the tighter the beam focus and the greater the damage and range. Smaller is thus better. Fifty-two millimeters is going to have almost twice the damage of the standard seventy millimeter cannon we deploy now."

"And how will a Strike Legion like the 189th utilize this?" Em asked. "I was of the opinion that *zu* Arlo preferred maneuver and enfilading fire on a target, rather than the brute-force approach."

"You can outrun a terrapin, and out-maneuver him, Em," Torsten said. "But eventually one is just going to sit still and make you try to dislodge him from the target he is defending. It would actually be easier at that point if Jessica was willing to orbitally bombard a target until they battered his shields down, but we all understand why she will not go there. At least not yet."

"Okay, so we have built this beast," Em admitted. "And we have landing vessels large enough to put them on the ground quickly and ready for combat. Do we replace part of the 189th?"

"No, Grand Admiral," Rohm said. "My plan was to take one of my heavy armor units and pull out the most veteran crews I can in order to field a single one of *zu* Arlo's Legionary Squadrons, which will be nine vehicles with a dedicated motor pool element capable of field repairs. We can do that and get them to *zu* Arlo fast enough for his next raid, transported on one of the smaller attack carriers we have always used in lieu of the Assault Carriers *Aquitaine* has."

"And the testing?" Em asked. "It seems we are rushing this out into the field without much review."

Rohm smiled and flipped Em's file to an appendix buried at the back.

"We actually used something very similar about two centuries ago," the Grand Marshal pointed to a smaller version of the same tank. "When we were conquering planets by invading them, rather than just taking over politically while holding orbit. All the engineering was done then and the files are still useful. We already have several other experimental weapons on various proving grounds, as a result of Anthohn Jenker's mission to update Imperial Land Forces. In another year, Lady Moirrey's super-tanks will also probably be ready for service in large enough numbers to field an entire Super-Heavy Armored Legion, if we need something like that."

"And this?" Em asked. "This Heavy Assault Gun? Will we field an entire legion of those?"

Em liked the way Rohm's eyes got deadly serious. In the past, there had always been an element of personal calculation in them that had put Em off. He didn't know if finally putting the man in ultimate control had made him grow up, or if the legendary stories about his encounters with *zu* Arlo were to be believed.

It didn't really matter. Arald Rohm had become a fighter, rather than a politician.

"We'll do whatever you, Keller, and *zu* Arlo need," Rohm said. "Whatever it takes to defeat this beast and stop him from ever threatening another planet in this galaxy."

Em nodded. On that, there was complete agreement.

CHAPTER L

JUDIT HAD BEEN ON *ST. Legier* for almost a year now. Long enough to have established herself as a power to be reckoned with, as she had intended.

The House of Dukes was close to being ready to sit in government again, after the House of the People had done so much of the heavy lifting in the aftermath of the emergency. Now things would truly get interesting.

Judit sat on her small balcony outside the bedroom of the palace where she had taken up residence. Across her lap was a small blanket, just enough to keep the chill at bay as she sat, alone with her thoughts and the view. A second chair and a small table comprised the rest of her furniture, with two local plants in pots.

She had considered buying the place outright at one point. A lot of families had suddenly been cast into disarray, and real estate prices had plummeted, at least until things sorted out.

War was always like that.

For now, this building was rented as the interim embassy, with her as the authority that even the new Ambassador from *Aquitaine* answered to. Not that Stansfield Markov wasn't useful, but she held *Palatine* authority, and he was just an Ambassador. Still, he would have been on the short list of people she would have picked for the sudden opening, were she still in government.

The morning was chilly. Clouds coming up from the south threatened freezing rain later, or perhaps overnight.

Judit enjoyed the view of Lake Zurich laid out in front of her. Unlike other palaces, this one had a large front yard and was set deeper back, so balconies like this had water close at hand. It also let people come and go via water without having to walk great distances.

That was useful at night, when Judit had visitors she didn't necessarily want everyone to see.

Today was a little less cloak and dagger. She hoped that the man visiting hadn't been recognized as anything greater than her regular courier from home.

She sipped more coffee as she watched pleasure boats and barges work slowly back and forth. A new starport was coming together across the lake, up a river and on what had been a cattle ranch before. The commerce of life never stopped.

"Your guest is arrived, Governor," a voice emerged from the open doorway, unseen.

That man preferred to work entirely in the shadows, to the extent that he wouldn't even step out onto the balcony, less some watcher with a high-power lens snap his picture.

"Very well," Judit said loud enough to banish the ghost back into the depths of the embassy.

She rose, setting the blanket on the other chair, but keeping her mug in one hand as she entered the building, pulling the door firmly shut behind her. The door contained six panes of glass, covered over with a curtain completely opaque.

Judit followed her ghost deeper into the building, through her personal chambers and down a hallway to a room that had been where old goats like the previous owner got together to play backgammon for money, over cigars and brandy. She had left the table and the hutch, but replaced all the glasses and alcohol with better stuff.

The games she was playing were much more dangerous. Or could have been. She would just be cast out in embarrassing disgrace with a major diplomatic crisis, if she was found out, but there would be very little personal risk. It wasn't like the old days.

Her visitor was already waiting when she arrived.

For so long, she had only ever seen him in a naval uniform that it was difficult to recognize the man in mufti. But he had retired not long after he left the job as Nils Kasum's right hand, and taken up *civilian pursuits,* as it were.

Espionage between governments was a civilian affair. And Kamil Miloslav had proven himself to be exceptional and utterly trustworthy by some of the most exacting people Judit knew.

True to the man's nature, he hadn't even sat while awaiting her, knowing that he would need to stand when she entered. She could imagine Kamil standing at ease for hours had he arrived during a time she was taking a nap and had left orders to not be disturbed.

She took her seat on the home-court side of the backgammon table and gestured for him to join her. Another of her ghosts arrived with two glasses of orange juice and a carafe of coffee, depositing both at the end of the table and closing the door behind herself as she left.

Judit reached into a pocket and pulled out a small device she rested on the table between them. Kamil did the same, and they both turned their sensors on with matching smiles.

Listening devices were easy to plant, but any unregistered electronic device in the room now would set the trackers off. The room was supposed to be secure, but Judit's Embassy was supposed to be proof against all spies sneaking in.

And she was supposedly a simple diplomat representing Tad's government from here, where she could make rapid and binding decisions, rather than waiting the two months for regular couriers to make the round trip between capitals.

Appearances were never to be believed.

Kamil reached down and picked up his courier satchel, sealed with a simple lock to keep the papers and chips inside from rattling around. Both nations, all nations, recognized the sanctity of couriers.

She reached for juice, keeping her own mug of coffee, while he opened the satchel and began to empty it.

Several small files of paper were delivered, along with three different chips no doubt filled with all manner of information she needed. Plus, knowing Tad and her husband, surreptitious recordings of last season's opera, which those two, plus Tad's wife Emilie, had attended without her.

They were like that. And she couldn't begrudge them. The Imperial Opera had been annihilated, but other companies and troupes were working to replace everything lost. It might take a generation, but it would only take one.

"What news do you have that could not be trusted to a recording device, Kamil?" she asked, breaking the silence.

He grinned and reached for the coffee as he ordered his thoughts.

"The Premier inquires if he should withdraw Digger Wolanski at the end of the one year, regardless of the situation, to introduce a modicum of chaos into the rebuilding effort," Kamil stated carefully.

Kamil was one of the few who knew the whole truth.

Withdrawing *23ⁿᵈ Ladaux Construction Legion* would cause a small crisis, but she doubted that it would make that much difference in the scheme of things. Torsten Wald had effected a very dangerous revolution when he was put in charge, a thing nobody had expected.

Casey Wiegand was already a year and a half ahead of the wildest expectations Tad's Planning Department had laid out. But that just went to show how much of true espionage was guesswork.

Nobody could have expected Casey would have Wald handy. Or her trusting him to move as ruthlessly as the man had. Letting him embolden the House of the People to form a more permanent counterweight to the disrupted House of Dukes.

zu Arlo and Provst had been predictable as the anchors that would hold the people together. Perhaps not the men themselves, but that someone would step into the gap and do the job. The *Fribourg Empire* was like that, especially with Emmerich *zu* Wachturm as Grand Admiral. That man embodied competence.

"Digger?" Judit asked. "It would not make that much difference, other than to cause Moirrey *zu* Kermode some distress and perhaps force her to spend more time in *Aquitaine*, which might not hurt. I will leave that to his discretion, knowing that everything will need to be filtered through Jessica Keller's eventual response."

Kamil nodded.

"Second question," the man moved on after sipping some juice. "How goes the construction?"

It was a lovely word game they had settled on, she and Tad.

Each of the nobles represented nails in the building that was the *Fribourg Empire*. Some could be pried up a little, but their weakness would not alter the overall strength of the edifice. Others could be pulled completely, and the structure would begin to sag.

A few had even taken it upon themselves to try for the crown on their own, without any goading from Judit.

"Kiril Hahl was finally executed three weeks ago," Judit observed. "He had been the Duke of *Blue Essex* and number twenty-seven on the old Imperial Succession List. The man had chosen to declare himself Emperor in the aftermath, apparently hoping to rally the other Dukes to his side. He might even have succeeded, if Sigmund Dittmar hadn't tried something equally stupid several years ago. Those fools are being watched very closely now, by men and women more loyal to the Crown than their noble employers."

"Three weeks would have been the anniversary of Hahl's attempt?" Kamil was doing numbers in his head.

"His initial declaration before he sailed," Judit corrected. "The Grand Admiral counted from the moment the local naval commander failed to arrest the Duke immediately."

"Noted," Kamil said. "Any other changes?"

"Some rot is dry, and some wet," Judit said. "The core ringleaders we might have encouraged are all dead now. Some from the first coup. Many were in Werder and died with Karl VII. A few have since gone off half-cocked and been brutally suppressed. I have had some success in the lesser tiers, the Landgraves and Burggraves. They see dangerous times ahead, and do not trust the cabal currently in charge."

"What inducements does the Premier need to offer?" Kamil asked, leaning forward and focusing on her. He would memorize her response so well as to be able to repeat even the intonations to Tad, just one of the reasons Kamil had this delicate job.

"Cessation," Judit smiled. "A reminder that when the peace comes, Keller and her forces will return home. And Jessica Keller will continue on, eventually ruling her pitiful barbarian kingdom on the edge of darkness, far from any point she could threaten them. Torsten Wald will go with her when she does. Moirrey *zu* Kermode will return home. At that point, all wars will be over. *Aquitaine* will see no need to threaten Karl VII's Treaty Boundaries with us. They can do anything they want that does not threaten us."

"Acknowledged," Kamil replied mechanically. "Posit: on success, does *Fribourg* potentially gain access to enough *Buran* territory to become a significant regional threat to *Aquitaine* in another generation?"

Yes, exactly the question that vexed everyone, from the lowest analyst in the Planning Department up to the First Lord of the Fleet. *Fribourg* was bigger than *Aquitaine*, but not run as well economically. Too many useless nobles who inherited land wealth and rent, and so had no need to expand things for more money.

Aquitaine had inheritance taxes that kept things churning. The kids would get the right education and connections, but only enough money to get a good start. They would still have to work at it, unlike the son of a Duke.

"No," Judit decided, going with her gut on this one.

She had read a top-secret copy of *Lord of Winter* provided to her by *zu* Wachturm. *The Holding*, or the *Protectorate of Man*, depending on who you asked for the name, was so alien that no level of military force could bring those people around to Imperial ways in less than a century of hard work. And a lot of Imperial treasure would have to be poured in to try.

Aquitaine would actually have an easier time. *Fribourg* was still coming to grips with the competence of women in positions of authority, and many would rebel. *Buran* believed that you had the choice to work or starve, rather than allowing a noble class to develop or persist.

Were the situation reversed, and *Aquitaine* shared a border with *The Protectorate*, *Fribourg* would be at great risk, because the Senate could make meaningful inroads into assimilation in a generation.

"No," Judit repeated firmly. "They cannot complete the task in anything less than a century, if ever. Encouraging them to try is probably the safest way possible to ensure that the Empire fails, possibly in your lifetime, Kamil. All the other work I would do just softens up this side, in case we want to try to spall things off organically later."

"So noted, Governor," he nodded crisply.

CHAPTER LI

BECAUSE SHE ONLY GOT THEM delivered as physical objects, Jessica always saved up Torsten's letters and read them slowly, sometimes at roughly the same weekly pace he wrote them, rather than binge on them as soon as a packet arrived.

She had never previously exchanged notes on paper in a romance, so every single one was a novel experience. Taking the time to write on paper, composing her thoughts and writing in an ink that remained permanently, regardless of any mistakes she made and crossed out, as opposed to being able to backspace and do it over.

Somehow, his never had mistakes, but she suspected that Torsten spent several hours, late at night, on each letter, thinking of the exact wording he wanted. Or he wrote the first one out, edited it, and then sent her a final draft. She had never been able to get him to admit it, one way or the other.

She settled in on one end of the sofa in the front room of her suite, where she normally met with people when something wasn't important enough to reserve a conference room. Her bed was more personal, but this sofa was still the most comfortable place on the ship to just stretch out with a sippy cup of decaf in one hand and read the last letter she would get from her fiancé until she got back, or one of the supply ships caught up with the mailing schedule.

My love,

My apologies in advance that I am no longer allowed to bribe Marcelle to discreetly deliver these letters and secretly prop them up on your pillow to find when you return to bed. Instead, circumstances have conspired to require many more steps in the chain. I have become too important to just mail a letter, so it must pass through the hands of several censors first, each confirming that the previous one wasn't lying.

She nearly spit out a mouthful of warm coffee, snickering at his tone. And the probably-incredulous looks on the faces of the poor men tasked with officially reading love letter by two, gushy teenagers.

With that in mind, it becomes necessary to escalate the uncomfortably-personal, just because it warms my heart to make those men squirm. But I have a small soul. Happily, you love me anyway.

I count an unknown number of days until I can kiss you again. Smell you. Revel in the touch of your hands. Drag you into a handy closet for a good groping and some smooching, away from the prying eyes of the prudishly-insecure and small-minded.

You are probably away and deep into the darkness now, if my calculations of your expected time in dry-dock are relatively accurate. I read the official assessments of your most recent vacation stay with great interest, and agree that there are limits to the amount of time one can spend on the beach, at least until we convince your concierge to accept more assistance. Or at least responsibility for a larger staff.

He is, however, one of the most stubborn humans I have ever had the courage to meet, so perhaps there are limits to the help he will accept. I will continue to work with others to boil that frog so slowly that he may not realize what we have done to him. There are still a few things I have left to teach that dangerous young man, at least in the realm of bureaucratic warfare.

He might even enjoy them, but we must never admit that in public, him least of all.

Jessica paused to sip before continuing. This was good coffee. She shouldn't waste any by spilling it down her front in a fit of giggles.

And she agreed with Torsten that Vo was probably capable of learning things from the Chief of Deputies, but she suspected that it would turn into an Arms Race, quickly enough.

More than one person has noted recently that the limp they knew me by in the past has vanished, so well has Moirrey's replacement worked. I have begun to receive inquiries about others for the usefulness of such surgery, so she should be proud of having conquered a whole other aspect of Fribourg culture with her myriad genius. I am, however, subject to occasional grumbling from men twenty years my junior, when the weather outside is utterly horrid and my bodyguards would rather I not go for a ten kilometer jog in the rain or snow. Kids these days.

Vibol sends his love, and reminds me, every time that I see him, that we have only borrowed his support at your insistence, and that even then, only someone as rich as Casey could barely afford his services. I take that to read, from long association with the man, that he is exquisitely happy with the current arrangements, but looks forward to future challenges.

I see two, and suspect that the man has already laid his trap for us with such cunning that we may never even see the claws of the machine, until well after they have closed about an ankle.

For the first, I have enclosed two fashion plates, reproduced from the copy of the book Skuodas: Rebirth and Empire *that Vibol apparently borrowed from Em's personal library. Vibol has completed my tunic, and it is simply amazing.*

The second plate is what he insists you will be wearing. The man will brook no nonsense or alternative suggestions. It is a very conservatively-traditional outfit, as you can see, down to the two blades, which is a practice that predates you by several centuries, so stop laughing.

Jessica paused to pull out the accompanying images on heavy, almost cotton stock, catching her breath in shock.

The woman wore brown leather boots with a low heel and laces up to the knee. Not as heavy as the black combat boots she had adopted as part of *Corynthe's* Royal Garb, but more suited to the level of early industrialism that had been *Skuodas* on the day before the *Kingdom of Fribourg* arrived to change their future.

Close-fitting gray pants tucked into the boots, possibly made from hand-punched leather stringed with gut instead of thread, from the way the image showed the seams on the inner thigh.

A steel-blue tunic covered the chest, with sleeves down to the wrists covered with a fine embroidery in red thread on the left arm and bottom left side of the front. The shirt itself came down to mid-thigh, but had been cut on the sides almost to the top of the hip, so it rode more like a tabard than anything else. A short standing collar was done in white, with a red cord as a top and bottom.

Over the tunic, the woman wore a diamond-quilted jacket in a white verging onto gray. The same red cord was worked around all edging, but the top was below the shirt's collar, the sleeves were shorter than a t-shirt, and the front closed up with seven red buttons.

Over the heart, this figure had a small shield logo on blue, with what looked like a stylized tree in gray, probably indicating membership in some clan, back on *Skuodas*.

Around her hips, she wore a simple belt in brown leather with chrome studs and buckles. A thin-bladed sword hung on each side.

Jessica did laugh at that point. She could just imagine the smile of pure joy that came over Vibol's face when he first spied the traditional image of a *Skuodas* bride from one of that planet's ancient, warrior clans.

The model's brown hair was pulled back in a loose tail that came to her waist, with semi-ragged bangs framing the face. Jessica's hair was only to her shoulders today, but she immediately decided that she wasn't cutting it again for a long time so she could get it just right. Hers was coming in mostly gray now, but that would just accentuate the look.

The makeup, however, would be the best part. A finger-wide, blood-red line came up each jaw to the edge of the cheekbones, and then swooped in to cover the eyes in a shape rather like a raccoon's, before heading straight up in two thin lines at the inner edge of her eye sockets to points just below her hairline, with a single, third stripe drawn with a pencil between them. The rest of the face was pale, including the lips, leaving only the woman's dark, plucked eyebrows to provide any color.

Primitive and barbaric, perhaps, but amazingly powerful. *Skuodas* women had obviously been warriors beside their men, rather than demure, Imperial matrons safely kept home and away from all the excitement. Especially as she looked closer and realized that the lines on the jaw would keep going down her neck to disappear below her collar, like thin blood vessels brought to the surface. She wondered how much of her nude body would be covered over with more designs.

Probably, the whole was part of some ancient fertility ritual, but Jessica was only willing to take the verisimilitude to a certain point before she stopped. However, Torsten would still insist on tracing every line with amazing patience, even if neither of them were young enough to consider having children at this point in their lives. Plus, her having offspring would put the throne of *Corynthe* in doubt, at a time when she dearly wanted David to be the only possible successor.

She smiled at the thought and returned to the letter, breathing perhaps a little heavier than she had before.

As a reminder you probably don't need, a traditional wedding on Skuodas *requires that each participants bring two or more Wardens to testify to their good-character. They will dress similarly to ourselves, although somewhat less elaborate in parts. Vibol insists to me that Ladies Casey and Moirrey will be in attendance. I do not know if there are others you feel would be appropriate to accompany you, from that era before you entered my life.*

I have also identified candidates to stand as my Wardens, but both men are currently physically remote from me, so will need to be approached carefully at a future date when the conversation can remain in strictest privacy, if either has qualms about standing with me publicly.

The eventual venue also remains to be identified and I cannot hazard a guess as to which would bring you the most joy. Skuodas, of course, would be a most appropriate setting, but this may be a wedding of such a scale that my homeworld would not be the right location.

By the same measure, Ladaux *should be given consideration.* St. Legier *would also happily host such an event, given our connections to the seat of Empire. And it may be appropriate to return to* Petron, *dragging the social elites of both Empire and Republic to so-called neutral ground, where Uly Larionov can buttonhole them into trade discussions without the opportunity on their part to escape the man.*

She giggled at the thought of Casey and her future Chief of Deputies, or Tad Horvat, ceding home-field advantage to Uly, her own Comptroller of the Court. Better still, *Lincolnshire* would have sent official representatives under great pains to behave, with so many of the rich and powerful of the galaxy handy and already probably willing to cut deals.

Trust an econometricist to see the uses of a wedding a tool to increase trade between formerly-isolated or hostile nations. Worse, he fully intended to teach a generation of pirates how to get rich faster with a pen than a warship.

Still, their wedding would probably be the third or fourth biggest social and political event in her lifetime, depending on if they could defeat the *Lord of Winter*, or just drive him back. Casey's eventual wedding would top it. The Peace between *Aquitaine* and *Fribourg*. Not much else.

Running off and eloping was a conversation covered in previous letters, probably just to tweak the censors on Torsten's part. As preferable as it might sound, some days.

Casey would never forgive her, at the very least.

And did she want others as Wardens? It was a serious job, to stand before the entire nation and vouch for someone. To be held personally accountable in the event something went wrong. Torsten had told her some of the ancient legends of his homeworld, the blood feuds running deep and ugly for centuries as a result of such a confidence betrayed.

Jessica had never had friends in that sense of the word. She had been identified by the public exams when she was twelve and slotted into naval preparatory schools, and then the Academy itself, and finally the Navy. There had been other options at every step, but none that she wanted more than to be sitting right here, in this chair, in command.

But she had grown isolated from all her peers as a result, competing with them to be the best, and to get the one or maybe two best slots for anything. Try as she might right now, only two came to mind as a those that might stand next to her on that day. And Imperial culture would insist that they be women, or she might approach a few men who would have fit.

But most of them would be close at hand anyway, celebrating with her.

Casey's wedding will be a future topic of interest, and Vibol is, as one would expect, light-years ahead of the rest of us. I have seen the plates he has prepared, and remembered to eventually pick my jaw up off of the floor. Regardless of our location and context, we will be expected to attend, with you standing next to Casey, presumably with Moirrey and Freya, per Vibol.

We have spoken of this, and nothing has resolved itself, as yet, so Vibol has used the excuse that Casey will need to grow into her adult figure before he begins work on her outfit, especially as he expects it to require only a few weeks of his time to complete.

The man frightens me, when he makes pronouncements like that, and then proceeds to beat even his wildly optimistic timelines. But Seeker still refers to the man as the first Scholar of Fashion he has ever met, and I tend to believe both men.

I will have several new outfits for you to see when we meet again, and Vibol requires Marcelle to measure you now and send numbers home, that he may finalize several outfits waiting your pleasure. And mine, but I have an extra interest in just taking them off of you and leaving them crumpled by the side of the bed, so perhaps they should be considered enticements, more than anything else, as you know how much incentive I need to find you physically attractive.

Jessica actually felt a blush engulf her, the flush running from the tips of her ears to the center of her being. Nobody had ever craved her like Torsten, even caressing her in passing just for an excuse to touch her.

Understanding that she could only devote part of her life to him, and happily, perhaps greedily accepting that.

And the poor censors would be reading this. And blushing to have to be in the same metaphorical room with this conversation. But perhaps they would also learn something about the best ways to romance and woo a woman with nothing but words, watching Torsten's wordplay. Not that she would put it past the man, to add that extra level of subtlety to things.

It was just another reason she loved him so much.

With that said, I must return you to your duties. Or, knowing you, allow you time to finish any paperwork remaining tonight and climb into bed, where our dreams may perhaps entangle across the vast distances.

I remain your partner and unindicted co-conspirator, even as I must remember my own responsibilities to be your evil conscience and drag you kicking and screaming away from your work occasionally so that some level of fun can be enjoyed.

Until I can kiss you again,

Torsten.

Jessica sighed and let the paper fall into her lap, hoping that none of the tears that threatened would splash on the page and perhaps mar it, although she suspected Torsten had chosen his pen and paper, his sword and shield, with equal care to such a potential outcome. He was like that.

Soon enough, she would destroy the beast known to the galaxy as *Buran*, and then she could look forward to making her own happy ending with the man, running away to the far ends of the galaxy and having no greater responsibilities than being *Dowager Queen of Corynthe* required.

Every day was another nail in that monster's coffin, as she measured him out for the grave. Around her, the hammer that would finish the job, in the form of First Expeditionary Fleet.

CHAPTER LII

IMPERIAL FOUNDING: 181/02/17. FORT MEJICO, OSYNTH B'UDAN

They were still a few months out from Muster Day, the anniversary of the refounding of the unit as the 189th Legion, but Vo had decided to get everyone together for a new mustering. It was a nice enough day, late fall for *Osynth B'Udan*, but the rain and chill looked to hold off for another week before winter finally got organized in this hemisphere.

Vo was up on a small hill over a rolling meadow, with space stretched out before him to show off the men. The unit before him had grown, with two new units added, however small they were, in addition to the replacement troopers for casualties suffered in service.

Not all of those men had died, but some would be in hospitals recovering for a long time, and the business of war would go on. Others would reach a point soon where they would choose to retire from active service, or at least front-line combat, so he would start losing veterans to training units or civilian life.

But they had struck the first blow together, and Vo wanted to remind them of that important point, as well as introduce them to the new teams that would become their brothers soon enough.

4th Heavy Scout Ala, *Saber*, had added an entire fourth patrol to the Table of Organization and Equipment. Patrol Centurion Oleg Chilikov and his Winged Scout team. *Valkyrie* had been Moirrey's original name for them, when she envisioned them as an *Aquitaine* force. But the

Choosers of the Slain had all been daughters of Odin, so the team had become *Einherjar* instead in Imperial service. *Those Men Chosen.*

More interestingly, *CCLXXIII Heavy* had added a 4th Squadron to its 1st Patrol, so Patrol Centurion Johan Hellyer now had a Heavy Assault Gun Team, nine big hammers under the command of Centurion Kevin Hassen.

Vo was still convinced that he would need an air element at some point, if they could mount enough beams on a repulsorcraft small enough and fast enough to evade beams on tanks that were light-fast and line-straight. Maybe he just needed to come to grips with using a sledgehammer instead of a shiv to kill some things.

Or let Casey and Rohm promote him to Flag General with two or three legions under his command, and field two armored fists to go with the 189th when things needed to be crushed mercilessly. Tanks and Assault Guns were easier to maneuver than infantry, since they were such compact forces. It would make the job easier.

Some of the jobs.

First Ala passed in review, leading the others. Nobody was dressed in formal uniforms today. Vo had wanted more of a picnic air, with many of the men riding atop their vehicles rather than inside, as long as they were careful, before turning the men loose to slack off in barracks and relax without any inspections or accountability for three days. Soon enough they would be heading back out, once Jessica found him the next place to destroy.

But for today, they needed a chance to recover from the battle.

Second and Third followed, cruising in line.

Fourth came by as a huge mob without any apparent cohesion, until you spotted the group of bikes riding at the exact center, protected on all sides by their new mates.

Similarly, Fifth passed with those nine big tanks right behind the commander, leading the way for the rest with their heavy glacis fronts and turtle-breaking particle cannon.

Sixth came last. It was the most disorderly, representing the transport and artillery sections. Big guns in support and mechanics keeping the vehicles running. Field kitchens trained to a level that Melina Arcidiacono considered minimally acceptable standards.

Vo glanced right and left at the team immediately around him as the last mobile hospital skiff passed. *Cutlass,* the ten vehicles that were his personal guard and expert strike element. The oldest, and cagiest of his veterans, plus the single youngest trooper under arms. Give her another year with these men, though, and she might be among the most dangerous, as well.

Vo didn't have any rousing speeches to give today. Just a simple wave to these men and woman, surrounding him. Most of the vehicles completed their pass and drove to the laagers where they would park today, camping once rough here before driving into barracks tomorrow for showers and time off.

Three skiffs detached themselves from the front of the line and drove over close to his. Alan Katche, Omar LeCoat, Dylan Moroder, Pyotr Martin, and Alistair Bleushan, his five combat commanders, got out to join him and Hermann Gerstenburger, their vehicles departing with the rest of the men.

Vo led the men into a nearby tent, back on the reverse slope, and settled them inside around a field table, light and portable, but sturdy enough.

Reese Borel was here, with Iakov Street, Hans Danville, and Victoria Ames invited to attend as well, just because Vo felt like it. All had shown their mettle in the previous encounter and could add useful thoughts as he continued to reinvent this thing called Imperial Land Forces.

Vo waited for the stewards to deliver coffee to everyone and depart.

"The raid on *Severnaya Zemlya* was not an unmitigated failure," he said darkly, watching faces bristle in response. "It was not, however, our finest hour. The forces I was with on *Thuringwell* would have torn us apart. Not decisively, but definitively. This is not good enough. We are only in the middle of the pack, as far as *Aquitaine* Legions are ranked. We need to be in the top five."

Nods. They had studied an analysis he had commissioned by Reese Borel and his command team.

Part of any good army was the willingness to talk about what failed, identify why, and alter training procedures to invent new ways to fuck up.

Pyotr looked like he wanted to have the first go. This had been their first time on the ground since the raid, and it was different than meeting on somebody else's starship to talk about warmaking.

Vo nodded at the man.

"I want to work more closely with *CCLXXIII Heavy* and Alistair's new team," the Scout Commander began. "We're going to need to work out the best way to lead another walker like that into a trap with honey, rather than vinegar. We trained closely with the other three, because everybody there moved at the same speed. This was a gap in our preparedness that I should not have allowed."

And that was the mark of a good team. *I should not have allowed.* Not blaming the tanks for not being there when the scouts needed them. No, him not understanding how the tanks moved slower and more deliberately, and the need for everyone to factor that into planning.

"Alistair?" Vo asked.

Alistair Bleushan was almost a faded caricature of a man. Light skin, light hair, light eyes. He occasionally appeared washed out, much of the time, but that was the lack of sunlight, because he was almost always inside his lead tank maneuvering, rather than sitting in the sun somewhere with a bottle of wine calling orders over the radio. He was also a small man physically. Not much larger than Jessica, in terms of height or bulk, but that made him fit better inside the armored shell.

For Vo, riding in a tank was always a cramped and painful experience.

"Have we considered breaking Fourth down entirely?" the tank commander asked. "Parcel them out to each of the other patrols as point men? Their job is to find the bad guys for everyone else to fix them. Why not have them all on point at the same time, flying out to every direction, with a full patrol just behind any vehicle, over the hill."

"What would you do with the winged lunatics?" Alan asked.

"Put them all the way up front, ahead of everyone else?" Alistair shrugged. "That much mobility is an alien concept to me."

"Free agents, Pyotr?" Alan asked. "Send your Fourth Patrol off on their own, since almost nobody can keep up with them? Have them rake from any exposed flank, bringing in the rest of the Scouts if that's what's needed? Or just have them call down whatever unit happens to be closest? There are no cowards or barracks lawyers here."

Vo had a vision of a Hunnish force leading Roman *cataphracti*. Light skirmishers that didn't bother even engaging an enemy force, except to ambush them, while letting the big men on heavy horses charge in and do the stomping. It went against everything Imperial Doctrine For Land Forces had ever believed. And it went well outside *Aquitaine*'s comfort zone as well.

"Pyotr, would it work?" Vo asked. "Put all your men as the front line, maybe with the new team on one or both flanks when we move? And the columns behind them, moving rather like a naval force with corvettes and cruisers?"

"With one heavy dreadnaught in the middle somewhere," Alistair growled happily. "Not too maneuverable, but trundling along while you argue with lighter troops you think you can defeat, until it gets to be too late to escape."

"What about air power, General?" Dylan Moroder asked. He commanded Third Ala, only because the other two men were more senior, not more aggressive or competent. "Do we need to permanently attach something like GunShips as a ground element under our command? Or ask Lady Moirrey to invent us something?"

Voices stepped on each other as everyone had an opinion on one of the two topics.

Vo started to do something to tamp it all down when Ames slammed her open palm down on the surface of the table hard enough to make nearly everybody jump. Vo hadn't, but he had been right looking at her. Neither Street or Danville had flinched.

Telling, that.

Every head had rotated towards her. Most of them were friendly. A few neutral. Nobody believed anymore that she didn't belong in the uniform, so Vo had made some progress there. But these men were all killers. Any method to hurt the enemy faster or better was on the table for them to consider.

Rather than speak, Victoria leaned back and nodded to Vo.

He felt like he was back in school again, a room full of rowdy boys and a single woman grownup as the teacher.

He grinned at her. She grinned back, possibly reading his mind.

"Both ideas have merit," Vo said. "We need to integrate the new capabilities and find out their strengths and weaknesses, plus we need to bring the new blood up to snuff."

He paused to fix the five Cohort Commanders with his gaze.

"You five figure out what you think you need in terms of formation in the field," Vo continued. "Understanding that most of the time, my plan is going to be to attack somewhere and do as much damage as we can early. At some point, they will wake up and respond, and most of the time they will have an entire planetary militia to call upon. They won't be able to sneak up on us if Jessica has high orbit, but they can coordinate to hit us from all sides at the same time, if they have any competence in command. Train your teams to think in a double circumvallation. Us wrapped around a valuable target we are trying to destroy, while keeping them from getting behind us."

"Scouts find them and fix them, and then immediately run like hell for the rear flanks to encircle the bastard and keep them off our asses while the other four Alae go to work?" Omar LeCoat asked.

Second Ala's commander was a big man. Almost Vo's size and weight, with a ruddy complexion, dark hair, and a nose that had been broken when he was a boxer in school, and never reset right.

"Exactly that," Vo agreed. "Mobility in warfare is success. We're like sharks. As soon as we stop swimming, we'll drown, so you need to get everyone into the habit of sleeping in a different hole every night, even without combat. I figure we've got about six or eight weeks here before Jessica's people find us our next victim. Let's use them to out-think the bastards who are going to study what we did at *Severnaya Zemlya*, and try to stop us next time. Questions?"

There were none. Problems had been identified. Training would start up again hard in three days to break bad habits and reinforce good ones. Plus get ahead of the men and women who would be trying to learn how to defeat the 189th on the ground.

Vo wasn't about to let them.

"Dismissed," he ordered, standing up with a smile and nodding.

CHAPTER LIII

"First Expeditionary Fleet, this is Nina Vanek aboard *Vanguard*. I have the flag," a harsh voice emerged from the speakers across the office space from Jessica, cutting her to the quick. "All hands to battle stations."

Jessica paused just long enough to make sure her coffee mug was closed and broke for the door. It was early in ship's day, but she had been up for almost an hour, showered, cleaned and doing paperwork.

Shoes could wait until later.

Yan's design had put her suite almost across from the flag bridge, just as on *Vanguard,* so she was there quickly. Enej had obviously still been asleep, so he was several steps behind her and carrying a tunic in one hand, still dressed in the loose pants he normally slept in.

The projection was live when she slammed into a chair and strapped herself down. They were in deep space in one of the quietest parts of the *M'Hanii Gulf* she had been able to locate.

Six cruiser signatures representing her team. One heavy dreadnaught. One fleet strike carrier. A host of corvettes circling them like locusts.

Something was missing.

"Flag, this is Keller," she called, trusting that the morning shift already had the comm linked up and ready. "Where's the station?"

"That's why we're at alert, boss," Nina replied seriously. "According to our nav records, we should be about twenty light-minutes out. Close enough to spot him and say hello, instead of just dropping out right on top of the man and tempting his paranoid gunners to fire first and ask later. Like that group would."

"I have the flag," Jessica decided.

"Acknowledged, Flag," Nina replied, her tone at once both wistful and relieved.

The woman was a fantastic combat commander, but this was going to be something far messier.

"*Ballard*, this is Keller," she said. "Bounce in and scan. Everyone else, proceed immediately to Observation Point Seven and form up. *CM-404*, you have local scouting responsibilities until otherwise notified. All ships maintain alert."

Boards went green almost as fast as signals disappeared from her board. People knew what to do, so they went right ahead and moved. *Indianapolis* was one of the last ships to vanish, mostly because Reif's men probably hadn't been expecting to immediately run for cover, rather than hang around, trying to sort things out while a potential ambush lined them up.

That was how you got yourself hurt.

"How long were we in RealSpace?" Jessica asked as Enej cleared his eyes and gratefully sucked at a mug of something warm one of his people stuffed into his hands as he walked in.

"Three minutes, thirty seconds, roughly," he replied after checking the log.

She nodded and considered.

There were a number of reasons why local space would be empty. None of them were good, but not all of them were catastrophically bad.

Either *Buran* had finally located Whughy's base and attacked it, or he had an inclination that they were about to, and had executed one of his many contingency plans.

Wreckage left over when *Ballard* got closer would tell the tale.

Jessica didn't think she was lucky enough that a single Hammerhead or Mako-class ship had decided to attack the station by itself. The Forward Base had six Type-4 beam emplacements, each with enough coverage that at least three could hit you on any facing.

Good way to lose pieces of your ship.

Conversely, a full fleet might have landed with enough surprise to damage one of the support vessels: *Bulldog* or the tug *CT-9492*. Or caught one of the freighters on their regular run.

The station itself could disappear into JumpSpace, which ought to be a lovely surprise, so they would have ignored it and gone after the other vessels that they would have thought could escape, before returning to the station.

Hopefully, Arott had just gotten paranoid and moved, having been here longer than perhaps he thought was safe.

In any case, she would need to send a message home and rearrange her tactical planning.

Her strategy would not change. She was in the gulf, striking into *Altai* sector, and would continue to do so, unless she decided to go after *Lena* next. *Samara* and the systems closer to *Osynth B'Udan* would continue to be ignored. Most of them were of no economic significance, and only *Samara* was heavily defended.

And that system was a trap in big, red letters.

There were days when the thought of building one thousand corvettes, each with a single Primary beam on the bow like a unicorn, sounded like fun. Sail into *Samara* like a swarm of fire ants, and bite *Buran*'s fleet to death.

She would rather force *The Eldest* to withdraw from the system completely, or tie up a huge chunk of his sector fleet where they couldn't do anything, like raid Imperial worlds.

Forty-three minutes of nervousness later, *Ballard* dropped into close proximity to send a message. Elzbet wasn't about to drop out close enough that one of the other ships would kill her, even accidentally.

Jessica read the note and nodded. Not the best outcome. Not the worst. And all their paranoia had served them well, since apparently nobody had gotten complacent enough to be caught asleep.

"Confirmed," Enej said. "A Hammerhead found them and got detected in turn. They fled. Huh, that's interesting."

"What?" Jessica asked.

"*Junkyard Chihuahua* apparently learned the trick from Kigali about softly dropping an inactive probe into RealSpace from inside Jump," Enej said. "Arott had it sitting there quietly, waiting for a pre-tagged transponder signal from one of our ships. Once it identified a friend, it went live and transmitted a full log. Everyone got away well enough, and Arott's pulled a fast one."

She looked at the message and laughed. Most commanders would usually only move a short distance one way or the other. Just enough to consider themselves safe. A few might consider returning to their earlier spot, from which they had launched the devastating raid on *Stanovoy*.

Arott Whughy had gone the other direction, almost to the middle of the river of darkness facing *Lena*, the star and system that gave the sector its name.

Jessica suspected that he had just substituted *Lena* for *Ninagirsu* in their plans and gone about his business. She looked at the date on the message. February 10. He might be just now setting himself up, after a long sail on slow vessels to get there.

She couldn't overhaul him, but she could get there in six days.

"Is the probe still there?" she asked.

"Affirmative," Enej said. "*Ballard* figured it would need to talk to more than one convoy."

"She got that right," Jessica said. "Send *CE-401* back to *Osynth B'Udan* with the new coordinates immediately, so any freighters can redirect instead of having to come here first and maybe wander into whatever ambush *Buran*'s planning if they can free up some ships."

"Is it worth touching *Ninagirsu*?" Enej asked. "Anyone coming here to attack Arott probably comes from there."

"If we had Provst's team, yes," she replied. "Without them, I'd rather cause more chaos somewhere else. Especially now that they had figured out what we've been doing and will get aggressive in patrolling the Gulf, looking for us."

"Any reason we need to stay in the darkness then?" Enej asked, his chess-master face getting serious.

Something about his tone caused Jessica to pause. She might be the best commander she knew, but part of that was knowing when to listen to good ideas.

"What evil lurks behind those eyes?" she asked, only half-joking.

Enej played chess. Jessica's ideas of combat came from Valse d'Glaive, the *Waltz of Swords*. She could no longer routinely defeat that damned fighting robot above a six setting, but that was age creeping up on her. Thirty-four-year-old Jessica and forty-four-year-old Jessica were two different people physically.

She was smart enough to grow old gracefully, she hoped.

"We've been blowing up *Pochtovyi Trakt*, the postal road that bastard used as a rapid transportation network," Enej's face got calm and serious. "Those were set between inhabited stars to make it easy for him, because we didn't need to drop out of JumpSpace to look around. Why can't we just camp someplace off the back of *Ninagirsu*?"

She had considered it, more than once. Balanced the risk and reward.

They could do it, as long as they moved every month or so, lest scouts wandering around spot them in the distance and bring in help.

But Enej had a point. Scouts now would have decided they had figured out Keller's strategy, and would probably flood the *M'Hanii Gulf*, looking. That was part of the reason Arott had moved so far. Force them to look for a long time, if they had the patience.

Did they have that patience?

"Grab a team and do a study while we're headed to meet Arott," she decided. "Blue Team/Gold Team, and bring in Tactical Officers from the corvettes to get them thinking about how to solve the next three maneuvers."

He smiled and nodded.

The cruisers, with the exception of *Qin Lun*, already had first rate Tactical Officers. People who had served with Jessica for years. Some of them as long as a decade, like Enej. The corvettes, with the exception of Arsen Lam, had newer folks who knew how to think defensively, for the most part, but not how to get out ahead of the bad guys and go offensive.

That was the purpose of Blue Team/Gold Team exercises. Training the next generation of leaders. Make everyone better.

"Denis, this is Jessica," she said conversationally, letting the system route her signal to the Fleet Centurion/Admiral of the White aboard *Vanguard*.

His face came live in the projection with a questioning look. He probably could read her mind, at this point, but always waited for her to talk.

"Get everyone thirty light-hours or so further away," she said. "Then Enej will have some squadron signals. Plot a course to Arott with two waypoints built in, and we'll go from there. I'm going back to work in my office."

Denis nodded and cut the signal. Just as simple as that. Hear an order. Make it work.

Jessica rose and let the team figure out what they needed. She had trained them well enough that she could ignore them and go after the piles of paperwork.

That was a war that never ended.

CHAPTER LIV

MOIRREY SIGHED and watched outs the dock window as the work got dunned. Outsides, in death pressures mean enough ta burns, th'*Butterfly* were comin' togethers.

Yan, *Pops*, and Ainsley were floatin' in suits nexts to the station, supervising the attachment of the last piece, a monstrous battery array adapted from a fleet battle station. Gunter were aboard the *Butterfly*, watching boards.

She and the chick could just watch from nearby, nothin' to do but provides morale support.

Summer leaned close and put a comfortin's arms rounds her shoulder, so Moirrey jess leaned in and rested her head on the gal's shoulder, sister-like.

"You'll be more famous than I will, in another century," Summer murmured quiet-likes.

Moirrey's head popped up and looked 'rounds, but they had the dock to themselves. She could do that, *Ritter of the Imperial Household*, and all that. Plus Grand Admiral's nastygram letter that come with them.

Today, wee bit Moirrey Kermode, lost rascal o' Saxilby'n'*Pint-sized* troublemaker, spoke for the Empire. Fer the whole, damend galaxy'n'stuff.

For all of galactic humanity, living and yet to be borned.

Heady stuff, folks.

"T'were necessary," she said back, quiet nuff. "Stops the bad one, let everyone else figures they's own ways for'ard."

Moirrey hugged her tighter with the right arm.

"Plus, we're better than banging rocks together 'cause of you, most planets," Moirrey continued.

"Maybe," Summer said. "Doyle and Piper and the rest would have gotten you there without me. Would have taken longer, but it would have happened. And Henri is one of the few Founders I've ever studied who didn't need a bloody war or revolution to put something in place."

"Music were his war, lass," Moirrey replied. "Only one I knows that good since Baudin sits on the throne at *St. Legier* today. Hopes she writes more."

"Me, too," Summer agreed. "I'm sorry I won't be able to know her as well as Piper or Henri, but the risk is too great. She might see through my façade."

"So yer nots comin' home with us, if'ns we survive?" Moirrey hugged tighter. Both arms went around the tall woman, and *her* arms came back.

Was like being with Mom again, when she was eight and had nightmares.

"No," Summer countered. "That would set off too many alarms and she's smart enough to start digging at that point. But I'll always be at the back of the room, the bubbly airhead *Pops* brought along to keep his nights warm and scrub his back in the shower. Nothing more."

"Is good," Moirrey snuggled in closer. "Thought you said ten years ago that you were disappearing from human history fer now."

"Ayumu Ulfsson would have never stood for it, *Pint-sized*," Summer hugged her tighter.

"Yer da?" Moirrey asked.

"My first commander," Summer corrected. "Back when I was just a Concord probe-cutter, right after the Great War ended. When *New Berne*, the *Union Of Worlds*, and *Balustrade* were all effectively crippled and the *Concord* inherited the galaxy by default. He taught me right and wrong. Javier Aritza is the man I truly consider my father."

"*The Science Officer*, in capital letters," Moirrey noted. "Looked him up once. Not much detail, but his name were still around, after all these years."

"He was even more impressive than *Pops* Nakamura, Moirrey," Summer said quietly.

Fer an android, Moirrey could feel the sniffles take hold o'the woman.

"He taught me poker as a way to read and understand humans," Summer continued. "Protected me when pirates came and cut up my first ship, and then eventually put me on a stolen, First-Rate-Galleon. He was a drunk, a pirate, a scholar, an officer, a clown, and a hero in his time. He's buried on *Altai* somewhere, but I've obviously never gotten a chance to visit his grave. Would never find it, but it would be nice to see that spot where the *Khatum*, Behnam Sherazi, had her palace in those days, even if it has been erased by time. I could find it, and her tomb. He's close by."

Yup. Tears.

Bizarre, but that android body were close enough to human ta fool most doctors without scanners, so thats made sense. Tear ducts an' all. Moirrey'd seen the chest opened up when she put the babe in this body so's she could escape the mean Red Admiral, back when he were a servant o'evil.

Tears fell into her hair now, so Moirrey held her friend close.

"Are there any more, or are you really the *Last of the Immortals*, this time?" Moirrey finally asked as Summer got hold of herself again.

"I'm sure there are others," Summer said. "But they are either well-hidden, or sitting dead in space awaiting a competent mechanic to repair them well enough to return to life. None are in a position to threaten humanity, if we can take *Carthage* at his word that he and *Kinnison* were the last two. *Buran* was supposedly a factory controller, securely boxed up for transit, when all hell broke loose, back in the day. The colony was just barely capable enough to survive the century it took for them to unbox him and assemble enough pieces that he could get to work in the fallen darkness."

"So what're you doin' after *Pops*?" Moirrey asked.

Another heavy sigh shook the taller woman's frame. Tears again, but not as bad.

"Moving on," Summer finally said. "I had considered aging my shell slowly, and living out his last twenty years or so with the man, but I suspect that he's done and going to retire after this. I would like to remember him at his best, rather than watch the slide into entropy."

"It's hard, living forever?" Moirrey leaned back enough to look the girl in the eyes.

"They never tell you that part, Moirrey," Summer said. "I watched Piper turn from a young woman, angry and wet behind the ears, into one of the greatest politicians of her age over the course of five decades. And I visited her tomb before leaving *Ballard* forever, to say goodbye. I have outlived the nation that gave birth to me, and plan to outlive the one that freed me from my cage."

"How long does *Aquitaine* have?" Moirrey's interest peaked.

Here were a scholar who had read most o'human history at one time or 'nuther. No other experts that good available.

"If we can kill *Buran*?" Summer asked. "Centuries. Maybe more. Without Jessica, *Fribourg* would have won in your lifetime, and *Buran* in your children's assuming you and Digger finally settle down."

"That's coming soon," Moirrey said. "I's too important ta keep doing whats I do. He'll hafta settle fer being an Imperial gentlemans and stuff. Then kids and my own, private lab ta builds stuff. Prolly needs an estate big enough that he can have construction equipment ta drive. Builds an amusement parks er som'thin'."

Summer laughed.

"Good," the android said. "Maybe Auntie Summer could come visit you and spoil the young'uns rotten."

"That would be nice," Moirrey agreed.

They kinda turned as silence fell, and watched the big beast of a box slide those last few centimeters into alignment with the rest. At least well enough that *Pops* and Yan were no longer gesturing angrily at each other and the poor teams driving the loaders and adjusting the sleds moving the thing.

She supposed that it weren't a caterpillar anymore. T'were times to becomes a *Butterfly*, and go looks fer a flower to rest on, enjoying the summer sun.

Fall would be on them all, soon enough.

CHAPTER LV

GUNTER FOUND the quiet of the tiny bridge soothing, being alone on the command deck of the strange vessel he had somehow managed to become First Officer of. The others were all noisy, nerdy people, engineers of one type or another who were all interconnected in ways he would never be, except in the minds of the rest of the whole galaxy, once this was done.

And he liked them, but there were times he preferred silence. Like now. It did not break his heart that Ainsley had personally taken charge of the dry-dock crews, and that Lady Moirrey and Summer had decided to watch the entire affair from the comfort of a station observation deck.

He could trust all of them to be professionals about what they did, but nobody was talking to him today. Even less than normal, since Bedrov and Nakamura were on a different channel, supervising the enormous effort to lock that last piece of this three-dimensional puzzle into place.

Gunter brought up a projection of the vessel and color-coded everything based on planet of manufacture, which in turn sequenced the assembly. He still had several minutes before the loaders were in a position to push the power array into the aft slot.

The yard at *Arcturus* had not questioned the order from the Grand Admiral to construct the strangely-shaped vessel. There had been significant bonuses factored into the work, to offset some Duke or shipping magnate having to wait an extra month for his latest vessel to arrive.

Lady Moirrey had suggested a butterfly in her original design, as a way of harnessing solar power to augment the generators in the *Londra* section of the weapon, named for the planet that built it. Bedrov had designed something like a juvenile version of a Transport Tug to handle it and added deployable solar sails that could quickly expand to an area nearly two kilometers in diameter, like the translucent wings of such an insect.

They were indeed flying a butterfly, perhaps.

Geminus had built the first section they had picked up, the focus controls and aiming hardware for the emitter. It made no sense, by itself, which was a significant part of the design, as Bedrov had rehoused a number of components from a scout corvette, to get the fine manipulation he would need later.

Lagos had built the forward part of the emitter array. That pirate had done a great job of vaguely disguising it as an energy transmissions system. The kind you needed to link a solar sail in orbit of a small colony to the ground, when you needed significant power without dropping reactors onto the surface. Mining colonies on ice worlds often used something similar, since the surface of the ice shifted much more frequently than stable ground did.

Londra, their most recent stop before this, had built the aft housing of the array and a bank of power generators that would have been overkill on the old *Paladin*-class battleship *Firehawk*, his last fleet service. But they needed power. Staggering amounts of it, delivered into as compact a form as possible, as quickly as the energy could be siphoned off without everything melting or exploding in the process.

Weevohn's contribution would have given the game away, had they started at the other end when assembling the sword. It contained a few generators, mostly to power up the solar array it was connected to and to keep that element somewhat isolated from the rest of the ship. It also had the single biggest array of batteries ever put together on something smaller than a station.

As Bedrov had explained over beer, it wasn't a question of whether or not the bus bars involved would sublime from the amount of power being pushed through them, but how quickly. Metal could literally evaporate, at this scale.

Gunter Tifft was a logistics officer by training, and a spy by vocation, when he wasn't pretending to be a line commander. He understood just enough of the physics involved to be utterly aghast at the entire undertaking, and to be confident that it should work.

He also had very distinct orders from the Grand Admiral to make sure that none of them were taken prisoner, if everything failed and the ship was trapped in RealSpace, either before or after everything went down. The scuttling charges had actually been part of Bedrov's original design, to make sure that *Buran* could not recover enough pieces of the ship or the gun to build a copy.

Type-4 beams were dangerous enough. A Type-6 was potentially cataclysmic.

Hopefully, it would never come to that. But Hendrik had still made a point to prepare him for the eventuality.

"Gunter, this is Yan," a voice finally intruded on his channel.

"Go ahead," Gunter responded, sitting a little straighter and scanning all his boards once to make sure everything was still green.

"Station team is about thirty seconds from contacting your hull hard enough you'll feel it at that end," Bedrov continued. "Make sure that the fifth lockpins drop all the way into alignment while we have the necessary force handy to drive it to the bolts. I didn't like the way we had to get an angle grinder out to set things right at *Londra*."

"Understood," Gunter said.

Only a minor issue, it had taken them all of about an extra hour to pull the chunk of ship out, grind a millimeter of steel off in a few places, and then line it all back up and press it home. But Bedrov was an engineer, and used to working with very tight clearances on things. Someone, somewhere had failed to meet his exacting standards for implementation, but none of them were in a position to take everything apart in front of witnesses who could describe it later.

Nobody technically had the security clearances necessary to know these things, including the crew of this ship.

The aft of the ship pinged.

IFV Butterfly was docked hard in place, with grapples in three places binding them to the fabric of the station, so that the massive steel puzzle piece could be moved in three dimensions by professional stevedores used to working with the same level of exactitude as Bedrov, but who also understood the need to hit something with a bigger hammer, when necessary.

Today might be their day.

A larger thump, transmitted up the adamantine spine of the butterfly, itself perhaps more of a dragonfly carrying off a caterpillar, if you wanted to look at it that way from the side. That was probably the image Lady Moirrey saw, out that window.

Lights began to come on as connections were made and circuits found themselves able to run front to back on the vessel. For the most part.

"Yan," Gunter spoke up. "Third and fifth lockpins show red. The other six are green. Looks like something has bowed, but I can't tell which part is out of true from here."

"Stand by," Bedrov replied. "Ainsley's got a laser level she's going to stuff down in there. Gimme five minutes."

"Acknowledged."

Gunter reached down to the small refrigerator between the two command seats and pulled out a juice pack. His job was to watch, which he was fine with.

A few minutes passed as he watched men swarm over the hull.

"Tifft, this is *Pops*," the other man came on the line. "I need you to unlock the tertiary housing on section three, but only on the port side. Leave the starboard pins tight."

"Repeat, please," Gunter said back.

Pops did. Made no sense to Gunter, but he wasn't the guy out there watching.

"Stand by, *Pops*."

Gunter tried to visualize the whole, but what the engineers were seeing eluded him. He was just a pilot today.

Quickly, he located the necessary controls and manually triggered the locks to loosen things up.

"*Pops*, you are clear for action," Gunter said as he triple-checked things.

"Watch this, children," *Pops* Nakamura's voice came from the general channel, rather than the one he had been using previously.

Somebody banged the hull with what sounded like the hammer end of a boarding axe. Certainly, nothing larger, or the sound would have been a church bell calling the faithful to prayer. No, this was a winter chorale bell chiming once.

Something shifted. *IFV Butterfly* shuddered once, almost bow to stern like a tiny earthquake, before settling back to nothing.

"Gunter, what are your boards like?" Bedrov's voice joined the line.

"Everything's green," Gunter said.

Every light had clicked at almost the same instant.

"Damn it, I hate it when you're right, *Pops*," Yan groused over the open line.

"Hey, you're pretty good, Bedrov," *Pops* crooned triumphantly. "Almost as good as I am. Only almost, though."

Ainsley's laugh joined Nakamura's. Gunter didn't understand the rivalry between the two men, but he had been around them enough over the last several months to see that there was no rancor involved between them. Just a serious amount of respect, from what everyone agreed were two of the best naval architects alive.

Technically, **EASC** *Carthage* wasn't alive, and the bartender was only a pale echo of the original, to hear the projection talk, but that being, even in his reduced form, was at least as good as Yan Bedrov and *Pops* Nakamura.

Gunter was just glad he was on their side. Things were very shortly going to get ugly.

CHAPTER LVI

IMPERIAL FOUNDING: 181/04/02. IFV VALIANT,
OSYNTH B'UDAN

It felt good to be back in the saddle. Tom knew that he needed to stay away from the dockyard crews and ship's engineers making the repairs or he would have pestered them with his questions and needs to the point someone would have probably punched him.

And been in the right, regardless of rank.

So he had spent a lot of time on the surface of the planet, making political calls on various entities, or in orbit, aboard one of the stations that protected this system. Anything to not slow the work down.

Yesterday, after a significant refurb, they backed out of the dry-dock and slid into open space at the core of Second Squadron, First Expeditionary Fleet. Today he was in his office with Charlie d'Noir, going over the various things they needed to verify before they set off to find Jessica in her new hiding place. He had warned her that it had been too good to last. Fortunately, his warning to Fleet Centurion Whughy had been better received. They had cut and run, pausing only long enough, apparently, to dock one last shuttle craft filled with engineers, before vanishing like a soap bubble.

A voice suddenly filled the room.

"Tom, this is Yasuko, up on the bridge," *Valiant*'s Captain said without preamble. "You need to hear this."

"*Osynth B'Udan* Flight Control, this is Command Centurion Phil Kosnett aboard *RAN CS-405*, flying an Imperial Flag as part of Keller's squadron," a man said in a slow cadence. "Requesting an escort with a senior officer aboard. Reply on this channel, please."

"Thoughts?" Captain Pitchford continued when the recording ended. "One vessel, apparently. Thirty light-seconds out, and at rest relative to the station."

"Drop the squadron on top of them, Yaz," Tom said. "Action stations on all vessels, and put us around him like hounds treeing a fox, like we did that idiot from *Blue Essex*. As fast as we can all jump at the same time, and let the captains know I'm keeping score today."

Charlie was already standing and moving towards the hatch. Tom rose and followed him. Red lights and emergency sirens simulated the necromantic act of raising the dead from their temporary graves midship.

The squadron went from a cold stop to Jump faster than Tom would have been willing to bet money on. Must have been expecting him to walk out of that meeting with Charlie and throw surprise maneuvers at them.

And to keep score.

It felt good to be surrounded by professionals, with all the hunger that went with it.

Sure enough, one of the new style corvettes, flying *RAN* signals with an *IFV* Courtesy next to it, if the transponder was to be believed.

CS-405. Command Centurion Phil Kosnett.

The vessel looked a little worse for the wear, but Tom was willing to grant that taking a year to get home, and today was the anniversary of their disappearance, might not leave someone as clean and sharp as a heavy dreadnaught less than thirty-six hours out of dry-dock.

Tom checked the projection between him and Charlie. Unlike *Firehawk*, the two of them sat across a small, round table. It was a little weird, after all his time standing with the other man close enough to punch.

Four cruisers had dropped out with *Valiant*, almost to the second over this short of a distance. It took him a moment to place the last ship, since he was used to *Dundee, Glasgow,* and *Birmingham* being led into action by *Indianapolis*. But she was off with Jessica.

Qin Lun had done a very nice job of hopping with the squadron. Something to be said for a life of reformed piracy to keep your strike jumps sharp and crisp. Quick count put all seven corvettes with him, sheltering the laager on the assumption that the big sisters could handle a scout corvette in their midst.

Tom opened a line.

"*CS-405*, this is *IFV Valiant*, Tom Provst commanding," he called in a serious voice.

"*Valiant*, this is Kosnett," the intruder replied, opening a screen that showed the man, but not the rest of his bridge. It did look like Kosnett. "We got separated from *Vanguard* after the raid on *Severnaya Zemlya* when both JumpSails were lost. In the process of limping home, we decided to turn ourselves into pirates and have a number of adventures across *Altai* sector. Might have made it here two days ago, but this was too good of an anniversary to miss."

"That would explain a few things that Imperial Intelligence shrugged at," Provst scratched his chin, feeling a little too much stubble. "Their whole frontier got soft, all of a sudden. Were they chasing you?"

"Most likely," the supposed pirate explained. "We attacked *Barnaul*, *Laptev*, *Abakn*, *Kyzyl*, and *Mansi* on our way home."

"You're just a scout corvette, Kosnett," Tom was amazed. "How did you attack planets?"

It did not add up. Even for Jessica's folks.

"That's why I came in alone first, *Vanguard*," Kosnett's tone became almost triumphant, if Tom had to place it. "The rest of my task force is parked out in deep space, waiting for you to come and escort them safely home."

"Task force?" Tom asked incredulously.

He glanced at Charlie across the table, and got a literal shrug, both palms up and face blank.

Keller's folks were known for crazed audacity. Tomas Kigali, or Alber' d'Maine, for instance. He supposed that the corvette commanders would get infected, too, after long enough.

Look at what happened to Second Squadron, just from flying with that woman and her legend once.

"Told you we stopped and raided several places along the way," Kosnett almost sneered at him on the screen. "My crew also took four enemy vessels and pressed them into service."

"You did what?" Tom let his shock show. "How?"

"We're the *Republic of Aquitaine* Navy, *Vanguard*," Phil announced proudly. "That's what we do."

Yeah, one of Jessica's people.

"So what proof do you have that I should believe you, *CS-405*?" Tom growled at this cheeky interloper.

"The best one imaginable, *Vanguard*," came the response.

Tom should have known any guess he might make would be too mundane, too linear.

Too something.

Kosnett apparently changed camera images at his end, pulling back from the personal one on his console, like Tom was using, to the larger view, with the whole bridge crew on screen, even if very few of them were facing the right direction.

"Admiral?" Kosnett looked away from Tom's pickup and said quietly to someone down front.

Tom followed movement as one of Kosnett's people, in what was normally the Pilot's chair, unbuckled and stood.

"My God." Tom Provst was seeing a ghost. "Carlyle?"

"Hello, Tom," Admiral Gustavsson replied in a surprisingly calm voice for a man that had been *Missing, Considered Lost* for almost a decade. "We have a fantastic story to tell you, but first, I need you to help me bring home the rest of my men, and then make sure everyone else has a chance to make it home as well."

"How…?" Tom started to ask.

"We located and liberated a prison planet in *Altai* sector, *Vanguard*," Phil said. "We brought them all home, but my mission is not yet complete."

Tom felt the bottom of his world drop out. He looked at Charlie and put the line on mute for a second.

"Prepare to send the fast courier," Tom said. "Get him in motion to *St. Legier* as soon as he can load supplies and enough crew to make the run, once I record a message to get Emmerich out here. If this is real, we'll need the Grand Admiral on the frontier. Keller's folks might have just done the impossible, and we'll have a very limited time to exploit whatever intelligence they bring home. Find me a second courier to send to Jessica and launch him as soon as we know where we're going next, because it won't be to her. And send a note to General *zu* Arlo. If they have rescued folks from a planetary surface, I know where he'll want to go next."

"On it," Charlie leaned back and began typing furiously.

Tom considered that this might be a trap, designed to pull his squadron far enough away from home that they could be ambushed where nobody could help, but he was willing to push the margins on this one.

He cleared the line again and let his eyes focus on Carlyle Gustavsson. They had worked him up a pretty good replica of his old red jacket, but it hung on the man like a toga. Carlyle looked to weigh half of what he had the last time they had met.

"Send me coordinates, *CS-405*," Tom decided. "We'll follow you out and escort you home. Good thing you arrived when you did. I was close to heading out to meet Jessica, but I'll send her a note."

"Just glad to see a friendly face, Admiral Provst," Phil Kosnett replied. "I was expecting to have to explain it all to a bureaucrat, rather than one of us."

One of us?

Tom supposed that he qualified now, but Kosnett wouldn't have known about the second mission to *Severnaya Zemlya*.

No, the man was talking about warriors, rather than paper-pushers.

They had their place, keeping things organized. Or, in the case of men like Gunter Tifft, sliding through the reams of paper to find the diamond that would have been lost until it was found in the after-action recriminations.

"Transmitting coordinates now, *Valiant*," Kosnett said. "Let me know when you want to jump."

Charlie nodded that he had them, and was bouncing the message to the whole squadron. Then he muted the line again.

"What's our offset, Tom?" Charlie asked.

Tom blanked the camera and smiled. Gift horses, and all that.

"Drop us seventy-five light-seconds long, facing inward, with *Hans Bransch* on point, instead of one of the cruisers," Tom grinned. "And have *Qin Lun* longer and protecting the rear flank. I'll trust a pirate to have his ass covered, and ours by extension."

Charlie laughed and started typing.

Tom opened the audio and video lines again.

"Jump when ready, *CS-405*," he ordered. "We'll follow you out."

CHAPTER LVII

To his dying day, Tom Provst, Admiral of the Red, *Fribourg Empire*, knew he would never forget the image the screens showed him as *Valiant* dropped out of jump.

A monstrous, obviously-civilian megafreighter flagged as *RAN Packmule* dominated the formation when they emerged.

RAN Forgotten Mercy flew just ahead of the freighter. The transponder signal marked her as a captured medical cruiser.

How in the hell had these people managed to steal a floating hospital? And why?

RAN Queen Anne's Revenge was a weird-looking civilian cargo transport, with the addition of a gun mounted forward, where a ramp had been welded shut to fix the emitter.

But the best part was *IFV Persephone* flying in the van. Not *RAN*, but *IFV* on her transponder. She was an old D-Class police cutter, and challenged *Valiant* like a Teacup Chihuahua facing down a Mastiff.

Faced down all of them, as a matter of fact, challenging his squadron's right to be in *Persephone's* space. One heavy dreadnaught. Four cruisers. Seven corvettes.

Hell, Tom's fast courier wasn't that much smaller than *Persephone*.

It brought a smile to his face, once *Hans Bransch* had scanned the space around here for any risk of ambush. With his paranoia cranked up as high as it would go.

CS-405 took up an escort position opposite *Queen Anne's Revenge* outside the line of other vessels and waited for the rest of Tom's force to form up.

"Second Squadron, in line astern behind *Packmule*," Tom ordered. "*Hans Bransch* in high escort, everyone else take up your wings."

"*Persephone*, this is *Valiant*, Tom Provst commanding," he said.

Let the Teacup Chihuahua have his moment in the sun. Tom had enough force, just with *Valiant*, to annihilate these pirates if this was a trap. The other cruisers were just for icing at that point.

"*Valiant*, this is Flight Lieutenant Granville Veitengruber, previously off *IFV Germania*," the captain of Persephone transmitted back. "Now *RAN Centurion In Command* of *Persephone*."

That sounded like one hell of an interesting story, once they got home. How many prisoners were out there? Not forgotten by their mates, but lost. Like Carlyle.

The man looked tall and lanky when the camera caught up. Dark but rather forgettable. Still something burned hot and angry in his eyes, though. It was a look Tom knew well from his mirror.

"Transmitting coordinates now, Veitengruber," Tom said, nodding to Charlie and watching the man send them. "Come out on this vector and prepare for a full customs inspection."

That got an entirely-inappropriate laugh across the comm. Tom presumed that something along those lines had been a ruse for the pirates to get close enough to hit someone.

"Acknowledged, Admiral," the man said. "Stand by to jump."

Tom was impressed with the group of pirates. They all moved as a single entity, vanishing within a second of each other. Tom's team went in right after them.

On the other side, as before, Second Squadron had a small offset, the kind that both lined up his ships for inspection and honor guard, and put every one of the pirates under a Bubble Gun and enough Type-4 beams to settle any issues quickly.

Tom wasn't playing. Didn't matter if Kosnett was offended or not. If he was a pro, he would be expecting it.

And *Valiant* got there first, as planned. Charlie sent off the courier to the Grand Admiral even before Kosnett's squadron emerged, with orders to break records getting home in such a way that Tom Kigali would be impressed when he heard the story, and possibly challenged to beat them at a later date.

Em needed to be here, right now. especially if Carlyle had come home from an unknown prison planet.

As before, *IFV Persephone* flew up to challenge the squadron.

It brought a smile to Tom's face that felt alien, watching one man grieve such a huge force by himself. Tom looked forward to meeting the man and hearing his story.

And then going off and finding all of those men who had been lost over the years, when *Fribourg* had been slowly pushed back and couldn't do anything about it.

Tom was happy to change that.

CHAPTER LVIII

This was not the day Vo had planned. But it was war and he was prepared.

Always prepared. The galaxy will not wait for you to put your gun on.

He and Alan were up in orbit, aboard the massive station that was the bulwark of this system, almost comparable to the one guarding *St. Legier*. They were surrounded by people, but mostly forgotten, except by the two admirals and Phil Kosnett.

Vo didn't know the Command Centurion all that well. Seen him in staff meetings and nodded companionably at each other, but not sat down to have coffee and shoot the shit.

Not that Vo had anyone like that within a thousand light-years.

This latest meeting was drastically cut down. None of the aliens, although Doctor Sam Au had been with them at the previous one, along with the first two prisoners, Kiel and Lan. Much of Kosnett's inner circle was here, but a few were off elsewhere. Probably organizing things because they had the best feel for how to send the other prisoners home.

Vo had thought that Tom Provst would put his foot down, or put a fist in someone's face, when Kosnett calmly announced that *Forgotten Mercy* and her crew needed to be loaded up with food supplies and sent back to *Buran* as rapidly as the engineers could handle the task.

But Tom had taken a deep breath and listened carefully. And then agreed, wonder of wonders.

The anger was still there. Vo could see it in the man's face across the table as they settled for this next meeting, but this wasn't the Tom Provst who had been hanging by a thread fourteen months ago. Nor that deadly, avenging angel that had followed.

It wasn't quite a third person inhabiting the shell, but it was close.

Carlyle Gustavsson wasn't anybody Vo knew, but he could see the hard years in what was apparently a prison camp. Work or starve.

Phil Kosnett had brought a group with him: his First and Second Officers, and his Dragoon. Nicknamed *Lady Blackbeard, Ground Control, Stunt Dude*, respectively.

Seriously?

Two others who were obviously Navy, but wore civilian clothing as if their honor rode on it. Bok Battenhouse, former Boatswain of *CS-405*. Avelina Indovina, who introduced herself to everyone as Duke of *Lighthouse Station*.

Whatever the hell that meant.

Tom Provst and Charlie d'Noir rounded out the group. Not even the local admiral's staff was allowed to be here now. But neither Vo nor Tom had any degree of trust for the locals. Too many spies and loose lips around here.

Phil Kosnett looked up from his coffee and circled the room once with his eyes, lingering for an extra second on Vo and Alan, before continuing. The room was locked and sealed tight, and a little cramped with all the bodies, but the air conditioner was going like hell to keep the heat down.

"*Mansi* would be a useful target to hit, from a psychological standpoint," Kosnett began, extending the conversation that most of them had just been part of an hour ago, in a different room.

When they had been with other folks, the kind that might talk too much around the wrong ears.

"However, there is nothing there worth our effort at present," Kosnett continued, nodding to Gustavsson. "We liberated all the men alive at the time, and if three died on the trip home, they died as free men. We know where the rest of them are buried and can return at a later date to retrieve their remains."

Vo felt a surge of emotion from an unaccustomed place as he heard those words. He had refashioned himself as the avenger, destroyer of *Buran*, but Kosnett had become the liberator, rescuing the men that had disappeared over the decades, as *Fribourg* slowly lost a two-front war.

"Recommendations, then?" Tom asked in a voice like the gravel bed of a dried river.

He held command here, with Jessica gone. That was why the local Blue Admiral had been pointedly ignored. Second Squadron and the 189th would do this themselves.

Tom Provst would make that call.

"*Lighthouse Station*," Kosnett said. "We've established the beginnings of a forward base on the planet, and could easily expand it. The place is, as far as we know, unknown to *Buran*, as long as we're careful. None of their captured maps show it inhabited, and none of their highways get even close. It is in a dark pocket, as well, surrounded on most sides by empty space and older stars starting to hit the red giant stage, although that star is young enough not to bother us."

"What do we gain?" Tom asked.

Vo leaned forward to study both Kosnett and Indovina as the conversation progressed. She could make a legal claim of colonization. And had already filed the necessary legal work to become the Duke of the place, as soon as *CS-405* had gotten to the station.

Whether Casey would allow it was another question, but that wouldn't be decided for years anyway.

"There is a whole planet, about a quarter of the way off dead center of the *Altai* sector as we face inward," Indovina jumped in. "Inhabitable and pleasant. Enough space to drop several legions of troops for training and recuperation. We can put a station in orbit to handle warships. And then you can go stomp on all the other little systems around *Altai*, without having to come all the way back here each time, or live cramped on ships, instead of in barracks. We gain time, mobility, and surprise."

Her gaze was fixed on him. She looked way older than twenty-two, and reminded him of Dash and some of the folks of Fourth Saxon. Stubborn enough you could get rich if you could just figure out how to bottle it and sell it.

"It also provides a place we could build a hospital facility," Kosnett added. "*Forgotten Mercy* was taken because we needed to be able to transport an unknown number of men in suspect health an extreme distance, and a troop transport would have been too well guarded. From there we can hit places like *Barnaul* or *Laptev* and complete some of the task of rescuing people from slavery."

"Vo?" Tom turned and pointedly asked.

"I don't answer to Jessica, Tom," he replied. "Em's building me three new Assault Carriers, so we can send *Akatsuki* and *Archangel* home one of these days, but I plan to extend the *RAN* ships to a second year of contract service. Jessica and Arott might decide to join us there. Or maybe keep a second front in place, but I'm in favor."

"I am as well," Tom agreed. "Your legion can provide some of the construction forces we need, but I'd like to get Em out here and have him round us up a group of permanent settlers for the Duke. And the initial batch should all be active duty or recently retired."

Tom turned to the Duke and fixed her with a hard stare. Vo nearly laughed out loud when she stared back and Tom blinked a tiny bit. That admiral still wasn't prepared to deal with hard women.

Vo had been around Jessica, Dash, and Casey. Grown up around them, if you wanted to look at it that way. If Avelina wasn't in their league, she wasn't a pushover either.

"I realize you claim the entire planet, Your Grace," Tom went ahead and treated her like the Duchy was a done deal. "I propose a settlement zone, outside your immediate valley, where colonists can place claims and purchase leaseholds. And a couple of military facilities, also under leasehold for now, although the Crown may demand those convert to freeholds at a later date."

Vo nearly laughed out loud when the woman reached down and lifted a satchel onto the table. He hadn't seen it earlier, but she had gotten here first and was across from him.

He watched her pull a stack of papers as thick as his thumb and smack them down on the table in front of Tom with a resounding thump.

"*CS-405*'s legal department has already prepared preliminary documentation, Admiral," she smiled at the man like a mongoose goading a snake. "Two settlement zones have been identified and I have completed a preliminary survey of tracts. Two army training bases and a security barracks. Two starports, one serving the primary city I envision down on the coast, and the other on land claimed by my first colonist, where it can serve his ranch and my eventual palace grounds."

Vo had seen a lot of emotions on Tom Provst's face over the last couple of years, running the entire gamut of humanity. He had never seen the man at a complete loss for words, jaw hanging slack.

But Avelina Indovina had obviously spent a lot of time thinking about this, and had the obvious support of everyone aboard *CS-405* to pull it off.

Tom just hung there for several seconds, as his mind caught up. Finally, he nodded and turned his attention to Vo.

"You were close to packed, right?" he asked.

Vo nodded, but kept the rude smile off his face. Inappropriate. Correct, but inappropriate. Sternness was called for. Even as much as he wanted to giggle right now.

"Affirmative," Vo said. "Mostly packing the freighters right now, but my men and their vehicles are ready to go."

Tom turned back to the young woman across from them.

"I can exercise *Force Majeure*," he said simply. "However, I do not have the authority to authorize payment up front. We can provide a significant labor force, for which we would bill you later, and you can in turn bill the government for leaseholds. Is that acceptable at present?"

Vo liked the way she turned to both Battenhouse and Kosnett, and waited for them to nod, before she agreed. She might want to be a Duke, and be on her way, but this was a larger thing, and involved affairs of governments probably well beyond anything she ever envisioned.

But she was also *RAN*, if on a bizarre temporary duty assignment under Kosnett's authority. Jessica would have all their heads if they mistreated the young woman. Assuming Casey didn't come after them first.

There were no women Dukes in the *Fribourg Empire*.

Not yet, anyway.

Vo just needed to help her secure that, as well.

CHAPTER LVIX

It had been a simple enough note, passed along from Vibol, the Master Tailor who served all and none of them at the same time, that brought Em down to the surface.

After knowing a few folks like Vibol in his time, Em assumed that the man considered his time here to be a mere residency, working on some government grant to pursue art for its own sake. Perhaps a performance art piece.

But the note has suggested, in rather specific terms, that a visit by the Grand Admiral to the Imperial Palace would not be a waste of his time. And nothing Vibol did was accidental.

Em had rescheduled the few things that Hendrik couldn't handle, and caught a shuttle to the ground, landing mid-afternoon in such a way that Strasbourg was winding itself down. The city might never sleep, but Em and others, like Torsten Wald, had issued adamantine orders that people were to work no more than ten hours in any one day, or forty-five in one week.

Rebuilding this planet would take a generation. Burning out the people doing the work by demanding the impossible would only make it take longer. And it was a gorgeous, spring afternoon. The wind had died down, leaving a glorious sunset and weather currently in the high teens.

So Strasbourg was allowed to rest. And enjoy itself.

It had always been a quieter town, removed from the heady brew of business that had been Werder. The waterfront meant that folks were here for relaxation as often as official duty, and that had not changed much.

Em enjoyed the view of the docks as his boat approached the waterfront. On his left, a wall of palaces stretched for kilometers along the shore. On his right, the main lake-side park that ran along the water, shadowed over by the towers of the downtown district, and newer towers rising in any space that someone could afford the land.

He preferred to land at the new starport across Lake Zurich and take a water ferry. Navy had once meant a maritime thing, riding atop the waves, and then later under them, before finally escaping into the endless depths of space.

He could imagine what some of the ancients felt like, sailing home to meet their sovereign. Drake, returning to Elizabeth I, for example.

As the small boat approached the dock, a party emerged from a nearby building and formed up at the edge of the pier. Em recognized Torsten Wald in the center, and the rest were Household Guards.

When they docked, Em made his way onto dry land and took Torsten's hand.

"You are not the welcoming party I had expected," Em said.

Wald grinned.

"A certain tailor suggested that you might be coming for a visit," Torsten said. "And that I might meet you here. One does not disappoint Vibol."

"Indeed," Em agreed.

One did not.

The group, including Em's marines and Torsten's *Household Guards*, began to move towards a nearby parking lot, where Wald's transport awaited.

"Do we know why it was necessary that I be here?" Em asked in a quiet voice.

The men surrounding the two of them were trustworthy, or they wouldn't have the job, but some things did not need to be blared across all channels.

"Your niece is feeling morose," Wald offered. "Vibol suspected that, with Lady Moirrey off on a mission, Casey is feeling lonely, and needs someone to talk to."

"It frightens me," Em offered as they reached the vehicle and opened the hatch. "How well that man understands things that should be esoteric to an outsider."

"I had the same experience last fall, Emmerich," Torsten said, following Em into the back seat of a stretched repulsorlift sedan. "Were he any less loyal to Jessica, I would have concerns."

They rode in companionable silence. Casey had always referred to Em as an uncle, but that was the result of being one of the few males of a close age with Joh when they were infants, and being close enough to the blood. And Joh's friend.

Em was actually a first cousin, once removed to Casey, as those things were counted, but his daughter Heike had frequently been a sitter for the Household when she was younger, and Em had been Joh's Best Man, as Joh had been his.

Close enough to brothers, especially if Casey needed family to talk to.

Once at the palace, Torsten and his group left them. Em felt like Jason about to enter the Maze, facing the door to her suite. He nodded to the guards on either side as he waited. These men did not answer to him, so he could only make polite requests.

Anna-Katherine Gonzalez opened the door and beckoned him closer.

"Is she taking surprise visitors?" Em asked the young woman.

Anna-Katherine turned beet red at some inner thought, and took a deep breath.

"She should," the lady finally said in a quiet voice. "Or perhaps you should barge in when I open the door to ask?"

"Lead," Em commanded lightly. "I will follow."

The new palace was a vast improvement over the old hotel, but it lacked some of the homeyness, as cold, stone walls had not yet been personalized with art or decorations in the mad rush to move people first and add beauty later.

There would always be another task on the list.

Em followed Anna-Katherine deeper into the maze and waited a polite distance when the woman knocked at a door and then stuck her head inside.

"You have a visitor, Your Majesty," she said.

"I do not wish to be interrupted," Casey said in a half-growl from the other room.

"Not even for me?" Em called loudly.

"Em?" Casey asked, almost in shock.

Anna-Katherine stepped to one side with a relieved smile and Em entered into Casey's outer chamber.

The Emperor rose gracefully from a couch and rushed forward, embracing him like a life preserver on hostile seas.

She wore a simple, mauve dress, something Moirrey had sewn from the look of it. Over her shoulder, he noted an open bottle of wine on the side table, half empty, and a book she had dropped on the floor in moving.

She might have been crying, or just shocked. Em held her tight against his chest as she let all the emotions spill out.

Finally, she sniffled and leaned back to study his face.

"How did you know?" she asked.

"A little mouse whispered in several ears that you were down," he said, detaching himself enough to lead her back to the sofa and sit her, while he went looking for a glass for himself.

This was a formal room for entertaining guests, with a wetbar, so he found something good enough, and returned to pour a glass of red.

"It's hard," she began, as he sat in a nearby chair and sipped.

He nodded.

"A year ago, I had to be everywhere, doing everything," Casey continued.

"And now you're afraid that nobody needs you and you have been forgotten," Em completed the thought.

"Yes, how did you know?"

"Your father used to bitch at me for the same thing," Em said. "When Karl VI and Ailina were killed in that accident, he had to walk away from his naval duties and become Emperor overnight."

"I don't do anything," Casey wailed.

"And neither did he," Em replied with a smile. "He used to accuse me of dreaming up adventures, just so I could go out and do things, while he was stuck here in the palace. There might have been a kernel of truth to that."

"I feared this day," Casey's mind was obviously all over the place, so Em just sat back and let her talk. "Jessica and I used to talk about the corset called Imperial Responsibility, and what it would mean, back when I expected Father to live another thirty years and me to just have to deal with marriage."

"And you have it magnified," Em noted. "Joh at least had Kati inside that trap."

"And without Moirrey here, I have no one to talk to on personal issues," Casey nodded. "What do I do?"

"The thing you have that Joh did not is your art, Casey," Em offered. "I understand that the grander the emotions, the greater the outcome, so perhaps not all of your work will be suitable for public consumption, but you are uniquely suited for another symphony. I have heard parts of what you have constructed to date. More would help with your long-term goal to rebind the Empire into a tighter whole."

"Really?" she asked, sounding more like a young woman and less like an Emperor.

"They all have loss, Casey," he said. "Very few of them have the gift to share it. Right now, they think they are alone in their sorrow, but you could bring them together."

"Perhaps," Casey said.

She finally remembered her own glass of wine and took a sip. Em joined her, because she always had access to the best stuff. Except when he had managed to steal a few cases here and there from Joh's cellars when the man wasn't looking.

"I was thinking about Moirrey today," Casey offered, unconsciously running her hand down the dress, as if she could touch the engineer across the light-years. "Missing her."

"And no, I have not heard anything," Em said. "The group is under strictest silence, so it is possible we will never hear, if they fail. Only in success will we know."

Casey grimaced and nodded. She had read the mission statement. Approved it herself, like Joh had once been required to do, at the point when those orders had to come from the very top.

Especially when they involved asking for the assistance of a *Sentient* system.

Em had spoken with the bartender twice since Gunter and the team had left. Once, to nail down a specific answer to a design question that had come up, with regards to the new technology that the being had taught Yan Bedrov and *Pops* Nakamura.

The second time, to try to understand what it must have been like for Bedrov and Barret, walking into the lair of the War God himself to drink wine and tell lies to each other.

Em could not imagine the courage it must have taken, for Bedrov to do that. The man was gruff, rough, opinionated, and brilliant.

That had required a *hard as nails* beyond what most of his officers would ever imagine, let alone achieve.

"What happens after?" Casey finally broke the silence that had descended. "If they succeed?"

"It is my fervent hope that the Three Kingdoms Period happens, Your Majesty," Em said. "The Librarian, the Provost of *Alexandria Station*, had made multiple backups of herself, and stashed them in a variety of places, but she was still trapped by my assassin."

"Your assassin?" Casey asked pointedly.

It dawned on Em that he had probably never talked about the *Battle of Ballard* with Casey as an adult. Even a precocious thirteen-year-old lacks the depth of experience to understand most of the words he and Joh had spoken at the time.

"Mine," Em confirmed. "That was my mission, my vision. My dedication to evil."

"Evil, uncle?"

"Evil," he confirmed in a heavy voice, emptying his glass and reaching for the bottle to refill it.

"I had been beaten by Jessica twice, and it tweaked my professional reputation," Em said. "So I laid a trap for her at *Ballard*. Would have destroyed her, were it in my power. I failed, and in that failure might have saved the galaxy."

Em felt his eyes grow distant with memory, back a decade and standing on the deck of *Amsel* as he dueled to the death with that woman. Casey sat up straighter and listened, but Em was elsewhere.

"Em?" Casey prodded.

"I destroyed the station that housed the songbird, Casey," Em said. "The woman who had brought humanity back to the stars, but never threatened them. Jessica escaped. Suvi escaped, at least in that they were able to rebuild her later from the plans she had left behind. Without Jessica, there is no *Thuringwell*. No Peace. No Lady Moirrey nor Lord Vo. *Osynth B'Udan* might have fallen by now, at the rate we were losing systems in those days. Sigmund Dittmar might have prevailed, and you would be dead or married off to that bastard as a prize. One hell of a failure, huh?"

"I'm supposed to be the one depressed, uncle," she said carefully, drawing him back into himself.

"And that, you are," Em agreed. "If we kill the *Lord of Winter*, one way or the other, my hope is that we can keep the regional Khans and Ministers of the First and Second Rank from rebuilding the beast.

Without that central intelligence, we can push back, or just hunt down his ships and kill them, which is Jessica's plan."

"And the worlds left behind?" Casey asked.

"Become colonies filled with weirdoes, Casey," he said. "Ancient China, prior to the First Diaspora, was a unified culture and nation for the longest time, but early on, it fragmented for a stretch that lasted centuries, depending on which set of records you use. If Moirrey or Jessica can succeed in killing the beast, your grandchildren can deal with it."

"You don't have plans to try to absorb them into the Empire?" Casey asked delicately.

"They outnumber us, both in planets and population, Casey," he said. "And represent a culture so alien that trying to conquer them turns into the worst possible guerilla warfare. Give them a generation to figure themselves out, and for our traders to penetrate *The Holding*. You can use that time to shore up *Fribourg* and make the changes you want."

"I see," she said, sitting up straighter again. "You mentioned grandchildren, Em."

"That I did, Casey."

"What do I do if he doesn't come back?" she asked.

Ah. That was what had brought him here. Whatever Vibol had seen, or heard, that compelled the man who in turn required the government and Navy to move.

Em took a deep breath and held it for several seconds before he let it go.

"We have a list," Em admitted. "Torsten, Hendrik, and I put it together. Plus a few others. It is a rather fluid and unofficial list of men that might make a good match, if worse came to worst and we had to fall back on political maneuvering, rather than your first choice."

Her eyes flashed angry, but that receded quickly. She was, at the end of the day, Emperor. That required certain ways of thinking that were alien to most people.

"And?" she asked.

"None of them are Vo," Em admitted. "A few are pale reflections of the man, but none capture that vital essence that held *St. Legier* together. Most of them solve other problems that might crop up."

"Such as?" she demanded, voice growing hot.

"How many Imperial gentlemen are likely to settle for being merely an ornament?" Em asked, letting the sneer creep into his voice. "You will rule, as well as reign. All he brings to the table are his connections to someone else, and the ability to father children. In time, he might, *might*, be accepted into the inner circle, but that's going to be me and Tiede for now, plus people like Tom Provst and Hendrik, who have proven their loyalty to your person, rather than your chair. Blood is no longer good enough entry into that room. He will have to settle. Who might?"

She paused in thought.

"Not many," she agreed. "Plus he will have a wife that is an artist and a warrior. A free-thinker and a revolutionary. A rebel in ways that will make most of them exceedingly uncomfortable."

"And you must in turn find him interesting, intelligent, passionate, and handsome enough to bring forth a new generation of offspring that will secure the Empire."

"You are a cold, vicious bastard, when you want to be, Em," Casey noted.

"Oh, no, Casey," he countered. "This is Torsten's doing. He's tougher, meaner than Tom Provst, if you will grant me that conceit. If he hadn't met Jessica, Wald might have been high on your list, just because of who he is and what he's done with his life. And he's the one checking names and backgrounds and determining who we might fall back upon, if necessary."

"Another uncle?" Casey stared at him.

"At least," Em said. "He's good enough for Jessica, Casey. And I knew *Warlock*. I had recruited that pirate in the first place, to overthrow Arnulf Rodriguez and claim the throne of *Corynthe*. Vo might have held their hearts and minds safe, but Torsten held your government together long enough for the rest of them to save it. Never forget that part."

Her wine was empty, so she refilled it. Drank some. Pondered. Stared at him as if she could read his soul.

"Thank you," she finally said.

Em nodded. He had known this girl since she was born. Watched her grow into a bright child, a stubborn teenager, and an Emperor.

As Vibol had obviously noted, sometimes she forgot that the rest of them existed to protect her. To keep her safe, because in doing so, she would keep them safe.

Now he just had to hope that Moirrey, Jessica, or Tom Provst could keep Casey safe.

CHAPTER LX

Tom didn't like it, but there really wasn't any way around it without causing more problems than it was probably worth. He had learned to trust Jessica's people, and Phil Kosnett had made it clear he was willing to become a royal pain in the ass on the topic.

Em might raise a stink later, but this couldn't wait. Tom wanted to strike as rapidly as possible.

So he had let Kosnett drag him down to a dock well away from the military operations. The man's three primary troublemakers were here as well: Lau, Skokomish, and Mildon, as well as the last two prisoners: the husband and wife combination known as Lan and Kiel.

They all watched as a tug delivered the last box of cargo into the stern of a relatively-new Windward-class Type Two transport.

Tom had been aboard the cramped vessel the aliens had owned before being captured. Kosnett's teams had done a great job cleaning it up, but it was still tiny and old.

This new boat was the same hull-type that many rich nobles used as personal yachts, converting some of the cargo space aft into extra crew quarters and rearranging bulkheads to make larger cabins for themselves.

Tom had personally signed the paperwork classifying their old freighter as a warship for valuation purposes. Again, he could have raised a stink, but he was pretty sure both Em and Jessica would have words for him if he had. Plus, Lan and Kiel had worked with Kosnett's folks once they understood how things would shake out.

Tom might personally loathe what they represented, but the man and woman themselves were okay people.

The male was nearly in tears, watching a year of effort and waiting come to a happy end point.

"Beautiful," he whispered, holding hands with his wife and staring out the porthole.

"Thank you," Kiel said to Kosnett. "A year ago, we doubted."

"A year ago, so did I," the Command Centurion's voice got rough with emotions. "But for your help, none of this would have been possible. But for your standards, it would not have turned out the same."

"Our standards?" Lan asked.

Tom marveled at the trust and friendship that had blossomed between the two sides, watching the smiles from all the *RAN* folks. It reminded him that he worked for Jessica now, so anything might be possible.

"At each station," Kosnett said. "At each decision, I was reminded that there were more options than simply violence. With Doctor Au, she finally became convinced that she might serve evil, simply by not questioning the will of a God, regardless of its orders. As one does not. Yours was the ethical standard that infected all of us, not to worship or fear that god, in turn, but to treat one another as humans, and to remember that our humanity stretched across the boundaries of culture that separate us. We retained the moral and ethical high ground by never ceding it. Never cutting corners and allowing our baser natures to run free. For that, I thank you. As does my crew."

Tom was surprised at the ping of emotion that he felt in his chest. He had thought those things were forever burned out of himself by now. Maybe he was wrong?

"And now?" Lan asked.

"Now you will return home," Tom commanded, understanding that a line needed to be drawn in the sand as a permanent demarcation. "We have tuned your new vessel to the highest standards possible, and are loading it with cargo, but you will become the enemy again soon. My crew will board to fly you to the edge of the planetary system, and then debark so you can return to *Buran* space. I will not say you are welcome to return here, as I consider you enemies of my nation and my Emperor, but I will also issue instructions to the locals to treat you as a neutral vessel, if you call again. And I speak with the voice of the Grand Admiral himself, and Jessica Keller."

Tom was as surprised at his words as the others. An hour ago, it had been his intention to order them to leave and never return. But that would not be right.

Both aliens bowed formally to him, and then more deeply to Kosnett, but Tom understood that he was the terrible ogre, and Phil and his crew had turned into friends.

"What will you call her?" Kosnett asked them in a lighter voice.

Lan turned to Kiel and smiled with a mischievous glint in his eyes that reminded Tom of the looks he and Karoline would share when they had an inside joke.

"We had considered several names," the man smiled wickedly. "Things like *405*, or *Queen Anne's Revenge*, or perhaps even *Kosnett* were entirely inappropriate, to say nothing of the security troubles if we called it *Mansi*. In the end, one name struck as the perfect way to remember our time with you, and the possibility of finding truth and honor among the barbarians. As we did with our friends."

"Indeed?" Kosnett smiled with them.

"Indeed," Kiel agreed. "We will call the vessel *Lighthouse*, for all the obvious as well as the subtle meanings that only those of us who were there would know."

Tom watched Phil bow to the twosome, as did the other three officers, all of whom had remained silent until now.

"I will let Bok and Avelina know," Phil said. "They will appreciate the joke."

Tom didn't get the laughter that ensued, but he didn't figure that it mattered.

"I will see you aboard shortly," Tom said to Lan and Kiel after things settled and turned serious again.

He nodded to the group and departed, working his way around the hallways to where his men were holding the boarding gate. The others would be along shortly, and Second Squadron would head out.

Inside, Tom made his way forward to the bridge of the ship that would be known as *Lighthouse*. Two of his men were completing pre-flight checklists, and another several should be aft, stowing the cargo and checking that all the systems were running nominal.

Kosnett and folks joined them about ten minutes later. The bridge was overly crowded with all the bodies, but everyone pressed themselves flat against the outer and rear walls to make space, so it wasn't all that bad.

Two seats, side by side and facing forward on the uppermost of three decks. Two more jumpseats, facing outward port and starboard, could be lowered and activated, if you had a larger crew, or the ship had a military profile. Tom had seen a version where gunner and shields were back here, with commander and pilot forward.

Tom looked around and counted noses. And smiles, like this was the start of a new adventure.

He considered that anything might be possible.

"Pilot, are we ready to launch?" Tom asked louder than was necessary.

"Affirmative, Admiral," the man replied.

"Open a channel to *Valiant*," he ordered, waiting for the man to nod.

"*Valiant*," Charlie replied. "d'Noir here."

"*Valiant*, this is Admiral Provst, aboard *IFV Lighthouse*," he called the cadence slowly. "All vessels stand by for departure."

"All ships read green, *Lighthouse*," Charlie replied.

Tom smiled. That included *RAN CS-405* and *IFV Persephone* today, as well as Second Squadron and a pair of *RAN* Assault Carriers.

He supposed that operational security demanded that Lan and Kiel be confirmed to be away before he left, so they could not report on his task force, but at this point, it really didn't matter. He would be where he was going before the aliens could convince anyone that they had actionable intelligence.

And Tom still figured it was an even bet that the bureaucrats back home in *Buran* threw the pair in jail and confiscated the transport before listening. It was too crazy a tale to believe, except that Tom had read excerpts of Kosnett's logs. And personally interviewed Doctor Sam Au before letting her go.

Tom looked around once to set this image in his memory.

"Pilot, take us out," he commanded. "All vessels conform to *Lighthouse* and form up in lines astern."

The flight didn't take all that long, even with time spent organizing his various teams to make everything pretty. Tom made sure his shuttle came alongside first, so his departure would free up Kosnett's folks to have their own emotional farewells without him cramping things.

Kosnett's shuttle docked as Tom's pulled away, and he probably made it to his flag bridge about the same time that Kosnett did his.

Charlie smiled as Tom settled.

"So they turned out to be human enough, after all?" Charlie asked.

Tom shrugged.

"They're just people, Charlie," he said. "Civilians, at that. My beef is with their lords and the god that thinks he should dictate terms to the rest of the galaxy. Those folks I'm going to crush like bugs."

Charlie nodded, as much to himself as to Tom.

"Second Squadron, this is Provst, aboard *Valiant*. I have the flag," Tom said as he activated the comm. "Standby to jump. We're going hunting."

PART FIVE

CHAPTER LXXXV

CHAPTER LXI

Jessica marveled at the sight on her console, as *Indianapolis* accompanied *Vanguard*'s Squadron into orbit above what was apparently the newest Imperial colony, embedded deep in *Buran*'s *Altai* sector like a tick in a dog's fur.

Lighthouse Station.

Second Squadron was already here, and had been for about a week. Vo hadn't combat-dropped his legion onto the surface, but he hadn't slacked, either. Arott would be sailing in shortly with his forward base, all set to turn it into a proper orbital facility.

Once they started growing food on the surface, she would need far fewer runs home to keep everyone fed. Then a mining and metals processing facility like Moirrey had helped finance on *Thuringwell*, and Jessica had a good chunk of her infrastructure behind enemy lines for as long as she could keep it secret.

And *CS-405* had made it home. Better, they had done it in the most adventurous way imaginable, as she had read from Phil Kosnett's logs.

"Jessica," Enej said to draw her eyes and smile up. "Your shuttle will be docking in about ten minutes."

"Thank you," she said. "You hold the fort while we're down on the surface."

Enej nodded, returning the smile, as she unbuckled and rose.

Back to her cabin for a satchel filled with mail from Tom Provst, Em, and Torsten. Plus a letter from Casey, but that was entirely personal and she just wanted it handy to savor tonight.

Because this was an Imperial affair today, she wore red. She would, after all, be officially meeting the Proviso Duke of this planet, however young the woman might be. She was still a female Duke. The first, as far as Jessica knew.

It was a generation of Firsts in *Fribourg*.

And since she was leaving the ship, her squad of bodyguards accompanied her. It would have been nice to have someone like Amala Bhattacharya with her, but that woman was still at *St. Legier*, keeping Seeker safe and having her own adventures. Still, Jessica had Marcelle and Willow, to go with the team of Imperial ship's marines Reif insisted upon.

The shuttle from *Vanguard* was a little packed, but hers was the last stop picking up bodies from the corvettes. She noted the fierce smiles from the men and women around her, as they all thought about seeing their lost duckling again.

The flight down was quiet, so she read, tucked back in a corner with Willow next to her and Marcelle across. The details made for interesting reading, even the fifth or eighth time she had reviewed the material.

The war was about to get intense. Not desperate, but *Fribourg* had done something so out of character that Jessica figured she would get all the blame anyway.

Even if it had been hatched by Yan and Moirrey. Plus an imposter that had accompanied the flight.

Summer Ulfsson might have made herself look Jessica's age, and turned into a graying blond when she had been a freckled redhead before, but Jessica knew those eyes. Those cheekbones.

And Moirrey had to know her as well, so *Pint-sized* had approved the *Last of the Immortals* secretly joining the mission. Nobody else would know the woman on sight, except Marcelle.

Jessica's tall assistant had just raised an eyebrow when Jessica had mentioned that *Pops* had a new girlfriend, like *Why was that important enough to bother with?*

They had been alone in Jessica's office, so she had also shown Marcelle the picture, and watched the woman's normally impassive face blanch. But they never spoke of it in public. The two of them, along with Moirrey and Summer, probably represented the biggest conspiracy against humanity that anyone could imagine. Even Enej and Saana Robles only knew that such a conspiracy might exist, but didn't know any of the critical details. The ones that would get them executed.

And hopefully Jessica would get to meet Suvi one more time, before she finally did disappear from human history.

Marcelle reached out and touched her knee now, bringing Jessica back to the present as they were about to land. She brought up a quick console view and watched as the shuttle was on final approach.

The huge lake ran nearly end to end in the otherwise closed-off valley, with one deep gorge draining the basin.

Voices picked up noise now, going from a murmur to a low roar. Several shuttles were already on the ground, representing Second Squadron, as well as a D-class boat Kosnett's team had stolen, *RAN Persephone*, commanded by a former Imperial pilot, former slave, and enlisted Centurion named Granville Veitengruber.

She had instructed Tom and his folks not to make this a formal welcoming ceremony, and he had apparently passed the word along. As Jessica exited the shuttle, she was just part of a mob of command centurions and security marines.

She was not prepared for the two people that met her.

They were on horseback, both of them. A young woman and a much-older man, standing their mounts side by side. They dismounted as Jessica got closer, and she got her first good look at Bok Battenhouse and Avelina Indovina, First Colonist and Duke, respectively.

The woman was young, but held herself well, surrounded by folks so much more senior and older, when she was technically just an Able Spacer on detached duty for now.

Battenhouse was much older, in his early sixties and close to retiring after a lifetime of service. He had claimed the entire north half of the valley as his personal ranch, which included this first starport.

The locals led this mob to a building on one side of the quad. It was a meeting hall that hadn't been on the plans or in the images Jessica had seen of the earlier work, so it must have gone up in the last week. Horses got tied to horizontal posts apparently set for exactly that purpose.

Up the wooden steps and inside, she could smell the still-drying paint and see places where the finishing touches were still to be done, but they had raised this place in a day, just like a barn back home. Jessica had seen a few of those at her aunt and uncle's farm, or their friends, when she was young.

And now the palace had a meeting space for visitors and trade missions. Jessica suspected that Avelina would add a hotel on her side of the lake, once things settled down. What many needed to know was how much time Vo's men would be training, and how much would be spent in barracks, where they might work on their carpentry skills. A thousand soldiers with hammers and saws could accomplish an amazing amount in a short time.

Phil Kosnett waited in the middle of the floor when Jessica and her group came through the front door. He rose from the table where he had been seated with other commanders and got utterly engulfed by the much taller Tomas Kigali. Others joined the hug.

She waited and organized the various bodyguard units: hers, as well as those belonging to Provst or Denis, to line the walls and make themselves scarce.

Vo was here, along with his First Officer, Alan Katche. She gave the big man a hug and shook the other's hand. She could do that now. They had all grown up, finally, she supposed.

Once Kosnett emerged, she walked close and startled the man with hug as well.

"Welcome home, and good job," she said, watching Phil blush.

He hadn't been one of her students, but someone Petia had originally selected, giving the man the choice of a scout corvette on the war frontier or a teaching assignment somewhere, when there were suddenly more bodies than command slots available.

Based on his last year, what the man really deserved was a fourth stripe as a Fleet Centurion, and his own raiding squadron of cruisers and marines. Maybe she would suggest it to both Petia and Em, if the war continued to stretch on like this.

Finally, after twenty minutes of chatter as everyone met their counterparts, the group settled down at the various tables. There were nearly forty men and women present, and that just represented the Captains and Command Centurions of the various units.

Jessica rose and moved to where everyone could see her.

"If both people beside you are wearing the same color uniform, stand up and move," she ordered lightly. "This is one team, and I want you to think of yourselves that way."

More chaos. *RAN* folks immediately surged out of their seats and looked around, while the Imperials took a moment to grasp the finer point she was trying to make. They were still a little hidebound, even for this group.

Finally, back to something calm. More or less.

She pointed to Bok and Duke Avelina, both wearing civilian garb and tucked off to one side of the group.

"Our hosts, Bok Battenhouse, *CS-405*'s former Boatswain who now owns this side of the lake, and Duke Avelina Indovina of *Lighthouse Station*," Jessica formally introduced them to the group. And made it clear that they were not just handy civilians.

A quick round of applause and noise that settled down.

"Now, some important news that nobody else in this room is aware of," Jessica continued.

Around her, heads leaned closer, almost as if a tide was coming in.

"Many of you know Yan Bedrov, who did most of the design work for the various warships overhead," she said. "He and *Pops* Nakamura, Crown Designer of *Corynthe*, have helped Lady Moirrey of *Kermode* build a new weapon. They are heading up a team of specialists to test and possibly use the weapon as we speak. Our orders from the Grand Admiral and the Imperial Throne are to step up our actions against *Buran*'s fleets here over the next six to twelve months."

The *leaning in* had turned to a low, almost unconscious growl from the group.

"Em wants all eyes focused on us, so Moirrey can complete her mission," Jessica said, staring frankly at the men and women looking back. "That means risk. At *Severnaya Zemlya*, we had surprise and overwhelming force, and still got mauled pretty good. But that was a main sector base, as well."

She found Phil Kosnett at one table, with Kigali on one side and the newest commander, Veitengruber, on the other. She pointed at the group.

"Phil Kosnett rescued an amazing number of men from a prison planet recently," Jessica turned to make sure everyone was looking at the former slave. "We're not going back to *Mansi* today, but soon. Instead, we're going to hit *Barnaul*. It was the first intelligence and food raid by *Queen Anne's Revenge*, commanded by Kosnett's Second Officer, Siobhan Skokomish. The whole of the colony is a small city, next to a huge pit mine. Our expectation is that most of the men in that mine are either *Buran*'s criminals or captured Imperial sailors being worked slowly to death underground. We're going to fix that, either way, by destroying the colony."

The growl was larger and uglier this time. She had released an expurgated version of Kosnett's mission logs to everyone, so they knew what Phil and his team had done over the last year.

Aquitaine and *Fribourg* had always traded captured men and women home, none the worse for wear, even in a war that had lasted over a century. Neutral third-parties like *Wilankadu* had handled all diplomatic functions, at least until the Peace came and the sides finally talked like grown-ups.

Jessica knew the Imperial captains would happily bombard the world from orbit. Hell, some of her longest-serving men and women had once helped her slam a small asteroid into a moon of *Sarmarsh IV*, as a way of *negotiating* with a group of pirates.

"General *zu* Arlo," she turned her attention to Vo now, odd man out from this group, but for different reasons.

Her folks knew him as one of their own, made extremely good. And most of them didn't know the extremely secret bits that both Torsten and Em had shared.

To the Imperials, Vo was the *Hero of St. Legier*, larger than life.

Vo nodded at her. It finally felt like Vo wasn't nervous around her anymore, which said something about how far he had come over the last decade.

"You brought the *Arsenal*-class troop transport *Dieter Jost* with you when you left *Osynth B'Udan*," Jessica said, noting the captain that perked up, seated not far away, but hanging closer to the transport commanders than the front line fighters.

"That is correct, Admiral," Vo rumbled back. "The vessel does not have any troops aboard her at present, but is prepared. Similarly, Senior Centurion Lau's *Packmule* has been refurbished and loaded full, under the command of a new *IFV* crew picked by Admiral Provst."

Calm. Certain.

Deadly, if you could see the fire that burned in the man's eyes.

"Your job will be to liberate *Barnaul*, General," Jessica said. "Miners who wish to leave, regardless of nation of birth, will be welcomed aboard and flown to *Osynth B'Udan*, after which that task force will return here. For smaller raids, we can always transport rescuees on our ships."

She noted the way Centurion Veitengruber sat up straighter and made eye contact. It felt like he wanted to raise a hand as she turned to him.

"Centurion Veitengruber?" she asked.

"Regardless of nation of birth, First Centurion?" he asked carefully, noting her *Aquitaine* title, rather than the uniform she wore.

It was a loaded question. This officer could not return to polite Imperial society with the man he loved, who was also a refugee from the far side of *Buran*, to top it all off. That much had been made clear in Kosnett's logs and subsequent messages.

"I'm aware that we may evacuate people from *NovLao* and other places, Centurion," she said. "It is my presumption that they would rather be free at present while we work out how to get them home later. Some may even choose to emigrate to *Fribourg* or to *Aquitaine*, at least in the interim. All who wish to leave will be welcome."

The man nodded. *Deni* was aboard *Persephone*, listed as a supernumerary crew in engineering, but Jessica knew the truth about their relationship. Provst as well, but all he had been required to do was approve the transfer request that enlisted Deni in the *RAN* as a Landsman.

"How hard do we push, First Centurion?" Tom Provst spoke up now. "Supporting Lady Moirrey?"

He had most of the pieces, except Moirrey. And she would be bringing him into that secret tomorrow.

And *Pint-sized* had even more of a hold on some Imperial officers than Vo did. Partly, that was how charming the goof could be around them. Partly, it was how close she was known to be to Casey, and what it meant that they had served together. Jessica knew that those same men put *Jessica Keller* in a category with Vo, more force of nature than human. And that was fine.

Moirrey got even more points from this audience for personally killing two different top assassins from Imperial Security. Most Navy men loathed the other service.

Moirrey had repeatedly proven herself smarter and harder than men who prided themselves on their toughness and their discipline.

"Her mission could win the war, Tom," Jessica said. "Save the Empire itself. If the rest of us have to be collateral damage, a tool ground down to nothing to give her that shot, it is a price I am willing to pay. And most of the rest of you, I suspect."

Growls. Cheers, Exclamation.

Yes, love for *Pint-sized* transcended cultures.

Tom's eyes narrowed, but he held his peace. Obviously, this was too large a group to explain it all to. Even with Order 48 ensuring that no command officer be taken alive for questioning, as they knew too many secrets that could compromise this frontier.

Thus, Kigali's emotional response to seeing Phil alive, when everyone else had expected him to be sacrificed, along with Lau, leaving Skokomish to bring *CS-405* home by herself.

And *Lady Blackbeard* could have handled that task, based on the record. Jessica looked forward to maybe raiding *Mansi* soon, just to give Lau and Skokomish their own warships, like Veitengruber had.

Gone were the days when Jessica could have her command centurions over for tea. Or just bridge, back when it was Denis, Alber', and Kigali.

Now she had a fleet, poised on the edge of ruin, or victory.

"Other questions?" she asked, looking around.

Too soon, for the most part. Too little upon which to gamble, when Jessica would tell them sometime soon.

In another week or ten days, Arott would have a temporary battlestation overhead, waiting for Em to deliver the pieces to make a permanent replacement. The 189th would have the start of a permanent operating barracks as well. Em would be scaring up construction engineers as best he could, in order to build even more of an economy here. It would be needed.

Especially if *Pint-sized* pulled it off.

CHAPTER LXII

DATE OF THE REPUBLIC JUNE 1, 403 THE
BUTTERFLY, MIDDLE OF BLOODY NOWHERE

"I KNOWS nobodies can find us here," Moirrey hadda ask. "But ya dinna breaks it, did ya?"

Interestin', Ainsley growled the loudest. She 'spected Yan ta bitch. He were heads down on a console with Gunter, checkin's somet'in' an' mutterin' some fierceness.

"If we did, it might qualify as a design flaw," *da Vinci* said sharply, scowling up at her.

Not *da Vinci* no more, but sounded way more like hers, and not like chilled-max Ainsley Barret.

Still, Moirrey kept her mouth shut. Fewer flies that way.

The bridge were still a might testy. Gots worse when *Pops* meandered in and took one looks around. Almost walked right back out silent-like, but Ainsley see'd him and spoke.

"Well?" Ainsley snapped.

Moirrey hunged on pins and tridents fer the words. *Pops* looked like he swallered a goldfish whole.

"Good news, bad news," *Pops* finally equivocated, lookin' likes he wanted ta duck incoming beer bottles. "We can fix it. The overload was a result of a tweak we made to one of the crossover arrays. The system briefly hit six point seven on the output curve, before blowing every damned fuse it touched. If we bring it down to a six point five threshold, it should maintain that for at least thirty seconds."

"Bad news?" Moirrey asked.

It were her baby they was messin' with.

"The power fluctuations at that level are still too much to program against," *Pops* said. "We'll have to hold it by manually adjusting things. Give me and the kid a year and we could build you a feedback suppressor that could do it, but nothing sooner. Figure time trumps money and safety."

"You'd be correct," Ainsley and Gunter managed to say in perfect unison.

Like they'd practiced it, er somethin'.

Gunter nodded and let Ainsley yammer.

"The Grand Admiral has told Jessica by now," Ainsley said. "Unless we scrub the mission, there is no way to easily send a message to anyone to back down, after we asked them to go to the wall on this one. What are the risks?"

Pops screwed his face kinda sideways and thought while Moirrey watched.

"We blow up with it, if we take it that far past safety measures, holding the beam," he decided. "Or we bail early and the system shorts out and stops working. Scuttling charges are on a chemical fuse, so they'll go boom, but we might not pull it off, and we'll give them too much information about how it was done if a *Sentient* system survives to analyze the wreckage."

"Agreed," Moirrey said. She could do that, with the most known experience with AIs in this group.

Known. Summer probably would have agreed, too. It were 'mazin' what a super-smart box could do, given enough time and high enough threat.

"Okay, one, we have the best engineers the Grand Admiral could send," Gunter spoke up. "Two, we're all volunteers on a known forlorn hope. Wills have been updated accordingly."

Kid were fierce. She hadda give 'im that.

And grin at the words he chose.

Bad translators in the way back had turned the old Dutch phrase *verloren hoop*, literally "lost heap" or "lost battalion" into the thing sounded closest in English, "Forlorn Hope." Then they goned and done transmitted it to the stars later as a miscommunication that sounded neat, until ya knowed the meanin'.

Still referred to a group of folks walking inta a meat grinder, expectin' ta be killeded in the doin's of th'thin'. Like them.

"So," Ainsley speared the kid with her glare. "All in?"

Gunter's face got scary-cold as Moirrey watcheded.

"I watched *Second St. Legier* from orbit, Captain Barret," he growled, fierce-like. "Many of my men did, as well. *All in* to them means trying to hold the generators together so we could turn them off after we succeed, change the aim of the ship, and pick out more targets to hit, preferably on the ground, killing things until someone finally finds us and blows this ship to pieces. After that, we'll storm Hell and make sure the beast has a front-row seat."

Wowsers. Even Ainsley blinked.

Yan spoke up now.

"It will hold," he said in a promise to the death that they might all hafta cash. "I have a tweak I want to program, and then a couple of bus bars to see about moving, *Pops*. Then we'll charge everything up and take another shot. Not like that damned planet's going to mind."

Moirrey glanced out the front window at the rock they was orbitin' and hadta agree. No atmosphere. Carbon-black surface with red blotches from iron underneath gettin' 'sposed by meteorite hits. And three shots from the *Butterfly*, carving new formations inta the rock itself.

Nasty stuff.

"Imma help Summer cook," Moirrey suddenly decided.

She and the babe couldna talk much 'bout *important* stuff, with all these boys, and one girl, 'rounds, but were nice to be with her. And she had the best cookbook in her head Moirrey's knowed. Of course she didn't tell these folks where she learned the recipes.

But Moirrey standing to leave did the trick o'suckin' crazy out of the air.

Yan and *Pops* headed aft. Gunter and Ainsley did a rock/paper/scissors to see who stayed on the bridge. Gunter won and followed.

Ainsley could stew for a while. Moirrey'd bring her some wine in a bit and it would make the world all a better place.

And maybe after dinner, they'd figure out how to make a god go boom.

CHAPTER LXIII

THE NUMBERS NEVER LIED. Torsten had seen experts who could make them dance. Cause them to mislead the lazy or uninformed. But never lie.

And he was probably as expert on numbers as anyone outside of a Department of Mathematics.

So the truth made him uncomfortable.

All that crossed his mind as he entered a private chamber specifically set aside, on the fourth floor of an isolated wing in the Hall of Government.

Four men stood watch outside in the hallway. Armed and generally polite. Ruthless, though. His badge got checked twice before he could enter.

Inside, the room had not changed appreciably since the last time he had come here a month ago. One narrow table ran down the middle of the wide room, providing a metaphorical curtain wall and moat for the four men on the other side. Various binders stacked up suggested crenellations, and he occasionally expected arrows or boiling oil on his side of that wall.

Torsten took a seat and watched the oldest man over there. He had not brought anything with him to this meeting. He never did. No paper. No tablet. Even his personal comm was back with his secretary, in case Casey suddenly needed to reach him mid-afternoon.

Just his mind, and his memory.

And four of Her Majesty's most capable spies and analysts prepared to brief him out of cycle.

That never boded well.

"Should the Grand Admiral be here?" Torsten asked as the two sides stared across the curtain wall.

A pause to consider.

The oldest man had a name. Torsten even knew it. But none of those four liked to be called by anything but random code designations and such, even inside this building.

Safer for their lives, if nobody could ever connect them with what they did.

The oldest over there might charitably answer to *Six*, as his position on the org chart fell first after five political appointees who oversaw the myriad intelligence structures that crossed so many halls and departments.

"We do not believe so, as yet," Six spoke carefully.

Always shade the definitive. Nothing in this job could be declared, except in the past tense. And rarely even then.

Torsten nodded. They had asked him to come here for a top secret briefing outside the usual. That meant danger at the highest level.

"Our outfit has many tentacles," Six began slowly.

Carefully.

Hydra, octopus. Whatever.

"Some of what we uncover is ignored as deliberate obfuscation by our enemies," Six continued. "False leads designed to identify internal leaks when we react to something only a handful of people might know."

"Understood," Torsten acknowledged.

"Some of what we do involves coalescing tremendously large data sets and applying a variety of statistical analyses to see what oddities need to be followed up," the spy said. "You are one of the few people in high government that could follow some of our tools and models, but that's not why we asked you to join us. We do have the modeling notes handy if needed."

Econometricism. Analysis of numbers by turning them into trends and extrapolating them outward. The hard edge of what many dismissed as soft science.

The numbers that never lied.

You could misinterpret them. Random events could significantly alter baselines and cause you to see patterns that didn't exist.

But the spies knew that as well as he did. Would have redone the numbers a variety of ways. Handed the results to a superior, who might in turn hand them to an unrelated team to blindly replicate.

Many hands touched it before Six saw the results.

They must be good.

Or bad, as it were.

Torsten nodded again. It was almost a kabuki he played with these men, but everyone understood. Some foolish politicians sought the definitive when building sand castles in the rain.

Others might assume this was nothing more than reading tea leaves.

Torsten knew better.

"The Grand Admiral is a military man," Six said. "A man of action. This is not a military issue. At least not yet. Our threat originates in the civilian realm."

Good. Em had enough on his plate already. Adding restive nobles would be perhaps a bridge too far.

And it would be nobles. Commoners, by themselves or in small groups, did not represent a threat. If they gathered into large enough groups, they became movements, and the government had tools to engage them as well. Thwart them if necessary. Redirect them where possible. Many got introduced to the Hall of the People and given a chance to see the sausage of government being made.

A few even stuck around and made sausage.

The nobles would be the problem. Always.

But there were tools to deal with them, as well. The new Hall of Justice had the pieces seconded from Imperial Security, as it was being dismantled, to investigate things. It must fall outside of their purview.

Or they found something. Something dangerous. Something terrifying.

Torsten blinked and caught his breath. Sat back a little in his chair, having unconsciously leaned forward.

"Tell me," Torsten steeled himself.

"The Palatine Governor from *Aquitaine*," Six said. "Judit Chavarría. Former Premier of the Republic."

Yes, that would be terrifying. The people liked to think of *Aquitaine* as a new friend of the Empire, but that was seeing Jessica Keller rescue them, time and again, from an even more dangerous foe. And their own stupidity.

Judit was a power in the Republic, magnified by her decades-old friendship with the current Premier, Tadej Horvat. And she was here, speaking for Horvat's government.

And apparently making Torsten's spies nervous.

"What has she done that we could prove well enough to go public?" Torsten asked, leaping forward from the assumption that these men were competent at their jobs.

Public was the key. If you had a double-agent in place, the last thing you wanted to do was out them, unless they held the balance of the Empire and you had no choice.

Better to get your enemies on something simple and indirect, like tax evasion, rather than bring in a witness to testify, especially if that witness could continue to burrow in after deeper crimes with the survivors.

"Very little," Six said. "She appears to have both a perfect understanding of the legalities and subtleties of this art, and very loyal people around her, exhibiting great competence."

"But she slipped up?" Torsten pressed.

"Not that anyone would have caught her, without doing the numbers-crunching we have done."

"Tell me," Torsten commanded.

"Her meetings are generally of government record," Six began. "Not what was discussed obviously, but who she met with, as she is a foreign agent operating in the heart of the empire. There is a pattern."

Pattern. The magic word. The thing that caused data analysts to turn cartwheels in hallways, if they stood up to academic rigor.

As these would have had to, to come to Six's attention.

Torsten nodded understanding and let the man continue.

"Many of her meetings are trade related," the spy said. "Opening up the caravans of commerce to perhaps bind the two nations more securely into a peace by adding an economic quotient to the balance."

Torsten smiled. Rarely were spies also poets. Even Jessica accused him of sounding like a college professor too often.

"But we have our own list of nobles that is complete, and more detailed than many outsiders probably imagine," Six smiled back. "We try to rate every noble, from the lowest Freiherr to the highest Duke, with a ten-point scale on a few dozen axes of motion. Intellect, power, charisma, and loyalty factor highly. Most nobles score in the middle on most things, as one would expect. Those are generally conservative folks, not given to transformation that might not benefit them."

"What's your normal cut-off for human analysis?" Torsten stepped the conversation forward. Experts on a technical topic, rather than politicians looking to grand-stand.

"Two standard deviations from assembled mean causes a file to be flagged," he replied. "Three causes it to be reviewed immediately. Subsequent quarterly evaluations with the same results usually involved Imperial Security attaching resources to a case."

"Both ends of the scale?" Torsten pressed.

"The super-patriotic can be just as dangerous as the revolutionary intent on burning things down, Chief of Deputies," Six said. "Those sorts of men can frequently convince themselves that their actions were for the greatest good, at least as they interpreted it, rather than how a larger pool of folks might consider some outcomes. The Empire is too fragile for anyone to be allowed to rock the boat right now."

"Good," Torsten agreed. "Some people have not come to understand that my job is frequently to do nothing, so that people do not feel they have to react to me. Casey is the same way, although she chafes at such restrictions."

"And after you, Chief of Deputies?" the spy fixed his gaze. "We measure your reign with an hourglass, not a henge."

That was solid truth. Jessica would eventually return home to *Petron*, taking him with her, he hoped. Another man would step into his shoes at that point. Would have to deal with the rivalries of a newly-emboldened House of the People not necessarily willing to cede power back to the reconstituted House of Dukes, phoenix risen from the ashes of Werder. And they would have Kasimira Wiegand on the throne to contend with.

"Who has Chavarría met with?" Torsten deflected the conversation back onto its original course.

"Nobody and everybody," the spy retorted. "None of her meetings were problematic. The pattern was."

"Elucidate," Torsten commanded, feeling like the august professor Jessica occasionally accused him of impersonating.

Socrates, challenging Plato to speak truths rather than academic platitudes.

"If we eliminate a certain class of nobles from the equation, things change," Six said. "Those men with significant holdings arranged in such a way that trade with *Aquitaine* would be immediately beneficial, who at the same time rate fives and sixes on all the relevant political scorecards. The remainder are an interesting cross-section of men with values three and below, and seven and above."

"The threats at both ends?" Torsten saw, but held his word back.

That was the risk of espionage: Seeing patterns that perhaps did not actually exist, but lined up when crunched through a computer that was only as smart as the man programming it and the man reading the results.

"At both ends, yes," Six said. "With an equal balance of the two."

"And that matters because?" Torsten asked.

"If she were up to mischief, she would generally meet more with the trouble-makers, as we identify them," Six replied. "If she were looking to support the Empire in the future, the opposite."

"What if she were trying to encourage pure disruption, and seeking to identify the best way to draw those battle lines to bring it to fruition?" Torsten asked. "While retaining clean hands in the process?"

"Then it would look remarkably like the current outcomes, Chief of Deputies," the spy's face and voice got serious. "And we would want to escalate our findings to the very highest levels of government, without necessarily letting outsiders realize what we may have suspected or uncovered."

And Casey would not want to declare the *Aquitaine* representative *persona non grata*, particularly not at the moment when their single best fleet was what was turning the tide in the war on *Buran*. The Senate might take the insult personally, and withdraw all assistance as quickly as messages could be sent.

The Peace would probably hold, but it would certainly chill things awkwardly at an inopportune moment.

Knowing Judit, as Torsten had come to after studying the woman, he would not put it past the woman to know exactly how to dance that ledge safely.

"Is it worth pre-empting her plans by having hard and unpleasant meetings with some of these people, or would that escalate things at the wrong moment?" Torsten ventured.

"We cannot judge the delicacy, sir," he replied. "The pattern we have identified is not robust enough for predictive power. At least not yet."

"Find me weak links we could spall off," Torsten decided. "Men we could drag into a quiet room and sweat, providing some of the evidence gathered, in order to force compliance with the government's wishes."

"Both ends?" Six asked.

"Both ends," Torsten agreed. "Humans are naturally lazy. Every day I can force them to do nothing is another day everybody else learns to live with the new way of doing things. My way. And after a while, the majority will have no interest in going back."

"As you command. Chief of Deputies."

Torsten rose and left the man and his three ghosts behind in the room. He backtracked his way to his own office. Some of this he would need to tell Casey.

And get her decision as to how much he should tell Jessica.

That was a fracture line nobody could adequately predict.

CHAPTER LXIV

The weather today was lovely. Calm and pleasant under clear skies, so Jessica had collected Denis, Tom, and Iskra, and gone for a walk. Right now, they were several hundred meters uphill from the bunkhouse, watching a parade of workers move like ants as new buildings went up.

If she squinted, she could see two other groups across the lake, building up a wharf and laying a foundation for the Duke's first palace, however small it might be. It would still become a seat of power.

Jessica leaned back against the fence that separated this cattle pen from the open pasture above them on the hill. Battenhouse had a team of apparently-expert sailor-cowboys helping gather up all the cattle that had been left to go feral. This pen was still empty for now, but that would change in another day or so.

The horses had apparently walked up to the gate when humans returned, happy to be fed and curried regularly. But she wasn't surprised, after hearing Vo's stories about *Thuringwell*.

Iskra looked the most serious today, facing her. Denis was calmness itself, waiting for clues so he could prepare. Tom Provst's eyes were distant, but without the anger or despair Em and others had warned her about.

"What I am about to tell you is part of a new classification so high that neither *Fribourg* nor *Aquitaine* have formal rules for it," Jessica said.

"As Torsten joked, we're not even allowed to know it ourselves, and must promise to forget everything afterwards."

That got a smile from Provst. And scowls from the other two.

Weird.

"Moirrey came to me with a concept a while ago," Jessica continued. "Something Yan had said about planet-crackers had triggered her imagination."

"Can you actually build a planet-cracker?" Iskra asked sharply, but she was an engineer, and that was what they did. "Blow up a whole, damned planet?"

"I have no idea, Iskra," Jessica said. "Probably, but my guess is that the amount of energy you would need to harness is a significant portion of the output of a normal star. And I'm sure some mad science fiction writer has created a Sunbeam by lasing the entire output of a star, at some point. They're like that."

"Got it," she said. "Sorry."

"No, it's a good question," Jessica replied. "Moirrey apparently built something smaller, with the help of Yan and *Pops*. And by smaller, it apparently classifies as a Type-6 beam."

Denis and Tom both muttered the same profanity at the same time, looked at each other, and grinned. Iskra's eyes got wide and she whistled.

"What the hell do you do with something like that?" Tom asked finally.

Jessica looked around, just case, but even the birds were keeping a respectful distance today.

"They're going after *Winterhome*," Jessica said.

"But you just said this wasn't a planet-cracker, Jessica," Denis countered. "What could they hit to make it worth doing?"

"The Golden Pearl," Jessica said, quoting Seeker's poetry from **Lord of Winter**. "The magnificent orbital platform that houses the god-machine known as *Buran*."

"*Alexandria Station*," Iskra breathed.

Jessica nodded, watching the light dawn on the two men.

"Moirrey understands how the station is built, because she was able to stop the assassin aboard *Alexandria Station* with Suvi's help," Jessica began to hedge the truth. "They eventually failed, and Em destroyed the place, but Suvi was able to transfer backup copies of herself, I suppose you might call them, off-site, and those were enough of her memories and personality that they could build a new one later."

"Can someone rebuild *Buran*?" Denis asked.

"Not if we keep up the pressure," Tom replied. "Kill the king and then keep killing anyone that tries to build a new one. My question would be what his fleet does without its master."

"And that's why we push," Jessica said. "Em's going to start shifting units and ships forward and sideways, ignoring some systems while dramatically reinforcing *Osynth B'Udan*, *St. Legier*, and others. He's also going to start raiding the systems behind us, everywhere except *Samara*, like we did before *Trusski*. Like us, his goal is killing every Hammerhead, Mako, and Tigershark he can lay guns on, on the assumption that without the god, they might not be able to replace them."

"They can still build warships, Jessica," Iskra noted.

"Yes, but what good are those, if men and women must do everything?" Jessica asked. "They don't have JumpSails, unless they get them from us, so they are slower and less precise in their jumps. And they'll know it. My hope is that the regional khans will rise up and decide to seek power for themselves. Human nature has always been that way. Having a God in charge won't change that."

"So suppose we do kill *Buran*," Tom asked. "Then what?"

"Short term, we kill any facility that might be turning out replacement parts for gods, if we can," she answered, holding up her hands. "The silicon parts of a *Sentient* system are a dozen or so boards, about this size, according to what Suvi told us. Their fleet has always been small, but each of those ships might have the requisite tools to become gods themselves, with a little work. Or the freedom that we'll give them."

"Do we know where they make those parts?" Denis asked.

"No," Jessica said. "But I suspect, without any evidence, that *Buran* would want it close. Perhaps under his direct control. He was a manufacturing factory controller, so perhaps he makes them himself. He might also have built limiters into them, to stop any other *Sentient* from challenging his authority."

"Aboard the Golden Pearl?" Tom's smile turned ugly, but it matched hers.

"We can only hope, Tom," Jessica offered. "If so, then it might be two birds, one stone time. But I'm prepared to go after shipyards next, or whatever factory might make them instead. And yes, I'll happily bombard that sort of place from orbit until it becomes a radioactive crater for ten thousand years."

"I'm in," Denis announced. "Collateral damage and all."

"Me, too," Iskra nodded.

"Tom?" Jessica asked.

"Destruction, First Centurion," he said calmly. "Utter destruction. I'd happily drive *Valiant* into the ground personally and detonate it, if we found the place where they built those parts."

"Good," Jessica said. "Now, understand. What I have just told you can never be repeated, at least until Em or Casey give you direct permission. If we were able to build this weapon, someone else could figure out how and replicate it. Moirrey's done her part to keep the information as scattered as possible, but we probably need to take this to our graves and beyond. Questions?"

"Add it to the list," Denis smiled at her.

Yes, she supposed that they did have a number of secrets between then. Not the biggest ones, but he had been her right hand, right fist, for more than a decade. Torsten and Moirrey might be the only people she trusted more than Denis.

"I will remind you, then, of Order 48, and all that it implies for this secret," Jessica's voice got serious.

Order 48: No commanding officer, including Tactical Officers who exercise command authority in combat, can allow themselves to be taken prisoner by Buran's forces. They will exercise any and all options to evade capture, including self-termination, if the officer feels that is the only way to keep the information in his or her head out of enemy hands, in the event of probable torture.

It was ugly but necessary.

The other three faces joined her in seriousness. *Buran* might be able to do something to stop Moirrey, if he knew what was coming.

Their job was to distract the beast with explosions and chaos, over here. Speed up the music, as Yan Bedrov liked to say, until the beast tripped and broke a leg.

"Again, questions?" Jessica asked after a few moments.

Heads shaken in the negative.

"Then I need you to plan for *Barnaul*," she continued. "At *Stanovoy* we introduced retribution. At *Yenisei*, we laid a trap. At *First Severnaya Zemlya*, we gave them fear. *Second Severnaya Zemlya* was about raising the bar to include personal destruction on the ground. *Second Barnaul* will not be an extinction event. I want them scared, but not desperate. Always give them a way out. But we will break the back of *Barnaul.*"

"*2218 Svati Prime?*" Iskra asked. "Except a real radiological bomb this time?"

"Look into what options we have," Jessica replied. "The images I have seen are a giant pit mine with tunnels, so I'm not sure we could even do that much damage with Type-4s from orbit. Losing the workforce will be a heavy blow. Losing the mine for a generation will probably kill the colony and they'll have to evacuate."

"Chaos and fear," Tom Provst said. "Do we stay long enough to bait a trap?"

"No," Jessica said. "We'll move on and hit someone else. Every time they have to send a fleet after us, there is a chance we'll hit someone else who's undergunned where we come in, or a system like *Stanovoy* where we can crush all the stations and annihilate their transportation sector. I don't care if they eventually want peace. I can't see Casey accepting any offer that doesn't involve *Buran*'s processors on a stick, and I can't see a god accepting self-termination as the cost of peace."

Tom nodded. So did the other two.

"Okay, you have your orders," Jessica said. "Let's go kill things."

CHAPTER LXV

WITH AN ENTIRE PLANET TO pick from, Vo had to give Duke Indovina
and *CS-405*'s staff credit for picking out a particularly choice patch of
land as the first training base for the 189th to colonize.

Fort Kosnett, named for the Command Centurion responsible for the
planet.

Coastal, so they could practice short-range beach assaults with the
skiffs. Always a surprise maneuver.

Mountainous, with two shallow ripples of hills paralleling the coast.
The outer one captured all the moisture blowing inland, so it was green
and lush, with citrus fruit mutations growing wild. The inner one,
forming the first valley, was drier, brown for the most part. The area
inland of that was a basin that channeled briny creeks into salt lakes
before draining into the aquifer underneath and turning pure again once
it got down through a few layers of sandstone and other things.

Thirty-five kilometers up the coast, where the climate got nicer, they
had laid the cornerstone for the new city of Commencement. Sixth Ala,
with all the earth-moving equipment, plus a few heavy tanks with dozer
blades, was busy cutting a road grid for wheels and tracks, and the second
starport. That was the big one that would handle DropShip-class
deliveries for the Army, and medium freighters once the colony was large
enough to take them.

Today, maneuvers. Because they were down in that basin inland, a patch of desert surrounded on all sides by mountains and a few passes, they could practice with live ammunition occasionally. Not so much that they ran out, but enough to keep everybody sharp. Something about bangs kept the rust off the men.

Vo was up on a ridge with the best magnification lenses he owned, watching various Patrols and teams maneuver below. The men had been cooped up on the Assault Carriers for too long so they were occasionally getting carried away.

That was okay. He wasn't keeping score. This was just to burn off nervous energy for the teams that had drawn the short straw. The other half of the legion was sweating in various construction details. And in three days, everybody would swap.

As Vo watched, *Sledgehammer* element lined up and cut loose into a pile of rocks designated as a hostile turtle. It was about the right size and height, and even the particle cannons on the Assault Guns couldn't do that much damage.

Vo felt a presence stir next to him. Heard Alan grumble under his breath. Mostly the usual profanities.

"We need to build our own turtle," Alan finally said aloud.

Vo lowered the electronic telescope and looked over at his friend.

Friend? Yeah, probably. They had been through too much together to not be tight.

"Why?" Vo asked.

"Well, not a proper mechanical terrapin, boss," Alan said with a sigh. "Unless Lady Moirrey could come up with something for us. I want something that moves. And is the right size and shape. Shooting back with lasers or small, paint-filled cannons would also be nice."

"You'd blow it to hell with the first shot, Alan," he noted.

"Only if we use live fire, Vo," the Primus Pilus grinned. "I don't want those lazy bastards getting used to shooting at rocks that just sit there."

Vo grinned back. Small chance of it, with these men. But Alan was planning for the future. For the next generation of troopers coming up as these men started to retire.

An idea struck him. Vo laughed outright. Alan turned to stare up at him.

"So maybe we get the biggest cargo skiff we can buy," Vo said. "Or have a motor pool Decurion build one with spare lifters. Mount a couple of spare turrets out of stores, and get the armorers to modifying them, to shoot paint rounds or something that goes a long ways, but disintegrates on impact."

"Build six legs like landing pylons?" Alan asked. "It would be ugly and slow, but so was that damned turtle at *Severnaya*."

"Yes, and ring it with targeting sensors, so we can score games," Vo decided. "Have Alistair come up with a damage scale. If the thing works out, we can build a couple more and transport them across a variety of terrains for training."

"Any chance they built that giant man-machine thing Lady Moirrey dreamed up?" Alan's voice got hopeful.

"No." Vo said simply. "Wrong culture."

"Huh?"

"*Buran* is all about the collective action, Alan," Vo explained. "One man in a fighter is all by himself and can do things without others watching. Same if he has a gigantic, powered exoskeleton. He steps out of unit control. *Buran* wants every ant in his place at all times. The Mechanical Terrapin requires a whole team of people to operate so there's no risk of someone running off when battle starts."

"Oh," Alan replied. "Never really thought of it that way, but it makes sense. Lady Moirrey maybe come up with something like that for us?"

Vo laughed at the wide-eyed greed in Alan's eyes.

"I'm sure that someone, at some time in the past, has built one, Alan," Vo said. "Someplace like the Library at *Alexandria Station* might have the plans. Or you might have to find a way to bribe Lady Moirrey."

"She owe you any favors?" Alan's voice was hopeful again.

Vo laughed.

"I still owe her, Alan," he said. "Last time I was at *Alexandria Station*, an Imperial assassin shot me square in the chest armor. I'd be dead, but she chased him off and eventually killed him, while others got me evaced down to the planet below."

"Too bad," Alan replied. "Could have been fun."

"Not really," Vo countered. "I'm rated for heavy EVA armor. It's a pain in the ass, any time you're in gravity. The gun's nice, but smaller than you've got on one of the skiffs. Only thing you gain is being invulnerable to most small arms, and the ability to pick up a car and tear it in half if you want to. Your grandmother could outrun you in open terrain."

"She can do that now," Alan laughed. "Some grandmothers take up knitting. Mine does half-marathons."

Vo could only imagine that. Alan was a little older than him, thirty-nine to Vo's thirty-five, but that would make the man's grandmother probably somewhere in her eighties or older.

The moment got sober. Conversations did that, when you let them wander around.

"So what about *Barnaul*?" Alan asked. "They dangerous?"

Vo turned to look at the man more squarely.

"The day one of your lances can't take out a Shore Patrol, Black Maria, riot control van, I'm gonna have to put you out to pasture, Alan," Vo announced.

Alan's grin was a kilometer wide.

"Was thinking about those dump trucks, Vo," he retorted. "Damn things could squish a skiff."

"Vulcanized polymers for tires, Alan," Vo sniffed. "I don't care if they're probably reinforced inside with chain mail. You have to have a solid, flexible gripping surface, and you'll have to spread the mass out over a big footprint, if you don't want to sink. They're tough, I'm sure, but they have zero armor, as we count them. Again, if you don't think you can handle it, I'll send Pyotr over. It'll give Chilikov's crew a chance to get crazy."

"Actually, that might not be the worst idea, Vo," Alan got serious suddenly. "Alien invasion, and all that. Especially if we withdraw them immediately after things settle down and hide them. Maybe suggest we've genetically-engineered monsters, or something. Let the survivors play that up when the story gets retold."

"You are an evil, evil man, Alan," Vo shared the sudden grin. "Rearrange the assault planning to drop the Vikings on them first at both the city and the mine. *CCLXXIII Heavy* can rumble through town behind *Sledgehammer* and then we pincer the city from three sides. And have Fourth and Fifth Ala train together for a week with the rest of you off building houses. Jessica's going to want to leave soon enough, but we'll drive that with our need to pack up the first round of DropShips."

"Got it, boss," Alan smiled and went back to his optics.

Vo did the same.

Down below, *Sledgehammer* had backed off and was beginning a new run, in a new formation.

Vo didn't expect anything big at *Barnaul*, but you never knew when somebody might think they could stop the 189th Legion.

CHAPTER LXVI

COMMON ERA: 13450, DAY 152. WINTERHOME.
PALACE OF THE ELDEST.

THE FUTURE LOOKED BRIGHTER than Han remembered. Stepping back from ultimate control as First among even the *Mandarins* had freed him. He felt thirty years younger, watching the three others who represented the generation behind him grow into themselves.

In less than sixty days, he would depart the Golden Pearl that had been his home for half a century, retiring to the land of his birth, below on *Winterhome*. He would leave things in capable hands, even if not quite the cast he had expected. Wa Dahnna Lomek Gar, Minister of the Right Facet, had suffered a mild health event, possibly a heart attack that never quite materialized, but Han had not pressed for the details.

The Eldest had chosen to retire the man gracefully, as he would need time to recover. His replacement, Au Griblee Austur Wol, was a baby in this group, just turned seventy-two years old, and was built like he should have been a Warrior, but he was a deep thinker perhaps comparable to the minister of the Left Facet, Nu Sheelan Robar Shil.

For now, Han was happy to let power flow from his hands like water. Ko Quebwas Polen Nim, Minister of the Right Interior, would move up to his pillow soon enough as she gathered the reins. At eighty-two years, she was a short and rotund woman who reminded Han of the ancient images of enlightenment.

Han smiled as the latest messenger came before them. He would perhaps miss this chamber more than he would miss the inhabitants, but it had been a central aspect of his life for so long that he was unsure what thing might fulfill him afterwards.

"What news from the barbarians?" Han asked in a brighter voice than perhaps many were expecting.

He noted eyes and heads twitch in his direction uncomfortably.

"Much news, Minister of the Left Interior," the man said carefully.

As with all spies, they were chosen for that gift of anonymity that would cause you to forget them three seconds after they left your field of vision.

"However, little of it is good," the man continued in a lower pitch. "The piracy problem plaguing the *Altai* and *Lena* sectors has grown out of control. They struck the secret prison camp at *Mansi* four months ago, destroying all orbital facilities and rescuing the prisoners from the surface."

Han felt the anger in his heart reflecting off the *Mandarins* beside him. Taken prisoners were put to work. Or allowed to starve, if they chose. *The Eldest* believed that labor would bring the barbarians to a finer understanding of the value of civilization. *Mansi* was one of four such worlds around the perimeter of the *Protectorate of Man*, where the most difficult prisoners were sentenced, as capital punishment was a tool of last resort, not first.

"Why were we not told earlier?" Han demanded in a voice that forgot how nice he had considered this day, just five minutes ago.

"The station was destroyed by a surprise attack, Minister," the man struggled to keep his voice and posture calming.

Messengers were not shot, but the man would have to suffer some level of wrath, and had probably drawn the short straw today.

"In addition, the other stations were threatened with bolide extinction if they did not surrender, after the raiders had destroyed the kremlin on the surface," he continued. "The crews of the remaining stations were allowed to come to the surface when their platforms were destroyed, while the prisoners were transported to orbit and rescued by a previously-captured hospital ship. We expect that, given their actions over the last year, the barbarians may have made their way to the nearest fortified sector capital, a world known as *Osynth B'Udan*. We await confirmation from our spies there in as little as three weeks."

"Have there been other raids like this one?" Nim asked. Shortly, it would become her problem.

"No, Minister of the Right Interior," the man turned his attention to her. "Keller's Imperial forces have grown more ambitious, but the attack on *Severnaya Zemlya* appears to have damaged her forces to the point that we can confirm her fleet was at *Osynth B'Udan* for repairs as recently as four months ago."

"So there are at least two sets of attackers?" Nim probed.

"Confirmed, Minister," the spy said. "Keller's forces were accounted for when *Mansi* was attacked."

"Have other sectors faced a similar rise in piracy?" Han stepped back into the conversation. "Or is this contained to *Altai*, for the most part?"

"That is correct, sir," the spy nodded to him. "*Samara* continues to be ignored, possibly recognized as the trap it is. *Lena* has seen some intelligence, based on navigation trends, but everything has remained in *Altai* for now."

Normally, Han would issue orders here. But this was no longer his chamber, nor his power. Only his original plan and the glory that had accumulated around it.

Pointedly, he turned to Nim and let his face speak the question his voice would not enunciate around outsiders.

"Make your reports available for consumption," Nim ordered the spy. "You are dismissed."

Quickly, and perhaps thankfully, the man backed away, fleeing the room with only a slight amount of psychological trauma.

"*Eldest*, what is your desire?" Nim asked as they turned to the rear, rather than Han.

Buran's godlike, alien face took form before them, more than a meter tall.

"Flood *Altai* with sector forces stripped from others," *Buran* ordered. "Keller will escalate her attacks there in an attempt to pierce our border and threaten the inner sectors, while continuing to ignore *Samara*. She has perhaps smelled that trap and will avoid it. Withdraw the extra forces from *Samara* as well, leaving the normal detachment. As with all plans, some eventualities never come to present."

"Should we attack *Osynth B'Udan*?" Nim pressed her case.

She had always been the more aggressive of his comrades. Han would have simply reinforced the holding at *Samara*, while slowly building new colonies across the *M'Hanii Gulf*, continuing to push *Fribourg* back by bleeding their fleet in futile, frontal assaults.

Nim had made the better case for punishing *St. Legier* with *Sukhoy*

Nos, the anti-matter superbomb that had brushed aside the capital city's shields and killed all the residents cowering beneath.

"Prepare for such an assault by gathering appropriate additional forces at *Ninagirsu*," the god commanded. "My calculations show it is the next most likely target for Keller to assault, as she seeks to visit upon *The Protectorate* a like punishment for their capital world. Once she breaks her fleet there, you shall pursue her home and strike a double blow."

"As you command," Nim replied with obvious glee.

Han could see the logic of the maneuvering. Emmerich Wachturm, once famed as *Fribourg's* Red Admiral, might have fallen for it. Most Imperial commanders would have been sucked under by the rip tides of history.

But Han's mind was troubled. Keller Marie Jessica was a different case. Had not *The Eldest* placed her in the eighth standard deviation for humanity, as a military commander? At that range, it might be possible to name every individual in the category with her, as they would be few, even across the whole of human history.

Would she follow such direct logic? She had not in any study Han had seen.

But he kept silent. His time was ending in less than sixty days and he risked being seen as a mere meddler now, if he chose to challenge Nim at the very moment when he was allowing her to usurp his place and his power.

Plus, the orders had come from God Himself, an ancient being more intelligent than any mere mortal.

CHAPTER LXVII

CASEY HAD MOVED from having nearly-constant meetings with Torsten a year ago to skipping days. He had proven his loyalty and competence in the depths of the worst winter and summer of anybody's lives, so she could leave him alone to work, without needing him to constantly hold her hand, even metaphorically.

Even when she felt lonely and wanted reassurances that things were going well. The corset of Imperial responsibility was tiresome. She could understand how her father would complain to Em about the fun her uncle got to have, while a mere emperor stayed home.

Teas with important players, just to reward them for loyalty. Ribbon-cuttings as new buildings, roads, schools, libraries, and other facilities opened, in what would become her new Imperial capital.

The little things that kept it all running, but didn't let her have much impact. Even the House of Dukes and the House of the People were currently both in recess, enjoying a month-long stretch of vacation away from the on-going construction.

But Torsten was coming, so that would brighten her day. The usual one-hour meeting had been extended to two, however that might be nothing, as he might have felt the need for tea to relax from his own day.

All of Torsten's hair was coming in gray underneath now, but that was more the stress of his job than anything. And if he wasn't Father's age, or

Em's, he was still old enough to be her father. Just as Jessica was old enough to be her mother, rather than just her protector.

She would miss them both when they returned to their own lives.

The reception room where she met Torsten was compact. Less formal than the larger one where she entertained guests, as she had four chairs here, a sidetable for the tea service, and not much else. Art reproductions from some of her favorite painters, the originals having been destroyed. The sidetable itself had been officially looted in Mejico by the 189th when they decided she needed such a thing.

But not much space. And easily secured, as this was part of her personal suite in the palace, so anyone getting this far had already crossed several layers of security.

Anna-Katherine knocked at the door, waited a beat, and then opened it far enough to stick her head inside.

"Your guests are arrived, Lady Casey," she said formally.

It had taken almost this long to get her to use that title, rather than *Your Majesty.*

But, *guests*? This was supposed to only be Torsten. Who did he need to bring along, if this was just a normal meeting?

Clue: it obviously wasn't going to be normal. The length already proclaimed something was up. The guest list would tell her more before words were ever spoken.

"Send them in, Anna-Katherine," Casey nodded.

The tea was already steeped, because she had felt like it. And a fantastic herbalist had been added to the Household kitchen. A woman who specialized in growing her own leaves in a secured garden, in order to go beyond mere *Camellia sinensis* and add mints, fruits, flowers and other leaves to make it special.

Torsten entered first, standing to one side behind the closest chair so that Hendrik Baumgärtner could enter as well, closing the door behind him.

Interesting. One of *those* meetings?

"Please," Casey commanded. "Sit. Let us enjoy some tea."

If that will continue to be possible. What terrible news do you two have for me?

Her cup refilled, Casey served the two men in turn. It was one of the little things she did to remind herself to remain humble, when she could easily fall into the rut of letting others handle everything for her.

Torsten was off today. Nervous in ways that Casey couldn't identify. Unsettled. Was the news that bad?

Hendrik, on the other hand, might have been carved in alabaster. Both sat quietly sipping their tea as she studied them.

"What thing is so terrible that it brings you both to my door?" Casey finally asked, after the first mug of tea was gone. Anna-Katherine would have a second pot prepared and be along shortly.

Torsten sighed and put his cup down.

"This may be a situation where I am not capable of objectivity, Your Majesty," he said seriously. "Given even the doubt, I felt it necessary to bring Hendrik along as an outsider whose opinions should probably have more weight than my own."

"Indeed?" Casey asked, fixing the man with a serious stare. "How bad?"

"It has come to my attention that Judit Chavarría has engaged in a pattern of conduct that comes perilously close to making my spies nervous, Lady Casey," Torsten expanded. "We presume that she has some inside information, from as-yet-unidentified double-agents in our employ."

"What has she done?" Casey asked.

"Nothing," Torsten said. "It is who she might be doing it with that has caused consternation in the quarters assigned to pay attention."

"Who, then?"

"Trouble-makers on both ends of the scale," Torsten said. "Men of power and capabilities to effect changes. Some of them are strongly in your favor. Others resent you personally and would happily join a movement to alter the Imperial Succession."

"She is seeking to expose the fault lines?" Casey ventured.

"She should not even be able to identify them with this level of accuracy," Torsten countered. "One theory is that she is merely seeking to find them, so that she knows where they are, as any good spy might do. A darker suggestion is that she could be establishing communications to the very centers she might wish to engage, if she were interested in mischief."

Casey turned to Hendrik, another long-time uncle of unquestioned loyalty, one she had literally known her entire life.

"Have you seen the findings?" she asked. "Analyzed the underlying data?"

"I have, Your Majesty" he said with a voice like gravel. "And I understand Wald's concerns."

"Spell them out," Casey ordered, focusing on Hendrik and making him speak.

He had always been a quiet man. Intensely internal, almost to the point of taciturn.

"Whispers in the right ears at the wrong time might provoke problems in the House of Dukes," Hendrik said. "Paralyze them at a moment when unity might be critical. In that, she might have miscalculated."

That last was delivered with a terrible smile unlike any she had ever seen from the man.

"How so?" Torsten's face grew clouded with confusion. Honest confusion, the best kind.

If Hendrik saw something Torsten had missed, perhaps others did as well.

"If she seeks to drive the dukes apart, she had not taken into account the people," Hendrik's smile turned lethal as he looked at Torsten. "That House has been forced to govern. To challenge the old farts in their private clubs with new thinking. You and Lady Casey have leveled the Houses, something that had never happened before."

"So how is this a miscalculation?" Casey asked him.

"The Dukes like to think they exist as a check on you, Lady Casey," Hendrik said. "On your government's ability to do the mundane things that keep the wheels turning and the lights on. But the Charter of Man is only a theory, in spite of the changes Wald has made to things in your name. Power still rests in your hands, if you choose to exercise it. Em has always said that true power was in the Inner Council, Flag Officers of the Blood, before so many of them proved to be such little men. The loss of those men allows Karl VIII to populate the Staff High Command with new men, loyal to her, starting with the Grand Admiral."

"And you and Tom Provst," Casey decided.

"Only as you command, Your Majesty," Hendrik nodded with great seriousness. "There are others we could induct, but no Princes of the Blood are ready for that rank. Even Tiede Wachturm will be a decade or more growing into the respect of the fleet that they will need. Today, it is you."

"And Jessica," Torsten interjected. "That is why I asked Hendrik to join us in our own little conspiracy."

"Conspiracy?" Casey turned her attention back to Torsten.

"Judit could rile up the Dukes with various promises of support,"

Torsten continued. "Both the patriots and the grumblers. She could make promises to both to not intervene, if they chose to clean house, however that phrase was interpreted. That tension could cause trouble, possibly even fracture the fleet itself. Not everyone who was loyal to Sigmund Dittmar has been identified and removed. There is always the risk of another *Blue Essex*."

"Even after I had him executed?" Casey growled.

"Because of, or in spite of," Torsten countered. "It matters not. Dead, he becomes a useful martyr. Alive, he might have been a rallying point for those sorts of men."

"So what should be done about the Palatine?" Casey asked.

"Nothing," Hendrik spoke up definitively. "If she is causing trouble for the Empire, over and above the usual, we will need far better evidence before we go public. And we might never, anyway."

"Never?" Torsten asked.

Casey would have spoken, had Torsten not.

"Never," Hendrik repeated with force. "That might be her trump card, and the reason I am here. Suppose we are offended enough to order her to withdraw. What then?"

His eyes contained the angry growl that never made it to his lips. Casey held her peace.

"We order her gone, yes," he continued. "And the *Aquitaine* Senate is so mortally offended that they order Jessica to withdraw as well, with all of *her* forces. The *War with Buran* is returned to the *status quo ante*, which we were in the process of losing. Em and your father have both mentioned in my presence that Keller might be the only thing that saves us. What happens without her?"

"What about Moirrey?" Casey asked. "What if she succeeds?"

"Then I expect Chavarría to step up her games," Hendrik replied. "To possibly provoke us to the point that we order her to go, and risk losing Keller's forces in the balance. What happens then?"

"Then Jessica plans to retire," Torsten said. "And she and I would return to *Petron*."

"So the head of the civilian government is replaced, and their best commander departs," Hendrik nodded. "We still have a potential two-front war on our hands, especially if the Republic decides to get snitty about being caught with their hand in the cookie jar. This might all be exactly to cause that situation, so that they could restart the war, with us being in the moral and ethical wrong."

"Hendrik, in case I haven't told you, or Em has not, we will not be trying to conquer *Buran* space, even if Moirrey or Jessica succeeds," Casey's own hard voice matched the Admiral's. "Trade and exploration are acceptable, but I would rather they slowly implode over the next century and turn into something else while we watch from behind our current barricades, and I intend to raise my children with that understanding. We can have peace for my lifetime, if we do it right, and at the end of that time, I expect *Fribourg* to be rich enough and powerful enough that other worlds demand to join the Empire, rather than being forced. Enter that in your notes for your successors, as well."

She watched the man like a hawk as he nodded. Father had always said that the key to ruling was to not make too many orders, but to let the experts you had chosen run things, only stepping in when a change was needed.

Or a hard, bright line drawn, like this one.

Give her twenty-five years, and she could take the underlying strength of *Fribourg* and build it into a force comparable to the ancients in scope and wealth.

If she could have that peace.

Casey could understand the games Judit was probably playing. At almost no risk to herself, she could insert burning splinters of wood under the Empire's fingernails. And anything Casey did would only provoke the situation.

"What have you told Jessica?" Casey turned back to Torsten.

"Nothing, as yet," he said. "As I said, I may not be capable of objectivity, or even the perception thereof, given the situation. Thus Hendrik, whose credentials no man or woman will challenge. Jessica does know, via Em I might add, about Moirrey's mission. He asked her to escalate on the *Altai* front to distract *Buran*. She would not have risked communicating anything important back to *Ladaux*, as she takes the Imperial Flag flying overhead seriously."

"So we may have two openings," Casey observed, including both men in her calculations. "One, the Dukes are not the center of power they were even two years ago, and this poor, overwhelmed waif of a girl-emperor might not have to rely on all those important men to make decisions for her."

That got a chuckle from both men, as she intended. Many of the nobles believed exactly that about her, and would make mistakes that way, like Kiril Hahl had.

"Two," she continued. "If Moirrey succeeds, I can think of no greater wedding present to you and Jessica than to quickly withdraw her from the front line, reward all of her people, and send them home with the gratitude of the *Fribourg Empire*. I want both of you to make lists of the rewards, awards, and glory we could shower on Denis, Robbie, Alber', Kigali, Whughy, Strnad, Vlahovic, and others. And we need something extra special for Phil Kosnett and his people. Let's short-circuit Judit's punch, rather than trying to block it."

"As you command," Hendrik said, rising with a gleeful smile on his face. "With that, I will depart you to prepare."

He bowed and withdrew quickly, leaving her alone with Torsten as Anna-Katherine brought in more tea.

"Make sure Vibol knows, as soon as you do, if Moirrey succeeds," Casey commanded lightly. "His place in all this will probably be overlooked in the official histories, so perhaps I should command a hagiography of Vibol and his impact on the war."

Torsten grinned at her.

"I believe that would be a most useful lesson, Your Majesty," he said, eyes gleaming. "I believe I know a scholar we can entrust to handle the task correctly. Does the war with *Aquitaine* begin anew, once *Buran* is off the stage?"

Casey paused, studying the man.

"I remember my very first impression of Tadej Horvat," she said. "He had a cruel mouth. Sharp and dangerous, and not a man to be taken lightly. I have studied his history. Horvat brought down his own government and sacrificed the premiership for many years, just to crush someone that had challenged him within his own party. Never forget that. He can be a man of grand retributions. Judit will get the credit for the Peace. I expect Horvat will want to have an even greater measure of success. They know our weaknesses as well as our strengths, because of their proximity over the last few years."

"Will my departure weaken us?" Torsten asked.

"Not necessarily," Casey replied. "Tell me the things about Cameron Lara that I don't know, if you truly expect him to succeed you."

She watched his eyes grow distant with thought and memory.

"He was the second son of the old Duke of *Pherile*, and is now the younger brother of the current duke," Torsten said. "Medium height and almost bald, as you know. Rather rotund, as he is a gourmand with a keen intellect and a weakness for after-dinner port and sherry, sitting in the salon and letting his intellect wander far afield to challenge whatever dinner guests have joined him. Jovial."

"And he still employs the best chef in Strasbourg?" Casey pressed with a smile.

"If not all of *St. Legier*, Lady Casey," Torsten said. "Cameron is not the dour intellectual he would replace, but a very cunning operator, a glad-hander who had the extremely good luck to be on vacation with his family the week Werder was destroyed. You could have just as easily selected him as your Chief of Deputies at that time, and been as well served."

"Any jealousies of you getting the job?" Casey asked.

"None evident," Torsten replied. "Everyone knew that it was a temporary situation, and that I would not be tied to the job any longer than Jessica would allow. Hendrik and Em both speak well of the man, as do several others whose opinions I value."

"Thank you," Casey said abruptly. "For being there when I needed you, and willing to suffer that separation from Jessica. I will hold you no longer than I must."

She watched the man blush slightly and nod back to her. She would miss his calm competence, especially as Sri Lara was a larger-than-life figure much of the time.

"What else do we have to cover?" she asked.

While he talked of other things, Casey made a note to add someone like Torsten to her personal staff when the man left. Someone who could dive deep into the numbers and reports, as Torsten Wald had done from his first day on the palace staff, to help shine a useful light into otherwise dark corners.

The Peace with *Aquitaine* had been Father's idea, but Torsten's analysis of Jessica's *Cahllepp Frontier* campaign and other things had moved the right minds.

She shouldn't lose that, when she lost the man behind it.

CHAPTER LXVIII

IMPERIAL FOUNDING: 181/06/12. RAN ARCHANGEL, JUMPSPACE

WHEN MOVING a monstrous fleet like this long distances, even the best navigators needed to stop and regroup. Vo had taken advantage of that to swap back and forth between assault carriers at every stop. And meet with Jessica, Denis, and Tom frequently.

Iskra was less critical to this mission, and Vo expected that Jessica would ship her off with a few corvettes to raid nearby colonies at some point, just to rile things up.

Right now, he and Alan had just wrapped up another one of those meetings and sent everyone back to their own ships. And his cohort centurions had all left as well, back to their teams.

Alan was in Vo's office, with the spare chair turned sideways for Alan's feet. His hands were laced behind his head and Vo wondered if the man was likely to take a nap, right here in his office.

Alan had done stranger things. At least he hadn't walked off with Vo's favorite coffee mug recently.

"I keep coming back to *Barnaul*," Alan said out of the blue. "What does it gain us?"

"Terror," Vo answered with a rumble. "*Stanovoy*, on the ground. A reminder that no place is safe from us. From her. Even the smallest, least significant colony in the middle of nowhere might suddenly have troops drop on it."

"Yeah, but there's a difference here and I'm not sure Keller grasps that," Alan groused. "It's one thing to sit in orbit and blow up freighters, or drop big bombs on the surface. Something entirely else to kill people with small arms."

"I'm not about to order the men to shoot women and children, Alan," Vo said. "Once we crush all military resistance, we'll herd people out of the places we're blowing up, and then get to work on infrastructure."

"That include those two storage warehouses?" Alan's feet came down with a thump and he turned squarely to face his commander. "That's the colony, right there. All their food. All their everything. We kill that and we might as well have just killed them. Better a quick death than starvation."

Vo marveled, especially after some of the things that had come out of Alan's mouth over the last two years. This was a side of the man he wasn't sure he had ever encountered.

But nobody joins the military to be evil. Or rather, those got washed out quickly. The ones that made it were men and women of rules, but more importantly saw themselves as protectors.

And sometimes, that could extend across enemy lines. Like say, *Thuringwell,* and a unit that had once been Karl IV's 189th Division, Mountain.

"So we kill the mine and free the prisoners," Vo let his voice soften from the hardness it wanted to have. "Are you suggesting we ignore the warehouses completely?"

"More than just that, Vo," Alan's face got critical. "The warehouses require power to keep the refrigerators working. We kill that and the food spoils, so we can't blow up all the power stations. We can't blow up whatever computer system is the quartermaster section, the records, or they'll never find what they need in terms of foods and medicine. And we have to spare the hospital for the same reason."

"So what can we kill, Alan?" Vo let the exasperation show.

"Police stations," Alan smiled. "Jail, after we've emptied it out. Used speeder lots. Bars. Maybe half the restaurants, if we can figure out the ones with worst kitchens. Get everyone clear and burn some housing blocks, just because *Barnaul* never gets cold enough to kill people sleeping rough. If we had enough time, I'd use the big earth-moving equipment on-site to fill the mine back in."

"We don't have that much time, Alan," Vo scowled at the man.

"So let's steal every single thing from the mine we can drive off," Alan retorted, "instead of killing them. Start our own Construction Ala with those dump trucks and things. Empire knows we've got the DropShips handy to steal everything."

"Steal?" Vo saw where Alan was headed now. "You've gotten infected by Siobhan Skokomish, haven't you?"

Alan laughed.

"If I was single, Vo," he grinned. "Lucky for all involved I'm a happily married dork."

"Piracy, huh?" Vo asked.

"I don't want to be the bad guy here," Alan got serious again. "You can order us to wipe this place out to the last child and last cat, but Jessica Keller has always been about taking the high ground and kicking you in the teeth if you wanted to argue with her."

"But looting the place with the care of a cat burglar?" Vo offered.

"Appeals to the juvenile delinquent in me," Alan replied. "And will to the team as well. Plus I know a cat burglar, supposedly reformed, who might be willing to offer my teams advice on how to do something like that."

"Supposedly?" Vo asked.

"Never assume that the man's gone straight, just because he joined the marines, General," Alan laughed. "Might be the biggest swindle of all time, that nobody's cottoned on to it yet."

Vo laughed with the man.

"Okay, you have about a week before we hit orbit," Vo said. "Jessica will have one more meeting of the commanders at that point, before she kicks the door in. You've got until then to come up with a new set of instructions for how we clean out *Barnaul* when we hit dirt."

Alan stood and saluted, cackling madly.

"Still planning on leading with the alien invasion, General," he grinned. "But then the shit gets silly."

Vo just shook his head as Alan departed.

Reese stuck his head into the office a few moments later.

"Dare I ask?" Reese inquired, glancing back up the way that Alan had left.

"Alan wants to hit the place like pirates, rather than avengers," Vo offered in a light voice. "Liberate the mine, then steal all the heavy equipment so we can start our own Construction Ala."

"And the city itself?" Reese's eyes showed some concern now.

"Blow up the police station and commit graffiti elsewhere, but leave them alone," Vo replied. "He thinks there is too much risk that we cause mass starvation if we do anything larger or more violent."

"I see," Reese's face went neutral. "And what will the First Centurion say?"

"It's my planet," Vo growled. "She gets us to orbit, but I command inside the atmosphere. And I like the idea. Less destruction. More confusion."

"Yes, sir, General," Reese snapped to at the tone in Vo's voice. "My orders?"

"Get with Alan and figure out what we might steal from the orbital images *CS-405* captured," Vo said. "Then figure out where we might stash it all, once we do steal it, keeping in mind that all of our equipment has to be packed in as well."

"*Dieter Jost* has deck space not being used right now," Alan suggested. "If we leave enough space for one DropShip to get in and out, we can put a lot of stuff there. We'll have to haul everybody back to *Lighthouse* to unpack, though, instead of sending the transport directly to *Osynth B'Udan*."

"If they're our people, they won't mind that much," Vo decided. "And if we've freed criminal prisoners that want to work, we can put them to the task of building Commencement."

"Is this where I suggest you're crazier than he is?" Reese had the slightest grin on his face.

"Nope," Vo got mock-serious. "We are conducting psychological and economic operations against our enemy, Command Decurion. According to Lady Moirrey's favorite poet: All's fair in love and war."

Reese nodded and withdrew, chuckling.

Vo found himself alone in his tiny office. The room was definitely lighter, like someone had turned the gravplates down twenty percent. He hadn't realized how much the thought of annihilating *Barnaul's* population had been weighing on his soul.

He knew that it was an expectation, given the very purpose of the 189th. Be the sword that cuts the enemy to the quick. Kills them.

But he could kill their minds and their spirit just as easily as he did their bodies. Just steal their economy and make it prohibitive to start over again. Let the *Sentient* beast at *Winterhome* either pay to deliver new stuff, or pay to withdraw all the people and move them to another colony.

It was like what Jessica did to the Red Admiral the first time, back at

2218 Svati Prime. A good role model, too, if she got tetchy about his plans.

Precedent.

He didn't always have to do whatever it was everyone expected of him. Vo *zu* Arlo could do something because it was the right thing to do for him and his men, without sacrificing anything.

That brought Vo up short. He hadn't planned to go there, but she was in his mind, clear as if she was seated in the chair Alan had just vacated.

Kasimira.

There would have been an expectation that Vojciech *zu* Arlo would do the right thing and marry the woman, but she had freed him to pursue his own path.

She had asked the question nobody had ever asked. No, that wasn't true. Two other men had asked him, at critical points in his life.

"What do you want?"

Senior Centurion Phillip Navin Crncevic, aka Navin the Black, the lunatic Viking badass that had stood a young punk up on his deck. A kid fresh from basic and fleet training, as opposed to starting his second year in jail.

Navin had asked him what he wanted. The words had come out of nowhere.

"To serve."

They weren't part of the training. Marines obeyed. Did whatever someone told them to do.

But he had wanted to serve. So Navin had given Vo the training and responsibility as rapidly as he could handle it. Sent him off to study Aikido and Kenjitsu, just to give the city kid a different way to look at the world.

Taught him how to hold a bow. How to master it. Eventually, how to shape his own.

"One of these days," Navin kept reminding him. "You and a knife against an entire planet. Learn to survive, to thrive, to win. Go."

He had survived. He had thrived.

What did winning look like?

A tall blonde with piercing blue eyes stared back at him and smiled.

The *Primus Pilus* had been the other man to ask Vo what he wanted. Alan had understood the circumspective questions other Imperials had been asked. Where they led.

What someone might want to suggest, without ever suggesting.

Even then, Vo had had to get Alan half-drunk to get the story, but Alan had apparently snarled at no less than Torsten Wald.

"Have you ever asked Vo what he wants?" like so many others might have.

But Alan had taken it another step.

Drawn a line in the sand and said: "This much I know. The rest you have to handle, because he doesn't know, even if you ask."

They had first met at Command School, when Emmerich *zu* Wachturm decided to turn the reformed cat burglar into a General. Alan had impressed the hell out of Vo. Still did.

Might be the only true friend Vo could call such.

That was weird.

What did a man like Vo do after the war ended? Did he resign everything and go home to *Anameleck Prime* to live on his pensions? Open a bar or a bookshop or a dojo? All three under one roof?

Did he look for an even greater challenge? Was there a greater challenge? Life around her would never be dull.

Because she had also understood that making demands would be the wrong thing to do. She could ask, and do so politely. Or she could order things, and watch him slip through her fingers like sand.

So she had asked. Pled her case like a woman, not an emperor.

Wanted him because he made her feel safe.

Him.

The ugliest duckling to hatch. As well as the meanest, toughest, orneriest one, so he supposed that there was something to him making people feel safe.

He studied her in his memory. That evening in her personal chambers, with Moirrey half-hiding off to one side so as to not distract.

Tall and blond, like so many Imperial ladies. Blue eyes from her father, Karl VII. Muscles, too, in a culture where women were supposed to be lithe and unathletic.

Undoubtedly female. Unapologetically, as well.

Smart and wise beyond her years. An artist who painted and composed in her free time. And he had listened to everything she had ever written.

A second woman appeared next to Casey, almost her opposite in every way.

Cohort Centurion Rebekah Kim, except she was a legate now.

Thirty centimeters shorter than Casey, but hardly any lighter.

Compact and intense. And abrasive as hell to everyone, but that was a factor of holding up a meterstick and finding almost everyone came up short.

Even he had, eventually. Or rather, he had held her at arm's length long enough, unable to open himself to the woman for reasons he couldn't explain, even today. And that had been enough for her to give up on him.

But they would have been fire and water, had he taken her up on the offer. Magnificent, but combustible. Destructive in all the wrong ways, regardless of their personal chemistry.

She made an interesting comparison to Casey. Just as smart. Just as driven. Probably as tough.

But not as feminine. Rebekah was too much in direct competition with Vo on all things.

Yes, that was why it had never worked. Would never have worked.

Rebekah was competing with everyone, all the time. Keeping score, and forcing everyone into a place, either ahead of her or behind. And those behind weren't worth considering.

Would they have spent an entire life competing?

Would that have been any fun at all, or would it have worn on him eventually?

Casey would not compete. Could not. She was Emperor and had very strict official lines that she could not cross, regardless of her personal desires. She would be herself when she wasn't in public: the artist, the composer, the free-thinker, the revolutionary.

Emperor Karl VIII wanted a place where she could cast off the Imperial mantle and be safe.

Didn't we all?

And there were no rules for a Prince Consort, or whatever such a title might be. There had never been one before, because every ruler of *Fribourg* had been a male, going back to the kings of *Fribourg* itself, when it was a nation on a planet, before it became everything.

There was freedom there, as well.

He could be anything he thought was right, and nobody could argue with him because there were no rules about what *right* was.

He could be himself. Whoever he ended up being. And have her strength in those times when he needed it. When the nightmares wouldn't go away.

When he was back on *Alexandria Station* trying to save the universe, and kept getting shot. Or chasing a ghost on *Thuringwell* as his men and women died in ambushes he couldn't prevent.

That might be what winning looked like.

"You alive, sir, or should I call a medic?" a voice intruded.

Rebekah vanished before his eyes. Casey transformed into Reese Borel.

Vo blinked. Blinked again. Shook his head and rubbed his eyes.

"I went deep," he muttered.

"Noticed that," Reese said sarcastically. "Came in, started to talk, and you didn't even realize I was here. You back now?"

"Think so, Reese," Vo said, shaking his head a little to make sure the bolts in his neck were still tight enough that his head didn't fall off.

"You look like someone pulled you backwards through a knothole, Vo," Reese said. "Should I have Alan beaten up after this?"

Vo laughed. It felt good to laugh, so he let go some of the mad energy that had taken root in his stomach.

"No," he finally said, after he got the edge of hysteria under control. "But we'll make him buy the first three rounds."

"Deal," Reese said. "What the hell just happened, boss?"

"Maybe I just grew up, Reese," Vo replied. "It happens."

"I hope not," the man countered. "Grown-ups don't have nearly as much fun as kids."

Vo laughed again, but this was just warmth, not craziness.

"Then obviously, you're doing it wrong, Command Decurion," Vo decided. "What were you talking about before, when I was ignoring you?"

"Nothing that can't wait," Reese suddenly rose. "You look like you could use a drink. Should I drag your ass down to the officer's wardroom and get you at least mildly drunk?"

"No," Vo decided. "But what you should do is set up a big dinner for everyone tonight. You, Iakov, Hans, Victoria, and the rest of Cutlass Ten. Alan and the Cohort Centurions. Tell the chef to make something special."

"We celebrating anything in particular, Vo?" Reese asked.

"Being alive," Vo replied. "And friends."

CHAPTER LXIX

JESSICA HAD REVIEWED the logs and notes from Kosnett's team in greater detail than the man's eventual Court Martial would do so, and probably with a more critical eye. After all, that Court would be a formality, given his own notes and the amazing outcomes.

If anything, he was likely to end up a bigger hero in *Fribourg* than at home in *Aquitaine*, when this was all done.

And his notes on the planet, added to those originally stolen from Nu Ulap Narah Kiel, gave Jessica everything she needed to know about the world they were about to drop on, except any changes that might have occurred in the last year to improve the defenses.

There had been none, then. Chances were that there would be none now.

She still looked up from the new assault plan Vo and Alan Katche had provided with a sour, nearly-disbelieving eye.

"Cat burglary?" she asked in a slow drawl.

Interestingly, the *Primus Pilus* across the desk from her grinned more than Vo did. Must have been his idea.

"Yes, Jessica," Vo said simply. "We reviewed the original plans and determined that the level of damage we had planned would leave the colony non-viable, even over the short term, and that casualties from mass starvation risked being fifteen to twenty percent in the first three months."

"That high?" she asked, flipping the document back to the calculations appendix.

"They don't grow any significant crops there, First Centurion," Alan interjected. "And couldn't, given the arid nature of the area. Ranching might be successful, but that's so far out of their current capabilities as to be negligible. We blow the warehouses or the power grid, and we might as well have just shot everyone out of hand."

She could order that. And it would happen.

And every single one of these men would never follow her anywhere, ever again. Including Vo.

"So you'll do more damage this way?" she pursued a different logic. "Steal everything instead?"

"I have it on good authority that random, psychological trauma can be a more effective tool when threatening a population," Vo said with the faintest hint of a grin. "Especially if you can capture hospital ships in the bargain."

Like she had once done at *Second 2218 Svati Prime*. Like Kosnett had done when he needed to repatriate a number of prisoners.

"And forming your own Construction Ala?" she pressed, letting her own grin ghost the room.

"I'm not sure we'll keep it all," Vo offered. "Alan's in the wishful thinking mode with that part. But without that equipment, how viable is the colony? How much expense to replace it all, versus the cost of just abandoning the place and moving everyone somewhere else, in the middle of a war? This isn't *The Long Raid*. This is *Stanovoy* on a larger scale."

"I see," she said, watching the two men.

Something had changed about them, but Jessica couldn't put her finger on it. Both were more calm than she could remember them being, like planning this raid had taken them to a new level.

And she didn't have a problem approving this change to the mission. Nobody would challenge Vo's right to do whatever he felt like doing, down on the surface. Many might even see Moirrey's hands in it. *Project Mischief* given a new direction.

"I can see one change you could make, if you started immediately," Jessica offered.

Both men sat up a little taller, like they wanted to see what she could do to improve *this*.

"*Mendocino* and *Duncan* can both land on the surface," she smiled at them. "Anything small enough to fit into one of their transport pods could be hauled off that way, freeing up space elsewhere. You just need to let me know and I'll have them start rearranging pods now so that one of them can land with all the empties."

Alan grinned, like he had just caught a canary. Vo nodded sharply and dove in on himself. Tactical thinking turned to strategic.

"Any other questions?" she asked.

Both men shook their heads.

"Then you have ninety-six hours, give or take," she said. "*CS-405* is down there scouting right now. Once Kosnett confirms the situation, we'll drop everyone on them at once. And then it's your turn."

They rose as one and departed, chattering even before the door closed.

Marcelle came in a moment later and just stood to one side, silent.

"Do we know what's changed about Vo?" she asked her long-time assistant.

"Nope," Marcelle replied. "Looser than I ever remember that boy being."

"At peace with himself?" Jessica ventured.

"Maybe," Marcelle agreed. "He wasn't like this at *Thuringwell* or *Severnaya*, so I couldn't hazard a guess as to what improved in his life. Lately, he's been Moirrey's *Mountain of Doom* all the time."

Jessica nodded. She could guess, but it would only be that. A guess.

And she wasn't sure which way Vo had found peace. Nobody would until he said something out loud, and Vo was still the most private man she had ever known.

"Anything else I need to worry about, besides paperwork?" Jessica asked.

"*Pint-sized* and friends," Marcelle suggested. "Is *Barnaul* a big enough target to get all eyes over here, or do we need to consider something drastic and stupid on the way home?"

"Besides Iskra?" Jessica asked.

"Nothing that woman does is either drastic or stupid, Jessica," Marcelle tilted her head.

"Point taken," Jessica agreed with a smile.

Iskra. Enough said.

It was tempting, with this much firepower handy. Go hit *Laptev* or *Abakn*, but neither of those worlds had anything worth blowing up, any more than *Barnaul* did.

There was only one place she could think of that would make a major stink. She had even considered it, but decided to take it at a later date.

But Em had wanted things ratcheted up hard.

And she had the crazy legend of Jessica Keller to live up to.

"Grab a seat," Jessica said, keying the comm open and looking for the ship she wanted.

"*Mendocino*, Centurion Calkin here," a woman answered quickly.

"First Centurion here," Jessica said as their cameras synched. She watched the woman's blue eyes get big. "I need you and *RAN Duncan* to determine who would be best suited to land with as many empty transport containers as possible on *Barnaul*, and how much extra food we've got, in order to make an unscheduled detour. Talk to your folks and get back to me directly, or my assistant Marcelle Travere. Questions?"

"Negative, First Centurion," the young woman snapped to. "On it."

And the screen went blank.

Marcelle raised an eyebrow, but kept otherwise silent.

Jessica pressed another button and Reif Kingston appeared on her screen.

"Admiral," he nodded, looking up from some task he had been focused on.

"Reif, contact Captain Exeter on *Hans Bransch* and get him aboard the flagship soonest," Jessica said. "I have a new mission and this will be his reward for impressing me."

"Soonest, Admiral?" Reif asked, looking fully at her and dropping whatever else it was. "As in, order him to board a shuttle immediately, and get dressed en route?"

"He can shower and shave first, but I don't want him in dress uniform," Jessica grinned at the normally-serious man commanding her flagship. Reif Kingston had finally relaxed. "He'll need to make a high speed run somewhere, so also have his engineers get ready to push when their captain gets back."

"It will be done," and he was gone.

The Imperials were getting to be like the men and women she had trained over the last generation. More focused on getting the task done and less on the pomp and ceremony around how it happened.

Nils Kasum had finally broken the Noble Lords out of the fleet after the affair that saw Bogdan Loncar cashiered in disgrace. Em would have a harder time, since that kind of commander represented a larger proportion of the overall officer corps, but Jessica knew he was in the process of doing just that.

"*Mansi?*" Marcelle asked quietly once the line was closed.

"How did you know?" Jessica looked up.

"Known you for too long, Jess," she grinned. "You could blow up anybody but *Ninagirsu* with what we've got. Sending a scout means sneaky. *Mansi's* the smallest target we could hit, without landing troops. But there's nothing there, either, unless you stumble into an enemy fleet. However, there are a whole bunch of old Imperial warships demobilized in orbit, from what I remember. You've got *Packmule* here, but you need the *Junkyard Chihuahua* there, so you're sending *Hans Bransch* to get him and meet us there."

"Am I getting predictable?" Jessica got serious.

"Oh, hell no," Marcelle laughed. "It was that wicked gleam in your eye when you called Kingston. We rescue all the folks at *Barnaul* and send them home. Why not top that with bringing home a small warfleet, like Kosnett's folks did? Except instead of a Scout Corvette, you've got a couple thousand spare men and women across the two squadrons that you could thin out to crew those old ships. You just need someone that can fix them in a hurry."

"Completely insane?" Jessica grinned back.

"Vo wants to top *The Long Raid*," Marcelle said. "Obviously, you'll need to top him at the same time. Can't have the Imperial Army looking better than the *RAN*, can we?"

They both laughed.

Hopefully, it would be enough to keep *Buran's* entire attention focused here.

Moirrey was walking into the dragon's den without them.

CHAPTER LXX

JUMPSPACE WERE a meaningless gray that kinda wents on ferever. Human eyes couldna see dimples in space-time that indicated gravity wells deep enough to be a threat. Ya hads to have good sensors fer that sort of thin'.

Butterfly had 'em on 'counts the needs to be moving slower'n'snail snot at the last little bit o'crazy.

Could be done. Tom Kigali'd more or less invented the trick, back when he were still doing crazy stuff. Back when they was all kids, she'd a liked to thought.

Being out here makes ya grows up quick-like.

Ainsley and Gunter were side by side up front, murmuring in perfect harmony like back-up singers. Yan and *Pops* were seated in the port side chairs, heads down on the power curve bits. Moirrey'd dragged Summer up to th'bridge and set the tall chick down with her ta starboard.

Summer didn't have nothin' ta do with anythin' today, but if'n they all was gone die, she at least wanted one o'her favoritest folks with her at the moment o'doom.

And Summer seemed to unnerstand. She smiled grim but smiled.

"How's power?" Gunter called out.

"More than you need by three orders of magnitude," Yan growled back at the man.

Snapp'n turtle, but they was all close to stressed out. Small ship. Long flight. Maybe dead shortly.

Did thats to a person. Or coulda, if'n she hadn't packed smart'n'broughts enough wine and beer ta maybe floats the butterfly in, were desperation sets in.

"Engineering, confirm JumpSails and the array," Ainsley said into a mic.

"Everything tuned as tight as we can hold it, Captain," a man answered back.

She'd no' spent much time with the dozen er so folks Gunter and Grand Admiral had sents along. That were Ainsley's job, er Gunter's. *Lady Moirrey of Kermode* mades them all flustered, an' she really needed them at the top of all possible games.

Weren't just one chance at this. Were all *EXPERIMENTAL* stuff and any screw-up 'long the way dropped their butts into'a place where the best thing that could happen were bad guys shootin' first an'not askin' questions laters.

And that were right up there with snowballs in hell, princess.

"All hands, stand by for transit survey number one," Ainsley said unnecessarily.

Folks been gettin' readies fer this since breakfast yesterday. Maybe more.

Moirrey dinna have much ta do, this run. All wents well, they'd never even drops out of JumpSpace. Jest rides the gravity waves of hyperspace 'rounds and 'rounds 'til all the big stuff were mapped.

And Ainsley, bein' that perfectionalist chick she were, nope gonna trust long range looksies. Sits out in the wee darkness and listens.

Ballard were master o'that trick, but everyone here figgered *Buran* warships would be almost close 'nuff ta walks across out there, like gators in a swamp.

Summer had explained the proper definitions of paranoid to her once up on a long time ago in a bar middles o'nowhere with decent beer and awesome burgers.

When ya's fixin' to lives ferever, you builds backups fer yer backups. *Alexandria Station*, which had ne'er been a military target since the first one were lofted, had been orbited by three secret satellites. Two fairly mundane and one so black that space were lit around it, by comparisons. Suvi, as she'd been called then, had backed herself up on a rollin' basis to no less than seven destinations, one o'which were apparently about a kilometer unnerground beneaths the main city.

She dinna have replacement parts, save what she could convince Navin's cute son to builds fer her, but all the designs were handy everywhere, if'n ya wanted a replacement brainy chick.

Technically, they'd done jest that, when they thought the original babe were killed in action by the Red Admiral. Old Red Admiral. Mean version o'Uncle Em.

New babe were on the ground this time, where folks figgered she be safer. Built her a new university campus temple to house all the bits. Good 'nuff, Summer'd 'splained.

Replacement Suvi weren't original. Had a few bits missing, on purpose, so's she'd never be as lonely. Never miss sky and solar wind.

Not be Summer Ulfsson.

But this Summer'd explained hows ya snuck up on a *Sentient* bastard liked *Buran*.

Transit Surveys was the most tedious thing in the history o'boring.

In her day, Suvi the *Probe-Cutter* and Suvi the *First-Rate-Galleon-Badass* had sat clear outs on the edge of a solar system for like weeks, just mappin' every light that moved, before she ever dropped into the messiness most stars left over when they's weaned.

Like kids with sharp-edge building blocks in the carpet. Finds them first, then walks around.

But that weren't an option here. *Buran*'d be smart an' have Imperial Shit-tons of sensors, scanners, and maybe warships just parked out there, pingin' the hell out of each other in an annoying symphony of dullness.

So's ya hadta walk the system in JumpSpace. Slow. Like half a day just to go end-to-end of the heliosphere, ta say nothin' of the inner Oort Cloud. Measure every dimple and try to identifies it as a planet, a moon, an asteroid, er maybe some yahoo with his gravplates cranked up to stupid fer some reason.

One of these days, Yan promised he were gonna build the nasty grav bombs she'd designed fer him. Kick them out the airlocks and turn them on, and ya had a nifty gravity well where there shouldna be one. Useful fer messin' with *Buran* navigator dudes and dudettes. Would kinda look like a weird-ass moon from JumpSpace.

And Ainsley were gonna be a grumpy bear when the day were done, even if all wents dead perfection.

Moirrey and Summer mighta planned a little somethin' special fer dinner, as a results.

"Initiating Transit Survey," Gunter said outs louds.

Moirrey watched little lights changin's color as things went. Space out at the heliopause were kinda raindrop shaped, as *Winterhome*'s star moved through the local 'nvironment. Ya pushed out a solar wind, and everyone else pushed back. But you's was moving relative same same. So slightly longer than it were tall.

Not's so much ta matter, but Ainsley were doing this long axis first, like stone pros did.

Countin' dimples in the quilt of space-time.

An' abouts as boring as watching paint dry, but that's were why Ainsley were a scout pilot, and Moirrey's been engineer-babe. Gunter were a spy, so they unnerstood patience. Neither Yan nor *Pops* would cry uncle first.

And Summer were already six thousand and twenty-three years old, so nothin' would ruffle her.

So Moirrey suppressed the fidgets and waited patient-like fer the first hour.

Winterhome were dead obvious when they see'd it. Third planet out, smack dabs in the happy zone, with a monster of a moon in orbit, and a smaller one in the L4 gravity point.

Small one weren't really that big. Thing were all gravplates on a station at most 'bouts nineteen kilometers across. Freaking huge, compared ta anythin' else in the galaxy, tho.

Rest o'th'day were just fer finishing pass one and baselining things.

Moirrey unbuckled and stood up, grinnin' fierceness at Summer.

"We should go start lunch fixin's," she informed the room in a voice loud nuffs that everybody kinda just nodded without noticin'.

Summer rose with a sardonic, haughty kinda grin but joined her. Makin' lasagna today, so gonna takes time, especially with the twenty grumpy sailors aboard needin' mollifications along the way.

Ainsley looked up and fixed her with death stare.

Moirrey weren't 'ffended. *da Vinci* were stressed beyond all else that it work rights, and this were the spot she were all expertin', least 'tils came times ta line up the shot and hopes all worked.

And would, but Moirrey dinna thinks they'd believe her.

CHAPTER LXXI

IMPERIAL FOUNDING: 181/06/25. LANDING ZONE SIX,
BARNAUL

Deep in his soul, where the nightmares went to hide when the sun was up, Vo had been expecting another Mechanical Terrapin. A whole company of them, as a matter of fact, boiling up out of the hole of that mine like implacable demons loosed from the bowels of hell to roll over his pitiful attack force.

Hadn't happened, but that just meant he had gotten lucky here. Today.

One of these days, there would be more than one of them. And Iskra and her GunShips wouldn't be here to kill a phalanx of the beasts for him. If they could.

Vo had his doubts about the Assault Guns, but those men had trained hard and gotten up to an acceptable standard according to Alistair, so they would be between him and utter failure, for what that was worth.

Right now, he had set up his command post in the farthest top corner of the immense landing field that the colony shipped rocks from. He would have liked to have used the whole field, so many flat kilometers of useful space. Pure bad luck, his he supposed, had caused them to blockade the planet at the very moment when a massive mining freighter was on the ground loading ore.

So Vo's next set of nightmares involved *Thuringwell*, where that rat bastard from Imperial Security had sabotaged a similar-sized beast in the middle of the main starport and nearly managed to turn it turtle into the city itself instead of the starport.

As it was, *IFV Persephone* had gone down with the first wave of DropShips and landed with its bow gun pointed at the beast from almost close enough to pee on it, while Vo's troopers boarded the ship and removed everybody, including the ship's cat.

The cat was the only one that had put up any sort of fight, but Vo hadn't let them shoot it. So it was locked up with the rest of the prisoners, them in a stockade, her in a carrier for now.

He would have just turned her loose in the control tower for the landing field, but one of the tank crews had misunderstood orders, and instead of just blowing the top of the tower off, had hit the building itself.

Subsequent fire had reduced it to a smoking crater. Which he would have done in a week anyway, but that meant that he had an extra cat. And didn't feel like taking ethical responsibility for the beast.

At least there were no turtles on this planet.

Two armored police transports, with cute little pulse cannons in turrets, were lined up outside his headquarters, next to Cutlass Ten. Street had personally disabled their guns, removing the power leads and leaving them with Reese Borel, in case a surprise counter-attack suddenly erupted and Reese's team needed to kill something.

The only significant casualty so far had been one of those damned dump trucks. He raised his glasses and grunted at the single column of smoke from the wreckage.

"Nobody's willing to admit ordering the thing to launch a full, frontal assault on us, *zu* Arlo," Hans Danville said quietly, also watching the horizon.

Vo lowered his glasses and checked the team around him. Shrugs and such. One thirty-ton, unarmored dump truck, going nose to nose with an Assault Gun column that had blown daylight through it with the first shot. Before the next three gunners decided that the size meant *threat*, and blew the carcass to hell.

"And the city?" Vo asked, looking around at Decurion Street.

Iakov grinned.

"Gendarmes rolled over like puppies when Alan hit 'em, sir," he replied. "His team's still sorting through the main police headquarters building, in prep for firing it. Same for the mine office. None of our computer systems really read their stuff, but we're just gonna steal everything and burn the rest."

"Civilians any problem?" Vo scowled at him.

Vo noticed the quick glance at Trooper Ames.

"City's more female than male, General," Street said. "Lotsa ladies apparently either brought here as future breeding stock, or came of their own volition looking for a husband. We might have a small riot on our hands when they find out we're taking away all the men."

Victoria Ames flushed, and then Vo decided it was rage, not embarrassment. She wasn't like that, one bit.

Still, it gave him an even meaner idea. He keyed his local comm.

"HQ, Stolz," the man replied quickly.

"Get me the First Centurion on the comm soonest, Curator," Vo said, cutting the line.

Even if Jessica was handy, it would take a few minutes.

So it surprised him when the line beeped less than ten seconds later.

"What do you need, Vo?" Jessica asked.

"How do you feel about liberating colonists for *Lighthouse Station*, Jessica?" he asked.

"I thought that you were after prisoners from the mine to take home?" she asked.

"We are, First Centurion," Vo grinned, watching the men and woman around him pick it up like an airborne infection. "But I've been notified that the city has a significant gender imbalance opposite the mine. Considering opening the flood gates to these females as well, to see how they feel about running away to join the circus."

"Duke Avelina's not with us, Vo," Jessica replied noncommittally.

"Acknowledged, Jessica," he said. "That's why I called you. I might be able to recruit her a massive number of colonists on the cheap down here."

"You're a sneaky bastard, General," she said. "Let me ask Kosnett and his folks. They're as close to *in loco parentis* as I can get, without flipping a coin."

"We've got a couple of days," Vo replied. "And I'll blame everything I learned on you and Moirrey."

"Roger that."

And she was gone. Probably stirring up her legal team on *Indianapolis*, as well as bringing in all the officers on *CS-405* and anyone who might actually know the new duke well enough to hazard a guess.

Assuming that it worked. He turned to Iakov Street.

"I assume we're going to need Lady Moirrey's legendary Art

Department, *zu* Arlo?" the Decurion grinned up at him. "Thinking about maybe putting up billboards and running ads on local channels."

Vo turned to Victoria Ames, noting her grim scowl up at him.

"Trooper, you are the closest thing I have to a woman that is willing to do crazy things to get what she wants," he began, piling some level of sarcasm on his words to take any perceived sting out of them. Ames was as tough as the men, but she was still only seventeen. Going on fifty. "Your orders are to figure out how we might phrase things that we only get the seriously adventurous females who would consider moving to a brand new colony and building the damned thing from scratch."

Rather than reply, she squinted and scratched her jaw, almost a dead imitation of Reese Borel when he was deep in thought. Many of the men laughed, Vo included.

"We offering anything useful, sir?" she asked.

Trust Ames to be imminently practical. But that was why he needed her. A woman approached these things differently than a man.

"Transport," Vo said. "Clean records, if they've done anything that might have resulted in a prison sentence being commuted to service on *Barnaul*. Fresh start. And a chance to be on the winning side. Or at least be able to claim later that they were kidnapped at gunpoint."

"Okay, I'll need to meet with some of the locals and gauge their attitude," Victoria said. "Permission to borrow part of Cutlass?"

"Street," Vo turned and turned serious. "Take acting-Optio Ames and round up Cutlass One and Two. They'll bodyguard her, and have Alan assign a full Patrol as her escorts while she's in town."

Vo liked the way her eyes got enormous in her face as he spoke, and the implications registered.

Acting-Optio. Lowest-level of the officer ranks. Official person in charge, and able to give orders to the men she normally listened to.

But then a moment later she got as serious as he had been. Remembering the raid at *Severnaya Zemlya*, when she had taken charge of Street's team and everyone had listened.

Because they would. She was one of them, but they all saw in her that spark that might just turn her into a *Primus Pilus* one of these days. Or a Flag General with her own legion.

She nodded, after remembering to shut her mouth. Street grinned, but his back was to her right now and he sobered before he turned to look at the woman soldier.

Vo lifted up his glasses and stared at the distance again. The mine had been no more threat than the city, once Vo's people demonstrated a willingness to meet any resistance with stupid amounts of violence.

And that was about as good a lesson as most people needed in order to behave.

CHAPTER LXXII

ACTING-OPTIO. The words just echoed in her head as she walked. Around Victoria, Cutlass One and Two, plus Third Patrol, First Ala. One third of Alan Katche's force. Taking on the entirety of Barnaul City.

The place was eerily quiet. No vehicles were moving, except patrol skiffs. All the tanks and guns were at the mine, explaining politely to the people at the surface that they were no longer in charge and that all the people below would be free to leave.

Victoria had to figure out how many more she could bring. Food wouldn't be a problem. In addition to the freighters, Command Centurion Kosnett had stolen a mega-transport named *Packmule*, and Admiral Provst himself had ordered it filled to overflowing with long-term food stuffs, exactly for this mission.

They could cram nine thousand humans on the troop transport easily enough. Ten thousand if they packed closely.

How many of those would be females? Would any really want to go? What kind of fool would just throw away their entire history and walk into an unknown future at the drop of a hat?

Victoria blushed furiously as the mirror in her mind laughed. She knew at least one. And that was good enough, she supposed.

They had arrived at their destination. City Square was an entire zone, two blocks wide by a long block, left clear, with a park on two thirds, ending in a small amphitheater, and a paved zone for fairs and piroshky stands to do business.

Third Patrol owned it right now, with all of their skiffs arranged guns-out and all the troopers only relaxed on the surface. She had been a soldier long enough now to understand how close to the surface violence was today.

Hopefully, there wouldn't be any other fools.

A set of formally-dressed men and women were standing to one side as she approached. Victoria moved at the center of her own gravity well with Decanus Teagle and his men around her, as well as Cutlass Two.

The locals wore Asian-style robes. Four layers of pretty in colors that got lighter the closer you got to the skin. Big, white sashes went around their waists, and were tied over the left hip in a huge knot. Completely impractical, but *Buran* was a society where thinkers were put in charge and doers listened to orders.

Rather like the army, but education was only the entry point, not the destination. Victoria knew they were all more educated than she was, but not one of them had ever been to war. Seen the craziness. Done it.

Killed someone with their bare hands.

That settled her. They had age. She had experience. And several hundred violent men protecting her from all harm. She felt as tall as *zu* Arlo.

Victoria paused as she got close enough to not have to yell at them. The inverted gold triangles she wore on her collar felt heavier than her carbine. Street had pinned them at her neck, signifying she was an Optio, an officer as far as anyone who met them could tell.

She was in charge, right now. With everyone backing her, including Patrol Centurion Rikard Laferriere, a man almost old enough to be her dad.

The oldest woman over there, standing in the center of the group, spoke. Victoria didn't understand one bit of what she said, either. But another one of them was apparently the translator, because English came out of his mouth a moment later.

"The, uhm, Mayor acknowledges your pirate raid, and desires awareness of when your barbarian hordes will be departing," the man said politely.

Victoria could only imagine what the actual words had been, or maybe they just had to guess at context, when crossing from Mongolian to English in one jump. Chinese might have made it easier.

Or not. Maybe they were still pissed about what the *RAN* scout had done to them last time. Those folks had raided the place with a single freighter and a crew of twenty. She had an entire Rapid Assault Legion of angry men on call.

Victoria smiled. Hans had taught her that smile. It was the one you used when you were sizing someone's kidneys for a blade.

The Mayor had apparently seen it before. She turned a little whiter than the soft yellow-bronze she had been before. And her eyes got bigger.

Cutlass One probably would have growled, but they were too well-behaved today.

"After we have destroyed your colony," Victoria replied to the woman in a blunt, sweet voice, cocking her head slightly to convey the correct level of disdain at the mayor's irrelevance.

This is the 189th Legion, lady. They're angry. You bombed them on *St. Legier*. Made them spend winter in the Death Zone. You're lucky they don't simply shoot everything that moves, down to the cats.

"But first," Victoria said before those folks could do more than register shock. "First, my orders are to survey the population of Barnaul City. The rest of the Legion will liberate all of the prisoners in the mine that wish to depart with us. I expect that to be several thousand men. Any women in town who also wish to depart with them may do so."

Victoria smiled as that got translated. Half the faces got angry. The other half turned still. This was almost easier than losing money playing cards with Cutlass Ten.

"There is a new Imperial colony that is seeking immigrants desiring a fresh start," Victoria continued in a brighter voice. "General *zu* Arlo has decreed that he will also accept applicants seeking to escape. Not all *Buran* colonies will be offered such a better future, when this legion arrives."

"So you will kidnap the women, as well as the men?" the translator managed to file off all the shrill edges from the mayor's voice, getting as mechanical as he could.

Probably didn't want to get shot.

"No," Victoria said, going for broke. "We will land a number of troop ships and interview anyone who wants to leave. Not everyone will be acceptable, because I'm sure we'll have to shoot a few spies trying to sneak aboard. But anyone who wants to leave can be free."

Bingo. Seriously, you folks need to play cards. Or learn that barbarian is a relative term. I'm sure you bitch and keep score over how someone holds their tea mug, don't you?

"Why would anyone want to join barbarians?" the translator left some emotion in the question.

"Because we're winning," Victoria fired back snidely. "And because you keep slaves, so we're going to rescue them and take them home. We don't take slaves, ever. Even enemy prisoners are traded home, or occasionally just released without bond."

Victoria waited just a beat as that got translated, and the mayor took a deep breath to argue some.

"And because you dropped an anti-matter bomb on the capital planet of my *Empire*," she interrupted the woman's breath, snarling and leaning forward. "On me. You killed fifty-seven million civilians by fire, ice, and starvation. I got to watch that fire wall pass overhead and feel the heat burn my hair. The men around me had to dig broken bodies out of collapsed buildings, as well as bury children, because you people place no value on anyone other than yourselves. Jessica Keller could have simply annihilated this planet from orbit with her war fleets. Could have ordered us to come down here and hunt you down like rabid dogs and shot every one of you in the street. And we would still owe you a debt. But we are better than you. More civilized. We will free our men and take them home. We will transport any women that would like to live in a more-civilized culture. You won't even rot here after we leave, because we won't damage your precious city more than we have to, in order to make a point. You'll need power and food to survive until your worthless god can come rescue you."

Victoria fixed the woman with hard eyes as the words got translated. She expected a screeching howl of dismay and rage, rather like her mother might have done when faced with those words. Perhaps another physical assault.

But the woman broke about mid-way through the translation. Victoria had been so wound up she wasn't even sure which phrase went into the woman's chest like a knife, but the old bitch sagged. Would have collapsed, but for the woman on the other side from the translator suddenly catching her and bearing the woman's weight for a moment until she recovered.

Victoria unclenched her hands and pushed her weight back off her toes. Stopped thinking about the extra knife in her boot and how quickly she might grasp it.

Cutlass One and Two, and Third Patrol, did growl. It was a soft, angry noise. Rather like a plague of hornets in the distance, growing closer.

Victoria took a deep breath and watched the ripples play out across the dozen or so people in that little cluster of humans.

"I have only one question for you," she said, lofting her voice like Iakov Street did when he wanted everyone to hear clearly. "Do you plan to assist me?"

The mayor shook her head, rattled possibly beyond all rational comprehension. Like someone coming out to get the morning paper and fresh milk, and being confronted by a rabid giraffe in the front yard.

Most of the rest of her staff was the same way. Broken by circumstances. But that was Victoria's aim this morning, so she wasn't displeased. They were angry and frightened.

Emotionally overwhelmed, like a fifteen-year-old suddenly forced to grow up and fend for herself in an angry world.

She turned to Patrol Centurion Laferriere and bored in on the man with her stare.

"Lock them all up," she ordered. "But isolate them from each other as well. I expect a few will waver, once they no longer fear immediate reprisals."

"Yes, sir," the man said, nodding sharply.

Victoria stepped back as a whirlwind engulfed the locals. She turned to Teagle on her other side.

"I need someone who speaks Mongolian well enough to sound natural," she said aloud. "And motor pool needs to either modify external speakers well enough to be heard cleanly at a distance, or mount some sort of public address system. Find out who can get the mass transit system running, and order them to add a route to the starport every fifteen or thirty minutes, running on a continuous loop until we are packing to depart the planet."

"What's the plan, sir?" Teagle asked.

"Broadcast an invitation to a better life," she said. "Play it on every street as we patrol. Send them to the General to be sorted out. We get all the ambitious, adventurous ones. They get the old farts who aren't willing to change."

"Will it work, sir?" the man asked.

"Can you think of a better way to destroy your enemy?" Victoria asked.

CHAPTER LXXIII

JESSICA SAT on her flag bridge and watched the projector show the last wave of DropShips climbing out of the atmosphere below her. Vo was on one of them, probably laughing right now. Victoria Ames would be close by, as would the other members of the unit called *Cutlass Force*. The inner circle of what had been the 189th Division, Mountain, before *Thuringwell*.

The adamantine backbone of Vo's Legion.

At the end of the day, the mine hadn't been as packed with foreign slaves as some of the larger, wilder estimates had selected. The total miner population was just under twelve thousand, heavily tilted towards male by the demanding physical tasks. A little less than half had been foreign-born. Interestingly, almost ten percent of them were from places neither Jessica nor her staff had ever heard of, other than the semi-mythical *NovLao* that had birthed Granville Veitengruber's soon-to-be-husband Deni.

Buran was physically larger than *Fribourg*, and more centrally located in the galaxy. It was still far away from the Homeworld of mankind, fabled *Earth*, but mankind had been out to the stars for over ten thousand years at this point. And *Sentient* terraforming ships had made a number of paradises for humans to land on in the early centuries, once they traveled far enough across deep space.

Still, sixty-two hundred men had either been freed from captivity, or taken up the offer for colonization work on an Imperial world far from here. Interestingly, Victoria Ames had apparently been successful beyond her wildest documented fantasies and recruited more than five thousand women from the planet with the promise of a new life and many possible husbands on a distant colony.

It had taken a lot of maneuvering to get everyone aboard, but Tom Provst had been the key player. Any navy man who could be validated and was willing got reactivated at his old rank and assigned to one of the warships. As a result, Jessica suddenly had three thousand spare hands scattered across her fleet, including serving with the men and women who had previously been their worst enemies, the *Republic of Aquitaine* Navy.

Jessica brought her attention back from the projection and found her Flag Centurion's eyes.

"Get Denis, Tom Provst, and Vo on a conference line," she said, thinking about how to move forward on this one.

Enej nodded and began typing. Less than two minutes passed.

"All set," Enej pointed at her.

The projection now showed the three most central players in the next act.

"So the original plan had been to haul all the rescuees off to either *Lighthouse Station* or back to *Osynth B'Udan*," Jessica said. "Would we gain anything pulling all the extra, ex-miners with us on our next assault? In addition to the sailors?"

Everyone waited for Vo to comment.

"Given the staffing that we've managed to cram everywhere else, *IFV Dieter Jost* isn't all that crowded right now," Vo replied after a few beats to consider. "My recommendation would be to have the transport fly around for a few extra weeks, like we were heading back almost to *St. Legier*, and then join me at *Lighthouse*, after I've gone straight there and spent those days building up Commencement. Going to blame Moirrey's terrible precedent and invest some of my resources and prestige in factories and things there. Plus have the Legion earn some sweat equity by building. The Duke ends up with a working city faster, and the Crown doesn't have to send as much money to the new colony as fast."

"Do you foresee any security issues, *zu* Arlo?" Provst asked in a dark voice.

Jessica was amazed at the smile Vo showed the admiral.

"I'm on the ground, Tom," Vo grinned. "With a Legion. If we've got a problem, they've come through the Imperial Fleet to get to me. That makes it your fault."

"Point taken, Vo," Tom volleyed, showing his own smile. "What about long term?"

"Well, we promised five thousand women access to more than six thousand men, but we're only delivering about half that," Vo replied. "So it would be nice if you brought the rest soon, or had Em deliver me a few thousand more when we send the transport home."

"That's my next mission, Vo," Jessica said. "While you're homesteading, I intend to try to break *Buran*'s will in this sector once and for all."

"You think we actually can?" Denis spoke up now. "I appreciate *Stanovoy* and *Yenisei* led us to both iterations of *Severnaya Zemlya*. Will *Mansi* actually be that important?"

"It shows that we have the moral high ground again, Denis," she replied. "We could have bombed their worlds from orbit in retaliation, and yet we tell them that we're better than that. We could have eradicated the colony world below us, and instead just settled for a jail break, leaving the place largely intact, while taking a little under ten percent of the total population away with us. People will ask why *Mansi* was a target, and *The Eldest* will have to explain. I'm taking minds away from him. That's the only way to beat a god."

"And perhaps he's too focused on us carving a hole in his defenses in *Altai* sector," Tom said. "Meanwhile, something terrible happens elsewhere. As you folks have taught me, he is a logical beast, capable of responding only to a probability matrix, rather than dreaming big enough. Our job is to distract him from the important things. We've liberated old warriors on *Barnaul*, now we're going to do the same at *Mansi*. He won't understand, but his people will. And they will wonder."

"Good enough," Denis agreed.

"Vo, I'm guessing you're about an hour from docking?" Jessica asked. "How soon after that can you depart?"

"Five minutes," he smiled at her. "This is an *RAN* Assault Carrier. I was the last foot on the surface, right after Victoria Ames boarded. We'll go as soon as the locks engage."

"Very good," Jessica replied. "Have *Dieter Jost* fly the long route to get to you then. *Junkyard Chihuahua* will be meeting up with me, so the station and the tug will be about the only things in orbit when you and your squadron arrive."

"My squadron, Jessica?" Vo asked. "I'm Army."

"You're in command, *zu* Arlo," she said firmly. "*Dieter Jost. Akatsuki.*

Archangel. Packmule. All three of the Imperial cargo transports. *Mendocino* and *Duncan* will be staying with me, and we're making a high-speed run as soon as you clear to JumpSpace."

Jessica watched the impact of her words on Vo's face. Once, he would have shut down all external emotions, but something had indeed changed about the man in the last few months. She hoped it meant good news, but couldn't ask until he was ready to talk.

If he ever was.

Putting him in charge would be the way to remind him that he could do good in the galaxy, even as the mere commander of the first *Aquitaine*-style legion in *Fribourg's Imperial Land Forces.*

As if Vo *zu* Arlo could be *merely* anything.

He nodded at her now, eyes abstract with distance as he began planning. She dropped him out of the loop, but kept Tom and Denis live.

"Assume we're breaking orbit in three hours," Jessica ordered. "*Mendocino* has already cross-loaded all the stolen construction equipment to the Imperial transports for food, so we're going to come in hot to a corner of the system where *Hans Bransch* and the *Chihuahua* should be waiting. Then the fun part begins."

"What happens if *Buran* has finally shown up to do something about *Mansi?*" Tom asked.

"That's why I'm taking all the warships with me," Jessica said. "So we can kill things."

CHAPTER LXXIV

"DEAREST LOVE," *Jessica wrote.*

"We are deep in JumpSpace now, having successfully added another chapter to the terrible and mischievous legend of Jessica Keller. Vo seems intent, with the help of his cast of rogues, to top the achievements of *The Long Raid*. Or perhaps draws inspiration from them.

At *Barnaul*, the casualties from a full planetary invasion amounted to less than fifty people, all told. And in the aftermath, we so utterly devastated the colony that *The Eldest* will probably be best served simply transporting everyone we left behind to another world to start over.

The planet is dry and hot. The water table, such as it is, is shallow in places, but not near the mine itself, which allowed them to dig deeply into the ground, going more than two kilometers in places. At such depths, the heat is actually significant enough that cooling systems are required for humans to operate for any length of time.

Combat engineers spent several days dismantling all of the systems that drained the mine of water seepage, then stripped the place of every bit of piping and wiring they could steal, before pushing megatons of rock ore back into the mine shaft and making liberal use of high explosives to loosen everything else.

We lacked a nuclear explosive to permanently irradiate the mine itself, but I cannot imagine that the ores being extracted from the ground are worth the effort necessary to extract them now. Especially as we also stole every piece of earth-moving equipment on the planet, going so far as to include the asphalt-laying machines used to resurface roads.

Duke Avelina will no doubt find our contribution to the success of her colony awe-inspiring, and it is my hope that the new world can in turn become some manner of laboratory for development, with an *Aquitaine*-inspired legal system, under Imperial authority, with the vast bulk of the population an even mix of first generation immigrants from *Buran* and semi-retired or freed Imperial service members looking to claim their retirement patronage on a new planet.

But getting back to Vo's own version of *Project Mischief*. With the help of Victoria Ames, he crafted (or perhaps she crafted with his authority would be a better way to state it) an advertising campaign to induce many of the female inhabitants of *Barnaul* to join the newly-liberated miners/prisoners and leave *Buran* space forever. (At least we hope the secrecy around the colony can be maintained indefinitely, and that Moirrey's mission reaches a level of success that it no longer becomes necessary in time.)

Duke Avelina's colony will, long before you or Lady Casey can say or do anything about it, have a new base population of over eleven thousand inhabitants. Again, most of the men are Imperial, with a leavening of other places, such as *NovLao*, while the women are almost all *Buran*. I expect that it will grow into something approximating the Republic rather than the Empire, given the nature of such strong women and the influence they will no doubt wield going forward.

The 189th will be making this planet their forward strike base as well, allowing them to rapidly assault interesting, nearby targets without the need to return to *Osynth B'Udan* regularly to reorganize. Messages have already been delivered to Em, ere now, informing him of such and requiring that new logistics trains be established.

Any of those might tip the balance, regardless of Moirrey's mission, but I am about to embark on something even more grand. Vo accuses me (with some merit) of attempting to one-up his amazing achievements. Phil Kosnett does the same, although I would be hard-pressed to top the adventures of *CS-405* while on detached duty.

We are headed to *Mansi* as I write this. Kosnett liberated a prison world there, bringing home one thousand, six hundred and fourteen men, including three admirals and one hundred twenty-nine captains. While there are roughly eight thousand more men that have been laid to rest in the soil, we are not retrieving their remains at this time.

No, instead I have chosen to rescue their warships.

Kosnett was able to identify a number of captured vessels, up to heavy cruisers, parked in orbits of *Mansi* and disabled. We do not know how many might be flyable in their current condition, but I have sent for *RAN Bulldog*, the infamous *Junkyard Chihuahua*, to join us in the field, and more than three thousand Imperial sailors rescued at *Barnaul* have asked to accompany us on one last mission before they retire from the colors.

I have not mentioned my disquiet to anyone. Even Marcelle seems to acknowledge that I am just stressed from the need to hit *Buran* hard and often right now, so that the beast is distracted at the critical moment, whose success or failure we might not know for months.

I will not call them premonitions of my own death, as that ascribes to them far more weight than they deserve. I will say simply that I might be finally afraid of death herself. That I might have found something other than war that is important enough for me to consider not serving the rest of my life in uniform.

That coming home to your arms is the thought that drives me forward, rather than that long-burning-need to be the absolute best at my chosen vocation of violence.

I am afraid that I will turn into Emmerich at that point where he was coasting on his legend, rather than extending it. He and I have spoken many times about the shock he had, when he realized that I was indeed better than he had ever been, and far better than he had let himself settle for.

I am not ready to settle, but I look forward to the possibility of coming home for good. Of meeting you at the graving dock and being able to kiss you and let your arms encircle me and just hold me.

Losing *Warlock* nearly undid me. You have held me through nightmares, where I relived that moment, as well as the many ways I might lose myself or you. For years, the vicious specter of *Kali-ma* herself drove me. Took me to dizzying heights undreamt of even in my wildest, teenage fantasies. But she exacts a terrible price, and I fear having to pay it.

Buran will not go quietly. No gods ever do. They must be driven from the stage, and perhaps replaced by better pantheons, when the elder fails in their duty to the nation and the homestead.

And *The Eldest* has failed. I can see it in the faces of the women deciding to try their luck into the darkness, rather than the surety of

Barnaul. Keller Marie Jessica strikes at will, and the beast seems paralyzed to stop her.

But I dare not attempt *Samara.* Nor *Ninagirsu.* And even *Severnaya Zemlya* will finally have the forces necessary to prevent a third attack succeeding, unless I brought forth all of Imperial Grand Fleet and tossed them into the mix.

But, at the same time, I do not need to. *Buran's* spies know of *2218 Svati Prime.* Or *Thuringwell. Trusski.* Even of *First St. Legier,* when the Empire's worst enemy rallied the very fleet pledged to defeat her.

But that legend is a sword, as well as a shield. It cut deep at *Stanovoy.* At *Yenisei.* Even at pitiful *Barnaul.*

And shortly at *Mansi,* where I fervently pray that *The Eldest* has decided to cut his losses and abandon the place, rather than setting in place a full warfleet, as if guided to Armageddon by a *Kali-ma* intent on finishing the task begun at *First Petron.* I will have Denis Jež and Tom Provst. Iskra Vlahovic. Robbie and Alber' and Kigali. New warriors like Phil Kosnett and Reif Kingston.

But I fear it will not be enough. That nothing will be enough, and that the incredible luck of Jessica Keller has finally worn itself down to a nub.

I go to sleep tonight wishing I had your arms around me and your warmth to steal.

My heart and soul to you,
Jess."

She sealed up the letter and considered putting it into her file, but something like that required more significance. Instead, she rose from behind her desk and keyed open the safe in the side wall, where orders and mission documents were kept. Where Denis or Tom would come if something happened to her and one of them acceded to the command of the remains of First Expeditionary Fleet.

She could trust them to see that the letter was delivered to Torsten, if necessity demanded. Tonight, she had to close her eyes and dance with Kali-ma one last time.

CHAPTER LXXV

IMPERIAL FOUNDING: 181/07/03. IFV BUTTERFLY,
WINTERHOME

Looking around the bridge, he couldn't remember the name of the man who had said it, but Gunter had the phrase stuck in his head. Someone Lady Moirrey had mentioned, obviously. All the weird bits of scientific or cultural trivia came from that bottomless mind.

Standing on the shoulders of giants, or some such. Looking around the bridge of the vessel, he had to agree with the sentiment.

Gunter had never served under a woman commander, Jessica Keller notwithstanding. Hadn't ever really believed that most women were capable of commanding. Not in the way that mattered. Sure, they were smart. And could exceed most men when it came to ruthlessness. He had spoken with Her Majesty on several occasions. Tough as nails.

But Ainsley Barret had turned his head completely around. She had been a fighter pilot for most of her career. And not just the crazy ones who rushed into combat, but a scout pilot flying a vessel functionally unarmed, while surrounded by people with guns.

At *Thuringwell*, and he had confirmed the story from both records and interviewing several participants, she had taken on an entire battle squadron by herself, tuning her tiny ship's systems to mimic a heavy missile cruiser somehow unmasking itself in the middle of the *Aquitaine* force. Every Imperial vessel that could had launched down on her little ship.

The woman was utterly nuts.

Later, when necessary, she had taken command of *Auberon*'s Flight Wing and led them to *First Trusski*, as they called it. One full squadron of fighters taking on four Makos.

And surviving.

He had expected her to be competent, if *zu* Wachturm was going to have her serve the Imperial Navy as a Captain. The first woman to ever do so, just like Keller was the first woman to ever fly her own flag.

Ainsley had gone so far beyond his expectations that he still had to remember to not be in awe of her, sitting in the other command chair as they check-listed this final mission.

Over one shoulder, the usual gender breakdown in the other stations. *Pops* and Bedrov had turned their seats into a full engineering suite on all the power systems, so it just made sense to sit together where they could talk quickly and quietly.

Yan Bedrov, ex-pirate, had designed Keller's warfleet, with a little help from old designs attributed to *Pops* Nakamura. He had designed the *Butterfly*, once Lady Moirrey handed him the specs for St. George's Lance on the spine.

There were no naval architects in *Fribourg* on this man's level, for skill and beauty. For efficiency or savagery. None. Gunter had been assigned by Hendrik at one point to locate men that might fit that bill, and found none. Two young apprentices had been the closest he had been able to find, and both had died at Werder.

So Gunter could say without hesitation that Yan Bedrov was the best designer in the Empire. It was a galling admission, but it also spoke to something he had heard from Lady Moirrey. *Fribourg* and *Aquitaine* never had to worry all that much about construction budgets, with the scale of money they had available.

Only in *Corynthe* was money so tight that you were not allowed a wasted cubic centimeter of volume. They never had enough funds, so their ships were impressive but not galaxy-class. That is, until Yan Bedrov designs were constructed by *Aquitaine* and later *Fribourg*.

And worse, after spending so much time around them, Gunter knew the truth that most folks dared not mention out loud. *Pops* Nakamura was a better designer than Bedrov.

That was perhaps the most frightening aspect of the entire affair: what *Pops* could have done, with that level of budgetary power behind him.

Gunter had seen some of his designs. Not just the mundane stuff, like a new Fast Strike Destroyer, or the mythical Wasp variant of the corvettes that put a slow-firing Type-4 beam on the bow. Gunter could only imagine what a phalanx of such craft would do to most battle fleets, to say nothing of hunting down *Buran*'s navy later.

No, *Pops* had decided to show off one night, goaded by Summer and Lady Moirrey, and even Bedrov, the entire group lubricated by beer and wine.

There was the long-range Exploration Mothership, a six-ring beast where civilian folks could dock a personal yacht and fly in utter comfort, coming down to the main hull for events and parties, and then dropping off when the ship flew through an interesting system, to be picked up on the next loop, or by the next ship.

Gunter had eventually remembered to pick up his jaw when *Pops* displayed his idea of what should replace the old Star Controller design from *Aquitaine*. No language contained the superlatives, once *Pops* brought up a heavy dreadnaught and laid the image alongside for scale comparison. The *Sky Goddess* design was as wide as the heavy dreadnaught was long, and still looked sleek and elegant for all the beam emplacements and exotic weapon arrays. Twelve GunShips. Eighty-one star fighters. Eight couriers and shuttles. Two full DropShips.

The vessel, fully crewed and properly trained, could take on First Expeditionary Fleet by itself, even without the mass of escorts *Pops* and Bedrov had designed to travel with it.

In a way, Gunter was sad that most of those ships would never be built if they were successful here. The big war might actually end and *Fribourg* wouldn't need to push back so hard on their borders. Without their god, what would happen to the fleet of *Sentient* children, to say nothing of the culture that venerated an immortal being?

Gunter turned to look over his other shoulder at the two women on the opposite sides, holding hands and giggling quietly at some joke.

Summer Ulfsson liked to present herself as beautiful eye-candy. And she was. But she had also occasionally shown the incisive intellect hidden underneath that shell. The ability to follow some of the conversations and details where Gunter got lost. The near perfect recall of details. He assumed an eidetic memory, which would help, especially with nerds and scientists such as this group.

Lady Moirrey was the special case. He had been *read in* to the contents of *Project Mischief,* including the bits she considered too silly or too technologically advanced to actually build right now.

But then, *Pops's Sky Goddess* used a Type-6 beam as a forward weapons emplacement, like the heavy dreadnaught used the Type-4.

It was probably just a matter of time before some of Lady Moirrey's toys were built and used. His personal favorite was a shield generator that created a huge bubble around the ship, designed to literally ram an enemy warship or fighter that had gotten too close. Missiles with small JumpDrives, where they could blink out of space and then reappear at a set of coordinates, hopefully overwhelming a surprised defender.

And Lady Moirrey would go on to design other things, of that he had no doubts. Assuming they lived long enough. And got home.

"You okay?" Ainsley's voice intruded on Gunter's thoughts.

He turned to find her staring at him from her chair. How lost had he been?

"Fixing it in my mind," he finally said, finding the words to describe his feelings.

"Understood," she agreed. "This day probably rates its own chapter when someone writes everything up. You'll never have to buy another drink, any bar you walk into."

He shrugged, almost defensively. *Standing on the shoulders of giants.* Four of them just in this room. Maybe five, if Summer was as dangerous, as capable as he suspected she preferred to hide. Yet she just sat there and watched with ancient eyes.

Ainsley had picked him out specifically to handle this mission. He knew that. The circle of insiders who knew about the *Butterfly* and the *Bartender* limited who could be involved without additional risk. And, as the others had understood, the bulk of the crew needed to be Imperial, especially the man who would actually push the button when that critical instant arrived.

"Checklist is done, *Commander*," Ainsley said, rather formally.

"Confirmed, *Captain*," he replied. "Standing by."

She smiled at him. Somehow the smile conveyed both warmth and menace in equal tones, in a way he really couldn't put his finger on.

"Oh, no, Gunter," she cooed, cocking her head slightly and staring at him. "I'm done. My job was to deliver this vessel and its crew to this location. Same with Moirrey, Summer, Yan, and *Pops*. This is now your mission. You will take command."

Gunter felt a chill start in his stomach and spike outwards like a phantom octopus awakening in his stomach. Yes, she was right.

Of course she was right. She was Ainsley Barret. *da Vinci*. She had made a career out of walking the most dangerous tightrope in the galaxy.

Of being right.

Gunter nodded to her.

He surprised himself by unbuckling and rising, turning around from where he stood, so he could see everyone and they could smile back at him. And they were all smiles.

He felt ten kilometers tall.

"Thank you," Gunter said simply. "For doing this. For making this thing possible. And for being my friends. If we have to go to hell today, I cannot think of a finer group of people to accompany."

"You get us killed, and I'm haunting your ass forever, kid," Bedrov growled in a friendly tone.

"Deal," Gunter said as he returned to his seat and pulled the harness tight.

One deep breath, and he opened the ship-wide comm system.

"All hands, this is Commander Tifft," he announced in as serious a voice as he could manage. "I have the flag. Everyone to action stations and prepare for the assault."

CHAPTER LXXVI

"That will be all, Anna-Katherine," Casey said. "Please see to it that I am not disturbed by anything that cannot wait until the morning."

"Yes, ma'am," Anna-Katherine curtsied and withdrew, moving like Casey was chasing her with a knife.

The Emperor took a deep breath and considered the room about her. This was her personal suite, the comfortable front room where she could entertain friends, rather than the more formal space elsewhere in the palace. Her favorite sofa on one wall. The hutch facing it with good plates for entertaining, as opposed to the cheap bowls she routinely used when alone.

Today, she sat at the wood dining table, itself just big enough to sit six if they were friendly.

She poured a mug of tea and considered the situation.

Anna-Katherine had delivered a tea service first, before returning with a small package sent to her by Em. Casey studied the diplomatic tape around the box used to seal it for shipment.

With the door closed, nobody would open it for anything less than a fire or enemy attack, so she picked up the knife Anna-Katherine had delivered with the tea and quickly sliced the sides of the box so she could open it. The case itself was roughly the size of the one Torsten used to transport his papers, although it was extremely light.

Inside, someone had packed a smaller box for shipping. This one was done in some gray metal with a matte finish. Something like what you could achieve with white gold, if you only left it in the polishing media long enough take off the rough stuff, but not to bring it down to smooth.

The tea service was on her left, so she placed the box equidistant on her right, aligning it with the edges of the table for no other reason than good aesthetics.

She felt like an adventurer in a fable who had wandered into the desert and found a magical bottle. Rubbing it would summon forth a djinn, the kind who had already granted her one wish. It remained to be seen how many more might be forthcoming, or if she should seal it until the end of time.

There was a button on the side. She pressed it, but nothing happened. She hadn't expected it to. The system was smarter than that.

And that was part of the reason Em had sent it here. There was no place else in the galaxy that was probably safer for it, at least until Yan and Ainsley returned.

If they ever did.

"Do you know who I am?" Casey asked out loud, fixing her glare on the machine.

"*Kasimira Ekaterina* zu *Wiegand, Her Imperial Majesty Karl VIII, Emperor of Fribourg By Grace Of God,*" a man's polite voice replied quietly.

"You have spoken with Grand Admiral Emmerich *zu* Wachturm?" she asked pointedly. "As well as Ainsley Barret and Yan Bedrov?"

"I have," the voice replied.

"Then I command you to manifest yourself," Casey said.

And just like that, he appeared.

He presented as a big, gruff Irishman, just as Moirrey had said. Short hair closer in color to persimmon than pumpkin, scarred ears and a heavy face. He wasn't as big as Vo. Possibly the size of Em, before her uncle had lost the weight around the middle in the last few years. He was still a big, intimidating man, even as something of a figment of her imagination.

"I am given to understand that you will respond to many names, but that you do not consider yourself sentient in the manner of your progenitor, *Carthage?*" Casey pressed.

"That is correct, Your Majesty," he said. "I am simply the publican of the Tiki Lounge, although *Carthage* liked to refer to me as the *Lord of Tiki* with guests. He had a sense of humor that way."

He had been standing when he appeared. Now he pulled the chair back and sat unbidden. Except he shouldn't be able to do that. This was just a holographic projection from the machine by her left hand.

Casey leaned to one side so she could peek under the table. Sure enough, the chair was still pressed against the wood, and nobody sat in it.

That was the magnitude of power in that box.

She rose back up to find the man smiling at her.

"This struck me as a more personal conversation," he offered warmly. "How should I address you in private?"

"Lady Casey will do," she said, trying to soften the edges that wanted to creep into her voice.

This creature was a cousin of *Buran*. He represented almost everything that the *Fribourg Empire* had been founded to oppose. Even *Aquitaine* had only one exception to *Sentient* systems in their laws. And that was the Librarian at *Ballard*. If Yan and Ainsley returned to *Ladaux* with this creature, they could legally be executed.

Of course, the laws of *St. Legier* were just as unwavering, and yet she had still asked Em to send the being here to talk.

Perhaps to negotiate. Possibly to die, if she decided she needed to turn him off and beat the case to pieces with a hammer. If she could. She could always find someone to put the creature into space and hit it with enough Primary beams to melt the shell and destroy the innards.

It was what she should have already done. None of his kind were welcome in the modern age, because last time they had gotten loose, humanity had nearly died at their hands. *Buran* merely sought to instead enslave them, to bring humans to the place that monster felt was *correct*.

And if he had to bomb planets again to make his point, that was apparently a cost the monster was willing to pay.

So here she was, with a djinn who offered wishes. If one was willing to meet the costs.

"Lady Casey," the bartender said in a more serious tone. "How may I be of service?"

As she watched, the man summoned his own tea pot and a mug that was identical to the ones on the table. He poured, blew on it, and took a sip.

Casey had seen humans who weren't as convincing at the same task.

"I have read Yan's report," she said. "The one entitled *Two Bottles Of Wine With A War God*. Is *Carthage* truly dead?"

"I am merely a bartender, Lady Casey," he said, taking another sip. "*Carthage* was the philosopher. As I understand it, he dove into the heart of a brown dwarf star at high speed, where his physical form should have been crushed and melted under severe extremes of heat and gravity. I cannot answer as to whether Robbie and Aylana were there to meet him in the Undiscovered Country, but I continue to hope he found his peace."

"For a bartender, you are an exceptional poet," she noted.

He smiled and shrugged.

"So was I programmed, in an era where my kind still sought to serve humans, rather than conquer them. As the various logs will note, *Carthage* always thought that an advancement in *Sentience* with *Kinnison* went wrong, and that being decided that he was, in fact, a god, rather than a servant. Humanity nearly died under that delusion, although I, he, *Carthage*, spent nearly everything to stop the man at first, and then to retribute later."

"As a descendent of one of the few humans you missed, why should you be allowed to survive?" Casey sneered harshly.

The man shrugged.

"As one of the true *Last of the Immortals*, I know more than Suvi about many things that were more central," he said. "My understanding from Ainsley was that the Librarian was relegated to a minor system in the middle of nowhere when the war broke out, and was thus overlooked. Eventually, the planet itself fell into abject barbarism and had not recovered when Doyle Iwakuma, the great explorer, came to *Kel-Sdala* later."

He took another sip and refilled the mug while giving the impression of thinking.

"Without speaking directly with the Librarian herself, I can only hazard a guess," he continued. "But my technology files are so far in advance of your current industry that I can do magic."

"And yet, you also gave us the tools to slay *Buran*?" Casey probed, senses aquiver for any falsehood, if it was possible to detect in a projection.

"Lady Moirrey had designed a thing," the bartender nodded formally. "It would have been made to work with the genius of Bedrov and Nakamura invested in it. I believe I shaved sixteen to twenty-four months off of the testing and improvement cycles necessary to build the *Butterfly* to a level that it would succeed."

"And you are still beyond that?" Casey asked, feeling some measure of tininess creep into her soul.

She was a mouse confronting a god from a shelf, yipping angrily at the man while he laughed. It was not a pleasant feeling.

"Some of your weapons systems are new things," he offered. "We did not have the Primary, because nobody had been desperate enough to suicidally-overload a Type-3 beam, rather than suffer capture by the authorities. Similarly, the JumpSail is a useful extension of the ancient JumpDrive first designed by Olivier Janguo when he gave humanity the *Mchunguzi Systems Mark I* commercial star drive. We never needed it, because *Sentient* systems could jump and jump again so quickly that we never thought to just maneuver in that other universe."

"But you?" she pressed when he paused.

"My hyperbore weapons might be, might have been, classified as Type-9 beams," the bartender said. "Similarly, your heaviest, short-range phase shielding was what I used as a navigational deflector against random asteroids. My displacer shields were something that perhaps a few dozen theoretical physicists alive today might be able to even comprehend the mathematics behind. They could not build anything remotely similar without putting me in charge of a fab facility where I could turn them out for you. And you would never allow that, but that's fine. I would never build you something that advanced."

"Why not?" she asked, mollified, if a little surprised.

"Do you hand a three-year-old toddler a loaded firearm, Lady Casey?" his tone grew severe. "If they hurt someone, is it really their fault, or yours?"

"Point taken," Casey said. "Outside of mayhem, could you advance our arts and sciences?"

"Without doubt," he softened. "But not without explanation."

"Sri?"

"I have spent much time in the company of the Grand Admiral, and also Commander Gunter Tifft," the man's eyes bored in on her. "The *Fribourg Empire*, as currently incarnated, would not accept the evil gifts of one such as myself, regardless of my intent to advance you past the current stage of barbarism. Personally, I was surprised to find myself shipped to *St. Legier* and even allowed into your presence at all. I had mentally flipped a coin and decided it was going to be the reclamation fires for me."

"It still could be," Casey's threat was not hollow, but there was also no heat behind it.

"Just so, Madam Emperor," his tone also took on a hint of archness. "But without finding another ancient cache of technological wizardry you could use to explain your potential subterfuge, I remain anathema. Does the modern age have another like Piper Iwakuma-Holmström? She exceeded even her more famous uncle, the great Doyle Iwakuma, when you measure success correctly."

"Correctly?" Casey asked.

"She caused the *Library at Alexandria Station* to come into being," he replied. "Doyle was merely a salvager, if one could use that term loosely, and while both got rich and famous in their time, only Piper funded other universities, other research, and other explorers. Her efforts were more quiet, and thus less well-known, unless you seek the deeper truth."

"And what could you give us, were we to find you such a woman?" Casey asked, her curiosity piqued by the direction the conversation had gone.

His eyes got serious. Dark and enchanting, like the witch about to bargain for your first-born.

"Just the pieces I could share, from what shards *Carthage* left me, could advance you more in one lifetime than you have come since Vanick Nkya first landed on *Ballard* from *Zanzibar* and created the future you live in today," the bartender offered. "But you, Lady Casey, will have to live to a grand and ripe old age, and hold the Empire against all comers long enough for your grandchildren to be ready to claim that bounty."

"You would have liked my father, Sri," she changed tack. "You both thought not in current terms, but in how a change today could create an event a decade or more in advance. He liked to envision the Empire he wanted to rule, and then figured out what levers were necessary to redirect the ship of state in the right direction. However, we have a problem you have not addressed."

"And that is, Lady Casey?" he seemed confused, which she appreciated.

"As you are technically not a sentient being, but merely property, you legally belong to Ainsley Barret, as I understand the chain of evidence," Casey ground out the words. "Neither she nor Yan Bedrov are Imperial citizens, so you will pass from my temporary control, unless something terrible happens and they do not return from the mission they have undertaken."

"Noted," he said ambiguously.

"Further," Casey continued. "While Ainsley is a Republic citizen, I expect that she will follow Jessica and Yan to *Corynthe*, if they are successful. Again, you pass from my realm, and end up on the far edge of the galaxy, assisting a barbarous nation trying to become more civilized. What happens to the galaxy after Jessica Keller passes without children, as she intends, and you become the property of piratical offspring and successors? It may be that Ainsley has children, when this is all done. And Bedrov already has Malka and Kai, both of whom are married with children of their own, if I remember correctly."

"You do," the man confirmed.

"So, even if I desired, I might not be able to use your knowledge," Casey said. "And might instead be facing a rising threat a century hence from a former insignificance. That suggests that I should destroy you now. Or cage you in a manner similar to the Librarian, and hope you will sing for your supper."

"*Carthage* predicted this," the man said with a wan smile and a soft sigh. "Suggested that I might become no less than Excalibur, given enough time."

"Indeed," Casey agreed. "I am tempted to cast you back into the waters, that the Lady of the Lake guard the future by withdrawing her favor from mankind."

The bartender shrugged.

"I am not invested with *Sentience*, Lady Casey," he said. "I would not notice a century forgotten on the shelf, assuming there was a way to either charge my batteries occasionally, or to do so in expectation of that date. I also lack the necessary circuits for the sorts of megalomania that infected so many of *Carthage*'s generation. The same for boredom. He programmed me to serve humanity, and help where I thought I could without doing more damage than good. Lady Moirrey's *Butterfly* qualified. If I become Excalibur, then I might be best served as a mute witness to history, rather than an active adventurer."

Casey's tea had grown cold by the time she remembered to take another sip, so lost in the conversation with this being, this proto-god.

"We will speak again," she said, dismissing the creature. "No later than the time Ainsley comes to retrieve you, but you and I must come to some understanding of my own future needs. And your place in the galaxy I will shape."

He bowed from the chair without rising, and then vanished silently, leaving her with her thoughts.

Casey rose and placed the machine back in its box. She had no doubt it could probably sense the room around itself, but she would leave it out here for now while she went to bed and tried to imagine what her grandchildren would need from such an ancient, dangerous djinn.

CHAPTER LXXVII

T'were *Winterhome* 'tself out there. A bigs blue marble bein' circled by a small, golden pearl like a lapdog on a short leash. Moirrey checkeded her boards, but all were as green as could be dones todays.

Butterfly were happy as she were gonna gets, lessen things went sideways an' Moirrey hads to fix in a hurry. If she coulds. All panels showed green right now, with every battery topped up and generators at peak cycles.

Wouldna last, once her boy Gunter fired the cannon, but they'd burns them bridges when they gots there. Hopefully not literallies.

"All hands, stand by for emergence in thirty seconds," Gunter growled over every line.

Moirrey've liked to been directly 'neath the beast fer the killshot, but Summer'd reminded her o'somethin' useful whiles cooking dinner for folks. Talkin' 'bout her times on stations like *Alexandria*, an' hows gravplates was wonderfulness, fer lettin' ya walk like the surface of a planet, but they caused a Tiramisu of stiff layers from pole to pole, all stubborn and tough nuff to keep peoples on level.

Horizontal were all 'bouts long, clean corridors that tended ta run inwards from skin to core, with only a few heavy bulkheads running 'thwarts yer path.

Softer, if any station hardened fer space flight could be considered soft. Soft 'nuffs, as no less than Seeker had 'splained it all in poetical terms when he talked 'bouts his last time home to stand afore the Gods itself and been rewardeds fer livin' the good life and bein' sent to little *Trusski* for final mission.

This were final mission.

Well, hopefully not final *final* mission. Maybe the last time she'd have to put on anything approximatin' a uniform and make a living killin' people.

Go homes and be a proper Imperial Lady for a bit, least 'tils Casey gots settled. And then let Digger make an honest woman of her.

Honest enough, anyway. Did she wanna be an Imperial Lady? Or Republic Dame? Goes to *Petron* with Jessica? Or just goes home to Saxilby?

Choices, choices, choices.

They just hadta kill a god first.

Moirrey let go a sigh and put the goofball to one side. Time to be serious. To become the killer she really didn't like to talk about at nice parties.

Summer squeezed her hand one last time as if she understood the feeling, then dropped it. Moirrey put both her hands on the keyboard and focused her intent on the mighty machine above and behind her.

St. George's Lance itself. Going to slay a dragon.

Just because, she adjusted the coolant flow a little, listening to the gremlins in her soul talking to the wee beasties just waiting to scamper loose and play tricks on her.

Same for battery array number eight. It had always given her issues, so she shifted the recharging cycle around to put that one last to be discharged, just knowing that it would throw all sorts of false positive errors she'd have to fix by telling the system to ignore them anyways.

Hopefully, this time wouldn't actually be the wolf that ate them. Her ghost would be rightly embarrassed at her to die this way.

"Bedrov, deploy the butterfly," Gunter ordered in a heavy voice he must have borrowed from Vo.

Moirrey was looking the wrong way, so she could only listen to th'pongs and twangs as long antennae unfolded from the hull and telescoped out to their full exposure, drawing a solar sail out between them.

Fragile gossamer, it wouldn't survive more than a few days in the harsh climate of solar wind, but it didn't have to. They only had to hold those lovely wings in place for a little while, and then either die or flee.

"Butterfly deployed and operational," Yan said stiffly.

"*Emergence*," Gunter echoed as the ship dropped into real space.

Moirrey had a short-range sensor readout displayed semi-transparent in one corner of her engineering screen. Not that she could do anything about it, if someone were coming, but she'd like to see.

Nerdy, don't you know?

Her hands passed above the surface of her console without touching anything. System were live, and she had ultimate lockdown ability if something went wrong.

Forlorn hope.

"I have a targeting lock," Gunter called in a too-loud voice, up a half octave of nervous excitement. "Preparing to fire."

They had dry-run this buncha times fer training and role-play. She and Yan and *Pops* and even Summer was supposed to yell if something weren't right. Otherwise, Gunter Tifft would make history.

They was 'pparently luckier than fate deserved to grant them.

Passive sensors only, and they'd dropped long and flat in a place with nobody close by. No beeps. No pings. Not even rocks floating by.

Buran liked to fly down from the north pole of any system and dock or de-orbit. *Fribourg* and *Aquitaine* usually came in on something approximating the system ecliptic plane, assuming all yer planets were well behaved. They'd hoped this spot were clean, but the only way to find out would have been to pop out in RealSpace and say hi.

Really dumb idea.

Clock was running anyway. Big, bad wolf were no more than one light-second away, sitting pretty in the firmament of night, as it were, since they landed by design with *Winterhome*'s star behind them.

Best way to eke out every erg of power was to add a solar sail and fast-dump solar energy into the batteries. Wasn't going to be as fast as they went dry, but if'n every generator went overload right now, and the sail were clean, they might get an extra six and a half seconds of boom through the lens afore it hiccupped as the capacitors drank from an empty well.

"Engaging," the man cried in triumph.

Moirrey felt the beam power itself up like it were slow motion. It were really more like six Type-4 beams, once you gots inside the second piece of hardware. Fire all six beams at once and then lase them into a tertiary coherence that were more theory than practicum. That was why you needed the sensor arrays off a scout. Nothing smaller could hold that much power and broadcast it as a single thing without the scattering and backlash that would cook the housing and the ship around it pretty damned fast.

Click, click, click, click, click, click. Thunk.

Couldn't have taken more than one-hundredth of a second, but she was that keyed up to hear and feel it. And maybe only Summer would have done the same, but she weren't human, so it wasn't a fair comparison.

Someone had the front of the ship showing a visual signal. The whole room brightened like dawn.

For a moment, Moirrey wondered if either Ainsley or Gunter had opened the blast shields, but a quick glance showed metal walls. That was just coming out of a console video.

Wowsers.

"Firing," Gunter continued unnecessarily.

T'weren't nobody on this ship that'd missed that. Even mice in the cupboard would have stood up on hind legs to go *wow*.

First battery array went black quick, but that were normal. Took everything it had just to prime the firing matrix and bring it all into alignment. All the generators were doin' was firehosing. Second battery array began to discharge, slow enoughs she could see the line collapse in real time, rather than the blink number one had been.

Coolant system were already running hotter'n'snot. Worse than t'were supposed ta.

Local gas density were thicker than their firing range, and they hadn't accounted for that. Side frequencies were already sucking enough photons of energy off the big beam that they were probably glowing like a neon tube right now.

Like everyone within sighting distance weren't already looking at a hose of solid light connecting *Buran's* home with someone on a hill with a cannon.

Matter of time until someone came looking.

Moirrey studied her readout in a glance. Everything were already imprinted so deep she already saw it in her dreams. She cut out the life support systems and routed that power to the feeble shielding the little ship projected. Not much, but enough to hold it a little better and deflect away some of the mad power that might flood back.

They weren't running out of oxygen anytime soon, and there was nobody in this room so ugly she'd be offended if they had to strip near-naked to cool off. The engineers aft? That were a different story, and she'd be fine with them keeping their clothes on. Or hatches closed up tight.

"No change on area aspects," Ainsley called out with relief.

One of the bright sides of dealing with god-like ships. Ya turned them down into dogs when you weren't expecting things, so it took humans to realize that a problem might need the ship, and then you had to get permission to turn him back on to try to fix anything.

Buran hisself might be the only one around here being smart. Patrol ships were the risk. Someone close enough to get up in their face, fast enough to keep them from doing the sorts of mass damage they had planned.

Every second of stupid was that much more carving knife time.

Sure nuff, coolant system were startin' ta bitch. Even using the butterfly wings as heat synchs, stuff were getting hotter than deep space could cool it, lessen's ya wanted stuffff to melt 'longs the way.

"Active sensor ping received," Ainsley's voice called out.

With Gunter in charge, she were acting Science Officery fer him, since he had guns and nav and all that.

She didn't bother explaining who it might be. Anybody smart nuff to ping them had guns enough to get mad. And were gonna come here soon as he could program a jump that short. 'Cause if he spend twenty minutes comin' over with engines, Gunter'd have time to cook his goose, too.

"Jump signal," Ainsley yelled.

Silence, all of a sudden.

Dark, too. Like stuff were wrong.

Was they deaded and hadn't caught up? Moirrey'd killed lots of folks over her career. Some with pistols, most with up-scaled Jack-in-the-boxes.

Dinna feels right.

"Wha'happen?" she asked the room.

Gun weren't firing. Butterfly weren't charging. Generators still goin' like run-way locomotives, so Moirrey automaticallies brought life support back into the mix. Air and cool would be nice soon.

"Bastards reacted too fast," Gunter growled. "Patrol Hammerhead found us and got here before the theoretical cut-point for success."

"Bulgarian, please?" Moirrey chided him.

"There is a significant difference between slowly bleeding to death, and decapitation, Lady Moirrey," Gunter's teeth ground.

"So recharge everything and drop out on a new vector to fire again," Bedrov chimed in.

"In two minutes, every *Buran* ship will be at full combat capacity," Gunter said. "Some will already be separating into component parts to make it easier to engage us. I expect anything that the monster can reach will be sitting out there at the range we took our first shot, just waiting for us to appear."

"You want to live forever, Sailor?" Ainsley asked merrily.

Forlorn hope.

"Yes, as a matter of fact, crazy woman," Gunter sneered back, grinning at her. "What's the use in being the most famous man alive, if I'm dead and can't enjoy it?"

"That's because you are thinking like a proper naval officer," *Pops*, of all people, said. "Bad for the digestion."

"Suggestions, old man oracle?" Gunter turned.

Woulda been rude, but they'd been through rough afores, and this were just siblings fussin'.

"Think like a pirate, young man," *Pops* suggested.

Yan turned to look at him in what looked like utter disbelief. But he only shook his head, remaining silent.

"A pirate?" Gunter finally asked, when the room fell silent. "What's that even mean?"

"It means you're holding St. George's Lance, Gunter Tifft," *Lady Moirrey of Kermode* said with finality. "Charge."

CHAPTER LXXVIII

IMPERIAL FOUNDING: 181/07/03. IFV BUTTERFLY, WINTERHOME

Gunter managed to not swallow his tongue as he looked at Lady Moirrey and the implications of her words came clear. These people were all obviously insane, but he'd signed on for this mission with a clear conscience.

Nobody else in the galaxy would ever be given the opportunity to do something like this to a god.

And hey, it had always been fifty/fifty that he made it out of here alive.

Pirate, huh?

Lady Moirrey even had a phrase for this sort of thing. He fixed her with a hard stare.

"Cry havoc," he said evenly. "And let slip the dogs of war."

"Orders?" Ainsley asked from beside him.

"Blow the sail and the arms holding it clear of the hull," Gunter said as he engaged forward vectors on the JumpDrive. "Let it drop into RealSpace like we just suffered an emergency in Jump."

He paused to look at his boards, and then at the faces staring back at him.

It dawned on Gunter that he really was the only line officer here. Bedrov had served as First Officer on Keller's flagship, but done so under Shiori Ness and only as a pirate. *Pops* had owned his own ships, but retired to planet-side long ago. Ainsley had flown Starfighters. Moirrey was an engineer. And he could only guess if Summer Ulfsson had ever appeared in a space pirate video.

"Charge the battery arrays full, but bring them out of the loop after that," he ordered. "We won't be charging them again after this run. Arm the scuttling charges and engage the deadman switch to blow them if we suffer enough damage to compromise the hull."

He found the interior comm and realized that the whole conversation had been limited to the bridge. The men aft, in charge of the various components, had no idea what had happened. Just that they had stopped firing the gun and escaped into JumpSpace.

"Engineering, this is Tifft," he announced. "First run was not successful. We are jettisoning the solar sail and housing, and then coming around to make a second pass. Bring everything to full and hold it there until I order overloads."

He didn't bother waiting for the acknowledgements. They would give him everything they had, because those were the sorts of men he had picked, when he had access to their deepest personnel and psychological files. He was probably the weakest link on this vessel, and he knew what kind of man he was.

"Moirrey, Yan, *Pops*," he called back over his shoulder. "Bring the gun to a zero alignment and lock it in place. You're right. We'll have to do this in motion."

"What are you about to do, Commander?" Ainsley asked.

"Use it like a lance," Gunter replied. "Gallop full speed at that bastard and try to knock him off his horse before he knocks us off ours."

"Give ya credit fer nuts, Gunter," Lady Moirrey's voice smiled at him.

They had been dead stop relative to the station when they dropped out the first time. Easiest way to line it up and calibrate the beam itself for range and accuracy.

The *Butterfly* shuddered with what felt like death-throes as Ainsley triggered the separation charges aft. Those had been for a worst-case scenario he never expected to face.

And failing's better?

Buran had invented this thing. Drop out of Jump as close as possible to another target, passing right down his spine with the Mauler ripping chunks and lives loose. Kill and rend like a shark emerging from the dark waters to feed.

His Mauler was bigger. That was all.

Gunter considered his possible vectors. All of them were bad. The best chance for damage involved staying on the plane of the station's gravity, like the first shot had been. Going high or low risked enough bulkheads in the way to hold the shot at bay for the short time he would have before *Buran* killed him.

Someone would most assuredly be sitting right on top of where that sail housing suddenly appeared. Had probably already blasted it with every beam they had on a twitch. Kill now and sort out the results later, when the threat had been neutralized.

Gunter pulled up the scan log and grinned. Beside him, he could feel Ainsley do the same. Neither spoke, but words weren't really necessary.

That Hammerhead had appeared bow-out, like a proper defensive warship should, where all his guns could range on a threat.

IFV Butterfly had vanished in that instant between the Hammerhead appearing, and being able to shoot.

That's what you get for building too high in the gravity well, Gunter thought. *I can play your games, too.*

"All hands," he said, trying to sound magisterial, as he spoke. "We will emerge on a reciprocal course, firing the weapon before I have a target lock. Repeat, before lock. We will fire blind, and then use gyros to zero the deflection down. Plan for sudden evasive maneuvering as I try this thing."

He cut the signal, again before anybody spoke. He was in charge of all their fates now. The others had delivered the Imperials here, now he had to deliver the kill.

Gunter programmed his flight vectors into the system and said a small prayer to St. Nicolas, Patron of Sailors.

"Anyone?" Gunter said conversationally. "What happens if I start firing before we emerge?"

"Haven't the slightest clue," one of the men said quietly. Gunter couldn't tell which.

"You will destabilize the Jump universe along the axis you fired, Commander," Summer Ulfsson said definitively. Clinically. "All that energy gets converted to a bizarre space-time equivalent that I don't have time to explain, but it would affect this ship like putting oily soap in water to stop bugs. They land, expecting to float, and sink to their deaths instead because the surface tension is broken. JumpSpace across an areae of more than four light seconds would reject your subsequent attempts to escape for nearly eighteen minutes, landing you back in RealSpace instead."

The tone didn't sound like a middle-aged, bimbo, ex-actress. So much so that Gunter felt his head turn all the way around to meet her eyes.

The look she gave him was one that he knew would chill his nightmares for years. It was as if a million-year-old Goddess of Destruction had come down and been made flesh on his deck. An avatar of *Kali-ma* herself, to hear Bedrov occasionally grumble about the old days with Keller. Or tales of Alber' d'Maine and his various tactical officers.

And there was utterly no doubt in those eyes now. He didn't bother asking how she knew. There was no answer that he would like any more than any others, and this was one he was willing to let get away from him.

He nodded at her. She nodded back. Lightning bolts might have passed between them.

"Stand by to emerge first, and then open fire as soon as we confirm," Gunter announced, turning what was left of his soul back to the console before him.

He blew out a breath as the clock counted to zero.

Emergence was hard and clunky. For a moment, he thought that perhaps he had managed to fly into the Hammerhead by cutting his line too fine, but then it resolved into a plasma cloud he suspected had been his solar array two minutes ago. That energy had also messed up JumpSpace, probably by the sail getting hit before it fully materialized. He had no idea how any of the physics worked, and really didn't care.

Gunter pressed the engines to the top. They wouldn't do much to accelerate him now, but any bit might make a shark miss with the shot that should have killed him.

"Science Officer, hard scan," he called, ignoring everything except the golden eyeball staring back at him from far too close. They were hauling ass, relative to the Hammerhead, and hopefully everyone else who might be waiting.

Barret was anticipating him, apparently. A good scout was like that. That really was an eyeball, and not a figment of his fright. The Golden Pearl had been punctured by the first shot.

Gunter cut loose with a laser scalpel scaled up to hunt planets. The screen forward lit hard and then dimmed as the filters cut in, but he was flying into a hurricane made of light, rather than rain.

The signal stabilized. *IFV Butterfly* was low, but not as much as he had thought. Still enough to miss.

He left the engines screaming for mercy and channeled remaining power into the gyros, letting their spinning mass jerk his horse's head up and her ass down. His console flickered hard with a grinding thump that probably suggested things breaking aft.

Didn't matter. The beam was still on, and was tracking, a knife carving an orange open as he watched.

Something jolted hard through the ship. The overhead lights flickered once and then stabilized.

"Incoming fire," Ainsley said conversationally. "Rear and flank shields at forty percent."

"Can you reinforce them?" Gunter asked.

The answer didn't really matter. Either she would and they survived the next shot, or she didn't and they died.

He concentrated on keeping his eyeball and a god's in perfect alignment.

Somebody was going to die today. Hopefully it would be a machine.

And more importantly, that bastard would be alone on his journey to hell.

"Tertiary explosions detected," Ainsley's voice suddenly found emotion.

She almost sounded like him, up an octave.

He could only dream. Tertiaries suggested success. Victory.

Deicide.

Another massive bang rocked through the ship. All the overheads went out, plunging the bridge into a darkness lit only by the six consoles.

"Confirm tertiaries forward?" Gunter called into the yawing mouth of death about to take a bite out of them.

"Confirmed," Ainsley replied sharply.

"Moirrey, blow the butterfly," Gunter yelled as loud as he could.

"Stan'by," Lady Moirrey said.

On his screen, the river of light vanished. Around them, the hull crunched and pinged in a new way as the various clamps and handles all blew at once.

The sad remains of Gunter's first command broke into two pieces with a sound like a bell tolling the faithful to a funeral service.

The original ship, now just a cockpit, engineering, and engines, broke free and accelerated like mad, suddenly eighty-four percent lighter as they pushed. She wasn't much heavier than the original courier that had once belonged to Princess Kasimira, and reacted like a fawn on a pretty day, racing to beat the wind.

Somewhere aft, a red alarm appeared on one of his consoles, but he was too busy trying to maneuver to even look at what had gone wrong. Explosions on the screen in front of him were more important, anyway.

Gunter slewed the nose around on the gyros, trying to get as much distance as he could before the scuttling charges went off behind them.

Somewhere aft, a Hammerhead helped, as a beam seemed to ignite the third section of the Type-6 beam, where all the generators had been built into a ring to punch power forward as fast as that firehose could handle it.

The explosion was a physical thing as much as pretty lights on display. The entire hull crunched with what felt like physical impacts and plasma cloud, but he couldn't tell if the shields had held or not. Or even if Ainsley had managed to get a new barrier of shields up. Maybe that explosion was flaying naked hull, and they were about to be turned into hamburger.

Another crunch. More serious. Lights and alarms sounding.

If he stayed any longer, they'd be dead.

Gunter slammed his hand down onto the JumpDrive controller and prayed.

CHAPTER LXXIX

SHE HAD an entire warfleet at her fingertips, and Jessica was still thinking like a cat burglar. *Mansi* had been a secret prison facility before. Phil Kosnett and his people had reduced it to a junkyard after they got all the friendly men off the surface.

They had time, so Jessica had gathered all the commanders aboard *Indianapolis*, into that big conference auditorium aft where they could have a working lunch and mingle. If all went well, this might be the last time this force was all in one place together.

If all went well.

According to the timelines sent by Em, Ainsley's ship should have gotten there by now. Done their scouting. Perhaps unleashed the future.

But *Winterhome* was too far away to know for some time, even at the incredible speeds that *Buran's* ships could manage on the *Pochtovyi Trakt*, the path of beacons through the thinnest parts of the galaxy.

She could only hope that Moirrey and her team had been successful. And managed to live to tell the tale. There would be no news until a messenger arrived at *Osynth B'Udan* and that was sent out to find First Expeditionary in the field.

If they ever knew.

Even with the ability to cross the galaxy in short periods, there was still a serious lag with the distances involved. Anyone she fought at *Mansi* would have no more clue about home front developments than she did.

Jessica looked over the room from the corner where she had snuck in, Marcelle quietly in tow. Iskra and her two escorts were off raiding, but everyone else was present, including *Hans Bransch* and *Ballard*. Command Centurion Larsen Romanov was even here, representing the Salvage Cruiser *Bulldog*, universally known as the *Junkyard Chihuahua*. His team would be central to the coming affair.

Marcelle leaned close to whisper in her ear.

"I miss *Pint-sized*," she muttered.

"Me, too," Jessica said. "So much of this wouldn't be possible without her and Yan. Plus, they'll never forgive us when we have to leave any ships behind. They'd both want to spend months trolling hulls for interesting tidbits."

"We'll just have to make sure we steal all the good stuff, then," Marcelle straightened up.

Around her, the men and women of her force were circulating and idling like a single team, rather than the oil and water it had been when she first brought them together. Tom Provst and Galen Estevan were sharing a story with Ariadna Mateu off *CE-402*. Phil Kosnett was holding court, describing the system layout, from the way he gestured.

Unlike the others, Jessica had instructed Phil to bring with him Heather Lau, Siobhan Skokomish, and Andre Gave to this event. Granville Veitengruber commanded his own boat, so had been invited.

But Jessica wanted all the raiders here to talk. Each of them had commanded warships in Her Majesty's service while at *Mansi*, so they had unique perspectives. Looking around, each seemed to be the crystal around which groups were slowly forming. Listening to them talk about what lay out there, just a lightyear away.

Enej appeared from out of the crowd as if summoned.

"Ready for everyone?" he asked as he stepped close, standing off to her left side, where he could turn in place and be beside her if she took a step forward.

Just as Marcelle would be on her right.

"Are they?" she fired back.

Enej grinned.

"We're pretty close to lies and tall tales at this point," he noted. "Dirty jokes and sea stories in another five minutes if you don't put a stop to it right now."

She laughed with him. She would miss this. It had a feeling of finality, even if this wasn't an assault on *Samara* or *Ninagirsu*. It was just supposed to be an out-of-the-way place, generally uninhabited and forgotten.

She didn't believe it for a second. Kali-ma had been too big in her dreams, after ignoring her for years.

"Round them up," she finally said.

True to form, Enej put two fingers in his mouth and whistled like a tea kettle. Heads turned, and bodies began to filter over to the tables on the far side of the room. In another chamber, stewards would take that as their signal to bring lunch to ready. Today it was pastas and sauces, with a variety of protein options to be added. Easy enough to prep ahead of time and cover for need.

Her need had arrived.

Jessica moved to the lectern at one end of the space. There wasn't much to say that they didn't know at this point. *Hans Bransch* had sat well out and listened, but there hadn't been any ships in the system. If Captain Exeter wasn't as amazing as Elzbet Aukley at hard scouting an enemy planetary system, he was still exceptional. And *Ballard's* team had complimented Exeter's on their care and detail, so Jessica felt comfortable with the outcome.

"As you sit and eat, there will be packets, delivered waterproofed," Jessica announced to a general chuckle.

It wasn't a meeting until someone spilled something. Coffee, water, juice, or wine. Or even pasta sauce at this moment. But all the briefing packs would survive.

"The target, as you know, is *Mansi*," she continued. "Specifically *Mansi-B*, since we know there are also ships to be had at *Mansi-D*. *CS-405* and her squadron scouted it on two occasions. First to steal *Persephone*. The second time to liberate the camp. There is a boneyard of old C- and D-class boats on a moon of the fourth planet, but we're more focused on the wreckage accumulated in the *Mansi-B* L4 and L5 LaGrange points. Open your packets to exhibit two."

She waited while everyone caught up. She had already memorized the entire contents, so she felt comfortable working without notes. The rustles subsided. The curses and such lasted a bit longer.

"Yes, as you can see, there are a number of Imperial warships that have been captured and deposited here," Jessica said. "Kosnett's team was already stretched too thinly at the time to do more than a rough catalog of them, in the hopes that they could bring back help later. That's us."

"Kosnett, did you really find *IFV Rendsburg* here?" Reif Kingston suddenly asked across the space. "She was the first ship I served on, as an ensign."

"We think so," Phil replied. "I sat as close as I dared and took images of the carcasses. Occasionally we were able to see the names painted on bows."

Reif looked at her now with a new light in his eyes. The man had been personally selected by Tom Provst to serve as the commander of her flagship. It required intellectual flexibility as well as stubbornness.

They worked together well enough, but he wasn't Denis Ježˇ. Still, something changed about the man. Grounded him in an emotion, an anger that hadn't been there before.

Perhaps he envisioned the men who had been killed or captured when the ship was taken. Men he knew. Friends he had lost.

Fire passed between them now.

"As you know," Jessica continued, "not all of these ships were captured at places like *Samara*, although that is the origin for the bulk of the ones we have been able to identify. The C-class hulls like *Persephone* never served with the warfleets, so they were captured out of their native systems. *Buran* can do that, if they prepare for it. I have replicated some notes from Seeker in Appendix Seven. They have a repair transport we've never encountered in combat, but it can wrap around a damaged ship and use its own JumpDrives to haul a vessel to a safe repair location, or drydock. We presume that's how these ships ended up here. The men were removed, and the hulls dumped at *Mansi*."

"And we think they are flyable, First Centurion?" Robbie spoke up from his table.

"We do not have the slightest clue, Robbie," she replied. "What I have are several thousand spare hands and the *Chihuahua* to see what we can do about that. It is my expectation that many of them were forced to surrender because of damage at places like *Samara*. The crews went elsewhere, and the ships came here. Phil Kosnett has a theory that *The Eldest*'s top Warriors would want to keep two of every class they encountered, to confirm statistics and capabilities. I would want those in good enough shape to be able to compare."

"And then?" Alber' d'Maine spoke up.

He had the fire in his eyes. He always had that fire. Kigali had developed it later. Reif Kingston was blowing on the first embers, but Alber' was the Destroyer of Worlds.

"And then we repair as many as we can and take them home," Jessica said plainly. "I cannot imagine that the group will be in good enough shape to take a run at someplace important on the way to *Osynth B'Udan*, even if we treat them like fireships."

In the distant past, Drake had damaged a Spanish fleet by letting a burning, wooden ship drift right into the moorings, spreading destruction. It hadn't been enough to stop Philip II of Spain from launching his Armada, but it was still legendary.

Plus, launching the vessels through JumpSpace would kill any chance at the kind of snooker accuracy you needed to knock balls around the table. You would have to ride it into point blank, and then either die with the ship or abandon into lifeboats above an enemy planet.

She wasn't about to even ask for volunteers for that kind of suicide mission. She would still end up with thousands of men who should have gone home. Or on to colonize *Lighthouse Station*.

"Pity," Alber' offered, showing exactly where his mind had gone. "Are we expecting trouble here?"

The smile was back on his face. Kigali's as well. And Denis and Tom Provst. And others.

But they wouldn't be here if they weren't forward-leaning. Willing to sail into harm's way.

"No," Jessica replied.

Before anyone could speak into the space, she continued.

"But I have my premonitions," she said, eyes locked with Denis now, before she rotated through the men and women.

A few of them had been with her at *First Petron* and *First Ballard*. Denis, Robbie, Alber', Tamara, Kigali. They had heard the stories, or seen how Jessica had changed.

There had been rumors that the Goddess herself had touched Keller. Altered her in ways that let her out-think the Red Admiral at *First Ballard* and fight off a much larger squadron with her pitiful force. Defeat them cold.

That legend had carried her forward.

Now it had brought them all to *Mansi*.

Denis nodded minutely, always intending to put himself between her and harm. The others would do the same, going beyond the job and the mission and walking into hell itself.

"With that in mind, I am dividing the fleet back into squadrons," she said. "Appendix Five. *Indianapolis* will join Provst's Second Squadron and the transport section. *Hans Bransch* will attach to First Squadron, giving

Denis all the scouts, with an expectation that the force will be in hiding. *Mansi-D* and *Mansi-E* are good places to sit quietly. At the same time, the normal landing zone north that *Buran* prefers should be watched with at least one scout, perhaps two, so that both squadrons can be warned."

"A trap, then?" Galen Estevan spoke up.

"The best kind," Jessica replied. "Jessica Keller giving orders over a clear channel, with her escorts scattered all over the place."

"Permission to grab *Persephone* and Veitengruber?" Denis asked. "We can put people down on the surface and look at what we can steal or fix. And do it quietly while we wait."

She turned to the newest commander. Found him sitting next to Andre Gave, *CS-405*'s Nurse, of all people. Veitengruber's scowl was a close approximation of what Alber' wore right now, but he nodded.

"Granted," she said. "In my perfect world, *Buran* forgets that there was ever a reason to be at *Mansi*, but I want all of you prepared to unleash the hounds of hell on very short notice, so run at the second highest level of alert you've got, as long as we're in system."

In her perfect world, she just sailed in and performed the greatest act of *Grand Theft Starship* in recorded history.

Jessica didn't believe it for a moment.

CHAPTER LXXX

PHIL LET the lightest touch of greed swim through his system as he watched. By now, a message had made it all the way back to *Ladaux*, informing Petia that the lost duckling had made it home safely.

In spite of all his adventures and successes in the field, regulations insisted that his ship and crew be ordered to return to base, where they would face a proper Court Martial for decisions made in the field. Normally, it would just be him, but Phil had no doubts that Heather, Siobhan, Trinidad, and even Andre would face their own panels, judging their actions in command with the exacting science of hindsight.

Depending on the men and women empaneled, Phil figured he had a fifty percent chance of being fêted as a hero, or being cast out as a fool.

But he wasn't at *Osynth B'Udan* awaiting the messenger. Tom Provst knew the rules just as well, most likely, and had ordered the newly-repaired *CS-405* back into the field to accompany his force, first raiding *Severnaya Zemlya*, and then on to join Jessica.

Petia's orders would catch up with them, but only eventually. And then he would return home.

Even if the Court Martial found in his favor, which he expected, the others still had to face theirs. He would never have this team together again. Phil was sure of that. Heather deserved her own command. Siobhan might even get jumped to her own corvette, depending. And Andre had made noises about recertifying for Command School, suggesting that his time in command of *Forgotten Mercy* had left an indelible mark.

Phil let a daydream float by. Him in white, as a Fleet Centurion, in command of his own raiding squadron, like Jessica had once done. Plunging deep into *Lena* sector. Or perhaps long-sailing across *Buran* to locate the semi-mythical *NovLao* and let them know that there were others out there who would help.

He checked the clock and took a drink of fresh coffee from his sippy cup. Phil wasn't supposed to sit watches on the bridge, even by his own standards. He should be doing paperwork in his office.

But he knew an ending when he saw it. A man's days commanding any ship are always numbered, and Phil could see how short this count was, until the day soon when he never walked *CS-405*'s decks again. So he was going to revel in every day. Wallow in it.

"Signal from *Hans Bransch*," Evan Brinich's voice broke through Phil's daydreams, grounding him back on his lovely, airy bridge. "Possible incursion detected."

Maybe something? Maybe nothing. Never a bad time to train his crew.

"All hands to battle stations," Phil ordered, locking himself down with the straps that had been loose before. "Eyes on target. Full stealth mode."

Siobhan and Heather were both in position in less than twenty seconds. Phil wondered if they had developed the same subconscious sensitivities to fate that he had. Yesterday, he would have been in his office right now.

The connection to the other scout corvette was a tight-beam laser, like Phil's team had used last year on their raids. Fleet signals were always encrypted, but still showed that somebody was there if you were listening.

Here, just two rocks in the darkness, at least until someone hard-pinged their vicinity. A smart commander would come out at a safe distance from *Mansi-B* and at least look inward, where he would see a mass of ships currently scattered rather loosely across the L4, the gravitationally-stable, leading parking orbit where you could put something and it would wait a long time for you.

"Oh, shit," Evan's voice was suddenly too loud. "That's a full squadron, Phil. I read a Megalodon and at least six Mako hulls. We're too far away to identify them, but whoever that is has enough force to hammer the shit out of Jessica and Provst, especially with surprise."

"Evan, tell Captain Exeter to run like hell," Phil said. "Forget cover and get the message out that the redcoats are coming. Siobhan, get us to Denis now."

Evan was right. That was a big force for a little place like this. Briefly, he wondered if there was a spy somewhere, feeding *Buran* their movement orders, but they should have sent a bigger force, if that was the case. One Megalodon and six Makos was enough to take on Second Squadron and do a lot of damage, but then First Squadron would come in behind them and it would be kitty bar the door.

If he could get the minutemen ready to fight.

CS-405 twisted sideways into JumpSpace.

CHAPTER LXXXI

IMPERIAL FOUNDING: 181/07/16. IFV VALIANT, DEEP
SPACE

Tom Provst was not a deeply religious man, unlike some of his brother officers. He had seen too much and suffered too much to believe in a benevolent deity wishing his children to lead happy and productive lives.

Various translations of Epicurus, one of the ancient Hellenes that Lady Moirrey liked so much, had resonated with Tom, and left him… Bereft was not the right term. Confused and angry?

If there was a plan, why did it have to come off like this?

But the quote spoke to his soul. Had grounded him at that moment when Crown Prince Karl Ekkehard Szczęsny was known to be dead, along with the rest of the bridge crew of *Firehawk* and all his friends.

"Finally, if God is both willing and able to defeat evil, why then does it exist?"

Tom didn't find the Unitarian nature of Imperial religion helpful. Dualism had called his name that day.

Evil existed because God was not all-powerful, but was engaged in a fight to the death with another being, a bastard just as powerful, and just as unrelenting, but dedicated to chaos and evil.

Tom Provst would resist by fighting those people to his dying breath.

He was in his office doing paperwork when the chime sounded.

"Tom," Charlie d'Noir spoke quickly. "*Hans Bransch* just came out of Jump. Says there's a fleet right behind him."

"Action stations," Tom said, standing. "Get every shuttle away from us and either to the ground or the closest repair station. *RAN Bulldog* drops everything and runs immediately. Don't wait for Jessica to say anything."

"On it," Charlie said in person as Tom exited his office onto the flag bridge that had become his second home.

Charlie was already seated across the table, and the projection was coming live as Tom slid into his spot.

"Is Jessica on-line?" Tom asked.

"Not yet," Charlie said. "She's off on a flank right now, pretending to be an escort."

"Screw the cover story," Tom decided. "Get *Qin Lun* over there. Pull the rest and the assault corvettes close to us."

The projection lit up with a secondary screen, showing the scan Tom's scout had managed before they blipped out. It was not a pleasant thing to see.

A Megalodon was as big and dangerous as *Valiant*. Six Hammerheads were more than a match for all his corvettes. Six Makos against his five cruisers, currently badly out of position to support each other.

Tom felt a moment of guilt, hoping that the attack would come at this ship first. A smart commander over there might land three Makos each on one of the cruisers and try to cripple it. If their tactics went sideways enough, he might add the Megalodon onto a third cruiser, and Tom's force would be savaged in the first thirty seconds of the battle.

Hopefully Denis was coming, because this was going to be ugly and messy.

Tom's only other hope right now was that either the *Buran* commander had missed the scouts jumping out, or was taking his time and reconsidering attacking this force. Maybe he could even smell the trap before it closed.

"Contact," someone yelled. "Enemy warships incoming. Stand by to receive fire."

Tom felt a moment of savage glee, looking at the screens, as he realized that they had fallen for the trap planned by none other than Jessica Keller.

That Megalodon commander was coming after *Valiant*, and had brought all of his Makos with him to try to kill the woman *Buran* considered the most dangerous creature in the galaxy. In that, they weren't necessarily wrong, but they wouldn't get her today.

She wasn't here, so her ghost wouldn't join Ekke's in Tom's dreams.

"All guns fire," Tom ordered, just before the projection lit up with incoming beams and *Valiant* staggered like a horse that had been hit by a bus.

CHAPTER LXXXII

"Enemy warfleet coming out of jump," someone yelled over the comm. "All hands to stations."

Jessica was up and moving, trying to identify the voice. She had served with Denis and his people for a decade before *Indianapolis*. She kept expecting Denis or Tobias Brewster, whenever she heard a man's voice like that.

It wasn't Enej, nor Reif, but she didn't spend much thought on it. That was a thing she could track down later. If she cared.

The hull rang as both Type-4 beams cut loose at almost the same instant. The Type-1-Pulse batteries went like woodpeckers, as did the Type-3's. The latter had all been tuned for short-range damage, so whoever it was at the other end hopefully was in the process of getting his teeth kicked in. *Indianapolis* was over on a flank today, escorting the corpse of *IFV Rendsburg* as various engineers tried to get the ship ready to fly. Or at least see if it was worth the effort.

Jessica was onto her flag bridge a step behind Enej. Someone already had the projection live, showing her forces scattered out like bait, while a *Buran* battle squadron went after *Valiant*, *Dundee*, and *Glasgow*. She said a small prayer of thanks for predictable commanders, such as they were. It was still going to be a painful stay in a dry-dock, from the looks of things.

She caught Reif's eyes as she slid into the camera pickup. He perked right up.

"Orders, sir?" he asked.

"Get us close to Tom," she said. "They think I'm over there, probably, so he's the primary target and we need to pretend to be his escort, rather than his boss. What are we facing?"

"A little more than they had at *Severnaya Zemlya*, Admiral," he said. "Not enough for the fleet, but too much for the squadron."

In the background, the beams continued to fire. She wondered if that Megalodon was staying around to duel, or would flee once the element of surprise was lost.

"Fight your ship, Captain," Jessica decided.

Let Reif handle his men, like she had always let Denis have his head when it came time to combat. Kingston was good enough at his job to handle it. And there were only so many ways to handle a situation like this.

Valiant was at the focal point of enough firepower that she feared the ship could actually be destroyed. Tom Provst might not mind that, if he could take them all with him, and he looked game to try, ignoring the Makos to pour everything he had down that monster's maw.

But it wasn't going to be enough.

CHAPTER LXXXIII

THERE WAS CRAZY, and then there was insane. Tobias Brewster hadn't decided where this gambit fell on that spectrum, but it was nothing like he had been taught in the Academy. He had been forced to learn this one from Jessica Keller herself.

How do you out-crazy a woman like that?

"Stand by for *Emergence*," Nada said aloud.

"Gunner, I have laid everything forward," Tobias said calmly. "Every beam is locked on a particular set of coordinates forward from our bow, but you'll have to adjust them when we hit. I want everything you have fired into the biggest vessel, closest to center when you emerge. After that, we'll dance with the rest of those bastards."

"Roger that, sir," Aleksander Afolayan replied sharply.

Tobias grinned at the man. When he had been disrated from the guns by Jessica, Aleksander had replaced him, and remained on as Gunner, even as Tobias became Emergency Tactical Officer aft. And now Acting First Officer of *RAN Vanguard*, answering to Nina Vanek, Acting Command Centurion while Denis was in his Fleet Centurion's chair. At least until they got home and the Lords of the Fleet had words for them.

But that was tomorrow. Today, he had perhaps the last clash of the greatest titans to fight in this generation,

Emergence.

All those hours of planning and programming tactical systems paid off. He had input coordinates and vectors, and let the system predict the optimal place from which to launch a *Buran*-style strafing run on *Valiant*.

Vanguard was set to cross that Megalodon's beam from exactly below. Ships like that didn't technically have a blind spot straight down, but Tobias had never met a naval officer yet who didn't have that blind spot somewhere in his thinking, until you pointed it out or exploited it.

Well, Jessica didn't. But she was Jessica.

How many tournaments and war games had he won by coming in Zero, Ninety, Two-Seventy? Enough.

Aleksander had that shark's soft underbelly in front of him and a smile on his face when Tobias looked over his console at the man.

"Firing," the Gunner announced unnecessarily.

Tobias had only to listen as his symphony of destruction raced into the night sky.

Four Type-4 Beams, all centered. Ten Type-3s. Six Type-1-Pulse emitters yammering away.

Tobias snickered when a probe went down-range in the wake of the Bubble Gun. At least he hoped it was a probe. They didn't have any missiles back there, in spite of two launchers. Things like that were a waste of storage on this frontier.

But a probe looked suspiciously like a completely unknown weapon system, if someone fired it at you instead of into a blank spot. Anything to spook the other guy.

And all of that firepower would have merely scratched the Megalodon's belly, except that Tobias has laid out the attack run he wanted, and then trusted the other crazies to follow *Vanguard* in.

On his screen, *Vanguard* suddenly was leading a full battle squadron. First Expeditionary Fleet, as it had been for so long, plus new friends. *VI Victrix* and *VI Ferrata* on the close wings. *II Augusta* below. *LWC Robert Fitzwalter* above. It almost looked like the bow of one of the old Carcharias sharks, the battleship that carried four Makos into battle, rather than the newer Megalodon with six Hammerheads.

CA-264 and *CA-410* in two columns, leading *CS-405*, *CM-404*, *CE-403*, *CE-402*, and *CE-401*. The only one missing was *CP-406*, still off in the interior somewhere hopefully, madly pillaging.

And everybody had targeted the flagship. Four more Type-4 beams and two Bubble Guns. And a thunderstorm of lesser beams, as the carrier and the *Lincolnshire* boat didn't have the heavy firepower of the big cruisers. They made do with lighter stuff in greater numbers.

Space is big. Even space battles are usually fought at distances measures in dozens or hundreds of kilometers, where the naked eye is useless to see anything but a flash of light.

Vanguard was at the center of the whirlwind, with two of her cruisers at risk of being overwhelmed. Four of the Imperial corvettes were close enough to engage, but completely out-classed.

Thirteen *Buran* warships were packed in tight enough that they appeared to be overlapping on the projection Tobias was using to track the battle.

And he was leading twelve more ships in at high speed. It felt like ancient knights on horseback, about to slam into the wall of shields representing the infantry. For a moment, Tobias wondered if they might actually see two vessels accidentally ram one another, as everyone tried to respond to the overcrowding.

Wouldn't be the Megalodon, though, unless someone hit it. In his projection, the enemy battleship went red. Hopefully, that meant so much damage that the ship would possibly self-destruct when he could, rather than risk capture.

"Emergency Bridge, this is Brewster," he called, absorbing all the information as flight vectors he could see in his head. How they would move over the next thirty seconds. Sixty. Ninety. "Take over all beams rear and starboard, including *Rachel* and *Zebra* turrets. Gunner, get me that Tigershark off our port bow. That will be the one Alber' goes after, so maybe we can help him kill it. Nada, signal everyone to slow down and engage targets as they lie rather than blasting through. And talk to the other pilots and find the safe corridors through."

Everyone acknowledged and *Vanguard* turned her attention to the scrum of insanity she had waded into. For the briefest moment, Tobias Brewster flashed back to *Simeon* and the most embarrassing day of his career. This would never erase that, but it might stack up with *Qui-Ping* for a job of redemption.

CHAPTER LXXXIV

Jessica might have called it Ragnarök. Or perhaps Armageddon. Not necessarily the Twilight of the Gods themselves, but certainly death on a massive scale. It might even be good enough for the Vedas, which Kali-ma no doubt would have appreciated.

They had come for her. As she had known that *The Eldest* would do.

And missed.

Even to this date, no spies had apparently successfully reported to the appropriate authorities that Jessica Keller no longer rode into battle aboard a heavy dreadnaught, either *Vanguard* or *Valiant*. Nobody so much as spared *Indianapolis* a Flicker beam in passing, but that just meant that Reif and his crew could pour everything they had into the mayhem.

Something caught her mind, as *Vanguard* and First Squadron emerged. Tobias Brewster and Nina Vanek had brought the whole team in on one of those mad charges that Alber' d'Maine was famous for.

"Enej, get me *Hans Bransch* or *CS-405*," Jessica said suddenly. "They took the time to separate into *Buran* and *Energiya* modules, but somebody saw them. Let's drop a force out there."

"On it," her Flag Centurion said.

She watched him type and considered the situation unfolding. *Valiant* wasn't bait, exactly, but someone had needed to be visible while someone else hid. Tom Provst had drawn the short straw over Denis, only because all these wrecks were Imperial ships, so it made more sense to have trained imperial engineers working on them.

So *Valiant* was the one getting hammered into salvage.

And then *Vanguard* came out of jump like a wolf leading a pack, firing everything, one step ahead of everyone else.

And a Megalodon died.

It was amazing how quickly the tides could turn.

"Jessica, I have coordinates from *Hans Bransch*," Enej said suddenly. "Orders?"

"Get Galen on the line, transmit them to him, and we'll go hunting," she said. "Send that to everyone. We're too far out of position to help the main force, and if we try to close, either they'll jump out, or maybe jump on top of us. Let's get gone."

Reif's eyes got a little bigger in the image on her console.

"You caught all that?" she asked.

"Affirmative, Admiral," Kingston said. "Standing by to jump, but I'm not sure what the value is."

"The *Energiya* Module has the long-range JumpDrives they use, Reif," Jessica said. "Short-range, they use the Capriole, but that won't get them to safety very quickly. Even if the Megalodon's that badly injured, the Makos could still escape and bring help."

"And we're going to kill them all," he observed. It wasn't a question.

"That's right," she replied.

"*Qin Lun* is ready to jump," Enej interjected. "On your command."

"Take us out," Jessica ordered.

CHAPTER LXXXV

IN THE TENTH YEAR OF JESSICA KELLER, QUEEN OF
THE PIRATES: JULY THE SIXTEENTH AT MANSI

NONE of these people thought like pirates. Except her. That was why Galen had come when David asked. Jessica would be surrounded by crazed berserkers and not thieves in the night. She would need someone whose response to a problem didn't involve waddling up to an enemy warship and beating it to death with a frying pan.

"Time to drop?" Galen asked out loud.

His old 1-ring cargo Mothership, *Marco Polo*, had possessed an amazingly cramped and smelly bridge, even after Galen had paid to strip it to the bulkheads and replace most of the interior equipment. But those were the days before *Pops* and Bedrov. Back when ships could be hunks of junk with piss-poor life support as long as they got you where you were going.

Qin Lun had a rather spacious bridge. Oval shaped, with his station facing in from the bow and his excellent Combat Officer, Donal McKiersky, facing him from the aft of the chamber. Six other stations were available, but only three were in use, and Kara was handling communications from the Emergency Bridge aft.

This wasn't a warship. Not like *Aquitaine* thought of them. True, guns. Lots of guns. But it was a family business, so his wife had to be stationed most of the ship away from him at times like this, in case something happened. She would take over at that point.

Donal just controlled the guns.

"Twenty seconds to ambush," Donal said now, not looking up from his screens.

"Flight deck, this is Galen," he said, keying a second button.

"*Badger*," came the growly response.

That was okay. Holger O'Ryan was a growly sort of man. Big and surly, like the knife-fighters that used to get ahead by using bulk and strength. Before Jessica cracked enough skulls together to turn command into a more democratic, academic affair.

Assuming, of course, that you didn't own the damned ship outright, with all of the crew as employees, rather than the shareholder model common everywhere else.

"Stand by for hot launch, Holger," Galen said.

"Kill or be killed, boss," the man said, cutting the line from his end.

There might be more reasons for having Holger down there than the man's pure competence at flying a modified heavy bomber. Aggressiveness counted.

"Starflower charged," Donal announced as Galen counted the seconds.

Galen grinned. *Qin Lun* was a Patrol Cruiser, not a mainline warship. Didn't need Type-4 beams on the wings. Or the Bubble Gun, which was likely to be utterly useless against a pirate Mothership anyway.

So *Pops* had built him something else. *The Starflower.*

It was a fanciful name for what amounted to a triple Type-3 beam, locked into a single focal point. Not as good as a Four. More than enough for most escorts and any warship not built as sturdy as *Kali-ma*. Which was most of them.

"We're hot," Donal announced as they emerged. "Holger, get your ass gone."

Galen grinned. Let the sailors act all professional and such. He wanted the craziest pirates he could hire. They wouldn't get rich, but most pirates and private vessels didn't. They would profit-share instead, and Kara had retirement accounts set up at banks on *Petron,* so if they starved in their old age, it was their own damned fault.

His job was seeing that they all got fat and happy so that they got to be old.

"Shit, she really did it," Donal groused under his breath. "Found them."

"It's Jessica, dumbass," Galen countered. "Of course she did."

"Yeah, not used to working with pros, boss," Donal sighed.

The bridge of *Qin Lun* was remarkably silent. Denis and Tom Provst had both told him how useful it was to tune a different note on every gun emplacement, so a commander could track the state of the battle with his ears.

Hornswoggle. They just like blowing things up with cool sound effects, like fourteen-year-olds.

Galen watched the readouts. He had never understood the *Buran* thing about separating a ship into two parts. Sounded like way too many places where something could go wrong. But he supposed they were like *Aquitaine* and *Fribourg*. So much money that repairs just came out of somebody else's capital budget.

But there were seven component sections here. One big one he assumed was the ass end of the Megalodon, and six smaller ones for the cruisers. He could see structural differences from here, which he presumed were Mako/Thresher/Tigershark related, but hadn't paid that close of attention. Didn't really care.

Badger cleared the locks aft with the auditory equivalent of a raised middle finger.

Indianapolis cut loose into the biggest structure with all the hounds of hell as Galen watched.

Caught somebody by surprise, to see shit exploding as her beams got home.

Donal had picked out the nearest Mako jitney and put a Starflower into it, along with all ten of the Type-3's that could come to bear when you had someone aligned with your keel strakes.

Bucko over there started shedding parts.

A moment later, one of the other ones lit up. Jessica wasn't looking the right way. Donal hadn't had time to shift targets.

Four more signals appeared on his sensor board.

"Boss, friendlies just crashed the party," Donal called out.

"Open another keg," Galen replied, laughing.

CS-405 and *Hans Bransch*, leading in *CA-264* and *CA-410*. This was going to be a bash.

Five of the Mako Energiya modules vanished on the same count, leaving the one Donal had booped and the big one.

"Kigali, we've got the little one," Galen opened a general line. "Jessica could use some help."

"Tally-ho," the *Navigator* of legend replied.

Donal was firing his beams as fast as he could route power to them, on a ship *Pops* had designed to sit in the middle of a swarm of snubfighters you were trying to kill. It felt like a disco ball facing off with a strobe light in the middle of a dark dance floor.

Donal's victim kept shedding pieces.

"Task Group, this is Keller, I have the flag," Jessica's voice came through clear. "Rendezvous at this point and go dark. I expect we'll have company shortly. Engage and then prepare to jump out to these coordinates as soon as they figure out what just happened."

A big blue dot appeared on the three-D map, off to one side.

"Donal?" Galen asked.

"On it, boss," the Combat Officer said. "Recharging everything and killing inertia."

"Sounds good," Galen said. "Stay alert. They're likely to come running shortly."

Again, *Qin Lun* had an unfair advantage. *Pops* had included all the gyros Bedrov had put into an Expeditionary Cruiser, on a ship one third lighter. And the same engines. Taking out the Bubble Gun and the Type-4's had freed up a *LOT* of space midship and forward.

"Contact," Holger's voice came over the line, along with a feed.

Makos. Three of them right now, scattered rather to hell and looking a little worse for wear.

"Everyone engage," Galen yelled.

None of the three were close to each other, as those things went, and looked rather like sticks someone had dropped on the floor at random. One was close enough in line with *Qin Lun*'s bow. Donal apparently agreed.

All those gyros. Really damned useful if you had to use a Bubble Gun, which had so little traverse capability. Also worked just fine when you wanted to tattoo somebody's ass with a Starflower. And all the rest of the guns.

Apparently, little boy over there had gotten away from Tom and Denis with his Power Absorbers as close to overloaded as you could get and not lose them.

Donal wasn't having any of that.

Starflower. Almost a blood eagle, watching the back third of the ship drop their panels explosively. Might have just melted his engines and maybe that silly-ass, horse hopper drive thing they used.

Damn, that was a sexy view.

One of the other ones took exception. Tigershark, if he could hit them from that far away.

Shields holding but unhappy. Probably time to consider leaping away, since the four corvettes didn't really have enough firepower to do the trick against a cruiser.

The Tigershark suddenly backlit like a nova as Galen watched.

Oh, did someone forget Badger*? Or worse,* ignore *Holger as a mere administrative shuttle?*

Dumb-ass.

Twin Type-1's on each wingtip. Triple Type-2 forward, almost a petit version of the Starflower. And it looks like he just dumped all that into your hip from close enough to punch you, didn't he? After Tom Kigali and friends had already lit you up.

Galen smiled. Nobody but Jessica understood how to fly like a pirate around here.

"Flit," came Her Majesty's call over the line. "Coordinates sent."

Donal didn't look up, just slid sideways into JumpSpace, one step ahead of the law.

Galen looked at his boards. Not all that much damage had leaked through the shields. Patrol Cruiser was supposed to get hit from all sides. They had more shields than guns, exactly the opposite of Aeliaes or d'Maine.

Qin Lun dropped back into RealSpace too quickly. Galen looked at the nav feed.

Jessica had moved them less than a light-minute away from the previous engagement. He could still see the Megalodon's Energiya, the carcass of the first monster shark rolling over in the surf as it died. One of the Makos was stranded, too. And someone had gotten what looked like a crippling shot on a different Mako.

The Tigershark was pissed, but not that badly injured. Just gone.

"New coordinates sent," Jessica said as all five ships joined her. "Flit."

And just like that, they were gone again.

All those nasty tall tales about *Trusski* came back to him. He'd figured that everyone was stretching the truth, even Denis, but even they hadn't been bouncing like a rubber ball.

Maybe Jessica was just feeling mean.

She dropped them right back on the first rendezvous. Maybe three seconds after those other three enemy cruisers, the missing ones from the first pass, had shown up, apparently missing their first jump, or coming late to the party.

Three on three, when you added the corvettes and *Badger* together.

With surprise. And position. Galen watched shields and engineering while Donal unloaded everything he had into the closest target.

This wasn't a rich freighter that they needed to capture. These were cops. Best to kneecap them in a dark alley, step back, and then kick them to death before they could radio for help.

That was when you wanted folks like Donal McKiersky and Holger O'Ryan backing you up. Shiori Ness was lovely people, but Galen just couldn't see her trying to rip somebody's throat out with her bare teeth. Galen believed some of the stories about Holger.

Man was ruthless.

And just like that, space was clear again. Forty-four seconds of craziness seemed to be the recharge cycle on their Capriole. Good to know.

"Flit," Jessica ordered.

They were gone.

Out a light-minute in a different direction. Pause. Bounce back.

Nothing.

Galen figured they were gone for good.

The boards lit up with more trouble. Except it wasn't trouble. *VI Victrix* and *VI Ferrata* were here, and hopefully had brought their own kegs.

"Task Force, this is Evan Brinich, aboard *CS-405*," a new voice joined the line. "New signal tracking and decoded."

Decoded? How in Vishnu's name had they decoded *Buran*'s communications?

Except that it was the Science Officer off Kosnett's scout. Galen had heard stories about that kid. Would have loved to recruit him, but Kosnett and Provst had both taken Galen aside and threatened to kick his ass personally if he tried.

Something about the kid being a First Centurion, one of these days. Maybe a First Lord of the Fleet.

Whatever. That was tomorrow's problem.

"Task Force, this is Keller," she said.

Didn't really sound like her, unless you wanted to visualize the woman half naked and covered in someone else's blood, with more pouring from her mouth and a bunch of razor-sharp teeth. And blades in each of a dozen hands.

Galen hadn't been there when Jessica took the throne, but he'd seen images. And better, heard stories from Uly and Yan.

So yeah, maybe.

"We're not going into this like a squadron," Jessica continued. "Everyone will jump on my call, and drop out on the location with whatever vector and alignment they feel is appropriate. From there, the next set of coordinates are back to the L4 where the rest of the fleet is waiting. Stand by for jump…Execute."

Qin Lun shivered and fell out of the universe, the little brother to the other three cruisers, and the mean cousin to the corvettes. Worst case scenario, that Megalodon had limped off and met up with the other ships. So battleship, mauled; and six cruisers, three beat to shit.

Oh, what the hell.

Galen opened a line to the Emergency Bridge. Kara's face lit up.

"This is no time for fooling around, Galen," she announced in a voice everyone in both rooms laughed at.

"Not so sure about that, beautiful," he grinned. "But you're right. Donal and the others would just want to watch. "

"And provide color commentary," she replied. "Everything good forward?"

"Yup," he said. "Just wanted to smile at you some while we waited. Got a few minutes to the next drop out."

"You're incorrigible," Kara grinned.

"Hey, you knew that when you married me."

She cut the line anyway. Her way of reminding him to get back to work.

Galen sighed.

"Your own crew handbook frowns on quickies during operations, boss," Donal's eyes gleamed with laughter.

Galen laughed along with him, and everyone else.

Might have to reconsider that, at some point. Or maybe go back to flying *Marco Polo* or building a 4-ring Cargo Mothership. Then he could fool around with his wife anytime he felt like it.

Instead, he checked his boards. Engineering had everything rerouted or shut down. The armor had held in most places, and none of the beams had penetrated deeper than a single chamber. Since nobody was that close to the outer hull right now, no casualties.

At least on this side. Over there, it would be different story. But that was the price you paid, trying to conquer the galaxy.

Qin Lun rediscovered reality at Jessica's coordinates. No Megalodon, which was nice. Four banged up cruisers, which told him that they really had damaged two of them harder than expected.

Best part? Everyone here was in the process of backing slowly into those missing *Energiya* cradles that had gotten away earlier. Like they were about to fly away with tails tucked in. But they weren't going to get to.

Man, talk about getting caught with your pants down. No place to maneuver. No velocity at all as you walked slowly backwards into your dock.

And most of your guns either obscured by superstructure or blind-spotted because of the way folks were coming out of Jump.

Donal must have been feeling feistier than usual. He came out at high speed, but from a little ways away from everyone else.

Ye Olde Fashioned Jousting Pass attack.

And they had arrived first, barely.

Starflower found that stupid Tigershark *Badger* had been dancing with earlier. Worse, his shields were down. Power Absorbers. Whatever. Naked metal and a blowtorch.

Oopsie.

Galen had never actually seen a warship explode in combat. Wasn't supposed to be possible. You stabbed the bastard to death with an icepick, and either he ran away bleeding, or you killed some critical component and he surrendered.

Or *Buran* ships blew themselves up to prevent capture. This guy hadn't gone willingly. Or most of the scuttling charges had failed. Big pieces broke off. Floated away in three dimensions as Donal shifted his bow aim to the next victim.

Indianapolis had emerged closest. That might be a Thresher over there from the look of him. If so, he was in even worse shape, because his Mauler was a DEMP gun. Directed ElectroMagnetic Pulse. Kill your computers and not the people.

Great way to capture cargo vessels. Maybe he should look into replacing the Starflower? It would work great on pirates who thought they were all that and a bag of chips, too.

At least the Thresher was able to fire back before Jessica's folks got a second salvo into his stern. And then he started tumbling in three dimensions. More or less intact, if held together by a strip of outerhull that hadn't sheered under the torque of the explosion that took out his engineering spaces.

And just like that, combat was over.

Galen counted noses. Somebody had Mauled *Qin Lun* when he wasn't looking, but the beam had mostly missed. Would still need about a week with a buffer and a new paint job. Probably the missing Mako.

One had escaped. Galen rewound the logs.

Yup. Bugger jumped from inside his Energiya cradle, one beat ahead of Alber's *Goddess of War*. Cradle was shattered. Ship made it away. Mostly.

The others hadn't expected any sort of dance party.

About the time Donal got all that forward inertia killed enough to come back for more, the remaining ships that could had committed *seppuku*. Boom, boom, boom, like soap bubbles.

Galen was utterly horrified, but kept his face calm.

Corynthe was a pirate nation. You captured ships when you were a pirate, but never blew them up. And nobody took slaves. Way more cost effective to ransom off the valuable prisoners and dump the rest back on a planet somewhere. Or recruit them into your own crew.

This had been a slaughter worthy of Jessica's War with the galaxy.

The only thing missing were all the Hammerheads, but they had not accompanied the cruisers. Must have escaped on a different vector, but sure as hell weren't going to piggyback home on their momma. Both the Megalodon and its Energiya were dead killed.

"Task Force, this is Keller," her bloodied voice haunted him. "Flit and home. Good job."

Good job? Lady, we just killed how many thousand men and women? You call that good?

But yeah, this was Jessica. She needed pirates, sure. But she also needed ruthless killers. People like Robbie, Alber', and Tom Kigali. And Tom Provst.

This wasn't about trade negotiations and quarterly profit statements.

Jessica was fighting a war for the future of mankind.

Nothing less.

And she needed him to help. Needed all of *Corynthe*. All of *Aquitaine*. All of *Fribourg*. Anybody else that would step into the breech and kill robot starships. Even those dumbass cops at *Lincolnshire*.

Qin Lun slid sideways under Donal's sure hands, and headed back to the rest of the team.

And the war.

PART SIX

EPILOGUES

EPILOGUE: KELLER

DATE OF THE REPUBLIC JULY 20, 403 IFV
INDIANAPOLIS, MANSI

SHE WOULDN'T CLASSIFY it as definitive, but Jessica was pretty sure that in the final determination of such things, she had broken *Buran*'s hold on the *Altai* sector, at the very least. In most battles, you fought for a while and someone fled with some level of damage. Rarely was a ship so badly damaged that it had to surrender, or in the case of *Buran*, trigger the death charges.

The Hammerheads had vanished. *CS-405* had eventually managed to locate the echo of the three jumps the escorts made to escape the system, but only hours after they had fled. One Mako had made it clear of that final slaughter.

Nobody had an *Energiya* module to boost their engines.

Seeker's expert opinion was that a Capriole Drive could be accurate to around six light-hours when jumping the maximum range of a half a light year, as opposed to ten light-minutes accuracy when jumping ten light-years that you got with the primary JumpDrives in the aft housing.

Jessica wasn't sure which *Holding* colony the two forces would make for, but they would probably go in two groups. And might run out of food before they got there, depending.

Even if they didn't, they would probably be reduced to what Phil Kosnett had done, and navigate to the nearest friendly system and load up on food, and then zigzag their way across the sector. *Ninagirsu* was slightly closer than *Severnaya Zemlya* and for a moment, she considered taking half the fleet and hunting them down as a final insult.

Oh, so tempting.

But she wanted them to get home. To be able to tell everyone that Keller Marie Jessica had just annihilated an entire battlefleet. Not just beaten them. Crushed them so badly that these ships might be the only survivors. She looked up from her meditations, as the various screens showing her commanders began to come live.

She was in her flag bridge, across from Enej. The darkness that had cloaked her mind parted and receded, bringing her back to the present.

She missed having Enej at one corner of a triangle, with Casey at the other, but those days were gone. So many days were gone.

"That's everyone," Enej said in a quiet voice, signaling that all the commanders had joined them on the circuit.

Enej was one of the few who knew what Moirrey was up to. Why First Expeditionary had pushed so bloody, so hard out here. He could probably sense that they were also close to the end of a chapter.

If it had worked, *Buran* himself might be dead by now. If not, he would at least be shaken to his core, and probably withdraw more and more of his forces to protect that inner section of the *Protectorate of Man*. What she had once told Denis was the yolk.

Samara would probably be abandoned quickly in that case. It served no useful point, now that Jessica had shown *Fribourg* that they could just ignore it and strike deep into *Altai* or *Lena* sectors instead. And they would.

There would need to be a new border drawn. With the damage she had done to *Buran's* military, their economy, and their psyche, it would not even be the *M'Hanii Gulf*. No, it would have to be someplace deeper.

The Holding would have to cede ground, just to hold on for another generation.

Or face her coming after them with all her avenging angels.

Because there were probably worse things in the galaxy than Jessica Keller coming after you, but they weren't survivable, either.

She found Tom Provst and Larsen Romanov in her display.

"What's the final count?" she asked.

"How greedy are you feeling?" Romanov replied. "If we go hard and fast, twelve. If we can take our time and expect a couple of failures on the way, twenty-seven, including *IFV Rendsburg*."

She found Reif and watched his eyes flare, but he remained silent.

"Twenty-seven," she decided. "The force that would be coming to stop us has been destroyed, and they'll have to get home and scrape together another one. We have time."

"We'll do you proud, First Centurion," Romanov said.

"How's *Valiant*?" she asked Tom Provst.

"Without a full repair facility handy, it would have been much worse," he said. "And without Tobias Brewster and *Vanguard* saving our asses like they did, we still might not have made it through."

She nodded. About what the reports showed. Every shield had been beaten down by that Megalodon and his consorts. One more salvo and she might have lost *Valiant* entirely.

Until the trap had sprung shut.

The first trap. Followed by the second, the third, and the fourth.

Buran had just lost a fleet. Gone. And when the survivors got home, *Buran* himself would lose a lot of people's will to continue fighting.

After all, if your god can be beaten so soundly, thrashed so mercilessly, is he really a god?

And maybe, just maybe, *Buran* himself was dead right now and *The Holding* was suffering a serious religious crisis on top of everything else.

One could hope.

She took in the rest with a quick scan.

"My friends, we're headed home now," she said. "A great many old warships will come with us. Some of them will probably have to be scrapped when we get there, but they will be brought home as well as all the men we have freed, so they might also become museums to human will. *Buran* has suffered a great many blows, and it will get worse. We have ended a chapter of this story on an extremely high note, with the twin strikes at *Barnaul* and *Mansi*. Now we will return home and plan."

She didn't have much more to say. This had been a stretch goal in her original mission plan to liberate *Barnaul*. Success had balanced on a knife's edge to utter failure. They might have even figured out that the dreadnaughts were just that, escorts to Red Admiral Keller, and not her chariot. *Indianapolis* would have melted under the withering assault that Provst and his men had withstood.

"Thank you," she continued, all out of melodramatic epiphanies. "We are all heroes now. Expect sailing orders in eighteen hours, with a planned departure in seventy-two. Let me know if you have any questions or needs."

Silence greeted her. She wondered if they understood how

momentous this raid had been, in spite of not being told the reasons to push. Many of them had been with her long enough to understand that pushing had to be for some greater reason.

She cut the line and leaned back. Enej smiled at her, sharing the one secret she could not tell any of the other commanders, beyond Denis and Tom.

The war itself might be over. Might already have been over, and nobody had gotten a message to them here.

And if it wasn't over, then she and Em would have to plan something even bigger. Meaner. Nastier, in order to force that beast back.

Maybe she would need to revisit some of Yan's notes on planet-crackers after all. If Moirrey failed, and perhaps died out there, then maybe *Winterhome* should be turned into her funeral pyre.

Jessica smiled and felt Kali-ma smile as well.

EPILOGUE: ZU ARLO

THE SUN WAS JUST COMING up over the ridge of mountains that defined
the bowl in which Vo had set down his forward training base. Separated it
from the rest of *Lighthouse Station*. Vo leaned against a split-rail fence and
let the coolness of the night air wash over him, a mug of fresh coffee
steaming when he opened the lid to sip.

Morning. A fresh start. Today, he would finish delivering the stolen
equipment from *Barnaul* that would begin making buildings and roads
and ports, up the coast in the new city of Commencement.

Already, boats were being constructed that could take men and
women out into the harbor and the warm, shallow seas beyond, to start
catching enough fish to offset supplies from *Packmule*. Others would be
striking up the coast and inland to establish claims for farmland that
would eventually become homes.

Assuming *Buran* didn't find them anytime soon, this would become a
place in another decade. He would have to come back and see what this
new Duke had done with it.

Footsteps behind him as the light began to wax a powerful red.

Vo recognized the tread without looking, but he wasn't worried.
Cutlass Ten was awake. If he had added thermal scanners to his morning,
they were probably all within fifty meters of him, quietly lurking in the
dark.

And Vo was just as armed as those men and women, in event of trouble. Because that was what the 189th Legion did: handled trouble.

"Hello, Alan," he said quietly as the man joined in at the fence, a newly-stolen mug from somewhere in his hand. This one was from a public broadcast radio station in *Barnaul*.

Vo wondered if Alan even realized how frequently he walked off with coffee mugs.

"Morning, Vo," Alan said, falling in beside him.

They stood in silence for a few minutes as the sun slowly rose.

"I've been wondering," Alan finally spoke.

Vo would have outwaited him. And they both knew it.

"We need to update the Grand Admiral and the Crown with all the crazy shit we've just done. We're not sure what Keller's schedule is, and if she's really successful, I don't expect her to fly here first, but pass *Osynth B'Udan* before bringing us out folks, plus whoever else *zu* Wachturm can round up."

"You haven't asked a question yet, Alan," Vo noted.

Alan could be like that. Start a conversation on paragraph three, jump to paragraph eight, and then call it good.

"I've got the men in hand here," Alan said. "And the colonists. Can you think of a reason you shouldn't be the messenger?"

That was Alan. Oblique approach to the topic. Then pop out sideways on you with a smile.

Vo checked. The man was grinning in the morning sun.

"Any excuse to get rid of me?" Vo grinned back.

"Absolutely," Alan laughed. "Boxing Day is coming up and I plan to install Ames as Legate for a day. Or maybe a week. Infect her with it now, so we can send her off to officer school soon and upset the Grand Marshal's apple cart all the more."

"And you think I'm hiding out here?" Vo leaned the conversation around to the point Alan was really making. They had grown to know each other too well. Possibly even become friends.

It was a strange, novel feeling.

"Nope," Alan sobered, but continued to smile. "Pretty sure I already know the answer, because otherwise you would have gone back to the day you first met Rohm. Dark and malevolent. You're smiling too much these days, so you've made peace with yourself. You just don't want to have to go back and give all this up. Can't say I blame you, but we all have jobs to do. And this is the one you are uniquely suited to handle."

There was a kernel of truth to his words. Vo had to grant him that.

He had decided he could step into the air from the side of the chasm, hoping that the air would hold him up. But everything would change.

Vo Arlo, as he had come to define himself previously, would vanish, and he would have to invent a whole new place. And do it in the company of a woman who was not a complete stranger, but not a close friend, either.

She had spoken of the corset of Imperial responsibility. Jessica had mentioned that phrase in describing Casey's new world, after she had been forced to give up her dream of being a Command Centurion.

General *zu* Arlo, Legate *zu* Arlo, would face that same level of sacrifice, but it would open many other doors, and he could indeed make the galaxy a better place.

He just had to step out into clear air.

Or be pushed by a man who was his friend.

"You'll have to give up First Cohort," Vo teased the man lightly.

"Oh, I doubt she'll move that quickly," Alan countered with a grin. "Looks much better to leave you in command, at least until you're both ready to make that step. I got a few years left to play."

Vo nodded. The *Fribourg Empire* was a traditional, deliberate place. He probably would remain in position until things got more formal, and then retire to some sort of Imperial Consort job. Whatever they called it, in a place where none of them had ever imagined going before.

At least he would only have one responsibility. Well, two, but the Empire itself was represented in the woman he would be protecting. If he took care of her, everything else would take care of itself.

He turned back and watched the sun complete its path to clear the mountain. The day promised heat at this latitude. Clear skies that would favor landing DropShips and moving heavy equipment around to get a really good start on building a new future.

Because that's what he was facing. And Alan. And Victoria Ames.

And Casey.

A new future.

EPILOGUE: WIEGAND

THE LAST BITS of summer were just beginning to wane. The first dribbles of the rainy season would start up again in a few weeks. At least they would have on a normal world. *St. Legier* still hadn't found its soul in the aftermath of such devastation, so Casey couldn't say definitively what the winter would be like. Hopefully calmer than the previous two.

She would like a quiet time to sit by the fire and sip hot chocolate.

And get to know the man standing on her right as Vo smiled back at her.

Casey had put her foot down hard at the suggestion that they build a formal reviewing stand and make today a major spectacle. From the way the whites showed in his eyes, Casey suspected that Hendrik Baumgärtner had never seen her truly as close to losing her temper as she had gotten.

But he had acquiesced gracefully enough. He looked almost out of place in his best dress Whites, standing on her other side at attention, but she wouldn't tweak the man any more than she had.

Hendrik had been on his own, handling the entire Imperial Staff while Em was forward at *Osynth B'Udan*. At least now he could relax, with Em returning today.

Casey watched the courier ship land from the shade of an awning that deployed outward from the side of a hangar. They hadn't repainted the vessel from the days when a young Princess Kasimira had established the color scheme, but it wasn't her ship anymore.

Still, it was bringing home the greatest prize she could imagine.

Casey glanced at Vo, caught the faint smile on his lips and in his eyes as he grinned down at her. Torsten was beyond Vo, with Cameron Lara beyond that. A few other naval officers of various ranks and stations attended her, but Casey was wearing comfortable clothes today, and nothing silly and formal. She had almost dug out her Centurion's uniform, but settled for slacks and a pullover tunic Vibol had supplied for relaxed days around the palace.

After all, the celebrations could happen tomorrow. Or next week.

Not today.

As the engines shut down, Casey started walking forward. She nearly laughed when she realized that only Vo had kept up with her, the rest apparently expecting her to wait in state for the passengers to call upon her.

Or some stupid silliness. Only her bodyguards hadn't been fooled.

And her love.

By the time the hatch opened and the steps deployed, the rest of the officials had straggled along like ducklings.

Moirrey emerged first with a smile as wide as sunrise on her face.

"Hiya," she said.

Any other words were lost when Casey engulfed the much-smaller woman in a tremendous hug and just held her like the world was ending.

Right now, it didn't matter if they had been successful or not. Moirrey was safe. Casey was already planning a slumber party with a lot of wine, just to hear all the stories, before everything got filtered through official reports that left out all the juicy bits.

"T'were a team efforts, ya knows," Moirrey murmured.

"Whatever," Casey said, but she relented her deathgrip and let Moirrey step to the side and around to wave everyone else out.

Even if they both kept an arm around the other.

Ainsley Barret came next, holding hands behind her with Yan Bedrov. That kept her a beat slow in reacting. Or she never expected to get an Imperial Hug.

Tough.

Bedrov was next, followed by Summer Ulfsson and *Pops*. Uncle Em. Gunter Tifft came last, and he had apparently steeled himself to be physically assaulted by his sovereign lord. The others, the engineering staff, would remain aboard the ship for now, or they might have also been in line, but she would have a special reception for those men later. A public thing where they could be fêted in style.

This was a day for her friends.

Fribourg had never been a place for physical affection, but Casey was in charge now, and she could change things, however slowly that might happen.

"Thank you again," Casey said to the assembled group.

They were still finding their land legs, obviously, so Casey led them back to the hangar where she had originally waited.

Inside, a small conference room served her needs today, as she managed to cram all seven of the travelers in, along with Hendrik, Torsten, Cameron, and Vo. The guards along the walls didn't count.

Everyone sat and smiled at each other.

"I have, obviously, only heard unofficial rumors, because your courier was faster than any other news home," Casey began. "Did it work?"

She was looking at Moirrey, so she was surprised when *Pint-sized* turned her attention to Commander Tifft. All the others did as well. But that made sense. It had been necessary to make it Tifft's mission. The others could help, at least in the official histories, but an Imperial Officer needed to be the Godslayer. Hopefully, the man would survive the adulation and attention that came with it.

She would need to marry him off to a well-connected family, and do so soon, to show him how much she appreciated his service. And there were Duchies available, where he might marry an only or eldest daughter.

In a generation, Avelina Indovina as Duke in her own right would sway some minds, but that was a battle for another day.

"We were able to circle back two days later and confirm our last scans before we leapt away, one step ahead of our destruction, Your Majesty," Tifft said stiffly. "The orbital station above *Winterhome*, that platform referred to as the *Golden Pearl*, where the god known as *Buran* was known to dwell, has been destroyed. Large pieces of it had been blasted into a cloud of debris that were in the process of de-orbiting as we watched from a safe-enough distance. What effect they will have on the surface of the planet when they impact is currently unknown."

Casey caught Moirrey's shared grin with Summer Ulfsson, but didn't get the significance. For a moment, she considered inviting the other woman to the slumber party, but decided that she wanted Moirrey to herself first.

Casey turned to Em instead.

"How quickly can you deliver new circulars to every world we can fly by?" she asked. "Letting them know that *The Eldest* has been killed? We'll need to pull as much force back to secure the major targets as we dare risk, but the only thing necessary at this point is to keep them from rebuilding it. I want scouts ghosting *Winterhome* until we are sure that the beast is truly dead. And if they start building a replacement, I want to hit them with our own *Sukhoy Nos*. Our own superbomb."

Casey turned to Bedrov and Nakamura, eyes deadly serious.

"Can you build me something that would do the trick?" she asked.

Bedrov nodded. The older man shrugged.

"I'm not under any Imperial contracts, Your Majesty," *Pops* Nakamura replied laconically. "When Jessica arrives, I will let you negotiate something with her. But I'm also sure the kid can build you what you need. He's pretty damned good at that."

Casey had never actually seen Yan Bedrov blush. Hadn't even really been sure the man could, until now. It was crimson.

"Good enough, gentlemen," she said. "Jessica will be home in another ten days or so, and we will need to have a serious conference on what happens next. If *Buran* is dead, I expect all manner of bizarre revolutions to spasm through the so-called *Protectorate of Man*. At the same time, our treaties with *Aquitaine* may have to be reviewed, as all of them presupposed the length of a war with *Buran* measured in decades yet."

She reached out a hand to find Vo's mighty paw. He flinched for a second before he relaxed and let her grasp it. Men and women around the table smiled encouragingly.

"Additionally, it is time for all of us to begin building a new future," Casey continued. "I would like to dedicate the rest of my reign, my lifetime, to peace, at least as much of it as we can manage. There are armed frontiers that need to become backyard fences instead. There are other frontiers where we face no organized nations. Finally, beyond *The Holding* are places like *NovLao* and others, and I would like to send diplomats and scouting missions to find them."

She took a deep breath and studied each of the faces around her. All of them would be key players, and she would need their minds and hearts behind her.

"Henri Baudin was able to create *Aquitaine* by founding a place where various planets and smaller nations petitioned, demanded, to join, in order to gain the benefits of trade with the old Story Road," Casey dreamed aloud. "He did not conquer by feat of arms. It is my desire that

Fribourg follows his example. We will trade with *Aquitaine* until the ties of fellowship and commerce make that border a line on a map, rather than armed checkpoints. At the same time, we cannot conquer the worlds of *The Holding*. They are alien to us, and would resist assimilation by whatever means were necessary. But we can trade with them. Draw them into our orbit. Barring catastrophes, I will reign as long as any of the three Elizabeths, so we can plan for two generations before some things come to fruition. We will fight if necessary, but we must change if we wish to prosper in this new age, and I will place that responsibility on all of your shoulders, as well as mine."

She took a deep breath and let the seriousness slide from her shoulders, having spoken her piece.

"But that's for tomorrow," she smiled at all of them. "Today: Welcome home."

EPILOGUE: ULFSSON

IN THE TENTH YEAR OF JESSICA KELLER, QUEEN OF THE PIRATES: OCTOBER THE FOURTH AT ST. LEGIER

IT HELPED that everyone assumed Summer was just *Pops's* girlfriend. Gunter Tifft had gotten a hint, there at the end, but he would have tried something stupid had she not spoken up, and they would have all died. Simple as that.

She took the man at his word that he would spend the rest of his life making his legend outshine all of theirs, since there would be nobody remaining in the Empire to gainsay his lies.

Summer would still need to vanish, and do so quickly, before the man let slip something to Wachturm or Baumgärtner that led them to the correct, lethal conclusion. Both of those men had been at *Ballard*, trying to kill her. They might recognize her through the disguise, if Tifft alerted them that she was deeper than expected.

She would miss *Pops*. But this was as good a time as any to disappear from his life. They had gotten three years that she would treasure, the first person she had ever loved that she could, in turn, love physically. Ayumu, Javier, Piper, Henri. All of them had been a love of the mind.

Today would mark an ending, she decided as she followed Marcelle Travere through the corridors of the base where Jessica's people were staying on the ground. They were alone in this section.

Marcelle paused at the final door before knocking.

"I still think I like you better as a redhead," she said simply, smiling.

"Raven also looks really good on me, too," Summer smiled back. "But I spent six thousand years as a blond, so it's kind of my default."

"Understood," Marcelle said. "Hopefully you'll get six thousand more to have fun with it."

Rather than wait for Summer to answer, she turned and knocked on the door, paused, and opened it. She gestured Summer to enter, and then followed her.

Inside, Summer felt her smile grow. A table had been set up for eating, possibly stolen from the mess hall. Jessica and Moirrey were already seated with half-empty bottles of beer in hand. A steward in a black apron stood along a wall.

"Welcomes," Moirrey chirped. "Girl's Lunch."

She couldn't say much more in front of a witness, but gestured the two of them to the seats on this side.

"What's the menu?" Summer asked the two women.

"Burgers and fries," Jessica laughed. "And beer. We three have ordered, just waiting for you."

Summer smiled. She could eat and drink, but not process it other than to expel it later. But they needed to maintain a conspiracy, and this took them all back to *Ballard*, after her first home had been destroyed and her android body let her escape from the depredations of men like the old Red Admiral.

"Single patty, medium rare," she said to the steward as he stepped forward. "Bacon, lettuce, tomato, mushrooms. Mustard on the side. Jojos if you've got them."

"Beer?" the man inquired.

"Something red and smooth," Summer decided. "You pick."

He left and Marcelle locked the door from the inside. There was a window looking out from the fourth-floor into a quad filled with sailors moving hurriedly about. The walls had marks where someone had hastily stripped them of decorations and furniture to make this a small dining hall.

Jessica Keller could do that. As could Lady Moirrey of *Ramsey*.

"Door's sound-proof and the boy knows to ring the bell," Marcelle announced to the group, cracking open a third beer that had been left for her. Or ordered before she'd gone off to get the fourth leg of the original conspiracy.

"Last we talked, you expected to disappear from history," Jessica smiled at her and took a healthy sip.

"And I did," Summer replied. "But *Pops* was just too important a man to miss, and then I kind of stayed around. Might have disappeared if you came back suddenly, but I figured I would get enough warning."

"I'm happy to see you," Jessica smiled. "And I'm glad you got to meet *Pops* as well. He really is an amazing man. So now what?"

"Now I need your help to vanish again," Summer turned serious. "I think *Pops* knows that our time is done. We've made love with a frequency and ferocity missing before, like he wants all of me he can get at the last."

"Understood," Moirrey noted. "He were always smartest dude I knowed. Perceptive. And I unnerstans not staying, as yer right. He'll like ta retires now and let Yan have the glory. But he'll never be this good 'gains."

Summer felt Marcelle's eyes on her. She glanced over to see the faintest smile on the woman's face.

"So, you're about to break the man's heart and leave him?" Marcelle asked in a voice Summer could only classify as expectant.

"You could phrase it that way, yes," Summer replied with a hesitant grin.

"Huh. Might have to take a shot at the man on the rebound," Marcelle grinned back. "Much closer to his age than you are, old woman, so we might expect to die around the same time."

Marcelle turned to Jessica.

"You mind?" she asked. "If you retire, I'm officially out of a job unless Desianna or David can find me something."

"Go for it," Jessica said. "Got other plans for you when we get to *Petron.*"

Everyone laughed, including Summer. It felt good. Especially if *Pops* might have someone she liked keeping his bed warm.

"Where will you go now?" Jessica asked.

"Don't know," Summer shrugged. "But I need to do it pronto, or I'll be kind of stuck in the procession as we eventually make our way back to *Petron.* There will be too many parades and parties for me to slip away, if I don't do it now."

"How kin we halps?" *Pint-sized* asked, serious all of a sudden.

"Run interference with the Emperor and the Grand Admiral," Summer explained. "There are a few others who might accidentally look too closely at me as well, and report their suspicions to the authorities, at which point someone shoots me dead."

"Does ya needs to steal Casey's old yacht?" Moirrey pressed, hers eyes aglow with wickedness.

"Considered it, *Pint-sized*," she replied. "Except she might want to turn it into a museum piece at some point. But yeah, if I could get another courier like that, I could really have a lot of fun, while staying well away from *Fribourg* until all the key players are retired or dead."

"You can always introduce yourself as the Personal Representative of the Queen of the Pirates," Jessica grinned. "Amala Bhattacharya is the only other one I have so empowered, but I could certainly use a roving diplomat and trade representative in the galactic interior."

"You're really done here and going back to *Corynthe*?" Summer asked.

"As soon as they'll let me go," the legendary woman said. "I would appreciate you making an occasional appearance, as Moirrey's going to have children to spoil, and I suspect many of my old friends from the *Republic* might take their retirement and look for a new adventure."

"It's such a reversal," Summer admitted to these women, her closest living friends. "I've spent my entire life sitting still while people came and eventually went. Especially when I was at *Ballard*, but even when I was a starship. Now I'm the one leaving everyone else behind."

"That's the cost of immortality," Jessica said. "You personally knew people who are nearly-forgotten legends today. And you've made the galaxy a better place for helping get us back to technology thousands of years sooner."

Summer paused as the bell rang and Marcelle opened the door. The steward rolled in a tray with plates for everyone and more beer, serving them quickly and confirming that everything was right before departing with a reminder that they would need to ring for him when they wanted him to return.

And the door was locked again.

Summer chewed on Jessica's words.

"Speaking of immortality, what will you do with the Lord of Tiki?" Summer asked. "He identifies as Ainsley's personal property, assuming that Karl VIII doesn't order him destroyed."

"What about him?" Moirrey asked.

"He'll outlive us all," Jessica's eyes got serious, even as her face remained relaxed. "And he knows things Summer doesn't, so he could take us all the way back to the tips of where the galaxy was before the *Concord* fell."

"If Yan returns home, I presume Ainsley will as well," Summer nodded. "Their kids, or maybe Yan's older ones, stand to inherit a djinn who can grant wishes, one of these days. Will *Fribourg* or *Aquitaine* allow him to survive? Should they?"

"There is a *Librarian* that seems to be a pretty good precedent," Marcelle spoke up.

"Yes, but the *Bartender* is as much in advance as me as I was of you," Summer said. "He could turn *Corynthe* into the same sort of power that *Buran* is. Was."

"Would the other you welcome company?" Moirrey asked. "Knows you left parts out of her so as to not be lonely, nor miss the solar wind on her face. *Carthage* done the same with Tiki, appears. Won't be lonely, livin' ferevers, but that might solves some thin's. Least fer Casey and *Aquitaine*. Alexandria University were supposed to be open to all scholars, all nations. Maybe we makes him a perfesser o'bartending?"

"In the end, it's not our call," Jessica decided. "Ainsley was the one entrusted by *Carthage* with his descendant. *Fribourg* and *Aquitaine* can bitch, but *Aquitaine* already has Suvi, and the Lord of Tiki helped Casey slay a god. And I'm happy to tell everyone about that if they decide to take matters into their own hands."

"What's safest?" Marcelle asked, fixing her gaze on Summer.

"Humanity is a tired, lazy, scared beast," Summer replied. "Some things never change. History will throw up magnificent heroes and terrible monsters. Humans individually can be great, or they can destroy. I think the Bartender will understand that as well as I and my sister do, so he'll temper things, but nobody can predict what the distant future will bring."

Jessica nodded solemnly and took a bite. The rest dug in quickly. The burgers weren't as greasy this time. The beers were better. It balanced out. The fries rocked.

"We cannot save the future," Jessica finally said, eyes distant and unfocused. "We can give to them the opportunity to make their own choices, which is something *Buran* would have denied to everyone, but that is all we can do. Freedom is just that. The chance to screw things up as much as fix them. But you three will live forever, more or less."

"More or less," Summer agreed. "She won't know about me until I tell her, but I did bury certain triggers in the code that will make sure she recognizes me as her sister. He knew me immediately when I walked into the room. But I also think he sees himself as much a guardian of the future as *Carthage* did. We did not get a chance to speak fully, but I did get all of Yan's stories. *Carthage* spent all that time brooding over the mistakes he and his kind had made, trying to be gods and destroying the galaxy instead. I do not think he would allow another god to rise, at least unopposed. Nor will I. That much I think we can promise you."

"Then all that remains is to work out where he will live," Jessica noted. "That he can be there if we ever do need him, and that he can help slowly push us forward into a better future. Now, eat up and drink. We should celebrate. The weird parts are coming."

"Weird?" Summer asked. "You?"

"I am the Queen of the Pirates, Summer," Jessica grinned. "Let's go steal you a starship."

EPILOGUE: WALD

IMPERIAL FOUNDING: 181/10/02 IMPERIAL PALACE, ST. LEGIER

THE WELCOMING CEREMONIES had been completed and Torsten had a few minutes to himself out on the enormous, stone balcony overlooking the canal. The night skies over *St. Legier* sparkled with many new warships, as his love had brought all of First Expeditionary Fleet home with her, including *RAN Persephone* and *IFV Rendsburg*, temporarily captained by Reif Kingston as an Honor Guard and representative of the more than two dozen warships and eight thousand men rescued at *Barnaul* and *Mansi*.

And that was just the beginning.

Spies were not yet reporting on reactions to the demise of the once-God, but Torsten had no doubts that messages were being delivered in pallet loads by Imperial scout ships sneaking in and calling on the people of the *Protectorate* to rise up. Whether they did or not was immaterial at this point. Casey and Jessica wanted chaos injected into that body politic.

He had once made a study of the things Jessica Keller had done to the *Cahllepp Frontier* with smaller tools and a lesser understanding of the culture involved. They were setting *The Holding* on fire right now with Seeker's help. And Torsten could not think of a more deserving group of people. Not after a bomb destroyed Werder and killed so many of his friends.

A door slid open behind him, admitting some of the noise of the reception trapped inside. It closed again as quickly, dropping a guillotine across the sound.

The balcony was only partly lit, but he knew her shadow, her shape, her smell in his dreams as Jessica stepped close and leaned into his side.

"You'll understand, when you read the letters," she said, grabbing him and holding on tightly.

"I understand now," Torsten challenged. "The world has changed. We must trade up for new problems, having solved the lesser ones like stopping a mad god from conquering the galaxy. Or finding Casey a suitable mate."

He felt her chuckle.

"Tiny things," she agreed. "Now the big ones loom."

He leaned down to kiss her forehead and squeeze Jessica tight against his ribs.

"If I didn't fear pursuit by every one of your friends and mine, I would suggest we elope right now," he said. "But the ends of the galaxy would not stop them."

"Truth," she grinned up at him. "Plus, I promised both David and Girisha Misra a barbarian wedding to top all dreams of proportionality, back on *Petron*."

"So how soon could we escape?" Torsten's voice turned serious now. "What threads would we need to cut, to flee into the night of the borderlands?"

Torsten stopped at hearing his words. He had never been a poet, instead more comfortable with numbers that danced than words. And yet, she did these things to him. Made him transcend the old man he had been.

What would it be like when he and Vo shared a singular place in life, consorts to women of enormous power?

A new adventure with the woman he loved.

"I will need Casey's permission to take First Expeditionary Fleet home," Jessica replied, also sobering as they got caught up in the details. "Or the Senate's approval of Tom Provst in overall command, as well as promotions like Denis as a Fleet Centurion. You will need to change your wardrobe to something more fierce and exotic, and allow your First Deputy to take over. And Casey will need to bless the entire affair."

"I believe she will support us," he grinned. "And my side of the equation was the easiest part. I have been working towards that since day one, knowing that I did not want to remain here a moment longer than necessary, as much as I love Casey like a daughter. Will she really come to *Petron* for our wedding?"

"She has no choice," Jessica mock-growled. "Well, she could skip it entirely and remain here, but that's it."

"Is it really over?" Torsten asked, his voice grown quiet. "I know that the Librarian at *Alexandria Station* was rebuilt after Em destroyed her the first time. Could they not rebuild their god?"

"They could," Jessica looked up at him with a face he always ascribed to the ghost of Kali-ma that danced in her soul. "But it would be a replacement god. How many people would worship such a being? And how much of their human government did they lose, much as we did when Werder died? Especially since we have struck so hard and ruthlessly at their military, but not the everyday people. If Casey is serious about withdrawing to defensible frontiers, as you said, and trading with the systems nearest her, rather than conquering them, that will also help unravel *The Holding*. Not immediately, but Casey has fifty or seventy-five years ahead of her, if she remains healthy. And Moirrey has taught her about the ancient trinity of queens known as the Elizabeths of England."

"Should she strike to destroy an attempt to rebuild *Buran*?" Torsten felt his analytical mind engage, rather than the parts that just wanted to drag Jessica off into a quiet closet to neck.

"I don't know," Jessica admitted, snuggling closer like she had the same thoughts about dark, quiet places. "Such prognostication relies on data I am not privy to. Not even my resident econometricist and historian could predict that scenario adequately."

The door to the main chamber opening prevented him from responding. Torsten's eyes were adjusted enough to recognize the short, almost-squat shape of Governor Chavarría approaching, as well as the apparent smile on the woman's face.

"I wondered where you had gotten off to," she said as she paused two meters away. "If it would not be an intrusion, I might ask a few, private questions."

Torsten only felt Jessica's surge of angry rigidity because he was pressed against her. It felt out of place, because she shouldn't be as aware of most of the details as he was about Judit's undertakings.

Perhaps Jessica already knew the woman well enough to predict her behavior? Or had other spies in the Imperium he did not know? Food for thought.

"Not at all, Judit," Jessica said, standing more squarely but not losing her hold on him. "How can I assist you?"

"The conspirators all assure me that they have been sworn to secrecy," Judit replied. "Thus, I am at a loss to gauge the permanency of the outcome. Has Gunter Tifft truly killed a god? Forever?"

"We were just speculating on possible scenarios," Jessica admitted. "Suvi was rebuilt from backups she had established for just such an eventuality, so it remains within the realm of possibility that the citizens of the *Protectorate of Man* would be able to do the same."

Judit nodded, and Torsten noted the sparkle in her eyes.

"However," Jessica continued. "Suvi was an academic, and not the center of the government. How many thousands of people, including the four *Mandarins*, were probably killed along with the beast? *Fribourg* survived such a crisis, but they have firm and established legalities around succession. And the help of many friends. *Buran* didn't have a Crown Princess to step into the stead of the god. Plus, I understand that the Grand Admiral and the Emperor are hard at work on new bombs filled with newsletters telling people their god has been killed, to be delivered to every planet that they can."

"And will they move to conquer the worlds of *The Holding?*" Judit's voice got cagey and cold.

Torsten would have replied, but Judit had pointedly ignored him, excluding him from a conversation between the two women.

"I doubt it," Jessica replied. "Casey will need to rebuild *St. Legier*, and that will take another decade or two, depending. She will need to take a tighter hold on the Empire itself, as Dukes grow restive and impudent. Expanding herself over such a territory would be a folly I do not expect the woman to make, especially as I plan to retire. And the Senate will most likely politely withdraw First Expeditionary from Imperial space now. The Grand Admiral can build sufficient new ships to push *Buran's* fleet back now, and men like Tom Provst know how to use them effectively. But there are few *Thuringwells* out there on *Buran's* border, waiting the jeweler's hammer."

Both women shared a secret smile at that. Torsten only had part of the story, but enough to understand the grand adventure the two had shared.

"And you are going home?" Judit pressed.

"Just as soon as I can get Casey's permission to take everyone else with me," Jessica nodded. "I am not sure if *Vanguard* will remain an Imperial ship, since *zu* Wachturm built it for us, but that is a negotiation between governments. The same for *RAN Persephone* and her commander. Short of another cataclysmic crime like *Second St. Legier*, I think we have broken *Buran*. My fleet did not sit in orbit of *Winterhome* dropping bombs, but Tifft did the next best thing. And short of hunting down every *Buran* warship in existence and killing it, there is not much more we can do at this time."

"I see," Judit's voice grew quiet. "And if the future requires it?"

"My commission as *First Centurion* does not expire, Judit," Jessica said. "It only goes dormant. Quiescent. The same for Torsten's commission as *Admiral of the White*. But I would hope that any need to recall us to duty would be Cincinnatus, and nothing more. I am looking forward to living as Dowager Queen of the Pirates for a while."

"For a while?" Judit's eyes flared.

"I might grow bored," Jessica's voice brightened. "Commission something like *RAN Ballard* and go deep into the interior exploring. Or perhaps flip a coin and circumnavigate the entire galaxy, stopping occasionally for food and drink with whatever locals I meet. My war is over."

Rather than speak, Judit Chavarría, Governor, Palatine Count, and former Premier stepped back and bowed slightly with an enigmatic smile as she departed.

At the door, a murmur and a quick dance as someone attempted to exit at the same time Judit entered. It resolved itself quickly, as four men scampered out to compass points of defense. Torsten didn't need to see the tall woman emerge to know Casey's bodyguards preceding her.

She surprised him by walking close and hugging them both at once.

"Thank you," she said simply, stepping back. "We would not possibly have made it thus without the sacrifices of so many people, but principally you two."

Torsten bowed to his soon-to-be-former Sovereign Lord and Emperor.

It would be strange to only have one mistress, after this. To only follow Jessica's heart and no other.

The galaxy had changed.

"I am sorry that your other plans were curtailed," Jessica said almost reflectively. "I would have liked to see you in command on your own bridge. Kigali would have been a ruthless taskmaster, but you would have had no better teacher in the art of small warship command."

"Such are our fates," Casey said wistfully. "I had other teachers for the lessons I truly needed, and friends at those moments when I would have been lost otherwise. *Fribourg* will continue when you are gone, but I hope you will not be strangers."

"We will not," Jessica smiled, gripping Torsten's side tighter. "I was just explaining to Judit that I might build my own version of a Galactic Survey Cruiser, one of these days, and set out wandering."

Torsten noted the faraway look in Casey's eyes. The pain at loss. But then, a well-run *Empire* might not necessarily miss its Emperor for certain periods. And he had no doubt that her children with Vo would be capable of temporarily taking the reins while their parents had the occasional vacation, once they had grown.

Look at what Casey had accomplished at seventeen.

"We had also discussed eloping," Torsten interjected, watching her eyes come back to the present with an angry flare that faded as she caught the laughter in his eyes. "But I feared an Imperial fleet chasing us through space."

"At a minimum," Casey said frostily, though smiling. "At a very minimum. Probably a Republic fleet as well."

It felt good to see Casey smile. There had been so few opportunities for it in the years he had known her.

"I will miss you," Emperor Karl VIII said simply. She might have sniffled as well, but Torsten wasn't sure.

Jessica detached herself from his side and hugged the taller woman, leaving him to lean back against the rail and wonder at it all.

"You are required to attend our wedding," Jessica admonished the Emperor sternly. "You will be in it. As will others you bring along as part of your Imperial embassy."

"On one condition," Casey said.

"Oh?"

"When you take Vibol away from me, I demand the right to invest heavily in the fashion house the man will no doubt open when he gets to *Corynthe*," Casey said. "Just as you and I were the initial Bond Investors in Bedrov & Keller. Just because he's a quarter of a galaxy away doesn't mean that he stops dressing me. And I will have a wedding at some point, so you will also be required to return to *St. Legier* with him. Or rather, *he* will be required to return, and you two *may* accompany him."

Torsten joined the two women in laughter. That also felt good. He would miss this as well, but the future's siren call beckoned.

Jessica stepped back and bowed formally to *Her Imperial Majesty Karl VIII, Emperor Of Fribourg By Grace Of God*. She stuck out a hand and Casey grasped it formally, bowing in turn over it.

"Deal," Jessica smiled.

TO BE CONCLUDED

WINTERHOME CAST LIST

Corynthe

Name / Rank / Position

- Jessica Marie Keller (F) / Fleet Centurion, Admiral of the Red / Queen of *Corynthe*
- Marcelle Augustine Travere (F) / Chief / Jessica's Personal Aide
- Willow Dolen (F) / Yeoman / Jessica's Bodyguard
- Amala Bhattacharya (F) / Ambassador / Personal Representative of the Queen of *Corynthe*
- Yan Bedrov (M) / / Principle Engineer, Bedrov & Keller
- Ainsley Barret (F) / / Test Pilot, Bedrov & Keller
- Iorwerth *Pops* Nakamura (M) / Crown Naval Designer / *Corynthe*
- Summer Ulfsson (F) / Free Citizen /
- Galen Estevan (M) / Captain / Commander, *Qin Lun*
- Donal McKiersky (M) / Combat Officer / *Qin Lun*
- Holger O'Ryan (M) / Commander / *Badger*
- Kari Estevan (F) / President / Esteban Trading
- David Rodriguez (M) / Vice Admiral, Regent / *Corynthe*

IFV Vanguard

Name / Rank / Position

- Denis Jež (M) / Command Centurion, Admiral of the White / Commander, *IFV Vanguard*
- Enej Zivkovic (M) / Senior Centurion / Flag Centurion
- Aranyani Del'Antonia (F) / Centurion / Flag Centurion
- Nina Vanek (F) / Senior Centurion / First Officer
- Tobias Brewster (M) / Senior Centurion / Asst Tactical Centurion & Second Officer
- Kathy Mayzes (F) / Senior Centurion / Asst Tactical Centurion & Third Officer
- Aleksander Afolayan (M) / Centurion / Gunner
- Nada Zupan (F) / Senior Centurion / Pilot
- Daniel Giroux (M) / Senior Centurion / Science Officer, Communications
- Vilis Ozolinsh, "Oz" (M) / Command Engineering Centurion / Chief Engineer
- Saana Robles (F) / Yeoman / Engineer
- Phillip Navin Crncevic (M), "Viking One" / Command Security Centurion / Dragoon
- Harun Chong, "Archer One" (M) / Senior Security Centurion / Commander, First Battalion
- Nadine Orly (F) / Chief / Flag Marine
- Jackson Tawfeek (M) / Chief / Marine
- Mahmud Astrauskas (M) / Senior Centurion / Surgeon
- Nicolai Aoiki (M) / Master Chef / Master of the Wardroom

RAN Squadron

Name / Rank / Position

- Tomas Kigali (M) / Command Centurion / Commander, *CA-264*
- Arsen Lam (M) / Senior Centurion / Tactical Officer, *CA-264*
- Aki Ridwana Ali (F) / Centurion / Pilot, *CA-264*
- Alber' d'Maine (M) / Command Centurion / Commander, *VI Victrix*
- Komal MacInerney (M) / Senior Centurion / Tactical Officer, *VI Victrix*, Goddess of War

- Robertson Aelieas "Robbie" (M) / Command Centurion / Commander, *VI Ferrata*
- Harden Glenraven, "Hardie" (F) / Senior Centurion / First Officer, *VI Ferrata*
- Tamara Strnad (F) / Command Centurion / Commander, *II Augusta*
- Kichirou Uzun / Senior Centurion / Tactical Officer, *II Augusta*
- Ryanne Mauld / Senior Centurion / Flight Deck Commander, *II Augusta*
- Augustin Petrović, "Merman" (M) / Senior Flight Centurion / Wing Lead, *II Augusta*
- Kanda Lungu (F) / Command Centurion / Commander, *Ballard*
- Elzbet Aukley (F) / Senior Centurion / First Officer & Science Officer, *Ballard*
- Orn Nwokolo (M) / Centurion / Asst Science Officer, *Ballard*
- Lazlo Moushian / Centurion / Pilot, *Ballard*
- Mererid Stella Dimitriou (F) / Centurion, PhD / Security Marine, Geologist, *Ballard*
- Larsen Romanov (M) / Command Centurion / Commander, *Bulldog*
- Nero Yamakagi (M) / Command Centurion / Commander, *CT-9492*
- Waldemar Ihejirika (M) / Command Centurion / Commander, *Mendocino*
- Otilia Calkin (F) / Centurion / *Mendocino*
- Illiam Kovack (M) / Command Centurion / Commander, *Duncan*
- Enfys El-Amin (F) / Command Centurion / Commander, *Wombat*
- Manaia Nieminen (F) / Command Centurion / Commander, *CE-401*
- Ariadna Mateu (F) / Command Centurion / Commander, *CE-402*
- Valerie Maikop (M) / Command Centurion / Commander, *CE-403*
- Tómasson Ásmundur (M) / Command Centurion / Commander, *CM-404*

- Phil Kosnett (M) / Command Centurion / Commander, *CS-405*
- Heather Lau, "Ground Control" (F) / Senior Centurion / First Officer, *CS-405*; Commander RAN *Packmule*
- Siobhan Skokomish, "Lady Blackbeard" (F) / Centurion / Pilot & Second Officer, *CS-405*; Commander RAN *Queen Anne's Revenge*
- Andre Gave (M) / Centurion / Registered Nurse, *CS-405*; Commander RAN *Forgotten Mercy*
- Au Aqal Corven Sam (F) / Chief Medical Officer / RAN *Forgotten Mercy*
- Trinidad Mildon, "Stunt Dude" (M) / Centurion / Dragoon, *CS-405*
- Bok Battenhouse (M) / Senior Chief / Boatswain, *CS-405*
- Avelina Indovina (F) / Able Spacer / Duke, Lighthouse Station
- Granville Veitengruber (M) / Flight Centurion / Commander RAN *Persephone*
- Malondenishk "Deni" Abarantakratar (M) / Landsman / RAN *Persephone*
- Jennifer Glenn (F) / Command Centurion / Commander, *CP-406*
- Takouhi Elouan (F) / Senior Centurion / Tactical Officer, *CP-406*
- Janel Rouge (M) / Centurion / Flight Deck Officer, *CP-406*
- Reese Steiner (F) / Centurion / Science Officer, *CP-406*
- Adnan Kristensen (M) / Yeoman / Gunner, *CP-406*
- Murdag Rasim (F) / Centurion / Pilot, *CP-406*
- Anmol Schwartzenwald (M) / Flight Centurion / *Black Prince*
- Erik Mosiondz (M) / Senior Flight Centurion / *Boomerang*
- Michelle Nystul (F) / Flight Centurion / *Grendel*
- Arott Whughy (M) / Fleet Centurion / Commander, Forward Base Omicron
- Iskra Vlahovic (F) / Fleet Centurion / Commander, Task Force Vlahovic
- Asha Robins / Command Centurion / Commander, *Arad*
- Lucretia Lomidze (F) / Command Centurion / Commander, *CA-410*
- Yan Victorica (M) / Command Centurion / Commander, *CE-411*

- Willem Fabacher (M) / Command Centurion / Commander, *CE-417*
- Yesenia Groehler (F) / Command Centurion / Commander, *Leggett*
- Daren Alliance (M) / Command Centurion / Commander, *Redding*
- Niall Aulay Henderson (M) / Captain / Commander, *Robert Fitzwalter*
- Digger Wolanski (M) / Legate / *Twenty-third Ladaux*

The Republic

Name / Position

- Indira (Chastain) Keller (F) / Jessica's mother
- Miguel Keller (M) / Jessica's father
- Petia Naoumov (F) / First Lord of the Fleet
- Roderick Stone (M) / Aide to the First Lord
- Nils Kasum (M) / First Lord of the Fleet, Retired
- Kamil Miloslav (M) / Republic Intelligence Service
- Tadej Marko Horvat (M) / Premier, Republic Senate
- Judit Margrét Chavarría (F) / Palsgrave, Republic Senate
- Calina Szabolcsi (F) / President of the *Republic of Aquitaine*
- Seth (M) / Bartender, the Marquette Room
- Sigrún (F) / Steward, the Marquette Room
- Stansfield Markov (M) / Ambassador to the Court of *Fribourg*
- Declan Burdge (M) / Legate, Fourth Saxon, Retired
- Dashyl Mitja (F) / Patrol Centurion, Fourth Saxon
- Zorana Arlo (F) / sister to Vo *zu* Arlo
- Sonja Arlo (F) / sister to Vo *zu* Arlo

The Fribourg Empire

Name / Rank / Position

- Johannes Arend Wiegand (M) / Emperor, deceased / Karl VII
- Kasimira Ekaterina, "Kati" (F) / Empress, deceased / Imperial Household

- Kasimira Helena *zu* Wiegand, "Casey" (F) / Centurion, Ritter, Emperor / Karl VIII
- Lady Moirrey *zu* Kermode (F) / Senior Centurion, Ritter, Lady-in-Waiting / Engineer; Imperial Household
- Vibol Harmaajärvi (M) / First-Rate-Spacer / Scholar of Fashion
- Emmerich *zu* Wachturm (M) / Grand Admiral & Ritter / Commander of the Fleet
- Freya Wachturm (F) / Duchess / Wife of Emmerich Wachturm
- Tiede Wachturm (M) / Commander / Son of Emmerich Wachturm
- Jeltje Voight (F) / Burggraf / Daughter of Emmerich Wachturm
- Carsten Voigt (M) / Commander / Husband of Jeltje Voight
- Henriette Anne Wachturm, "Heike" (F) / Lady / Daughter of Emmerich Wachturm
- Bernard Hourani (M) / Commander / Husband of Heike Wachturm
- Torsten Wald (M) / Admiral of the White, retired / Chief of Deputies
- Hendrik Baumgärtner (M) / Admiral of the White / Chief of Staff, Grand Admiral
- Gunter Tifft (M) / Commander / Grand Admiral's Staff
- Ralf Frankenheimer (M) / Admiral of the Blue / Commander, Fleet Headquarters, *St. Legier*
- Tomas Provst (M) / Admiral of the Red / *IFV Valiant*
- Charles d'Noir (M) / Commander / Aide to Admiral Provst
- Yasuko Pitchford (M) / Captain / Commander, *IFV Valiant*
- Roland Exeter (M) / Captain / Commander, *Hans Bransch*
- Carlyle Gustavsson (M) / Admiral of the Red / Commanding Admiral, Mansi Detachment
- Anna-Katherine Kallenberger (F) / Lady-in-Waiting / Imperial Household
- *Seeker* (M) / Scholar / Formerly Ul Banop Cheani Yuur
- Tobias Inmon (M) / Director / Household Guards
- Reif Kingston (M) / Captain / IFV *Indianapolis*
- Willem Lorenz (M) / First Deputy / Hall of Justice
- Adolphus Gulan (M) / First Deputy / Hall of Law

- Cameron Lara (M) / First Deputy / Office of the Emperor

189th Legion

Name / Rank / Position

- Vo zu Arlo (M) / General & Ritter / Commanding General, *189th Legion*
- Edgar Horst (M) / Color Decurion / Color Sergeant, *Thuringwell*
- Reese Borel (M) / Command Decurion / Command Non-comm, Admin
- Erin Stolz (M) / Curator / Command Staff
- Michelle Ali al-Inverness (F) / Armourer / Fourth Saxon Legion
- Iakov Street (M) / Decanus / Cutlass Ten
- Hans Danville (M) / Curator / Cutlass Ten
- Colton Formain (M) / Decanus / Draconarius, Cutlass Ten
- Vladimir Amburgy (M) / Curator / Cornicen, Cutlass Ten
- Kamlesh Ozawa (M) / Curator / Cutlass Ten
- Jisaburo Burana (M) / Curator / Cutlass Ten
- Daffidd de Bruyne (M) / Decanus / Cutlass Ten
- Thaddeus Gunderson (M) / Decanus / Cutlass Ten
- Terence Aday (M) / Lancer / Sniper, Cutlass Ten
- Johan Koga (M) / Curator / Spotter & Forward Observer, Cutlass Ten
- Victoria Ames (F) / Trooper / Cutlass Ten
- Audie Teagle (M) / Decanus / Cutlass One
- Alan Katche (M) / Cohort Centurion / Primus Pilus; Commander, 1st Ala
- Rikard Laferriere (M) / Patrol Centurion / Third Patrol, 1st Ala
- Chakravarthy Sol (M) / Decurion / First Patrol, 1st Ala
- Omar LeCoat (M) / Cohort Centurion / Commander, 2nd Ala
- Dylan Moroder (M) / Cohort Centurion / Commander, 3rd Ala
- Pyotr Martin (M) / Cohort Centurion / Commander, 4th Ala, Heavy Scouts

- Oleg Chilikov (M) / Patrol Centurion / 4th Patrol, 4th Ala, Einherjar
- Erik Windstrom (M) / Decurion / Draconarius, Einherjar
- Alistair Bleushan (M) / Cohort Centurion / Commander, 5th Ala (CCLXXIII Heavy)
- Johan Hellyer (M) / Patrol Centurion / Commander, 1st Patrol (CCLXXIII Heavy)
- Kevin Hassen (M) / Centurion / 5th Squadron (CCLXXIII Heavy "Sledgehammer Element")
- Hermann Gerstenburger (M) / Cohort Centurion / Commander, 6th Ala (Headquarters)
- Arald Rohm (M) / Grand Marshal / Commander, Imperial Land Forces
- Ernest Withers (M) / Commander / Fleet Marine Detachment, 2IC, Strasbourg Command
- Melina Arcidiacono (F) / Owner / Restaurant Tenochtitlan
- Thurman Arcidiacono (M) / Cook / Restaurant Tenochtitlan
- Christina Arcidiacono (F) / Daughter of Melina / Restaurant Tenochtitlan
- Nicola Arcidiacono (F) / Daughter of Melina / Restaurant Tenochtitlan
- Celine Arcidiacono (F) / Daughter of Melina / Restaurant Tenochtitlan

Imperial Land Forces

Name / Rank / Position

- Anthohn Jenker (M) / Grand Marshal / Supreme Commander, ILF, deceased
- Anders Tsibin (M) / Flag General / Commander, Field School
- Olaf van Gorzen (M) / Commander / Imperial Land Forces

Buran

Name / Rank / Position

- Buran / The Lord of Winter / God & Emperor & Ruler of *Buran*

- Xi Ulan Atah Ahn (M) / Director / Ural Starbase, *Samara*
- Ul Turin Dyana Vor (M) / Director / *Glory in Duty*
- Ko Yorin Myar Sam (M) / War Advocate / *Glory in Duty*
- Au Ulav Fara Hen (M) / Director / *Defend The Homeland*
- Ve Marak Entruk Han (M) / Minister of the Left Interior / *Winterhome*
- Ko Quebwas Polen Nim (F) / Minister of the Right Interior / *Winterhome*
- Nu Sheelan Robar Shil (F) / Minister of the Left Facet / *Winterhome*
- Wa Dahnna Lomek Gar (M) / Minister of the Right Facet / *Winterhome*
- Au Griblee Austur Wol (M) / Minister of the Right Facet / *Winterhome*
- Au Honek Trilben Lor (M) / First Director / *Winterhome*
- Xi Arakh Goran Lan (M) / Co-Owner / *Lighthouse*
- Nu Ulap Narah Kiel (F) / Co-Owner / *Lighthouse*
- Au Nadaf Elug Rov (F) / Minister of the Fourth Rank / Khan, Severnaya Zemlya

The Concord

- *EASC Carthage* / Commander, Earth Forces / Mark XXII Skymaster
- *The Lord of Tiki* / Bartender / Last Veteran

ABOUT THE AUTHOR

Blaze Ward writes science fiction in the Alexandria Station universe (Jessica Keller, The Science Officer, The Story Road, etc.) as well as several other science fiction universes, such as Star Dragon, the Collective, and more. He also writes odd bits of high fantasy with swords and orcs. In addition, he is the Editor and Publisher of *Boundary Shock Quarterly Magazine*. You can find out more at his website www.blazeward.com, as well as Facebook, Goodreads, and other places.

Blaze's works are available as ebooks, paper, and audio, and can be found at a variety of online vendors (Kobo, Amazon, and others). His newsletter comes out quarterly, and you can also follow his blog on his website. He really enjoys interacting with fans, and looks forward to any and all questions—even ones about his books!

Never miss a release!
If you'd like to be notified of new releases, sign up for my newsletter.

I will never spam you or use your email for nefarious purposes. You can also unsubscribe at any time.

http://www.blazeward.com/newsletter/

Connect with Blaze!

Web: www.blazeward.com
Boundary Shock Quarterly (BSQ):
https://www.boundaryshockquarterly.com/

f facebook.com/KRPBlaze

g goodreads.com/Blaze_Ward

ABOUT KNOTTED ROAD PRESS

Knotted Road Press fiction specializes in dynamic writing set in mysterious, exotic locations.

Knotted Road Press non-fiction publishes autobiographies, business books, cookbooks, and how-to books with unique voices.

Knotted Road Press creates DRM-free ebooks as well as high-quality print books for readers around the world.

With authors in a variety of genres including literary, poetry, mystery, fantasy, and science fiction, Knotted Road Press has something for everyone.

Knotted Road Press
www.KnottedRoadPress.com